LIZZIE LAMB

Harper's highland fling

Get your motor running...

Published by Goldcrest Books International Ltd
www.goldcrestbooks.com
publish@goldcrestbooks.com
ISBN: 978-1-913719-25-8

This book is dedicated to
my mother Elizabeth Fell
1928-1993
and my mother-in-law Betty Lamb
who has supported me in so many ways
on my writing journey

Chapter One

The premises officer fastened the banner, proclaiming Polzenith Primary School 'OUTSTANDING' in its recent Ofsted Inspection, to the school's Victorian railings.

'What do you think, Jim?' The breeze tugging at the corner of the banner whipped Harper MacDonald's dark hair across her eyes. She pushed the strands behind her ears with an impatient gesture.

'I think you've done a bloody marvellous job,' Jim said, tying the banner more securely. 'So do the parents and villagers. The Triple Whammy. Not many headteachers can lay claim to *that*.'

'I meant about the banner,' Harper chided, laughing. 'But you're right, I *have* done a bloody marvellous job. We all have.' She smiled at the elderly premises officer who, like other members of staff, cared passionately about the school and the community it served. That was the kind of esprit de corps Harper MacDonald fostered in her staff.

'You've worked your socks off since you came to Polzenith and turned things around. Time you went off on your holidays and forgot all about us until September.'

'You're right.' Harper nodded, thinking *if only!* Dismissing the negative thought she concentrated on the moment instead.

And what a moment – the start of the summer holidays when the days stretched ahead, full of promise and infinite possibility. Two months during which she could forget about being executive headteacher of a federation of village schools. Schools threatened with closure until she'd rocked up five years ago and turned them round.

Now all three had a banner fastened to their railings, trumpeting their Outstanding status, The Triple Whammy Jim referred to.

'Mark my words, it won't be long before you're headhunted. Fame and fortune will come knocking on your door, and you'll be gone. *Pouf.*' Jim's rueful expression acknowledged that headteachers of Harper MacDonald's calibre didn't stay in one place for long. Especially not in a triangle of former mining villages known as *The Three Pols*: Polzenith, Poltreath and Polvennor.

'Hardly.' Waving away his extravagant praise, she picked up the large tote bag at her feet and hoisted it over her shoulder, sagging under its weight. Parents, staff and children had been unfailingly generous, loading her with end-of-term gifts and wishing her well for the summer.

'Need a hand?'

'No, I'm fine. You and Mrs Jim have a great holiday, it'll slip past only too quickly.'

'Ain't that the truth?' Tipping her a salute, Jim picked up his tool kit and went back into the school.

Harper walked to the edge of the small village green in front of Polzenith Primary, stopping by the sturdy fencing she'd campaigned to have erected soon after taking up her post. She looked down at the breakers creaming on the beach far below, soon it would be teeming with children swimming and hunting for crabs in the rock pools. During morning assembly she'd hammered home the pleasures and dangers of playing on the beach and hoped they'd all listened. She wanted to start the autumn term with all present and correct.

'Stand down, MacDonald.' *The children aren't your responsibility for the next six weeks. Enjoy the freedom.* Turning, she swung her bag off her shoulder, allowing it to trail in the grass and walked past the former School House which should have been her grace and favour residence. However, it'd been sold off to a banker and his family years ago and was rarely occupied. That saddened her as she made her way towards her rented cottage further along the street, her home for the last five years.

Jim was right. The time had come for her to make a choice.

Put down roots or move on.

She paused by her front gate. Now wasn't the time to be thinking about her future. There was a bottle of ice-cold Sauvignon Blanc in the fridge waiting for her. She had last- minute packing to attend to and her niece, Ariel, to sort out.

Gaining OUTSTANDING for three failing schools was a doddle compared to the headache which was her wilful eighteen-year-old niece. But she wouldn't think about her right now, she'd concentrate on the bottle of wine in her fridge. She experienced a fleeting pang of loneliness because she would be drinking it alone. Sweeping the feeling aside, she slid her key into the Yale lock and considered the many positives in her life.

She was ending the academic year on a professional and personal high.

Tomorrow she was embarking on a three-week tour of Nepal.

And Ariel would be out of her hair for most of the summer.

Let that be enough.

'Ariel?' she called. Receiving no reply she dropped her bag and keys on the hall table.

The house felt empty, abandoned. Dust motes danced in a shaft of sunlight streaming through from the kitchen into the hall. Ariel's belongings, usually strewn about the hall as she headed for the fridge after school, were missing. Harper's end-of-term optimism evaporated, replaced by all too-familiar feelings of dread and anxiety. She glanced at her wrist watch. Ariel should have been home by now, dropped off by the school mini-bus on the edge of the village along with other teenagers who attended sixth form college in Truro.

Anxiety gave way to slow, burning anger. This was so typical of Ariel. She knew a taxi was booked for first thing tomorrow morning to take them to the station and then onto Heathrow where they would go their separate ways. Harper to a camp at the foot of the Himalayas from where her walking tour commenced. Ariel to stay with her mother in L.A to await her A level results. If either missed the connection, their holiday plans were well and truly screwed.

Was this part of a massive sulk on Ariel's part because Harper had refused to buy her a car after she'd passed her driving test? Or was she exacting revenge because Harper had insisted she spend at least part of the holiday working in the café in Polzenith, hopefully learning the value of money and how hard people had to work to earn it.

Another resigned sigh as Harper took her mobile from her tote bag and prepared to ring round Ariel's friends to see if they knew of her whereabouts. Ariel would be furious, natch, accuse her of spying on her, of ruining her life. But she'd have to suck it up, Harper was going to Nepal come hell or high water. And nothing, not even a stroppy eighteen-year-old, was getting in her way.

Whatever had happened to the sweet eleven-year-old who'd come to live with her seven years ago? Abducted by aliens, that's what! If she did encounter a Yeti in the Himalayas, it couldn't be any worse than Ariel in one of her massive strops.

Keeping calm, Harper waited for the dial tone.

Considering that Ariel had her mobile glued to her ear 24/7, it was strange how the one number she never rang was hers, Harper reflected. Receiving no answer from friend #1, Harper rang Ariel's number, steeling herself for the torrent of abuse that would bring down on her head. To her surprise, the ring tone from Ariel's favourite television programme rang out upstairs. Harper's shoulders relaxed, but her anger and exasperation increased. So – Madam was at home, but choosing not to answer her phone. Typical. Taking the stairs two at a time, Harper burst into Ariel's room without knocking, deciding that today the usual niceties didn't apply.

Sure enough, there was the iPhone Ariel's mother had bought for her eighteenth birthday complete with a data bundle which, seemingly, never ran out. Small wonder Harper's attempts to teach Ariel the value of money went unheeded. Picking up the phone she registered the caller ID: *Auntie Harper* and cancelled it. Her niece would rather lose a kidney than leave the house without her phone. That, coupled with the lack of her belongings in the hall, made Harper's blood pressure rise a few clicks.

Her gaze snagged on an envelope propped up on the dressing table, boldly inscribed: *Auntie Harper*. Heart thumping, she ripped it open. Inside was a letter written in Ariel's eccentric style: hearts over the letter 'i', sentences littered with emoticons. She stopped herself – now wasn't the time to get hung up on grammar and punctuation. She had to find Ariel, fetch her home – under armed guard if necessary – stand over her while she finished her packing and check that everything was in place for their departure tomorrow.

Passport. Visa. Dollars. Travellers' cheques.

The note, written on purple paper in magenta ink, was brief and to the point.

"FYI. I'm not going to stay with *MOM*." Harper pictured Ariel screwing up her face as she wrote. "Her douchebag husband spends all day *ogling me*, like I'm a piece of meat. She wants me to start calling him: DAD. Like *that's* gonna happen! Her husbands should come with name tag, serial number and health warning – like DAD #3. Douchebag #2. I'm with Pen and perfectly safe, so don't go getting your undies in a knot. He's not going to jump my bones the first night we spend alone.'

That sentence alone had the blood singing in Harper's ears.

'*Pen?*' Harper tried his name out for size. With uncanny ability Ariel had second- guessed her thoughts . . .

"You don't know him, okay? So, don't stress about it or even *think* of coming after us. And – don't go grilling my friends in that nauseating schoolmarm-ish way of yours. They've been sworn *to secrecy*. I'll buy a cheap burner, text Granny to let you know I haven't been abducted by the serial killer/rapist you imagine lies in wait round every corner. *PTO*."

Grinding her teeth, Harper turned the page. Any serial killer worth his salt would hand himself into to the police and claim sanctuary in the cells within five minutes of meeting Ariel. This *'Pen'* must be a saint to consider spending even part of the summer with her.

Harper didn't want to consider the inducements Ariel had offered. She hoped she'd rammed home the consequences of unprotected sex, recreational drugs and the danger of riding in high performance cars with friends who had too much money and too little driving experience.

Ariel's next sentence dragged her back to the present.

"Mom paid my allowance into my bank account a couple of days ago and, oddly enough, doesn't seem too keen to have me spending most of the summer with her in L.A. FYI – I'll be in Scotland."

Harper could well imagine sister Shona being in no hurry to have her nubile daughter lounging round the pool in a miniscule bikini while husband – number three, in case anyone was counting, compared Ariel's pert young body to Shona's saggy bits. How *could* Shona be so deceitful? Undermine her authority. Allow Ariel to play them off against each other, pretty much as she had since puberty kicked in giving her long legs, an enviable complexion and a scheming mind Machiavelli would've been proud of.

Did Shona want history to repeat itself? Ariel pregnant at eighteen, all hope of university dashed, her chances ruined? But, no – she wouldn't go down that road having travelled it with Shona almost twenty years earlier.

She'd find this mysterious *'Pen'*, track them down, bring Ariel home and put her on that plane to L.A, kicking and screaming if necessary – if it was the last thing she did.

Chapter Two

Harper's first port of call was Ariel's best friend, Tamsyn, who lived at the far end of the village.

Straightening the jacket of her business suit she pushed the gate open and marched up to the front door. She wished there'd been time to change, she looked – what was Ariel's expression? Schoolmarm-ish. But she hoped that would stand her in good stead. Her position as executive head of three schools set her apart from her contemporaries in the village, most of whom were wives and mothers in their early twenties and often on their second marriage a decade after that.

They treated her with respect but there was a wariness behind their smiles. Maybe that was why she'd never made a close friend since moving to the Three Pols. The reason why she often felt lonely? She pondered this as she pressed the doorbell with three sharp jabs. The door was opened by Tamsyn's mother, who looked shocked to find her standing there.

'Miss MacDonald!'

'Mrs Trethowan, I'm sorry to call without ringing first.' Harper's smile was designed to show she had nothing to worry about. 'Is Tamsyn in?'

'She in trouble?' Her eyes narrowed.

'No. I just wondered if she knew where Ariel was.' Harper kept her tone light, as though a disappearing niece was an everyday occurrence.

Their exchanged look of empathy acknowledged how wayward eighteen-year-olds could be, so full of hormones and attitude. Mrs Trethowan stepped back into the hall and shouted up the stairs. 'Tammy.'

'Wha'?'

'Get down 'ere. Miss MacDonald wants a word.'

'What do she want me fur?' Tamsyn stomped down the stairs, ear buds in place, phone cradled in her right hand. Her mother ripped the earbuds out of Tamsyn's ears and gestured for her to stand beside her on the doorstep. ''lo Mizz MacDonald.' Tamsyn affected an air of insouciance.

'Hello, Tamsyn. I'm looking for Ariel and,' she paused, 'Pen.' She spoke as though the coupling of their names was nothing out of the ordinary. Tamsyn glanced between her and her mother, plainly weighing up whether being loyal to Ariel was worth the hassle of having two adults on her case.

'I ain't *'zactly* sure where they are.'

'Tamsyn Trethowan,' her mother began, warningly.

'Pen lives above the garage at the other end of the village. Okay?' Having divulged as much information as she dared, Ariel could be an unforgiving enemy, she plugged the buds back in her ears, turned on her heel and returned upstairs.

Clearly hoping for a nice juicy nugget of gossip, Mrs Trethowan sent Harper a look of fellow feeling. 'What's your Ariel bin up to, then?'

'Hasn't done the packing for her holiday. Hasn't tidied her room. The usual.'

Mrs Trethowan's expression suggested that these were minor misdemeanours and that Miss MacDonald should spend some time with *her* brood if she wanted to know what life was really like. Picking up the vibe, Harper adopted the bright, professional smile she used to deflect the wrath of angry parents and defuse awkward situations.

'I'll try the garage, maybe I'll find her there.'

Unlikely. Ariel regarded dirt and grime as twin plagues and spent hours applying makeup and selecting her outfit before appearing 'selfie-ready'.

'Teenagers, huh? Little buggers, in't they?' Mrs Trethowan called after her.

'Aren't they just.'

* * *

Harper walked towards the end of the village where the garage was located. Her dander was up and there was a don't-mess-with-me glint in her eye which would have made even Ariel pause for thought. She recalled sarcastic snorting on Ariel's part when she'd revealed that her summer holiday would be spent on a rigorous walking tour in the foothills of the Himalayas.

'You oldies,' her niece had observed, 'are *obsessed* with walking. You've forgotten how to have fun. Go climb K2, or whatever middle-aged people spend their summers doing.' Harper had ignored that last jibe, too incensed at being described as middle-aged to think of anything to say. *Middle Aged?* She was thirty- seven, hardly in her dotage. Then Ariel had ended the discussion with indisputable logic 'If God had meant us to go on walking holidays he wouldn't have invented the car, would he?'

Car . . . The word stopped her in her tracks.

Her car was regularly serviced at one of the big garages in Truro. Maybe the local garage would be less than impressed that, during the five years she'd lived in Polzenith, she'd never once used their services. Ah well, offending a couple of grease-monkeys was the least of her worries. Quickening her pace she reached the garage where faded blue letters on a roll down metal door proclaimed it the business of one *Petroc Penhaligon*. Harper crossed her fingers, hoping that he was some crusty old gent in his sixties who'd sympathise with her predicament and help her to locate his – grandson?

Then she could be on her way with Ariel in tow, holiday plans intact.

For a moment, she saw herself as a redoubtable little tug towing a sleek liner into port, bucking against current and tide.

Radio One was blaring out when she walked into the garage. The music reminded her of the long drive home through traffic which had been her daily commute before moving to Polzenith. Did she miss it? Not for a moment. It had been a punishing schedule, a long day's teaching followed by the marking and preparation necessary to ensure her lessons were well prepared. Being able to walk across the village green and into her office, or driving the short distance to one of the other two schools was infinitely preferable.

Pushing the thought aside she crossed the garage threshold, pausing just long enough to allow her eyes to adjust to the gloom.

Middle-aged. Myopic. There really was no hope for her, she observed with a touch of self-deprecating humour.

After a minute, she picked out an inspection pit, cars up on ramps, and a pair of safety boots sticking out from underneath a Jaguar. Approaching an elderly man taking mugs of tea round to the mechanics, Harper smiled.

'Mr Penhaligon?'

'Can I help you, Miss? Here, Mick, take the tea.' He handed the tray to the nearest grease monkey.

'Yes, I'm looking for –' Before she could finish her sentence, someone started effing and blinding in the inspection pit, commenting on the strength of the tea and the fact that the Hobnobs were plain ones, not chocolate.

'Tone it down, lads, lady on board –'

A head popped above the edge of the inspection pit, blue eyes blazing out of a filthy face.

'Lady? Oh, sorry, Miss MacDonald.' Harper recognised the elder brother of twins in her class in Polzenith. Smiling, she turned back to the elderly mechanic.

'I'm looking for *Pen.*' She pronounced his name as though in italics.

'Pen?'

'Yes. Is he here?'

Instead of answering, the mechanic went over to the safety boots sticking out from under the Jaguar and gave them a none too gentle nudge with his foot. 'Lady to see you,' he said. There was a muttered expletive as the person under the car banged his head on the underside of the vehicle.

'Lady? Can't you deal with her? If it's Mrs Swift, tell her that her car will be ready tomorrow, as promised.' His tone suggested that he didn't like being harried by ladies, plural or singular. Harper frowned, his voice was deep, well-modulated and lacked the gentle Cornish burr of the villagers. More worryingly, it wasn't the voice of a young man. His annoyed growl suggested someone who'd left puberty behind many years ago.

Jeez – what was Ariel doing getting involved with someone who not only fixed cars for a living but sounded old enough to be her father. The MacDonalds – Harper's parents and sister Shona had higher hopes for her.

'Could you please come out and talk to me?' Her tone suggested that not only was she used to being obeyed, but that her patience was running out.

'I'm busy, get one of the men to deal with you –'

Rude!

'Excuse me? What is this – *talk to the feet*?'

The tapping stopped and the crawler board slid forward, revealing jean-clad legs poking out from beneath the frayed cuffs of dirty blue overalls.

'What's your problem, Miss –'

'Miss MacDonald,' the mechanic in the pit supplied, dipping his Hobnob in his mug of tea. 'From the primary school. You been a naughty boy, Boss?' Now the other mechanics downed tools and stood around drinking tea and enjoying the floor show.

'Who?' came back the muffled response.

'Harper MacDonald. And, since you ask, *you* are the problem. Would you please come out from under that car, give me your undivided attention and tell me where my niece is?' Her voice had risen an octave and ended in an feeble squeak. So not the impression she wanted to give to this – this, *Pen*. The crawler board inched forward, revealing that

Pen had long legs, a slim waist and broad shoulders. Lying prone on the crawler board he seemed a giant compared to the short, stocky men of the peninsular. Dismissing the thought as irrelevant, Harper folded her arms and waited, one foot tapping impatiently on the concrete floor.

Taking his time he got up and sauntered over, wiping his hands on a greasy rag hanging from the pocket of his overalls. As he drew closer, the smell of petrol, axle grease and oil wafted towards Harper. Wrinkling her nose she took a step back, she didn't want her business suit covered in diesel and Swarfega. He might have taken his time emerging from underneath the car, a tactic clearly designed to unsettle her, but he was quick to register her moue of distaste. Returning her inimical stare he gave her an unflattering once over which suggested she was a complete ball-ache, and the sooner she was out of his hair and his garage, the better.

'You've got my full attention, I'm a busy man, so get on with it.' Her cheeks flamed at his lack of respect, knowing that the Greek chorus over by the inspection pit would be sharing this exchange in the *Sailor's Arms* over a pint of Steaming Billy this evening.

Surely he wasn't this rude to all his customers? She gave him a more thorough inspection and then her brain kicked up a gear.

'My God, how *old* are you?' she blurted out.

The afternoon sun slanting through the skylight caught the gold earring in his left ear. An earring? For the love of all that was holy, Ariel had surpassed herself this time, becoming involved with a man who was a cross between a gypsy off the moors and the ancient mariner.

'Customers are usually more interested in my engineering qualifications,' he said, pulling off his beanie and tossing it onto the bonnet of the car. Unruly dark hair stuck up at all angles and it was plain from his expression that he wasn't pleased at providing a floorshow for his mechanics. 'Want to count my teeth?'

Keeping calm, Harper schooled her features, knowing that if she showed the slightest degree of disapproval over Ariel's choice of boyfriend – scrub that, manfriend, Ariel would elope to Gretna Green just to make a point.

''E's over forty,' Harper's former pupil put in helpfully.

'Over *forty?*' She rounded on him. 'You should be ashamed of yourself. Encouraging a young woman half your age to turn her back on university, ruin her chances and . . . get up to, I know not what.'

I know not what?

Harper groaned, inwardly, She might teach in a Victorian school building, but she was no shrinking violet in a crinoline reaching for the smelling salts every time a man crossed her path.

'I have no idea what you're talking about, Miss M –'

'Don't come the innocent with me. I've read the note. I can guess pretty accurately what your game is. You might impress silly young girls with your – your show of machismo and passing resemblance to a wild corsair. But you don't impress me. Not. For. One. Second.'

'Wild corsair?' He grinned, plainly amused by her choice of words. 'The village headmistress, huh? That figures.'

Feeling she was losing the moral high ground Harper pulled herself up to her full height and straightened her jacket. 'Executive head of three schools, to be precise.'

'Well, Miss Executive-Head-of-Three-Schools, you don't call the shots round here. I do. Let me apprise you of a couple of things –'

Apprise? Where had that come from ?

'For starters, my name isn't *Pen*. That's my son. Given your aptitude for figures, I'll let you do the maths; he's half my age and a bit less, having recently celebrated his eighteenth birthday. And for the record, I don't imagine for one minute that he's gone off with your daughter. He's got more sense than that.'

Daughter? Just how old did he think *she* was?

'Niece, to be precise.'

'Niece, daughter, whatever. Pen has a bright future ahead of him, a place at Oxford after the summer and a year at Harvard if he gets good grades in his fresher year. He wouldn't jeopardise that by going off with some –' Reaching out for his beanie he pulled it over his wild dark hair. 'This discussion is at an end.'

'Some *what*? Please continue. As for this discussion being at an end, we haven't even started. Maybe, once you learn all the facts, you'll discover that you don't know your son quite as well as you think.'

That stopped him in his tracks. 'Meaning?'

'It's all here. In this letter.' She waved Ariel's note in front of his face. 'I suggest that you read it before you say another word.' Snatching it out of her hand he leaned against the bonnet of the car he'd been working on and read it.

When he reached the end of the second page his expression darkened. 'No. Pen wouldn't,' he said, almost to himself. Then he slipped the note into its envelope and handed it back to Harper, a tell-tale pulse ticking on his firm jawline.

'Wouldn't he?'

Turning, he called over the mechanics standing by the inspection pit. 'Anyone seen Pen?'

'No Boss. He was here last night, working on his Mini after school as usual.'

'Quite.'

He gestured towards a corner of the garage where a car lay covered by a large tarpaulin. His told-you-so smile made Harper want to brain him with one of the tools on the workbench. His smug smile vanished when the mechanic received a 'go-on-tell him' dig in the ribs from one the others standing beside him in the inspection pit.

'B – Boss? Miss MacDonald's niece was here with Pen last night. The one with the long legs and . . .'

Harper shot him a quelling look. No need to be reminded that Ariel's luxuriant blonde hair, lithesome figure and endless legs drew admiring glances and trouble in equal measure. However, for the purposes of this exercise it suited Harper to portray her as chaste as a nun.

'What time was this?' Pen's father demanded, taking a step nearer the hapless mechanic who held up his hands in a *don't shoot the messenger* gesture.

'About ten o'clock last night. I noticed the lights were on when I walked back from the pub.'

'No, that's impossible,' Harper interrupted. 'Ariel came home and then went straight to bed. Around half past nine.' Her voice trailed away. She recalled thinking at the time that such behaviour was out of character. Ariel was a real night owl. But she'd been so busy dealing with end of term admin that she hadn't thought to look in on her and bid her goodnight, as was usual. It wouldn't be the first time Ariel had climbed out of her bedroom window to meet her friends in defiance of house rules.

Pen's father was quick to pick up on her hesitation. One dark eyebrow raised sardonically as he sent her an eloquent look. 'Let's settle this before I ring Pen.' Walking over to the Mini, he pulled back the tarpaulin to reveal, not the ancient Mini his son had been working on, but a collection of cardboard boxes fashioned into a Mini-shaped silhouette. Tossing the tarp aside he waded through the boxes, as if expecting to find the Mini beneath them.

'The little bugger,' the elderly mechanic exclaimed. 'He's gone off in it.'

'You think?' Penhaligon sent him a scathing look. He seemed poleaxed by his son's deception, Harper, however, was unsurprised. This had Ariel's name all over it.

The men backed away from their boss's wrath and would have dived into the inspection pit as quick as any Tommy in the trenches at the Somme if Penhaligon hadn't stayed them with: 'Hold it right there.'

'He won't get far, Boss. He tried to drive it round the yard a few weeks back but the engine wouldn't turn over,' the older mechanic informed.

'But he has been working on it since then. And I've –' the mechanic in the pit, hesitated.

'Go on,' Pen's father urged, tight-lipped.

'– been helping him.'

'Pen wouldn't drive around in a Mini without tax, insurance or an MOT. I've taught him better than that.'

'To be fair, Boss, because of its age the Mini doesn't *need* an MOT, or to be taxed.'

'Thanks for pointing out the obvious.' At that, the mechanic shrank back into the inspection pit.

'*What?*' Harper exclaimed. 'Let me get this straight. On top of everything, Ariel is a passenger in a death trap driven by a boy who's just passed his test?' She rounded on Pen's father standing amongst the cardboard boxes. 'Don't just stand there, man. Ring your son. Immediately.'

In that moment she was very much *Miss Executive-Head-of-Three-Schools* he'd mocked earlier. To emphasise her point, she marched over to him and tugged on his sleeve with both hands. She was a bantam weight by comparison but anxiety endowed her with unusual strength. Caught off guard, he staggered sideways before righting himself and shooting her a dark look. She'd delivered a dressing down in front of his workforce and practically assaulted him, plainly that didn't suit.

'Let's go somewhere more private to discuss this, shall we. This way, Miss MacDonald. If you please.'

It was a command, not a request.

Harper followed him over to a flight of rickety wooden stairs which led to a floor above the garage. Her brain was in overdrive. By her reckoning the teenagers had a day's start on them and were, according to Ariel's letter, well on their way to Scotland. Runaways no longer rocked up at Gretna Green and got married the next day, she knew that. However, she also knew that if she was to find her niece and bring her to heel she'd need the wild corsair's help to achieve it.

Chapter Three

Petroc Penhaligon opened the door at the top of the stairs. Despite knowing it would only make matters worse, he couldn't resist a mocking bow to indicate that Harper should precede him. She inclined her head gracious as a queen and walked into his sitting room, taking care to keep as much space between them as was physically possible. As though brushing against his oily overalls would contaminate her in some way.

Man, did she need taking down a peg or two. It'd give him the greatest pleasure to be able to do so, once he'd sorted out this business with his son and her niece. He longed to prove her wrong about Pen, hear her stammered apology for sounding off at him in front of his men. By this evening it would be all round the Three Pols that Miss MacDonald had, metaphorically, slapped Petroc Penhaligon's wrist and accused his son of kidnapping her niece.

Now, too late, he recalled seeing Pen on the village green with his friends and in the centre of the group had been this creature with, as his mechanics had said, long legs, waist length blond hair and . . . Little wonder Pen had been dazzled. Brought up in a small village and attending local schools and sixth form college meant he'd led a sheltered life.

Petroc couldn't remember him having a girlfriend, serious or otherwise. Whereas, this Ariel seemed as if she knew exactly how it worked and had probably learned everything from her infuriating aunt.

Sighing, he rubbed a weary hand over his eyes and then grimaced. His hands were covered in engine oil and made his eyes smart. Walking over to the sink in the corner of the open-plan sitting room-cum-kitchen, he washed them thoroughly, giving himself breathing space. Then he turned back to Miss MacDonald who stood in the middle of the room, looking madder than hell.

And, with good reason.

How could Pen have been so *stupid,* so lacking in judgement, so . . .

He remembered how it felt to be eighteen years old and on the brink of manhood, driven by hormones and needs that were all consuming. At that age he'd wanted nothing more than to travel the world, sow his wild oats and have fun before settling down to a career. Being a father at twenty-one hadn't been part of the plan, but that's how it'd worked out. Like father like son. Isn't that how it went? He should have seen this coming, should have sat Pen down, and had *the talk* with him. However, he thought they'd had all the time in the world and had planned to take him away for a father-and-son camping holiday before he went up to Oxford.

Looks like he'd left it too late.

Turning his attention to Miss MacDonald he watched her walk round his small living space, taking it all in. The shabby furniture which had seen better days, the patchwork quilt draped over the sofa that didn't quite hide its sagging springs, the floorboards he and Pen had painted last summer and the rickety kitchen table displaying the remains of a hurried breakfast.

Her expression said it all. She'd weighed him up and found him wanting.

He felt he should be rushing forward, clearing the mess away, offering tea. Or whatever one did when the village headmistress came calling. Then he thought, no; it suited him and Pen to live like this. Like proper males. Like mates. Now he suspected that he should have been less of a mate and more of a father. Damn her for making him reach that conclusion.

He'd bet her house was neat as a pin. Full of those perfectly matched things spinsters collected because they had nothing else to spend their money on. Hell, he'd wager there was even a cat or two asleep in a basket in the sitting room, waiting for her to return every night. And cushions; there'd be loads of cushions with no practical purpose other than to get in the way, and lifestyle magazines on the coffee table, arranged in chronological order.

'Sit down. Please.' He gestured to a desk in front of a large picture window through which the small high street, shops, bakery, village green, sea and the wide curve of Polzenith Bay were visible. 'Don't worry, the chair is perfectly clean. You won't get your suit dirty.'

'That,' she breathed, 'is the least of my worries.'

Sweeping the palm of her hand over the seat of her skirt, she sat down, crossed her legs at the ankle and swept them to one side before spinning the chair round to face him. Contained, controlled, in command. He longed to shake that composure, to wrinkle her suit, to make her dark hair fall free of its pins, her blue eyes widen in shock and surprise as they – He stopped there. There simply wasn't the time for this, he needed to re-read her niece's letter and work out his next move.

'May I?' He held out his hand.

She handed the letter over, reluctantly, as if it was Exhibit A. He read it again, skimming past the bits mentioning three husbands, douchebag surrogate fathers and a mother in La-La Land who appeared to have even less sense than her airhead daughter. He handed the letter back and she put it in her handbag, snapping the clasp together in a way that told him her patience was running out.

'Look, Mr Penhaligon. Ring your son. Find out where they are and then we can bring them home.' When agitated her voice rose an octave, maybe not as cool, calm and collected as she first appeared. He derived a certain grim satisfaction from that.

'I take it that you've rung your niece?' Picking up his mobile off the tattered arm of the sofa, he rang Pen on speed dial.

Rolling her eyes she let a sarcastic 'duh' hang in the air. 'Of course, but –'

'But, what?'

Harper regarded him with a cold stare, lips clamped together, evidently having no intention of divulging more than was strictly necessary. Plainly, she wanted more from him before she gave out classified information.

'Never mind. Just find out where they are.'

'Are you always this bossy?'

'When the occasion calls for it, yes.'

Pen's phone rang out and voicemail kicked in – *Hi, you've reached Pen's phone. But he isn't answering. You know the drill. Leave a message. I'll get back to you.* Petroc glanced over at Harper who was tapping an impatient tattoo on the desk, clearly anxious but taking pains to conceal it.

'Well?'

'It went straight to voicemail.' He rushed on before she could ask more questions. It seemed that his son had gone AWOL, and willingly. It wouldn't do to let her know that, at least, not yet. Not until he had all the facts and then he'd go after him – *them* – and when he found Pen deliver the biggest bollocking of his life. 'Look, I trust Pen. They'll be driving round the lanes having a wild adventure, thinking how clever they've been to get one over on their parents – sorry, responsible adults. They'll be home before we know it.'

At the words *I trust Pen,* her eyebrows shot up and she regarded him as if he was an idiot. One of those indulgent fathers who wanted to be his son's best friend, hang out with him and go on buddy-bonding weekends white water rafting, tombstoning off cliffs, paintballing.

'I don't think you quite comprehend the seriousness of the situation. It's all very well for your son to take off without notice. It's different for my niece, I am responsible for her welfare. I don't want to ring her mother at the end of the summer and tell her Ariel is –' She balked at the word. 'Do I have to spell it out?'

He knew it was wrong of him to insist. But he had to unsettle her, gain the moral high ground, be the one in charge.

'I'm rather afraid you do.'

'Bottom line? It's different for girls.'

'I think you're overreacting.' He agreed one hundred percent with her misgivings, shared her anxiety, but had no intention of letting her know. Surely Pen wouldn't be so irresponsible as to . . . to make him a *grandfather*? His blood ran cold and memories circled his head like angry birds. He'd handle this his way: find his son, sort everything out and bring them home before the weekend was over. But he'd do it alone.

No way was he forming an alliance with her.

'Don't you think you should check his room? In case he's left a note?' Again that look, as if she couldn't quite believe that she had to spell it out.

'If it makes you happy and . . .'

'Gets me out of your hair?'

'You said it.'

She stood up, making it plain that she found his attitude highly irritating. 'Shall we?' It was several seconds before he realised that she meant to enter Pen's room with or without him.

'Hold it right there. I'm not sure that Pen would . . .'

'What? Like us poking around in his inner sanctum. We're not looking for drugs or porn hidden under his mattress, we're looking for clues as to their whereabouts.'

'Drugs? Porn? You know nothing about my son, Miss MacDonald.'

'Neither it appears, do you.'

Without waiting, she pushed the bedroom door open and walked in. In contrast to the slovenly sitting room/kitchen, the bedroom was neat, tidy and showed no signs of a hurried departure. It was now a matter of honour to prove her wrong. However, a quick glance round the room showed Pen's large rucksack was missing from on top of the wardrobe and his bed hadn't been slept in.

Harper cut to the chase. 'Didn't he come home last night?'

'He texted me to say that he was staying over at a friend's house.'

She gave a snort of derision, 'Know what?'

'What?'

'We've been played. By a couple of experts.'

She sat on the edge of Pen's bed, looking defeated. Penhaligon didn't like the way she paired his son with her niece, but in that moment he felt sorry for her. He had no one to answer to but himself while she, he surmised, had a sister and anxious grandparents to explain things to and a reputation to maintain. He groaned inwardly. He would have staked his life on Pen not having a deceitful bone in his body.

Looks like he was wrong.

How could Pen be so stupid? Jeopardise his future and the girl's, too?

Harper's head was bowed, but when she looked up he detected the bright sheen of tears in her eyes. God, he hated it when women cried, it quite unmanned him. He adopted a deadpan expression to hide his feelings. Gaining mastery over her emotions she pointed over his shoulder.

'I think that's for you.'

Turning, he saw an envelope pinned to his son's notice board. Retrieving her niece's letter from her bag she invited him to join the dots. Same purple envelope, Pen's name written in magenta gel pen exactly like Ariel's. Keeping his expression neutral, Penhaligon opened the envelope with a calmness he was far from feeling.

After reading it through – twice – he passed it over to her.

Dad, I'm taking off for the summer with Ariel MacDonald. A Levels, the thought of more studying is doing my head in. I need to kick back, think what I really want from life, not follow the path mapped out for me. Ariel says we're young, we have to 'live the dream', and that's what I plan on doing. Ariel's great fun; a laugh a minute and I know she'll make this a summer to remember. Don't worry about me, I'll be in touch. See you in September – Pen

'September?' she gulped, folding the letter and sliding it back into the envelope. 'No indication of where they've gone,' she added a tad unnecessarily.

'None.'

'If Ariel says they've headed for Scotland then that's where they'll be.'

'You sound very sure.'

'I am. One thing about Ariel, she doesn't lie. She doesn't see the need.'

'No? Merely takes off, dragging an impressionable boy behind her?'

'Oh pu-leese. Don't give me that, it takes two to tango. I don't imagine for a minute that she had to bind and gag your son before throwing him in the back of his Mini and driving off.' Forced to acknowledge there was more than a grain of truth in that statement, he nodded. 'So, Mr Penhaligon, what next?'

Shocked that she'd deferred to him, it took him several seconds before he responded.

'I have a shrewd idea where Pen's headed. He won't get far before the Mini overheats, breaks down or, literally, blows a gasket.' Just like he felt like doing. 'I gave him the Mini to learn practical engineering skills, something to do in the long summer holidays, something to counterbalance . . .'

His voice trailed away. She didn't need to know that, proud as he was at Pen winning a place at Oxford, he didn't want him graduating with a PhD but incapable of changing a fuse. The Penhaligons had made their fortune from being at the forefront of the aeronautics industry, flying Sopwith Camels before the Great War, working as part of the team which developed Spitfires before moving on to the development of jet engines in the late forties. Then, in the fifties, inventing and designing better ways of taking to the air, becoming part of the burgeoning aerospace industry emerging around Bristol which had developed Concorde and satellite technology.

He wanted the same for Pen, but if the boy's aptitude lay in other areas he would have to accept that with good grace and not stand in his way. Snapping out of his dream he heard her say something.

'I'm sorry?'

'I said – what next? My car's in Truro being serviced while I'm – *was* planning to leave for a walking holiday in Tibet, first thing tomorrow morning.'

Penhaligon stopped himself from pulling a sardonic expression. Tibet? Of course, no doubt reliving Eat. Pray. Love as befitted a single woman focused on her career.

'I'm going after him, them. If they're headed for Scotland they'll have made for the M5 and the road north. I think I know where they'll spend the night.'

'The *night?* Oh My God.' Her veneer slipped and she invested the word with images neither of them wanted to contemplate.

'Exactly. Time is of the essence. I'll get cleaned up, head north and ring you when I catch up with them.'

'You're going nowhere without me, Mr Penhaligon. If you think you can make Ariel change her mind once it's set on something, you clearly know nothing about teenage girls. I'm packed and ready for my holiday. Sure, I'll have to do some ringing round, cancel things. After that, I can throw a couple of cases in the back of your car and –'

'No, you'll slow me down.'

'Slow you down? Don't be preposterous. I take it we aren't going to make our way along the M5 in a covered wagon? How could I possibly slow you down?'

Penhaligon frowned. It hadn't taken her long to return to default position. Plainly, she regarded him as an uneducated mechanic capable of nothing more demanding than getting a car through its MOT. A passage from the scriptures came to mind, something about the roman centurion giving commands and their being obeyed.

Go and he goeth? Isn't that how it went?

Well, not today, Princess. I'm the one in charge.

'Very well, Miss Macdonald. On your head, be it.'

It was plain from her expression that she expected more of a fight. She regarded him with suspicion, as though it was his plan to lull her into a false sense of security and then shoot off without her. Mind you, that wasn't a bad idea, but he didn't do sneaky and underhand. He left that to other men.

'I'll be outside your door in an hour. If you don't show I'll take it that you've changed your mind.'

'I won't. I mean, I will. Show that is.' Plainly caught on the back foot she stammered out: 'Th – thank you Mr Penhaligon.'

'Don't thank me, yet. And, for the sake of brevity, call me Rocco.'

'Rocco?'

'Short for Petroc. My Sunday name which no one uses apart from my parents.'

'Very well, Rocco.' Judging from her expression she thought his name, especially the shortened form, was pretentious.

'No need for the face, Petroc is the Cornish form of Peter. Anyone who has a niece called Ariel, shouldn't throw stones.'

'Really?' Her affronted expression showed she wasn't used to being spoken to in such a manner.

'Really.' He pushed back the sleeve of his overalls and checked the time on a vintage Rolex mariner's watch. 'One hour Miss MacDonald, clock's ticking. I'd get a move on, if I were you. Time and tide wait for no man, and that includes the headmistress of three schools.'

She looked as if she'd like to say more. Instead, she sucked in a breath, walked back into the sitting room and picked up her bag. Next thing he knew she was clattering down the wooden stairs and out of the garage. He watched as she walked down the high street and across the village green, her shoulders stiff, bristling with anger. He could almost find it in his heart to feel sorry for the errant niece once they caught up with her.

Almost, but not quite.

He walked into the sitting room and read his son's note through again.

'Pen. You idiot.'

His shoulders sagged as he recalled another time when he'd stood at this very window and thought his world had come to an end.

Chapter Four

Exactly fifty-five minutes later, Harper dropped her luggage in the hall. She'd packed lightly, not knowing how long she'd be away, or when they'd catch up with Ariel and Pen. She liked to be organised, prepared for anything. But events had overtaken her and that made her feel scratchy, uncomfortable. Placing both hands on the pier table she leaned forward and glanced in the mirror. This was her last minute ritual before leaving the house every morning to ensure that she looked as polished and professional as her position demanded. This evening, she didn't like what she saw: eyes large in her pale face and two hectic spots of colour on her cheekbones. Her hair had escaped from its usual chignon and curled around her face enjoying the unaccustomed freedom.

She looked disturbed, upset, out of kilter.

She would have to tread carefully. Petroc Penhaligon – she screwed up her face at the thought of him – was a wild card. He had a coiled strength which hid determination and the fact that he was used to getting his own way. He was trouble, the kind of man she usually avoided at all costs. Her reputation, position in the community and responsibility for a volatile eighteen-year-old meant there was little time for dalliance in her life.

Dalliance?

The quaint word, resonant of tea dances, dance cards and shy holding of hands in fern-filled conservatories, didn't quite cover the state of her love life. Make that non-love-life. Men – singular or plural, wild or tame, hadn't featured much of late. Dragging three schools out of special measures and keeping tabs on Ariel couldn't be achieved without sacrifice.

Her sacrifice.

As a consequence, Ariel was wont to remind her, her life was dull, dull, dull.

Another sigh. She had hoped trekking in the foothills of Tibet would free her mind and remove the weight of responsibility from her shoulders. That, raising her head each morning and staring into the bright blue skies and majestic mountains fringing the Gokyo Valley would restore her spirits. Or, practising yoga at one of the tea houses in Kenjoma would tease out knotted muscles and relax her frayed nerves. Part of her even hoped that she'd meet some like-minded trekker with whom she could explore oak forests, waterfalls and glaciers.

Dull. Dull. Dull.

The words echoed like the notes struck on the giant bell in one of the monasteries she would pass on her way to Cho Oyu. It felt clichéd, as if her life wasn't clichéd enough.

She was still dreaming of valleys below the snowline covered in rhododendron, frozen waterfalls and glacial lakes when a dark shape arrived at the door, blocking the light. A gloved fist banged on the glass and then the silhouette took a couple of steps back. Even through the opaque glass it was clear the shape was wearing a crash helmet and bike leathers. She sighed, the Pizza delivery boy. Ariel had the local takeaways on speed dial, despite the nutritious meals Harper prepared each evening. From the moment she'd seen manure being sprayed on the fields as organic fertiliser, Ariel had proclaimed that 'no way' was she eating anything that had had animal dung in it, or on it.

Vegetables, it appeared, were the enemy and not to be trusted.

To compound matters, the delivery boy had a crush on Ariel and brought left over pizzas to their door, mooning around Harper's kitchen in spite of Ariel's best efforts to put him off. Damn. She wasn't in the mood for love sick swains, bearing pizzas tonight.

'Hang on.' Harper's stomach gave a hungry growl at the thought of pizza. Her lunchtime sandwich seemed ages ago and her legs were beginning to buckle from a combination of hunger, stress and anxiety. Furthermore, she knew that once she and Rocco Penhaligon were on the A30, stopping for food would be out of the question. Her fridge was empty due to her holiday plans and the best she could rustle up was a tin of Cornish Fudge, an end of term present.

Coals to Newcastle.

She opened the front door prepared to give the pizza boy his marching orders but came face-to-face with Rocco Penhaligon looking tall and intimidating in bike leathers. Seemingly, thinking about him had been enough to conjure him up, and that unnerved her. Apparently picking up the negative vibes pulsing towards him Rocco retreated a couple of steps and flipped up the helmet's visor.

'Your carriage awaits, Princess.'

Glancing past him, Harper did a double take. Instead of the expected car waiting for her at the end of the drive there was a vintage motorbike. Her tired brain struggled to process this information.

She blinked. 'How? What the –'

'Can I come in? We wouldn't want to get the neighbours talking, would we?'

'Neighbours?' she asked, dazedly. Not waiting for her permission, he brushed past and was in the hall leaving her by the front door, mouth agape.

'Yes – you, me. Especially me. Miss MacDonald entertaining gentlemen callers? Shocking.' Tutting in a mocking fashion, he removed a set of bike leathers slung over his shoulder and hung them on the newel post. 'For you – and stow your gear in these.' A set of motorbike panniers landed at her feet, brushing against the Mulberry luggage she'd bought in anticipation of her holiday.

She might be trekking in the foothills of the Himalayas, staying each night at a different base camp or teahouse, but that didn't mean standards had to slip. Shaking her head free of inconsequential thoughts, she continued. 'It's been a long and stressful day. Would you mind explaining what's going on? Where's the car you promised?'

'Car? I never promised a car. I simply told you be ready within the hour.'

'Oh. You . . .' Exasperated, Harper stamped her foot and then kicked the panniers out of the way, as though they contaminated her designer luggage. So childish and immature, just like Ariel, she thought despairingly. Better calm down, she needed her mental faculties firing on all cylinders to deal with this man. Taking a deep breath she continued, 'You *implied* we'd be heading north in a car.'

'Are you mad? The first weekend of the summer holidays? The world, his wife, black lab and two point four children,' he pulled a sardonic face, 'will be clogging the road to Bristol with their Chelsea Tractors. The A30's already gridlocked thanks to an accident and that's before we even hit the M5. On a bike we can weave in and out of the traffic.'

'*Weave?* I don't think so.' Harper pulled herself up to her full five feet five, feeling very small and insignificant next to Penhaligon in his leathers. Time to assert herself. No way was he going to push her around. She would ring a car hire company in Truro or Newquay, and ...

'I haven't got time for this. Either you're coming with me, or not. The choice is yours.' Bending, he picked up the panniers and slung them across one shoulder like saddle bags. He was about to do the same with the leathers when she forestalled him.

'Wait, I –'

'Yes?'

'I'm coming with you.' It was as though every word was wrenched from her.

She couldn't quite see his mouth due to the chin guard on the helmet. But she'd bet a month's wages that he was grinning in that mocking way of his because he'd got one over on her. Turning, she picked up the bike leathers with a moue of distaste. They looked well-worn and she shuddered to think whose body had been encased in them.

Not his, surely?

'Don't worry. They're Pen's.' Mind reading, it appeared was another of Penhaligon's talents. 'I thought they'd be a better fit than a pair of mine, you being rather on the short side.' His look raked her from top to toe and implied that she could double as a Cornish pixie and probably sat on toadstools just for the hell of it. She opened her mouth to protest but he cut across her again. 'Anyhow, chill, Pen's had all his shots and I've sprayed the leathers with Febreze.' Evidently, he thought that was over and above the call of duty and sent her another dark look. Without meaning to, she'd implied that his son had been dragged up in the Three Pols and was no better than a mongrel.

'I –' She thought it diplomatic to apologise, but he cut across her.

'You'll be fine.' Taking them out of her slack fingers he gave them a shake down before handing them back. 'Five minutes, tops. Then I'm gone. A word of advice, Miss MacDonald –'

'Yes?' she asked through gritted teeth.

'We travel light. Dump the girly luggage.'

With that he left Harper standing in the hall cradling the leathers in her arms. She wondered, as he made his way down the path, if he could feel the poisoned darts her eyes aimed towards him, hitting him squarely between his broad shoulders.

* * *

He was sitting astride the bike when she walked – make that *squeaked*, down the path. The bike leathers were newer than first appeared and she suspected that Pen had only worn them a few times, hence their propensity to squeak. They did not smell of teenage boy, thanks to Febreze. They were too long, natch, but she'd managed to roll them up so she didn't look too ridiculous. She glanced around, but luckily most of the village was packing for their holidays or having their tea. No one kept sophisticated hours in Polzenith, it was the case of a quick tea/dinner and then on with the rest of the evening.

If he made capital out of this, so help her, she'd brain him.

'Good, you're wearing boots.' He glanced down at her feet. 'It'll get cold when we're travelling. Here, gloves; helmet, high vis jacket. Put them on.' While she did that, he took the panniers containing her belongings and secured them to the bike.

'My God, you're overbearing,' she said, forgetting her good manners and professional demeanour. How Ariel would laugh if she could see her kowtowing to the owner of the local garage. However, needs must and so she did as instructed, but the look she shot him warned him not to push his luck.

'Overbearing? Coming from the headmistress of three schools I'll take it as a compliment.' She couldn't see his expression but she suspected that he found her a total pain in the arse and wasn't bothering to hide it. *Believe me, mate*, she wanted to say – *the feeling's mutual.* Cramming the helmet over her dark hair she slipped her hands into the leather gauntlets and then stood around uncertainly. 'Hop on, Miss MacDonald.'

'You can call me Harper,' she muttered. 'If that isn't asking too much? I'm on holiday, remember?'

'Okay. Hop on *Harper.*'

She did just that, straddling the bike with difficulty. Penhaligon's booted feet were placed squarely on the ground, whereas she could only reach the tarmac on tiptoe. She squirmed around a little on the seat, wondering how she was going to stay upright as far as the end of the village, let alone Bristol. She envisaged him turning round miles down the road, wondering why it'd gone quiet, only to discover that she'd fallen off.

Wouldn't that please him!

'Look, I don't think I can do this,' she protested.

'Sure you can. Here. Put your feet on the foot rests, lean back against the rack and you'll be fine.' He revved the bike and shot forward. Harper let out an involuntary squeal and chastised herself for acting like a *girl*. So unlike herself. 'For the love of God. Is it going to be like this every time we travel faster than twenty-five miles an hour, or a turn a corner?'

'I'm just not used to riding pillion, okay, Evel Knievel?' She might be out of her comfort zone but she had no intention of giving him the upper hand.

'Evel Knievel?' She couldn't swear to it but she thought she heard a rumble of laughter deep in his chest. 'Okay, here's what you do. Put your arms around my waist and you'll feel more secure.'

'I'm not sure whether I –'

'Fine. Put them on my shoulders to steady yourself. But we've got a long way to travel, you'll soon get tired. And, to my certain knowledge, no one has even been ravished on the back of a motorbike on the A30 travelling at over sixty miles an hour.'

'Sixty miles an hour?' Another girly squeal. This was ridiculous, she would never reach Ariel before – she couldn't bring herself to phrase the sentence, before it was too late.

Ravished? The word crept up on her unannounced. What did he mean? Was it a case of like father, like son?

'And we're off.' He gunned the bike forward and her hands which had been resting lightly on his shoulders now wrapped themselves around his waist like a terrified boa constrictor. Worse was to come. There was no way Harper could wrap her arms around his waist without her breasts pressing into his back. Every time she pulled back, she wobbled dangerously and had to clutch him even more tightly. Good thing her helmet hid the flush of colour burning along her cheekbones and the unbecoming hives on her jaw line and décolletage.

She wanted to ask him to stop, to drop her off in Truro so she could hire a more conventional means of transport. But that would be to admit defeat, to show she was a prissy princess not up to the chasing half way across the county on the trail of the runaways. It killed her to admit that he was right, time was of the essence.

Grinding her teeth she let out an angry hiss. When she caught up with Miss Ariel Marie MacDonald she would be grounded.

For life.

* * *

Rocco could hear her chuntering via the Bluetooth connection between their helmets. Perhaps he should tell her that they could communicate that way – or maybe not. It amused him to hear her calling him everything from a pig to a dog and saying exactly what she'd do to her niece when this was over. How she'd be glad to see the back of him. The adjectives came thick and fast: *arrogant, egotistical, self-opinionated* and *way too full of himself.* Jeez, she never let up. He hoped she'd settle down and let him concentrate on his driving as they made their way towards the A30 and Bodmin Moor.

He might have guessed that she'd be a monumental pain in the arse, so starchy, so full of her own importance. The kind of woman he usually avoided at all costs. But he had to get Pen back home before he ruined his life and for that he needed help.

Her help. She was right, his experience of handling nubile eighteen-year-old girls was non-existent and her niece sounded a piece of work.

His expression grim, he remembered the first time he'd come to Polzenith. Rocking up for the surfing championships the same time as a group of New Age Travellers set up camp on the village green. He'd been young and impressionable, just like Pen, on a summer break from Bristol University where he'd been pressurised into studying philosophy, politics and economics and not aeronautical engineering as he'd wanted.

Predictably, he'd fallen head over heels for one of the travellers, a vision in layered tie-dyed clothing, multiple piercings and blonde dreadlocks. She'd set up a stall on the green selling friendship bracelets and necklaces, weaving shells, feathers and plaited leather together with nimble fingers. It was an idyllic summer and he spent every available minute with her when he wasn't surfing. In the long summer twilight he'd join the other travellers smoking dope and listening to their tales of the places they'd been, and where they were going for the winter: Goa. He thought he'd met the love of his life and had been rehearsing how he'd break it to his parents, that he didn't want to go back to university.

Then, as suddenly as the caravanserai of hippies had arrived, it vanished. Leaving behind a trail of garbage, debts, unwanted belongings and broken hearts. His among them. After that he couldn't settle. He'd dropped out of university, tapped into the trust fund set up for him by his grandparents and bought the garage in the village, hoping one day she'd return. And, when she did, he'd be right there waiting for her – like a faithful knight errant. Or a lovesick puppy.

He pulled a face, not sure, even after all this time, which was the more accurate description. 'Now what?'

'I said, can you hear me?' Her voice was full of suspicion, as if he'd played a trick on her.

'Oh, didn't I say? The helmets are linked by Bluetooth. So, yes, I've been listening to you talking rubbish for the last twenty miles. And, to be honest, I'm shocked that the village headmistress has such words in her vocabulary.'

'Ha, bloody, ha.' She removed her arms from round his waist, wobbled and then replaced them. 'I – I need to p-pee.' Her embarrassment was palpable, but he couldn't resist one last jibe.

'Didn't you go before we left?'

'Of course I did, you idiot. But nerves and, well, you know.'

He felt she was about to share secrets of a delicate nature and he didn't want that. 'Okay, there's some services ahead. I'll pull in there, but . . .'

'I know the drill. Don't take forever or you'll leave without me?'

'You're a quick learner Miss – Harper. I'll give you that.'

'Dealing with you, I'd better be.' She tutted, clearly annoyed at uttering such an ungrammatical sentence. 'Okay, where are we?'

'Indian Queens. Where Pocahontas is alleged to have landed from the New World.' He wanted her to know that he wasn't the oaf she imagined him to be. He might have dropped out of university but he was well read in spite of that.

'Alleged is about right. The name can't be traced back earlier than the nineteenth century and probably refers to a hostelry – The India Queen, which stood on this site.'

'Have you no poetry in your soul?'

'Since you ask, I have plenty of poetry in my soul. It's just that today it's gone AWOL, along with my niece – thanks to your son.' It was on Rocco's mind to defend Pen but he suspected that would only make matters worse. Better to save all that for when they caught up with the runaways, she admitted that her niece had lured him away and was forced to eat humble pie. Swinging off the motorway and into the area reserved for motorbikes, he rocked the Bonneville back on its rest and switched off the ignition.

Removing his gauntlets, he pushed back the cuff of his leather jacket and took a long look at his watch.

'You have five minutes, Miss MacDonald, starting from . . .'

'I get it!' Holding onto his shoulders, she swung herself off the pillion seat, making it plain that any form of physical contact between them was loathsome. She was about to walk off when he grabbed her by the arm.

'Helmet.'

'Oh!' Removing it, she threw it at him as if it were a rugger ball and then walked stiffly towards the brightly lit services. Rocco watched the way her neat buttocks rose and fell against the body-hugging leathers, how her hips sashayed as she tried to make her stiff muscles respond to her command. He let out a dry bark of laughter, and then – glancing at the male bikers leaning against their powerful machines, smoking or eating huge Cornish pasties, noticed that they were watching her, too.

Giving a humph of irritation, he got off his bike and shook his head. She might act all prim and proper but she was trouble, make no mistake about it. He'd be glad to see the back of her when they caught up with the youngsters. Rehearsing the speech to deliver to Pen, he picked up both helmets and followed her into the services.

* * *

Harper walked past the food hall, shutting out the happy families enjoying food from one of the many concessions around the hall. It was harder to ignore the tempting aromas wafting towards her: pizzas, burgers, pasties and the like. She'd crammed a small change purse and her credit card into the pocket of her borrowed leathers and wondered if she dared queue for something to eat, but decided against it. *Five minutes* he'd said and he meant it. It wouldn't do to show any signs of weakness in front of Rocco Penhaligon. If he didn't have the sense to realise that she was starving, she wasn't about to remind him.

He caught up with her at the huge doors leading to the car park.

'Okay?' he asked, catching her by the elbow.

'Never better.' She shook off his hand and walked ahead of him back to the area designated for bikers.

'I thought you might be tempted to grab a sandwich or –'

'Not hungry,' she lied. 'Let's get this over with ASAP and then life can return to normal. *Whatever that is,*' she muttered beneath her breath.

'Cool,' was all he said.

Harper curled up her lip: *cool*. Ah, she got it. He wanted her to know that he was down with the kids, knew the words they used, mimicked their phraseology. She wondered what his wife thought about all of this.

Wife. That word had an unexpected effect. It made her shiver and feel suddenly uncomfortable. What would Pen's mum make of her husband taking off with an unknown woman to track down their son? Surely, *she* should be the one riding pillion, not her. How would the rest of the village regard this escapade? Would her reputation be ruined after riding off into the sunset with another woman's man?

At that moment, if Ariel Marie MacDonald had walked across the carpark and thrown herself into her aunt's arms, said aunt would have found it very hard not to throttle her. A word which sounded very much like *fuck,* escaped from her lips. She turned it into a cough and then sneezed ostentatiously. Penhaligon looked down from his great height, a fleeting smile pulling at the corners of his mouth, amusement lighting his grey-green eyes.

'Indeed,' was all he had to offer. 'Shall we?'

'Let's.'

He retrieved the helmets, made sure she was safely seated on the pillion and then swung himself into position. This time Harper didn't need second bidding to put her arms around his waist. She was tired and hungry and found the physical contact strangely comforting.

Chapter Five

Harper had to admit that Rocco was right. The traffic on the A30 was horrendous. She admired the way he handled the motor cycle, weaving in and out of the gridlocked traffic, receiving glowering but envious looks from motorists confined in their tin cans with querulous children demanding: *are we there, yet, Dad?*

Passing the turn for Jamaica Inn off the A30 at Bolventor, Harper said, half-reflectively: 'We always took a break at Jamaica Inn when Ariel was younger. She loved the novel and read it many times, fancying herself as Mary Yelland. I had to play the part of the landlord's browbeaten wife, Patience Merlyn. No surprises there. When she discovered the brass plaque on the floor which said: On This Spot Joss Merlyn Was Murdered, she demanded that we return when they were conducting a ghost walk around the pub. But I felt she was too young for such activities.'

'Sounds like she has an overactive imagination,' Rocco ventured.

'Her mother is an actor,' Harper said. 'In Los Angeles.'

'Aren't they all? When they're not waiting tables or pumping gas?' Rocco inquired. The brief moment of empathy evaporated and, to signal her displeasure, Harper leaned as far away from him as she dared.

'Not all,' she said.

She zoned out, imagining herself in the teahouse at Dole looking out of her bedroom window at the stony beach and glacier lake fringed by mountains below her. The soft accents of the Nepalese staff contrasting with the languages of the different trekkers. It'd been a stressful day at the end of a long, demanding term and tears misted her eyes as she realised what she was missing. How she was going to explain Ariel's disappearance to her sister and parents, how would they react?

Unable to brush away the tears because she was wearing a helmet, she sniffed loudly instead.

'You okay?' Rocco's voice came through the headset.

Damned Bluetooth!

'Y- yes. Just tired and –'

'Hungry?' he supplied. 'Me, too. Can you bear it if we push on to Exeter and then take a break there?'

'Of course.' She blinked away the tears and leaned against his back, turning her head sideways.

'Don't fall asleep, will you?' Was that concern and contrition in his voice?

'I'll do my best. Not to – I mean.'

'Good girl,' He patted her hand. To her surprise, Harper didn't feel as patronised at being called a 'girl' as she might have at the outset of this venture. Which only went to show how hungry and thirsty she was. A pit stop, some food, a trip to the loo and she'd be fighting fit.

Then Petroc Penhaligon had better look out.

* * *

Sixty miles and an hour and a half later, Rocco swung the motorbike into Exeter Services. It being high summer and deceptively light, the services were busy and when Harper looked at her watch she was surprised to see that it was eight o'clock. They'd been on the road over three hours and her cramped muscles knew it. Rocco glanced over his shoulder as he rocked the bike back on its rest and, judging from the set of his shoulders, even he was feeling the effects of straddling the bike.

'We have over fifty miles to travel before we reach my parents' house. It's on the Somerset Levels. On an evening like this you can see Glastonbury Tor from the upstairs rooms.'

His voice had a quality she'd never heard before, wistfulness overlaid something deeper, something akin to bitterness and regret. Evidently heading home evoked memories for him, good and bad. There was a story behind his words, one Harper didn't have time for right now. All she could think of was catching up with the runaways, some nourishing food and a mug of extra strong coffee. Triple shot if necessary. She needed carbs and caffeine to fortify her for the ordeal ahead when she caught up with Ariel and ordered her home.

Good luck with that.

Giving herself a mental shake she swung off the bike and tried to stand, but her cramped muscles wouldn't support her. In one swift movement, Penhaligon was at her side, arm round her shoulders, holding her as if she weighed no more than a feather.

'Dead leg?' She nodded. 'Okay, you stay with the bike, I'll grab a couple of pasties, coffee, Krispy Kreme donuts and we'll eat them here.'

Harper gave a tired *whatever* shrug and then winced. Her shoulders ached too, a consequence of hanging on for grim death for the last three hours.

'Just make sure the coffee's so strong that the spoon's melting.' She frowned as he removed his helmet and hooked it over the handlebars, lips quirking. 'Now what?'

'You. I thought you'd be all – *fetch me a low-fat avocado salad, a bottle of spring water and a tall, skinny, latte, no sugar.*' He delivered the sentence in a mock-superior accent. Was that how she sounded? 'Looks like you're as ready for carbs-and-caffeine as I am.'

Hunger and tiredness made her feel out of sorts and in no mood for his barbed comments. 'So why are you standing there instead of queuing at Costa? Go. Be a hunter gatherer, or whatever macho Cornish men do.' His smile vanished and Harper experienced a moment of triumph at getting one over on him. Plainly, being characterised as a knuckle dragging Neanderthal didn't appeal to Petroc Penhaligon.

He looked as if he was about to deliver some biting retort but clearly thought better of it. Turning on his booted heel he headed for the food hall leaving a trail of unspoken words in his wake, spitting and hissing like firecrackers. After he'd disappeared into the crowd Harper removed her helmet, shook her hair free of its scrunchy and massaged her aching scalp. It was foolish to aggravate him when she needed his help. However, she seemed unable to stop herself. Sparring with him helped her to limber up for the massive confrontation ahead when she caught up with Ariel.

When Rocco returned ten minutes later Harper was surrounded by a group of bikers, ostensibly admiring the curves of the Bonneville and asking pertinent questions, none of which she felt qualified to answer. When they saw Rocco, they backed off, holding up their hands in an *no offence, mate* gesture.

'Nice bike, dude.'

'Yeah. Cool.'

'Thanks.' His dark brows drew together as he watched them walk back to their own bikes. 'New friends?' He handed Harper a paper bag containing pasty and a coffee with scant ceremony.

'Don't start.' Turning her back on him she gave the pasty her full attention. They ate in silence but Harper could almost hear the cogs in his mind whirring round as he revised his impression of her. Evidently he was back to believing Pen had been lured away by Ariel, just as she'd attracted a crowd of bikers the moment his back was turned. A case of like aunt, like niece? Her position as executive head of a federation of schools seemingly left behind the moment she'd climbed onto the Bonneville. Which made her – what exactly – a femme fatale in leathers?

After polishing off the pasty, Harper reached out for the paper bag of Krispy Kreme donuts hoping to find one of her favourites.

'So, what did they want?' He gestured towards the bikers with his coffee cup.

'I don't know. We didn't appear to speak the same language. I said we were travelling from Polzenith to Bristol and then all I heard was – M.P.G, two-hundred-and seventy degree crank angle parallel twin engine, sequential electronic fuel injection, and – oh, wait, what was it now – wet, multi-plate assist clutch.' She repeated the phrase like a child reciting the catechism. 'Almost as if they were talking in tongues.'

Detecting the chill wind of disapproval, she moved away and concentrated on the bag of donuts. Disregarding donut etiquette she selected one with strawberry frosting without asking which one he preferred. Biting into it she enjoyed the sugar rush and a small moue of pleasure escaped through sugar-coated lips. The frosting splintered, shards ending up near the corner of her mouth. Using her tongue and her little finger she guided the icing over her lips and onto her tongue.

Glowering – he seemed to do a lot of that, Rocco snatched the bag off her.

What *was* his problem? It wasn't as if she'd invited the bikers over to speak to her. Did he think she'd let them take turns riding on his precious bike, was that it? There was little time to speculate because Rocco drank his coffee, screwed up the cup and placed it inside the now empty bags and tossed them in a nearby litter bin. He glanced at his watch, looking towards the west where the sun was setting.

'We need to get going if we're to reach my parents' house before dark. I'm guessing that's where we'll find the runaways. Toilet?' Again, the curling lip.

Although she would probably be dying for a pee ten miles down the road, Harper had no intention of answering his question. She sent him a haughty stare, guessing he was one of those men who thought they knew everything there was to know about women. She bet he kept tampons in the bathroom cabinet in case any of his women friends stayed over. That was a disturbing thought – the women friends, not the tampons. Once again, it occurred to her that she knew nothing about the man she was about to spend another hour clinging to as though her life depended on it.

Her thoughts returned to his absent wife. The living quarters above the garage looked as if they hadn't seen a woman's touch in years and needed a 'good bottoming', as her cleaner put it. In fact, she recalled seeing more empty pizza boxes and motorbike maintenance manuals than novels, although from the way he spoke it was evident he was well read.

'Toilet?' he repeated, sending her a curious look. As though wondering what she was thinking. Better he didn't know!

'I'm good. You?'

'I think I can manage.'

Harper assumed that he'd probably used the facilities when he'd ordered the food. Still, they were only about an hour from his parents' home where he seemed convinced they'd find the teenagers. He'd better be right, she thought as she replaced the helmet, scrambled back on the pillion and curled her arms around his waist for the last leg of the journey.

* * *

It was always like this, Rocco thought, passing Taunton and heading into Somerset. Retina-burning sunsets, sky streaked vermillion and purple, night creeping up on them as they headed for his family home. His polarised visor cut out most of the glare; but unfortunately, Pen's helmet didn't have one so Harper was forced to turn her head to the right and press close to him in an attempt to keep low and avoid the sun's rays. Fixing Pen's helmet, that was something he needed to sort out when they were back in Polzenith. Thinking about that kept his mind on the task, which wasn't easy. Something in the way Harper curled her arms around his waist and moulded herself into his back made him shiver reflexively. It was as if they were in bed, naked and spooning each other's warm bodies after making love. His groin tightened and he gripped the sides of the motorbike to centre himself, stay focused.

Where had that last thought come from? 'Miss' had made her opinion of him quite plain. By this time tomorrow order would have been restored and they would go their separate ways. To be honest, she really wasn't his type – prissy, bossy, uptight. Every inch the village headmistress, a total ball ache.

However, being fair minded, and in view of everything that had happened today, he cut her some slack. As Pen's father he had no one to answer to but himself. She, on the other hand, had to explain to the girl's mother and grandparents how this half-baked plan to go AWOL had been hatched without her having an inkling of it. Which brought him neatly back to Ariel MacDonald and why Harper had become her guardian in the first place?

Then, as the bike ate up the miles, another thought occurred. How had they managed to live in the same village unaware of each other's existence. It wasn't a large village, but it was a straggling one. He lived at one end of it, she at the other and they had nothing in common. Nothing to draw them together. He couldn't quite see her propping up the bar at the *Sailor's Arms* on a Saturday night, knocking back pints of real ale. Other than her being a headmistress he knew nothing about her. Sixth sense warned him to keep it that way. She might project an image of efficiency and competence but he suspected that underneath that cute little business suit she was as much trouble as her niece.

Generally, he kept life simple. Just him and Pen. He rarely invited any woman to stay the night, using Pen as an excuse – an impressionable teenager didn't need to share his breakfast with a succession of his father's lady friends. And, as had become the pattern, after half a dozen dates he'd deliver the killer: *this isn't working, it isn't you – it's me* speech. After which he'd bid the latest in a line of short-lived relationships a friendly goodbye.

Perhaps, once Pen was up at Oxford he'd have time for a proper relationship with some woman. Find a like-minded spirit to spend the rest of his life with. Harper shifted against his back and this time he didn't shiver – hormones under control – but allowed himself a wry smile. He wouldn't have to deliver 'the killer speech' to her. She was totally focused on getting her niece home and picking up on that that trekking holiday in Nepal. He suspected, she'd be out of his life quicker than he could say *Ofsted Inspection*.

Which suited him just fine.

He shook himself free of his introspection, time for all of that once they'd caught up with the teenagers. Dipping his head, he saluted the iconic Willow Man coming up on their left-hand side. It was a ritual he and Pen observed when they reached this stage of the journey. He smiled, remembering how Pen had always been ridiculously excited to see the Willow Man and to pick out Glastonbury Tor in the distance as they headed up the A39.

Those days were over for good. Pen was growing up, becoming his own man. Time he cut the apron strings, but not quite yet.

With the sun streaming orange and vermillion through the gaps in the structure, the Willow Man seemed past his best. Rocco allowed himself a wry smile and sympathised with the wicker giant, recalling Harper's outburst when he'd wheeled himself from under the car. *My God, how old are you?* An unflattering observation, but he'd taken it like a man because she was upset over her niece's disappearance. It hurt to admit it, but she was right. The years were slipping by, it was time to re-evaluate his life.

Leaving the M5 at Junction 23 he slipped down a gear and headed towards the Somerset Levels and *Penhaligon's Court*. It hadn't felt like home for years, not since he'd moved to Polzenith to escape the overwhelming burden of family expectations. Then Pen had come along – unwanted, unasked for, but soon the best thing in his life. The reason why he got up every morning, the reason he worked all hours to make his business the best it could be. Something to pass on to his boy, should he want it. Prove to his parents how wrong they'd been.

About him. About Pen.

How could he advise his son: *Don't do what I did? Get an education, then step back, take stock and decide what you want from life. Running off with this girl is madness . . . don't let history repeat itself.*

Harper changed position, reminding him of her presence. How would it look, turning up with the village headmistress riding pillion on his motorbike? He allowed himself a sardonic smile. It would send his parents into a tailspin, which maybe wasn't such a bad thing.

* * *

Rocco steered the motorbike into a layby and switched off the engine. Harper raised her head and look around, seeing nothing but fields and the low lying pastureland of the Somerset Levels. She frowned, wasn't he – *they* – a bit too old for the 'we've run out of petrol' ploy? She was just about to say something suitably scathing when he looked over his shoulder and pointed.

'Look.'

They'd left the westering sun behind and Glastonbury Tor lay before them in the still July twilight. Behind the monastery which topped the Tor, the second 'super moon' of the year glowed like a searchlight. Harper had set her year five children the task of recording its phases over the coming weeks. A holiday project, not compulsory; just enough to keep them ticking over until school started back in September. She was just about to mention it to Penhaligon but stopped. He didn't need to know that she found it difficult to 'switch off' from her demanding role. Or that as soon as one term ended she was already planning the next, busy thoughts crowding in. He would probably think her a mad old spinster who lived for her job, with nothing better to occupy her waking hours.

Maybe he was right.

Taking a deep breath she composed her next sentence carefully. He must have felt the rise and fall of her chest because he turned around, flipped up his visor and sent her a steady look. 'Yes?'

Following suit, she raised hers. 'Nothing. Nothing of moment, that is.'

His green eyes appeared almost luminous in the fading light. 'Really? Not like you to run out of words.'

Challenged, she responded. 'I was simply going to say that I collect Moon Gazing Hares.' Moon Gazing Hares? Where had that come from? Next, she'd be telling him that she was born under Pisces, was sensitive to the moon's phases, the ebb and flow of the tide and the slow turning of the seasons. She cringed and then pressed the reset button. 'Got a problem with that?'

'Moon gazing hares? I'll be sure to remember. For your birthday.' She couldn't bear being mocked by him and realised that she'd been foolish to drop her guard and show him another side to her. A softer, less driven side. She wouldn't make that mistake again.

'It's eight months away, so unlikely. Can we get on?' Quickly, she reverted to type.

'Sure.'

His shrug suggested that if she couldn't see the beauty of the bright, white moon behind St Michael's Monastery, she was a creature without a heart, without a soul. He flipped down his visor and this time, when she wrapped her arms around his waist, his back was rigid, his dislike of her unmistakeable.

* * *

Dusk had properly taken hold when they pulled up in front of a pair of ornamental gates supported by Cotswold stone gateposts. Set into the left hand pillar was a brass plaque which announced they'd arrived at *Penhaligon's Court*. Harper pulled a face and pursed her lips, no wonder he had an overinflated sense of his own importance. Penhaligon's Court, indeed. Removing his helmet, Rocco raked his fingers through his hair before hooking the helmet over his arm and leaning forward to press the button on an intercom. A voice crackled on the other end, but Harper couldn't quite make out what was said because her helmet muffled her ears. She assumed Penhaligon had uttered the modern day version of *open sesame* because the gates slowly swung back.

Replacing his helmet, Rocco drove on.

Their progress up the drive was slow, the bike's headlights picking out an ancient avenue of trees, landscaped gardens and lake. Looking past Rocco, Harper saw a floodlit house with a porticoed entrance and sweeping lawns. Were those swans sleeping on the sloping terrace? This all seemed miles away from Petroc Penhaligon's loft apartment above his garage. Maybe his parents were the caretakers of the fine house and lived in staff accommodation round the back? Incongruously, the catchphrase from a TV show sprang into Harper's mind: *who lives in a house like this?*

She didn't have time to give the matter further thought because Rocco said: 'Look, Pen's Mini. We've caught up with them. Thank God.'

'Where?'

He pointed over to a row of garages next to a stable block. Sure enough, a clapped-out Mini parked alongside a horsebox and trailer was revealed as the Triumph triggered the security lights. 'Oh, thank the Lord,' Harper breathed, hugging Rocco more tightly, although there was no longer any danger of her falling off the bike. When they drew up alongside the Mini, Harper saw its broken window, smashed rear light and the passenger door without a handle.

For the love of God, Ariel could have been killed. When she met this Pen, she'd be giving him a piece of her mind, Ariel, too.

How irresponsible. How thoughtless. How typical!

Doors at the side of the house opened and a man walked out, letting a shaft of light stream towards them across the stone flags. Rocco removed his helmet and signalled for Harper to do the same. She did so, only too aware that she looked a total wreck, makeup ruined, hair a tangled bird's nest, body swamped by Pen's bike leathers. Hardly an ideal way to present herself as Ariel's guardian/responsible adult. If life had taught her one lesson, it was that you never get a second chance to make a good impression.

'Mr Rocco. Welcome home. We've been expecting you.'

Mr Rocco?

'I bet,' was Rocco's succinct reply. Then he slapped the man on the back and swung off the bike. 'This is Miss MacDonald. I'm sure you can guess why we're here.' The man hesitated and then gave a discreet nod which acknowledged it wasn't his place to comment.

Following Rocco's example Harper dismounted, but her legs gave way a second time and she staggered forward before regaining her balance. As before, Rocco was at her side, taking her elbow and supporting her, their earlier antagonism temporarily forgotten. He handed Harper's helmet over to the member of staff and she wondered where Rocco Penhaligon fitted into this grand setting of lake, listed building and uniformed staff. Putting the thought aside, she concentrated instead on the logistics of getting Ariel back to Polzenith tomorrow morning and salvaging her holiday plans.

She allowed herself a sigh of relief. This was what she was good at – problem solving, making things work. Tomorrow, she'd hire a car, drive them home and have a head-to-head with her niece en route while she was a captive audience. Ariel was wilful, but knew that once her aunt's dander was up it would be foolish to flout her wishes. Isn't that why she'd absconded without a word in the first place?

No way would Harper have countenanced her taking off with this boy and heading for Scotland. At least, not until she got to know him and felt assured that Ariel would be safe with him. And maybe even not then. She sighed. Ariel was eighteen and didn't need anyone's permission to do what she wanted, least of all hers. Once again, Harper pondered the question: *why Scotland*? Ariel had always been dismissive of their Scottish ancestry, regarding Scotland as the land of the Jocks, inedible food and musical instruments which sounded like a banshee on steroids.

What'd changed?

'Where are they?' Rocco demanded, breaking Harper's reverie.

'The yellow drawing room, sir,' came the reply.

Gathering her wits about her, Harper dragged her elbow free of Rocco's helping hand, straightened her back and walked into the house ahead of him.

Time to regroup; time to redraw the line in the sand.

Chapter Six

A short corridor opened into a vaulted kitchen dominated by a marble-topped central island over which hung a batterie de cuisine loaded with kitchenalia. A six-oven Aga, double Belfast sink and huge American-style fridge took up one wall, while twin dishwashers and a large chicken-coop dresser holding a harlequin collection of dinner plates, bowls and cups filled the other.

A young girl was scraping plates and stacking them in the dishwasher leading Harper to deduce that dinner was over. At that point, a woman, clearly not Penhaligon's mother judging by the discreet uniform she wore, entered the kitchen.

'Rocco,' she exclaimed in delight. 'We don't see you boys for months and then you and Pen roll up within a day of each other.'

'Like buses?' Rocco joked.

'Not at all, more like an unexpected treat,' the housekeeper responded.

Harper raised an eyebrow at Penhaligon being described as a 'boy', that took a stretch of the imagination, but clearly that was how the housekeeper saw him. She sent Harper a curious, friendly look as Rocco walked over and kissed her flushed cheeks. 'Lovely to see you, Angela.

Catch you later, I – we,' he glanced over at Harper, 'have things to sort out concerning Pen and Miss MacDonald's niece.'

At the coupling of their names the housekeeper became flustered and looked about to say more when she caught the eye of the major-domo carrying their helmets and changed tack. 'Of course, go on up. Would you and your guest like a sandwich?'

'No thanks, we've already eaten. But coffee would be good. And, maybe, some of your lemon drizzle cake?'

She brightened. 'Of course.'

'This way.' Rocco led Harper up a flight of stairs which doglegged off at an angle. Grasping the handrail Harper hauled herself up them, feeling she'd aged twenty years since they left Cornwall. If she never got on another motorbike it'd be too soon. And if she never saw Rocco Penhaligon after tonight, that'd suit her fine, too. She was bone-weary, had a rotten headache and her ears were buzzing due to stress. A confrontation with Ariel was the last thing she needed. However, needs must, so summoning up her last reserves of energy she prepared to do battle.

* * *

Rocco opened a green baize door at the top of the stairs, ushering them into a large square hall which affirmed the owners' wealth: black and white chequered tiled floor, expensive rugs, large fireplace flanked by two log baskets, family portraits dating back to the eighteenth century, antique furniture and a large pedestal table in the centre of the hall displaying a collection of enamelled snuff boxes, portrait miniatures and objet trouvé. The overall effect was designed to look as if it had all been achieved by accident, however Harper was prepared to bet a month's salary that a design team had worked hard to achieve the seamless look.

Which raised the question, again – why did Rocco Penhaligon live over a garage in a Cornish backwater when his family had money in abundance?

Wordlessly, Rocco led the way across the hall towards a wide, panelled door. As they drew nearer, the tension racked up a couple of notches and his expression darkened. That didn't make sense. Surely, now they had the runaways in their sight they could relax and concentrate on getting them home? No doubt Rocco's parents would support them in this. Pushing the door open, Rocco walked into a large sitting room leaving Harper to follow.

The sitting room could easily double as the set for a period drama: large squashy sofas, ottomans, opulent fabrics, gilt mirrors, with a low table holding a collection of pure white orchids completing the look. French doors opened onto a flagged terrace and landscaped gardens where the super moon revealed the lake and a huge orangery in resplendent glory. A couple in their late seventies was seated on opposite sofas reading and sipping cognac, very much at their ease.

Of the runaways there was no sign.

Rocco stepped into the room, seemingly not caring that his biker boots left a dusty trail on the white wool carpet. Unsure of her reception Harper hung back. Rocco hadn't deigned to introduce her to the housekeeper and she only hoped his mood had improved enough for him to introduce her to his parents.

'Petroc –' The man half rose, but Rocco stayed him with a gesture.

'Where are they?' His eyes swept the room like laser beams, as if half expecting Pen and Ariel to jump out from behind the thick, swagged curtains and shout: *surprise.*

'Not here.' The elderly lady on the sofa closed the novel she was reading and sighed. She didn't seem to find her son's behaviour out of the ordinary, making Harper wonder about Rocco's relationship with his parents.

'Not here?' Rocco's spoke softly, but his anger was plain. He balled his hands into fists in an obvious attempt to keep his anger in check. 'Would it be too much to expect you to tell us where they are?'

Us. At last, he'd acknowledged her presence.

'Come in and sit down Petroc.' His mother patted the space next to her but Rocco ignored her.

Showing him no such consideration his father regarded him coldly. 'Where are your manners, Petroc? Please introduce us to your,' he paused for a moment, 'companion.' Harper walked further into the room only too aware she looked far from the kind of sophisticated, educated woman the Penhaligons would doubtless expect their son to associate with. Hardly the ideal person to command respect and obedience from a runaway niece.

Rocco frowned. 'Harper MacDonald, my parents James and Heather Penhaligon.'

'How do you do?' Sidestepping him, Harper extended her hand, but Rocco held her back with an outstretched arm.

'No time for all of that. Would you please answer my question, Father?'

So this was how the Penhaligons played Happy Families? Rocco was about to say more when the housekeeper entered with a tray bearing a cafetiere, cups, plates and lemon drizzle cake. Picking up the atmosphere, she put the tray down on a side table and headed back to the kitchen.

'Pen isn't here,' Heather Penhaligon said, fussing over plates and napkins. 'Sugar, Miss MacDonald?'

Rocco looked fit to explode. Harper waved the cup of coffee away as politely as she could, although she was dying for a hot drink. Now wasn't the time. 'Thank you Mrs Penhaligon, perhaps after we've spoken to Pen and Ariel?'

'Oh, that won't be possible, my dear.' Heather Penhaligon poured out the coffee and smiled over at Harper. 'They left straight after lunch.' She glanced at her watch as if to confirm their departure time to herself and then smiled. 'Harper MacDonald? I take it your family has Scottish roots?'

'On my father's side, yes.'

'My family also, Miss MacDonald. Hence my Christian name, although I think Harper has a prettier ring to it. My ancestors were Gunns, from the far north east of Scotland, whereas my husband's family are Cornish through and through.' Another smile as she rattled on inconsequentially.

'Harper doesn't need to know about our ancestors, damn it, Mother,' Rocco fumed. 'What we need to know is where Pen and Ariel are headed.'

'Oh, that's quite easy.' His father folded up his newspaper and regarded his son over the top of his reading glasses. He took his time answering, as though he enjoyed goading his son.

'And?' Rocco prompted.

'Leicester,' he said eventually.

'*Leicester*?' Rocco's barked response made Harper jump. 'Why Leicester?' Now he was glaring at Harper as though she'd known the answer but was withholding it from him.

'My parents live in Leicester.' Harper stayed calm in the face of Rocco's anger. 'I'll ring my mother and ask her to hold on to them until we get there. Problem solved.'

'You think?' was his caustic reply.

'Yes, I do.' It was ridiculous for him to act as though Leicester was in another galaxy, far, far away, when it was at the opposite end of the ancient Fosse Way. Okay, Pen and Ariel had stolen the march on them again, but they would soon catch up with them.

She sounded more confident than she felt. Her parents had always spoiled Ariel and, knowing her mother, the runaways would be cosseted and fussed over. Never mind that Ariel had wrecked their holiday plans or that Pen had deliberately disobeyed his father. They were *youngsters*, her mother's favourite word, and should be allowed to live a life free from obligations and responsibilities. The very attitude which had paved the way for her sister's downfall.

How different it had been for *her* growing up, Harper reflected. Get top grades, graduate from a Russell Group university, set your sights on a good career, follow in our footsteps. Putting that thought aside, another struck her. If they'd left for Leicester, why was the Mini parked outside the back door? The same thought had evidently occurred to Rocco. He looked at his parents suspiciously, as though there was something they weren't telling him

'Pen's Mini's outside. If he's not driving that, what exactly *is* he driving?'

'Now, Rocco.' Getting to her feet, his mother walked over to him and stroked his arm placatingly. 'We didn't want Pen and Ariel – beautiful girl by the way, Miss MacDonald, and a credit to you – travelling another mile in that wreck of a car. Really, what were you thinking, allowing him to take it on the road in the first place, Petroc? I can understand you not wanting us to buy him a car when he passed his test. But to send him on his summer holidays in that jalopy, beggars belief.'

'Summer holidays?' Rocco exploded. 'Is that what he told you? And you swallowed it hook, line and sinker?'

'There was nothing *to* swallow, as you put it. They are simply a couple of teenagers taking time out after exams. Pen explained everything to us.' Getting to his feet, Rocco's father sent Harper a look which hinted that he hoped she'd side with them. And, put that way, it did all sound perfectly reasonable. Plainly, he was unaware that Pen didn't want to take up his place at Oxford after the summer.

She and Rocco exchanged a look before he went on to ask with deceptive calm, 'So, what car *is* he driving?'

'The Jeep we bought him after he passed his test. The one *you* so ungraciously turned down on his behalf, if I remember correctly.' Heather Penhaligon's reproachful look implied that being prevented from indulging their grandson was nothing new and was a source of friction between them. 'We felt sure you'd have no objection to us rewarding him for working hard to get good grades.'

'He hasn't got his results, yet, Mother.' Rocco pointed out. However, Heather Penhaligon was intent on acting the proud grandmother in front of Harper.

'Such a clever boy,' she explained to Harper. 'In spite of the odds stacked against him.' Another reproachful look over at her son.

'Odds?' Harper couldn't help asking, although it was none of her business. Scratch that! It had become her business the moment Pen had driven off with her niece.

'Yes. Odds.' Heather Penhaligon glanced over at her husband, openly seeking his support. 'Attending state school when we wanted him to board at Petroc's old school, as generations of Penhaligons have done. However, Petroc,' another reproachful look, 'would have none of it.'

'You won't find Miss MacDonald championing the independent

sector, Mother. She might not look the part,' *thanks!* 'but she is the executive head of a federation of local schools, has dragged them out of Special Measures and prevented their closure. She's regarded as a saint in the Three Pols.' Harper nearly fainted on the spot. Next time she needed a reference she knew who to ask. She didn't have time to bask in Rocco's praise, however, because he continued in the bitterest of tones. 'I think Pen's done pretty well, all things considered.'

'That's a moot point,' his father put in.

Rounding on him, Rocco replied in a steady voice. 'You lost the right to have any say in his life the day you suggested I put him up for adoption.'

Adoption? Harper looked from one Penhaligon to another, seeking enlightenment. During those drawn out seconds, Rocco gained mastery over his emotions.

'I'm sure Miss MacDonald doesn't want to witness us dragging skeletons out of the family armoire,' he said.

'At least we agree on one thing,' his mother replied.

'Quite.' James Penhaligon frowned at his son's lack of manners. 'Miss MacDonald looks exhausted. Judging from your attire, I'm guessing that you've ridden all the way from Polzenith on one of those infernal motorbikes you take such pride in restoring.'

'What of it?' Another bone of contention, clearly.

His father didn't elaborate. Throwing his son an eloquent look he walked over to the fireplace and pressed a bell to the left of the mantelpiece. 'It's late. Angela will show Miss MacDonald to the guest room and we will continue this discussion in the morning when we've all had time to consider our actions. Before we say something we'll regret.'

'Rather late for regrets, Father.' Rocco's shrug suggested that that this evening's family meeting was a follow-on from angry words spoken years before; words which could neither be forgotten nor called back. Harper glanced between the Penhaligons, each one bristling with anger and regret, searching for clues. Why had the elder Penhaligons wanted Rocco to put Pen up for adoption? Was he not Rocco's son? She wouldn't get any answer tonight, that much was certain.

She was glad when Angela answered James Penhaligon's summons and led her up a grand staircase to one of the Penhaligons' guest rooms.

* * *

After the day's events, Harper was glad to lie full length in the bath Angela had insisted on drawing for her. Her tired muscles relaxed in water liberally infused with Jo Malone bath oil. More products in the brand's black and white livery were laid out on a glass topped table next to the bath: body lotion, perfume, night cream. The panniers, which Rocco had thrown so cavalierly over the bike when they'd set out on the journey, had miraculously appeared at the foot of the bed and her meagre belongings unpacked and laid out next to a large fluffy robe and a silk chemise. Clearly, a guest's every need was catered for, which hinted at old money and an ease of living beyond Harper's dreams or means.

Ariel would have lapped it up she thought, turning the tap with her big toe and adding more hot water to the bath. Ariel considered herself a bit special, *understatement!* Coming to this grand house, complete with live-in staff would be right up her strasse. How she must have simpered and acted the part: *Let me help you with that, Mrs Penhaligon. I can see where Pen gets his good looks from, Mr P.* She knew exactly how to charm the pants off folk, when it suited her. In that, she was a better actress than her mother. Tears, tantrums and strops were reserved for her exclusively, Harper reflected, dribbling scented water from a large natural sponge over tired muscles.

Now Ariel had seen Pen's background, she'd be in no rush to dump him as she had previous boyfriends. Each one had been the love of her life until she'd discovered some trait or mannerism she didn't care for and had blown them out and moved on to the next hapless male.

Treat 'em mean, keep 'em keen seemingly her mantra.

Harper had lost track of the times she'd turned perfectly presentable young men away from the door because Ariel considered them 'dorks' or 'lame' or, current favourite expression – 'douchebags'. Nice. Harper didn't want her niece to get her heart broken, but it wouldn't hurt if, after a week in her company, Pen decided that joining the foreign legion was preferable to spending more time with Miss Ariel MacDonald.

Which brought Harper, uncomfortably, to another matter. Sleeping arrangements. Rocco's parents had offered her a guest bedroom despite probably believing that she and Rocco were an item. She hoped that they hadn't allowed Pen and Ariel to sleep together. That would complicate matters and make dragging her home twice as difficult. She thought of her sister Shona, pregnant at twenty and now on husband number three. She wasn't going to allow the same thing to happen to Ariel, although she guessed Ariel was probably savvier in *that department* than she was!

Groaning, she shifted in the bath and then shuddered. All this introspection had allowed the water to grow tepid. Climbing out, she quickly dried herself on an impossibly fluffy towel, slipped on the silk chemise, slid between the six-hundred thread count cotton sheets and was soon asleep.

Chapter Seven

Next morning, Rocco stood outside Harper's room bearing a cup of tea. Tapping on the door and receiving no answer, he tentatively pushed it open. 'Miss MacDonald?' he whispered and then shook his head at his own stupidity. *Miss MacDonald?* Surely they'd progressed *wa-ayy* beyond that? 'Harper,' he whispered, crossing the threshold and waiting as the mound of screwed up bedclothes on the king-sized bed shifted.

He tried again. 'Harper, are you awake?'

'I am *now*,' Harper murmured grumpily.

Placing the cup of tea on the bedside table, Rocco opened the curtains to let in the morning light. Harper yawned, gave him a sleepy once-over and then sat bolt upright in bed, all vestiges of sleep gone.

'What's this?' Her nod acknowledged that he was suited, booted, and ready for the road. Picking her mobile off the bedside table she checked the time and then exclaimed. 'Five o'clock!'

'Five o'clock on a fine summer's morning.' He gestured at the world beyond the window in what he hoped was a friendly, open manner. It wouldn't do to let her catch on that he intended to dissolve their partnership once she'd drunk her tea and was awake enough to take it in.

He owed her that much.

'You're ready to hit the road. Why didn't you wake me?' She sent him a suspicious look, reaching out for the dressing gown draped across the foot of the bed.

'I didn't wake you because,' deep breath, 'you won't be coming with me.' The killer blow delivered, he turned on his heel and made for the safety of the landing.

'Who says I'm not coming with you?'

'I do.'

'Really?' Her tone, suggesting that the matter was far from decided, stopped him in his tracks. Having learned that the best way to deal with Harper MacDonald was to present her with no room for manoeuvre, Rocco's reply was short and sweet.

'Yes, really.'

'I don't remember being consulted. Oh wait, I wasn't. You decided this all on your own.'

'You weren't consulted because I thought it was time we parted company and . . .'

'No need to elaborate. I get it.'

Reaching out for the cup of tea, Harper added the sugar lump he'd placed in the saucer and stirred her tea slowly. During the drawn out seconds neither spoke, which unnerved Rocco. He'd expected protest, arguments, a verbal fight to the death, questions about this house, his parents, what they'd said about Pen and why they'd said it. Instead, a show of sweet reasonableness. Why was she taking it all so calmly? Dismissing the thought, he decided to quit while he was ahead. It wouldn't surprise him if she leapt out of bed, threw a coat over her nightie and climbed on the bike before he could say: *hasta la vista, baby*.

'Good. Angela will make you breakfast and Williamson – the man who met us at the back door last night, will organise a car so you can return home. I'll catch up with the runaways in Leicester and bring them back to Polzenith. Take your time; drink your tea, there's no rush.' He started to back out of the room. 'Well, not for you at any rate.'

'Not for *me*? Of course, I understand. Fine.'

Meekness didn't suit her and Rocco was suspicious of her caving in so easily. But he was pleased that she hadn't put up a fight. Perhaps she wasn't as smart as she made out. He'd outwitted her easily. Too easily? Adopting a neutral expression, it wouldn't do to let her know that he considered he'd won the battle, he reached the bedroom door. Curling his fingers round the handle, he held his breath; three more steps and he would be on his way to Leicester.

'How . . . ever.' She drew out the syllables, forcing him to turn round. 'I *am* rather concerned.'

'You are?' He braced himself.

'Of course.' She regarded him over the rim of her cup, seemingly concerned for his welfare. 'Leicester's a sprawling city with many suburbs. You'll get lost without a navigator. That's me, in case you're wondering. I wouldn't *dream* of letting you leave without me.' Putting the cup and saucer down on the bedside table, she pushed back the covers and swung her legs out of bed. 'Give me a moment and I'll be good to go. I had hoped for breakfast,' she shrugged as if it was of no consequence, 'but we can easily pick something up along the way. As we did yesterday.'

He frowned. 'Not a good idea.'

'Breakfast, or my coming with you?'

'The latter. You aren't used to riding pillion, we've established that. Yesterday, I had to slow down on tricky bends because I was afraid you'd fall off.'

'Your concern is touching.'

He ignored the barbed comment. 'I need to make up for lost time and I can travel faster without you. If it'd been up to me, I would have got straight back on the bike last night and headed for Leicester.'

'Naturally, if I'm holding you back in any way, I'll bow out. Your major- domo, Wilkinson?'

'Williamson.'

'Whatever,' she used the expression ironically, 'can organise a car, as you've suggested. However,' *that damn word again*, 'you don't get rid of me that easily. I'll be heading up the Fosse Way, right behind you. But with one subtle difference.' Smiling, she walked over to the window and looked out across the landscaped gardens into the beauty of the dew-drenched morning.

'And what would that be?'

She took her time answering. 'I know where my parents live, whereas . . .' Turning, she smiled sweetly.

You don't –

The words hovered, unspoken, in the space between them. But Rocco wasn't conceding defeat that easily.

'I had thought of that, of course. *However,*' he threw the word back at her, 'I'm hoping that Pen, having realised what an idiot he's been, will answer his phone when I ring. With a bit of luck I'll catch him half-asleep and off guard, recently he seems to spend most of his time in bed.' The image of *his* son in bed with *her* niece did nothing for his blood pressure and left him feeling slightly nauseated. Shaking his head, he added: 'I'll make it plain that I expect him to return home ASAP.'

'Good luck with that. And what about my niece?'

'What about her? She can stay with her grandparents until you catch up with her and then –'

'Then?'

'To be honest I don't really care. She's your problem. I have Pen to deal with. I'll find somewhere nearby, a bed and breakfast most likely, where we can discuss this crazy idea of not taking up his university place. Doesn't he realise how lucky he is? How many sixth formers get offered an unconditional place at an Oxford college?'

Her eyebrows raised slightly at *unconditional*. Impressed, but not for long. 'And you think he'll listen?'

'I'm sure he will. He's never given me a moment's worry until now.' He zipped up his biker jacket, a precursor to leaving.

'That'll be down to Ariel, I suppose?' Her tone was really snarky.

'Well, isn't it?'

He might've known she'd be trouble. He should've followed his instinct and headed up the Fosse Way without taking his leave of her. However, abandoning her for his parents to deal with would have reflected badly on him and their relationship was already at rock bottom.

Had been ever since Pen had entered his life and complicated things. Well, now she knew where she stood and, having levelled with her, he felt honour had been satisfied and he could leave.

If Pen didn't answer the phone he would find her parents' address somehow. Even if it meant ringing every *bloody* MacDonald in the *bloody* phone book until he located them.

Assuming they weren't ex-directory, of course.

The more he thought about it, the more he realised that she was right. Trying to find the MacDonald household without her help would be like trying to find a needle in a haystack.

Damn. Damn. Damn.

Worse case scenarios began to crowd in. Pen and Ariel would get wind of what was planned and would be half way up the M6 before you could say: *Scotch Corner*. Pen would refuse point blank to leave his new girlfriend and travel home. There would be an unsightly scene on the MacDonald's doorstep, Ariel – from what he knew of her – relishing every moment and encouraging Pen to defy him. His confidence took a dive and he ground his teeth, angrier with his son than at any point over the last eighteen years. If Pen had been a couple of years younger, the law would've been on his side. At eighteen, Pen was an adult and could do exactly as he liked, and that bloody niece of hers doubtless knew it.

'Of course, they've gone straight to my parents,' Harper broke through his internal monologue. 'Ariel will be keen to show Pen and his Jeep to her friends. She won't pass up on an opportunity to crow over them, it's what she does.'

'Charming,' he commented.

She turned, leaned back against the window frame and sent him a straight look. 'You have no idea who you're dealing with. That's another reason why we shouldn't split up. Ariel takes some handling.'

'I think I'm capable of dealing with a stroppy adolescent.'

He sounded more confident than he felt. His and Pen's world was predominantly male: mechanics, suppliers, other workers, any females who came into their house were there fleetingly. He was out of practice dealing with younger women, teenagers in particular.

Harper's snort of derision underlined the fact.

'Think so? Pen sounds a sweet boy, malleable even. Ariel will have him wrapped round her little finger by now.' Once again, the image of her niece's legs wrapped around his son crept into his mind. He swallowed the bile in his throat and concentrated on what Harper was saying. 'Turning up on my parents' doorstep and coming the heavy father will play right into her hands. She'll laugh in your face, remind you that there's nothing you – we – can do about it. Then they'll leave us standing in a cloud of dust while they carry out their hare-brained scheme to head for Scotland and turn their back on university. On everything we had planned for them.'

We had planned for them? That made them sound like co-parents, partners even.

'Maybe we have overplayed our hand,' Rocco admitted, shoulders slumping as he leaned against the door jamb. The thought had occurred to him earlier when shaving. What if this disaster *was* entirely of their making? His blood ran cold. Pen would never have taken the Mini and headed north off his own bat. Ariel, doubtless telling him to *grow a pair* and pointing out how unfairly they'd been treated had been enough to turn his world on its head.

Pen was at that awkward age, just learning about girls and how they operated. In many respects he'd lived a sheltered life and was unfamiliar with feminine wiles, the weapons women had in their arsenal and how they used them to make you do exactly what they wanted. Harper was right, he did need an ally – and she was standing right in front of him.

Fuck. He'd been looking forward to travelling the next leg of the journey alone, collecting Pen, and then delivering the vintage motorbike to a friend's widow in Penrith. After that, he'd bring a chastened Pen back to Cornwall to work in the garage until he'd earned the right to be trusted. Until it was time for him to go up to Oxford.

What Harper did with her minx of a niece was her business.

'Very well, our partnership continues. But once we catch up with them, all bets are off and we part company.'

'Agreed.' She didn't seem unduly upset at the thought of ending their uneasy alliance.

Used to women hanging on his every word and keen to spend time with him, Rocco found her eagerness to be shot of him unflattering and disconcerting. A bit of an ego-crusher to be honest. He raised his head to speak to her but stopped dead in his tracks. As Harper walked away from the window the sun streamed through her diaphanous chemise, revealing every inch of her naked body. A jolt of sexual awareness shot from the pit of his stomach and zigzagged through his groin and all points south before petering out around his knees, leaving behind a shockwave of surprise.

Another inward groan.

Who was he to lecture his son on being lured away from Polzenith by a winsome body. Yesterday, when Harper had clung to him on each sharp bend pressing her body into his back, he'd experienced a similar reaction. A gentleman, he reasoned, would do the chivalrous thing and look away. Now it was his turn to be bloody-minded and disinclined to show her any consideration. She was the most aggravating, exasperating woman he'd come across in all his forty years. If that was a family characteristic, Pen hadn't stood a chance.

'You know the drill,' he said sharply, annoyed with himself and the sexual frisson over which he had no control. 'Be ready in half an hour or I'll leave without you.'

It was an empty threat and they both knew it.

'Of course.' Her tone, doubtless the one she used to pacify fractious four-year-olds on their first day in school, grated. 'I'll be ready. I'm guessing that you've already breakfasted? Maybe you could sling a couple of rounds of bread in the toaster and I'll grab them on my way through the kitchen.'

'Anything else m'lady requires? Devilled kidneys? Kedgeree? Eggs Benedict?'

'No need for sarcasm,' she reproved, 'toast will be just fine. Oh, and maybe some coffee?'

Shooting her one last – *don't push it* glare, he left the room closing the door behind him.

Harper, aware of how close she'd come to overplaying her hand let out a long, slow whistle. Her years as a teacher had taught her how to use sweet reasonableness to defuse awkward situations and it'd stood her in good stead this morning. Her lips curved in a half-smile as she walked towards the dressing table to collect her wash bag. She'd bested Petroc Penhaligon and that pleased her in ways she didn't quite understand.

Catching her reflection in the mirror her smile vanished.

The sun.

The chemise.

Oh. My. God.

She might as well have danced naked round the bedroom with a feather in her hair. Penhaligon had seen every inch of her: high breasts, flat stomach and rounded buttocks, shadowy triangle of hair, everything. All the way to her painted toes which were now curling in embarrassment.

And he hadn't said a word.

Chapter Eight

Rocco was astride the motorbike, gunning the engine impatiently when Harper joined him by the stable block. 'Shouldn't we say goodbye to your parents?' she ventured, climbing on behind him.

'What? And risk them telling Pen we're on our way? Don't think so. Ready?'

'Ready.' Then it was a reprise of yesterday, her clinging to him aware that she was surplus to requirements and 'slowing him down'. But with one subtle difference, she held the trump card: her parents' address, and she had no intention of revealing it until they were on the outskirts of Leicester. That way, he couldn't dump her without appearing, to use Ariel's expression, a complete douchebag.

Not that she'd put it past him.

* * *

They reached Leicester without incident and in record time. Rocco, ignoring her advice to travel along the Fosse Way, chose the M5 and A roads instead, making Harper suspect this was his way of establishing who was boss on this trip. She'd been half-joking when she'd said she was navigator, but clearly that was how he regarded her. Navigator, bomb aimer, excess baggage, annoyance. *Nice*, she fumed. However, she'd kept her counsel, knowing speed was of the essence if they were to catch up with the runaways. Hopefully, the fact that teenagers liked to lie in bed until noon would be in their favour and they'd reach her family home before Pen and Ariel were aware that they were hot on their trail.

At least she thought, as they drove the last hundred or so yards through the still-sleeping suburb of Stoneygate, she hadn't fallen off, wobbled or – worse – clung to him like a medieval maiden slung across a knight errant's saddle, cowering in fear of a dragon.

Knight errant? Ha! Anyone less gallant and chivalrous than Rocco Penhaligon was hard to imagine. She'd rather take her chances with the dragon.

Her huff of derision steamed up her visor.

Rocco slowed the bike and pulled up alongside the kerb. Flipping up his visor he turned towards her and waited, sending her a cool look which barely concealed his impatience.

'And?' he prompted.

'And, what?'

'House number?'

'Houses in the avenue don't have numbers, only names,' she said. He looked singularly unimpressed, given the grandeur of his parents' Grade II listed manor.

'Name, then?'

'Killiecrankie.'

'Killie-*what*? Oh, I get it – the battle where brave MacDonalds laid down their life for the Jacobite cause. 1689, wasn't it? Don't look so surprised, I do have Scottish ancestry and, despite all indications to the contrary, have been on the receiving end of a good education.' His voice trailed away and his expression clouded, hinting that boarding school hadn't been the happiest time of his life. Was that why he'd sent Pen to the local primary? Harper did the maths, if she'd rocked up in Polzenith a few years earlier she would have taught Pen in Year Six and met Rocco at parents' evening.

Giving her no time for further thought Rocco drove slowly along the tree-lined avenue until he located *Killiecrankie*. Drawing to a halt at the foot of the drive he signalled for her to dismount, then he wheeled the bike off the road and parked it behind a high hedge inside the property.

Removing his helmet he placed it on his seat and signalled for her to do the same. Then he raised his finger to his lips and nodded towards the house. Harper was quick to catch on; no need to announce their arrival, she would let them in with her key and catch Pen and Ariel . . . doing what, exactly? Up to no good? In bed together?

She gulped and walked over the grass to avoid walking up the gravel drive.

Memories came crowding in thick and fast, taking her back to the day she'd sat her last A level . . . After school, she'd run across the grass, whirling her school bag around her head, singing at the top of her voice and dancing a happy dance. Tomorrow she was setting off on a camping weekend with friends to celebrate the end of exams. She'd thrown her rucksack on the oak bench in the hall and burst into the kitchen, ready to be congratulated by her parents for sitting her exams without a fuss. Unlike her sister Shona who made a drama out of everything. It made her sick to remember the scene which had greeted her. Her mother crying at the table, her father standing boot-faced by the sink and Shona, seemingly without a care in the world, dropping scoops of ice cream into a KitchenAid blender announcing that she'd have to *up her calcium levels now there was a baby on the way.*

She couldn't go through all that again, she simply couldn't.

History would *not* repeat itself, not if she had anything to do with it.

Putting the thought aside she let herself into the house prepared to do battle. She tiptoed across the oak floorboards avoiding those which creaked, signalling for Rocco to follow suit.

'Kitchen . . .' she mouthed, pointing towards the closed door.

The house had a strange, empty feel. By rights, her father should have been at the kitchen table listening to Radio 4 and reading The Times. Her mother would usually be preparing breakfast, chatting to him as she scrambled eggs, even though she knew he liked to read his paper in peace.

Pushing the kitchen door ajar, Harper paused on the threshold and sucked in a dismayed breath. The kitchen was a total bomb site. Dirty dishes, cutlery and glasses, wine bottles, pizza boxes and her mother's favourite raspberry gin lay next to cans of mixers and hacked off slices of lemon and lime. The air was redolent with the smell of breakfast – bacon, eggs, fried bread. A cast iron skillet sat in a halo of grease splatters on the halogen hob.

The scene bore the hallmark of Ariel's haphazard cooking and weak grasp of what constituted housework.

With the skill of an Indian scout, Harper walked over to the frying pan and held her hand above it. She dipped a forefinger in the puddle of oil which had remnants of the fried bread floating in it.

Lukewarm. Clearly, the runaways weren't far ahead of them.

'I'll check upstairs.'

Leaving Penhaligon in the kitchen she took the stairs two at a time, bursting into Ariel's room. The bed was empty but had been slept in. Next, her parents' room. The duvet cover was wrinkle free, covered in the cushions and square pillows her mother considered a sign of sophisticated living. Then she headed for the guest room. Thank God, that bed had been slept in too, which meant they hadn't . . . *Calm down, MacDonald.* She was in danger of becoming obsessed with the notion of Ariel and Pen sleeping together. But she couldn't let go of the thought. As she'd remarked to Rocco – was it only yesterday? – it might be okay for his son to sow his wild oats, but in her niece's case they'd be praying for crop failure!

Raised voices reached her from downstairs and she sent up a silent prayer. Rocco must have found Pen and Ariel and was reading the riot act. Crisis averted. Her relief was short lived. When she entered the kitchen she found Rocco leaning against the sink, arms folded across his chest, trade mark sardonic smile in place. Standing in front of him wielding a cricket bat, was a man wearing an unflatteringly short towelling dressing gown. The bat-wielding assailant was on the scrawny side while Penhaligon, used to hauling car engines around like play furniture, had muscles to spare. Harper tutted, if it wasn't so ridiculous it would have been be amusing. However, her sense of humour seemed to have deserted her somewhere along the M5.

'Mother's ringing the police,' the man in the dressing gown said. 'For your own safety, I suggest that you stay right there until they arrive. I should warn you, I play cricket for the university and am pretty handy with a bat, if I say so myself.'

'Anthony,' Harper said his name. Anthony, evidently in full flow and running on adrenaline, didn't hear.

'We've never had Hell's Angels in the Avenue. You can tell your ch-chapter that I have no intention of allowing that to change. Or of permitting you to . . . to *squat* in this house while the owners are on holiday.' He froze, probably realising that it wasn't a good idea to let a gang of Hell's Angels know the house was unoccupied.

'Anthony.' Harper spoke more loudly this time. 'I'll take that. Thank you.' Holding out her hand she sent him the no nonsense look she used when confiscating Pokémon cards and other pocket games from inattentive pupils.

'Harper! Thank goodness you're okay? This thug hasn't . . .' He gulped, his Adam's Apple moving up and down convulsively, unable to say the word.

'Hasn't what?' Rocco growled, unfolding his arms and taking a step towards him.

'You know . . .'

'Assaulted me? Don't be so ridiculous,' Harper snapped.

For a moment, she thought Penhaligon was going to add something snarky like – *the school ma'am? Credit me with some taste.* Taking the bat from her neighbour Harper placed it on the kitchen table, passed a weary hand over her eyes and took a steadying breath. There was no need to vent her anger and frustration on her neighbour who'd been brave enough to investigate a potential burglary.

'Why are you dressed like a biker chick?' Anthony gave her a second look.

Biker chick? In spite of everything, Harper swallowed down a gurgle of laughter. She hadn't thought that Anthony, Admissions Manager at Leicester University, forty-five years old and living at home with his mother, knew such words.

'It's a long story. Would you please ring your mother, reassure her that everything's okay and ask the S.W.A.T team to stand down?' Anthony was Neighbourhood Watch co-ordinator and took his duties seriously. He frowned at her flippant reference to the S.W.A.T team, but let it pass.

'As long as you're okay, Harper.'

'I am.'

Retrieving his mobile phone from the pocket of his dressing gown, he called his mother and explained the situation. 'So, why are you here? Shouldn't you be in Nepal?'

'I should.' Harper brought Anthony up to speed regarding Ariel and Pen, aware that Rocco was eager to get back on the road.

'Ariel?' Anthony assumed the pained expression people usually adopted at the mention of her name. 'You've missed her by an hour. I was going to ring your parents last night because she and a young man, held an impromptu *party*.' He spoke as if Sodom and Gomorrah had relocated to leafy Stoneygate. Harper and Rocco looked round the kitchen, exchanged a glance and then shrugged. Party? The evidence suggested that a few of Ariel's friends had called round for beer and a pizza, nothing more.

Momentarily, they were united in defence of their wayward teenagers.

'And?' Knowing Anthony, she suspected that there was more.

'He stayed the night. Then I remembered that your parents were on a flotilla holiday somewhere off the Greek islands and couldn't be contacted. I was about to ring you when Ariel told me you knew all about her and the boy being in the house and were *cool with it*, to use teenage argot.' He glanced at Rocco, openly relishing his use of 'argot', a word a biker would be unlikely to have in his vocabulary. Then he gave a superior sniff and added, 'Considering, ahem, past history I thought that unlikely.'

Shona's misdemeanours were well documented and Harper didn't need a middle aged academic passing judgement on her family.

She didn't have time for this. All that mattered was that she and Rocco got on their way, pronto. Judging from Penhaligon's expression, he agreed. As she was steering Anthony firmly but politely towards the back door another thought struck her. Her parents hadn't mentioned a flotilla holiday to her, although clearly Ariel had known all about it, otherwise why had she stopped off at Leicester on her way to Scotland? Her grandparents, indulgent as they were, would have demanded to know why she wasn't on her way to L.A, and would have quizzed about her 'new boyfriend'.

'We're wasting time,' Rocco cut in. 'My life in Cornwall is on hold, jobs are stacking up at the garage, and the order books are full. So, if you don't mind?'

Harper held up her hand, she didn't need him on her case, too. 'Give me a few minutes to clean up, and –' She walked over to the sink to rinse plates before stacking them in the dishwasher. Rocco caught her by the arm, forestalling her.

'Oh, no you don't. Once we catch up with Pen and Ariel, they can travel back to Polzenith via Leicester and clean up the house. Beds?' Harper understood exactly what he was asking.

'Both slept in, but unmade.'

'Okay.' His brisk nod suggested that he was relieved to have that confirmed. Maybe he wasn't as cool as he made out about Pen sowing his wild oats? 'Anthony, is it?'

'Ye-es' Anthony edged closer to the back door, guessing that Rocco was about to demand something from him.

'How long are Harper's parents away for?'

'Two w-weeks I think,' he stammered.

'Okay, that gives us some leeway. Time to find the kids, bring them back here and make them clean up.' Releasing Harper's arm, he picked up the cricket bat. Anthony flinched, as though expecting Rocco to lay about him. 'Your bat.' He rested it across the back of his forearm, the handle pointing towards Anthony, as if it was a sword. Gingerly, Anthony took it and then allowed Rocco to escort him out of the house via the back door, all the way to the snicket gate linking the two properties.

'If this was my house, I'd have that gate permanently bolted,' Rocco said on his return.

'Really? Well, this isn't your house, so don't concern yourself about it.' It rankled that Rocco had assumed the role of dominant male and taken command of the situation.

'And, in case you're unaware of it, Miss MacDonald, the guy's sweet on you.' Rocco leaned back against the sink again, leaving the thought hanging in the air.

'Anthony? No way.'

'*Way*,' he replied, nodding for emphasis.

Harper's cheeks burned. She'd known Anthony all her life, he was more of an old maid than she was! If Rocco Penhaligon thought he was the best she could do, there was no hope for her. Looking up she saw a devil of mischief dancing in his eyes before it vanished and he turned away. When he swung back it was business as usual.

'Okay, so let's hit the road and see if we can catch up with them.'

Harper nodded. Unusually, she and Penhaligon were singing from the same hymn sheet. Seems like she'd have to forgive him for suggesting that if no one else wanted her, she had Anthony as backup. Rocco's stomach rumbled loudly, reminding them that it was several hours since they'd snatched a hurried breakfast.

Now Harper assumed command. 'I'll write a note for my parents in case they get back off holiday and this mess greets them. You make tea, look for biscuits in the cupboard over there, then bring it through to my mother's study, across the hall.

'Yes, Ma'am.' Rocco saluted smartly. Resisting the urge to say something cutting, Harper headed for her mother's study. Eventually Rocco joined her, not with tea and biscuits as requested, but slices of last night's pizza reheated in the microwave. To wash it down he'd made a weak shandy from beer and lemonade.

'No milk, so . . .' Rocco seated himself at her mother's desk. Looking round and taking stock as he chewed thoughtfully on a soggy slice of pizza it was plain he was gathering enough information from the surroundings to figure out what made her family tick.

'What does your mother do?'

'She's a forensic geneticist, semi-retired; her speciality is garnering genetic information from soil samples and other materials. She worked with the team which disinterred Richard the Third. The King in the Carpark? She's often called upon as an expert witness in tricky cases, some of them quite gruesome. This,' she indicated a filing cabinet at the end of the desk, 'contains her research into the link between British hereditary surnames and the Y chromosome.'

Rocco gave a long, slow whistle, showing respect for her mother's academic studies.

'And your father?' He pointed with his slice of pizza at a photograph taken at some formal occasion or other.

'Like me, he was a primary school head – but then he became an Ofsted Inspector before finally joining Her Majesty's Inspectorate of Schools, specialising in primary education. Although retired, he still undertakes consultancy work and is often called upon if there's a tricky situation to resolve. A failing school, an incompetent head, a vocal group of parents making life difficult for a school and its staff, for example.'

Rocco nodded. 'They must be very proud of what you've achieved.' This time there was no sting in his words.

'I guess.' Harper shrugged, but chose not to mention that becoming one of Her Majesty's Inspectors was the goal they'd set for her, not one she'd chosen herself.

'What's this?' He gestured towards a wall lined with photos showing Shona in different stage and television roles, each photo emphasising dramatic poses, her blond gorgeousness and confidence.

'Shona's Wall of Fame,' Harper remarked dryly. Reaching out, she touched a photograph of her sister wearing a Grecian-style costume, hair arranged in ringlets interwoven with fake seaweed. 'This is her at the end of her second year at the Royal Central School of Speech and Drama, playing Miranda in a production of the Tempest. Little did we know, that underneath those flowing robes was an embryonic Ariel.' She pulled a face at the very thought.

'I'm guessing that's how your niece got her name – *Ariel*? After the spirit rescued from the tree in which the witch Sycorax imprisoned him? Or is your sister drawn to the poetry of Sylvia Plath?' Evidently, he *had* been on the receiving end of a pretty thorough education. Now Anthony's ruse of using 'argot' to trip him up seemed even more pathetic. 'Don't look so surprised, after a year at university I decided that the world of academe wasn't for me.' A bit like Pen, Harper thought, sending Penhaligon an oblique look he was quick to pick up on. 'I know what you're thinking, given my history, bringing Pen to heel and expecting him to take up his place at Oxford isn't going to be easy.'

'Exactly.'

Then he adroitly changed the subject, deflecting her interest away from them. 'Ariel's father?'

'The actor who played Prince Ferdinand. *Oh, brave new world that has such creatures in it,*' Harper quoted the line when Miranda meets Ferdinand. 'He's a junior scion of a famous acting dynasty.' She mentioned his name and Rocco looked impressed, but not for long.

'Shouldn't he have done the honourable thing and married her?'

'Possibly, but his wife might've had something to say about *that.*'

'I see.' Another frown.

'Shona had no intention of marrying him, she simply used his connections as a stepping stone to building an acting career in the States. His name's on the birth certificate and that's about as far as it goes. Ariel prefers to call herself by our family name and, after a couple of ill-fated holidays with her half-siblings' family, hasn't seen her father in years.'

Harper finished writing the note and glanced over at Rocco. His expression suggested that Shona's story held a resonance for him. There was a long-drawn-out silence which she broke by rattling on.

'Shona declared that she could look after Ariel and pursue her acting career. What she meant was that *we* could look after Ariel while *she* got on with her life. Soon after Ariel was born, Shona got a part in a daytime soap, high-tailed it over to California and has stayed there ever since.'

'I've never heard of Shona MacDonald. Should I?'

Harper gave a dry laugh. 'Unlikely. Shona's been divorced and married three times. She's made more money from alimony than acting.' She stopped, aware she sounded rather un-sisterly. 'It's time she took her responsibilities as a mother more seriously.'

'And Ariel?' Rocco pointed at a different wall where framed photos of Ariel ranging from new born to teenager were displayed. Harper looked at her favourite, Ariel in uniform on her first day at big school, her blazer reaching down to her knuckles and carrying a rucksack almost as big as herself. In spite of everything that had unfolded recently, she smiled.

'We – mum, dad and me, decided that Ariel should stay in Leicester where she was secure and settled. As you can imagine, Shona was only too happy for that to happen. Then,' she paused and took a deep breath, 'when teenage hormones kicked in and Ariel became too much for my parents to handle, she came to live with me in Polzenith.'

'Fewer distractions?'

'Compared to Leicester? Yes.' She taped the note to the lid of her mother's MacBook as Penhaligon made his way round the study, examining every photograph, as though committing them to memory.

'So, why aren't you featured on the wall of fame, Miss MacDonald?' Walking over to a bookcase, Harper picked up two framed photographs and handed them to him.

'But I am! This is me, receiving my PGCE in Primary Education from Leicester University. And *this* is me, being awarded an MA in Educational Leadership and Management from Nottingham University.'

'I'm guessing that your parents' expectations are focused on you?'

'Yes. They want me to leave the Three Pols at the end of next term, follow in my father's footsteps and become an H.M.I.' She faltered, knowing that was the last thing she wanted. Then she laughed, and replaced the two photographs. 'I know what you're thinking, I was the one left holding the baby. That I've never had any fun.' She pulled a face. 'And you'd be right. But I couldn't leave my parents to bring up Ariel on their own.'

'Clearly your sister had no such scruples.'

Harper gave a dry laugh. 'That's not a word anyone would apply to Shona. Mother calls us Rose White and Rose Red. Like the fairy tale? Shona's inherited my mother's genes: blonde hair, winsome manner and a figure to die for and has passed those on to Ariel.'

'And *Harper* – where does that come from? Not exactly in the top ten of Scottish girls' names, is it?' Walking over to a bookcase filled with an eclectic collection of novels he pulled out *To Kill a Mocking Bird* by Harper Lee and raised an inquiring eyebrow.

Harper nodded. 'Mother's favourite novel. She wanted to call me *Scout,* after one of the characters, but that was vetoed by Father. He wanted to call me Eilidh, after his grandmother, but that . . .' Aware that she was gabbling, she drew the conversation to a close. 'Harper was a compromise.'

'I like it,' he said, replacing the novel in its rightful place on the shelf. 'It suits you.'

Harper blushed at the unexpected compliment. 'I'm a throwback to our MacDonald ancestors,' she explained matter-of-factly, 'dark hair, blue eyes, pale skin, and bloody-minded. Otherwise, quite unremarkable.'

'I'd agree with bloody-minded. Not sure about the rest.' He turned, his grin reminding Harper that he'd seen rather more of her than intended this morning. Quickly, she changed the subject.

'I'll take that as our cue to exit stage left. Ready?'

'Of course?' Her plan had been to get them as far as Leicester. She hadn't thought beyond that, having convinced herself that Ariel and Pen would be here.

'They both mentioned Scotland in their letters. That's where we're headed, but first I have an errand to carry out.'

'What can be more important than finding and bringing them back here?'

'Keeping a promise.'

'To whom?'

'A friend's widow who lives on the borders. That will be the limit of our travelling today.'

'Scotch Corner. Penrith?'

'You'll see. Ready?'

'Ready.' Her smile hid her irritation. Apparently, Penhaligon only shared information on a need-to-know basis, and as far as he was concerned, she didn't need to know.

It was only as she set the burglar alarm, locked the door and followed him down the drive that Harper realised she'd revealed much about herself and her family but had learned nothing about Petroc Penhaligon.

Chapter Nine

Rocco was glad to hit the motorway and head for Penrith and Morwenna Copperthwaite's farm. Once there, he could deliver the restored bike, swap it for the Land Rover languishing under a tarp in the barn and continue the hunt for the runaways. Hunt? Wild goose chase more like, although he did have a pretty good idea where they were headed. He felt uncomfortable about keeping the info on a need-to-know basis with Harper, but if they split up and he reached the teenagers first he wasn't sure he could handle her niece.

He thought over what he'd learned about Ariel and her much-married mother. It was remarkable that Harper MacDonald was so buttoned up, in control – a veritable Ice Queen. He'd like to rattle that self-possession, unpin her hair, spread it over her shoulders and kiss her until she begged him to stop. The tantalising image of Harper's body in the diaphanous chemise backlit by the sun made his imagination run wild.

Now he knew what lay beneath her neat grey suit.

However, she'd made it perfectly clear that she regarded him as an undereducated mechanic. His lips twisted in a wry smile as he recalled her surprise when he'd mentioned the Battle of Killiecrankie and his familiarity with Shakespeare and Sylvia Plath. It did no harm for her to have her prejudices challenged while, conversely, it did him a power of good.

Bringing his mind back on track, he kept an eye out for the exit for Penrith.

A group of bikers on powerful BMWs and Kawasakis overtook him, raising gauntleted hands in appreciation for the classic he was riding. Classic? Ha! Harper regarded the Triumph Bonneville as a pile of scrap, fit only for the breakers' yard. She didn't know the story behind it, how he and Pen had secured it on a low loader after Joe Copperthwaite's funeral and taken it back to Polzenith to restore.

Now he could hand it over to Morwenna and she could sell it for a good price, stave off her creditors and keep the dairy farm afloat another year. He'd hoped to make this journey with Pen, their last trip together, but that dream would have to be put on hold, thanks to Ariel – *bloody* – MacDonald.

Then he pulled himself up, sharp. Harper was right, Pen had played a part in all of this, it couldn't all be laid at Ariel's door. Another deep breath, this time for his parents who'd allowed Pen to drive off in the Jeep. He wanted Pen to learn the value of money, to know the satisfaction of taking a wreck and restoring it to its former glory. Pen had a trust fund waiting for him when he turned twenty-five, Rocco didn't want him to burn through it as so many of his contemporaries' offspring had.

If the Jeep hadn't been available he would have caught up with Pen and they'd be riding north to deliver the bike to Morwenna. Miss MacDonald and her troublesome niece would be heading south and their paths need never cross again, unless fate decreed otherwise. For a moment, he imagined how it would feel to bump into Harper in the village once all this was over, maybe be given the great honour of servicing her car. However, judging from the way she'd spoken of her parents' ambitions for her, he guessed she'd be leaving Polzenith before long. The thought brought him no pleasure. It was plain she couldn't wait to be rid of him, so why did he feel regret at the idea of terminating their partnership?

Go figure.

'You okay?' Harper asked via the Bluetooth intercom. 'All I can hear is heavy breathing, huffing and puffing.'

'The pizza's lying like a ton of bricks on my stomach.' The huffing and puffing he could pass off as indigestion. The heavy breathing, not so much! 'We're nearly there. Hang on; once we leave the M6 we'll be on B-roads and I don't want to discover it's gone quiet because you slipped off the bike ten miles back and I hadn't noticed.'

'You wish.' She tightened her grip around his waist, unaware of the effect on his blood pressure and libido. 'I've told you. I'm sticking to you like glue until we catch up with Pen and Ariel and take them home. End of.'

* * *

By the time they swung off the Penrith road and roared up a potholed farm track leading to Morwenna's dairy farm, every single bone in Harper's body ached. Riding pillion was more physically demanding than Pilates, power yoga and a spinning class rolled into one. She was relieved when Penhaligon rocked the bike back on its rest in front of an attractive farmhouse, snuggled in the lee of the land.

To her chagrin, Penhaligon dismounted with the grace of an athlete, removed his helmet and ran his fingers through his hair to restore it to order. She was about to make some scathing comment about vanity when the farmhouse door opened and three teenagers, long-legged as colts, came running out exclaiming: *Uncle Rocco!*

They were followed at a more sedate pace by a woman in her early forties. Her chestnut brown hair was pulled back in a scrunchy, her left cheek was dusted with flour and she wore a large, serviceable apron which had corkscrewed across her bosom. Tall like her daughters, she waited for Rocco and Harper to come closer, wiping her hands on a tea towel tucked into the waist band of her apron. There was a world of sadness in her brown eyes but she held herself with a certain grace, in contrast to her daughters who clambered all over Rocco exclaiming how much they'd missed him and where was Pen? He tipped the youngest upside down over his shoulder, making her sisters squeal with laughter and demand the same.

Morwenna stepped forward and Rocco moved the girls gently aside and held his arms open. Morwenna walked into them, pressing her forehead against his chest and taking a deep breath, all the better to inhale the scent of leather and musky maleness. She wrapped her arms around his waist and Rocco held on to her, kissing the top of her head and murmuring something soothing. The girls stopped laughing and, following their mother's example, pressed as close to Rocco as possible.

A sharp dart of emotion caught Harper off guard and she passed it off as a pang of empathy for Morwenna and her daughters' still-raw bereavement, their obvious sorrow. However, it stemmed from the less noble emotion of feeling excluded, of never having known friendship like theirs. Ashamed, she rebuked herself for harbouring such thoughts and hung back, waiting to be introduced.

Eventually the group unravelled and Rocco held Morwenna at arm's length, seemingly seeking assurance that she was coping. Morwenna smiled, but a slow tear rolled down her cheek.

'Oh, God,' she said. 'Sorry. It's just, seeing you and . . .'

'Come here, my lovely.' Rocco attempted to lighten the mood by speaking in an exaggerated Cornish accent, then brushed away the tear with the pad of his thumb. Taking a shaky breath, Morwenna pressed the heels of her hands into her eye sockets, gave a loud sniff and then wiped her face on the tea towel.

'Mu-um; gross,' her eldest pronounced.

'What? I didn't blow my nose on it, now did I?'

'Eu-ew,' the sisters chorused. Then they all laughed, crowding round their mother and hugging her.

'Seeing your dad's bike made me wobble, that's all.' Then she turned to Harper who was still wearing Pen's helmet. 'Who have we here? Not Pen, that much is for sure.'

'Not unless Pen's grown boobs,' one daughter observed, making the others giggle. Their mother sent them a reproving look and Rocco signalled for Harper to remove her helmet and step forward.

'This is Harper MacDonald, 'Wenna. It's a long story, one we'll share over tea and cake?' He looked hopeful and Morwenna laughed.

'When have you ever known me to have an empty cake tin?'

'Never.'

'Exactly.' Morwenna walked up to Harper and linked arms. 'Welcome, Harper. You look exhausted. I'm dying to hear why you've ridden pillion all the way from Polzenith on Joe's bike.' She turned to her daughters. 'Granny's tea set, don't you think, girls?'

'Oh yes,' the eldest agreed.

'Is this,' Morwenna's youngest daughter screwed up her face, keen to get the phrase right, 'a high day, or a holiday?'

'Now Rocco's here, both,' Morwenna affirmed, evidently proud that her daughter understood the importance of her father's bike returning home. 'Now come on, all of you, into the kitchen otherwise my cakes will be ruined and it'll be rich tea biscuits, instead.'

That was all the warning the girls needed and they ran towards the house to set the table. Morwenna linked arms with Rocco and Harper, gave them both a squeeze and then, with one last backward glance at the motorcycle, led them into the farmhouse.

***

If Survey Monkey devised a poll asking people to describe an archetypical farmhouse kitchen, Home Farm's would tick all the boxes. It was certainly Harper's idea of how a farmhouse kitchen *should* look: stand-alone antique pine furniture, refectory table, clothes pulley over an ancient cream Raeburn and other equipment not seen in lifestyle magazines since the eighties. The only pieces of modern equipment she could find were a huge fridge/freezer, freestanding mixer, food processor and dishwasher.

It was a country mile away from the Penhaligons' kitchen in Somerset.

Impressed, Harper watched the girls restoring order to the refectory table which was covered in flour and baking equipment, and laying it for tea. They simply got on with it, no posturing, sulks or *do I have to?* strops which seemed to be Ariel's modus operandi these days. She sighed, wondering how a bereaved mother could have made such a good job of parenting, whereas . . .

No, she wouldn't berate herself, she'd done her best after all.

'Take off those leathers and heavy boots and sling them over the settle. Harper, if you want to freshen up while the kettle's boiling Mary will take you through to the downstairs cloakroom and –' Her next words were lost as a dozen or more motorbikes roared up Home Farm's drive, stirring up the dust, sounding their horns and revving their engines.

The girls raced over to the window, domestic duties forgotten.

'The Penrith Pirates!' Morwenna's youngest daughter exclaimed, kneeling up on the window seat.

'How did they know Joe's bike was back home?' Morwenna mused and then turned towards Rocco. 'Any idea, Mr Penhaligon?'

'I have no idea.' He adopted an innocent expression. 'I mean, it's not as if I would have phoned them from Knutsford services, is it? Come on girls, let's show off your dad's bike.' Morwenna gave a comical, resigned shrug and they all trooped back out into the yard, leaving Harper feeling awkward because this was a family moment.

As if sensing her hesitancy, Morwenna signalled for her youngest to take Harper's hand and bring her along. Rocco, first out of the door, was greeted by a giant of a man with a bushy ginger beard. He picked Rocco up as if he weighed no more than a fly and gave him a bone-crushing man-hug. The rest of the bikers crowded round Rocco, pretending to spar with him and exclaiming at the transformation he'd wrought with Joe's bike.

'You've done Joe's memory proud, Rocco, no mistake,' Ginger Beard exclaimed before turning to Morwenna. 'Don't you worry, lass, we'll make sure it fetches a good price at auction. And if it doesn't reach its reserve, we'll make up the difference. Right, lads?' This was followed by a chorus of 'ayes' and 'rights' as they slapped Rocco on the back.

Morwenna's daughters sat on the much larger bikes and pretended to gun them until, losing interest, they went back indoors. After some time, the bikers' focus swung round to Harper who was standing slightly apart from the group.

'Don't tell us that you've finally found a woman crazy enough to take you on, Rocco, mate,' Ginger-beard commented. 'A looker who likes bikes? Ker-ching. You've won the bloody jackpot, man.'

'Result, dude.' Another biker high-fived Rocco while the others took in Harper's borrowed leathers and high vis vest, seemingly astounded that such a creature existed.

'Not exactly,' Rocco beckoned Harper forward. 'This is Miss MacDonald, the head of three local schools, including Polzenith. We're heading for Scotland and I thought that it'd be a good time to return the bike and take the Land Rover, instead.'

'A teacher!'

'Dude, they didn't have teachers like that when I was at school.' There was an appreciative murmur and Harper found herself blushing under their scrutiny.

'Better watch it, lads. Or you'll end up in detention,' Rocco joked, earning a *that-is- so-not-funny* scowl from Miss MacDonald.

'You look right bonnie in those leathers, lass.'

'Back off lads, looks like she's spoken for – eh, Rocco?' Another biker gave Rocco a hearty dig in the ribs. Harper was about to deny any connection with Rocco Penhaligon but changed her mind and smiled instead. The Penrith Pirates meant no harm, even if they were living in the dark ages, and as far removed from the kind of men she was used to socialising with, as to seem a different species.

'Can he come oot tae play, Miss?'

'We'll keep him out of trouble.'

'That'll be the day,' Harper added, giving them an arch look. Rocco watched her interaction with the bikers and their teasing, apparently amused that she could give as good as she got.

'Do you mind if I put the bike through its paces with the guys? Will you be okay?'

'I *think* I can spend half an hour without you.' Then, realising that sounded waspish, added, 'Off you go. Play nicely, children.'

'Yes, Miss.' With a wave the bikers walked over to their machines, laughing and joking with each other. Rocco joined them and they roared down the drive leaving dust in their wake. Harper stood looking down the drive until they were out of sight and the roar of their engines died away. She shivered, despite the heat, and an unexpected wave of loneliness swept over her.

She'd spent the last twenty-four hours with Rocco Penhaligon. They'd fought, argued, disagreed and made plain that they were together through necessity, not choice. Under other circumstances they would never have met and, to the casual observer, would appear to have little in common. Yet – being with him had become her new normal, and it felt strange to be without him.

Better get used to it, she advised herself, once this is over chances are you'll never see him again. Stay independent, be your own woman. There's no place for a man like Rocco Penhaligon in your life.

The last of the dust settled and she jumped when an arm slid round her waist.

'Tea?' Morwenna asked, 'I wouldn't put it past the girls to eat all the scones while they're hot.'

'Of course.'

'Now,' Morwenna said as they walked back towards the farmhouse. 'I want to know how you and Rocco met. Every last detail. Chapter and verse. No omissions. You can save the really juicy stuff for when the girls have gone to bed or are watching telly in the snug. I have to live vicariously these days,' she said, without an ounce of self-pity.

'It's not *quite* what you think,' Harper laughed as they walked into the house together, already on the way to becoming friends.

Chapter Ten

Cakes consumed, and with Rocco a no-show, the girls headed for their respective bolt holes. After explaining it was her late husband Joe's dictum that there should only be one family computer and it should be kept in the kitchen where they could monitor the sites their daughters accessed, Morwenna closed the door behind them. Standing still, she cocked her head on one side and listened. After some thumping on the ancient floorboards above their heads, the girls settled down.

Heading for the fridge she brought out a bottle of Sauvignon Blanc, wiggling it in front of Harper. 'Wanna sit on the decking and get drunk? Well, slightly tipsy as I have dinner to cook.'

'Why not.'

Morwenna took two large goblets down off the dresser and filled them three-quarters full. 'Nibbles?'

'Sounds like a plan.' Harper smiled.

Loading a tray with wine and bowls of crisps, nuts and olives, Morwenna carried it out onto a half-finished patio overlooking a valley where a herd of dairy cows chewed the grass contentedly. There were a couple of fold-up camping chairs on the decking and a rickety table. Morwenna gave an embarrassed laugh.

'Sorry about the rough and ready arrangements. The decking was Joe's project but he died before it could be finished.'

'I'm so sorry,' Harper murmured, knowing it sounded inadequate.

'Don't be,' Morwenna handed Harper a glass and then, sighing heavily, crashed down on the flimsy camping chair. 'It was a freak accident. They happen all the time on farms.' She stopped short of saying what had actually happened, but when she looked over at Harper, her eyes glistened with tears. 'Life can be an absolute bugger, can't it?'

'It certainly can.' They clinked glasses and neither spoke for several minutes. Then Morwenna gave a loud sniff and moved the conversation in another direction. 'How long have you known Rocco? Tell me *everything*.'

'Twenty-four hours, give or take.'

'Twenty-four hours? You're kidding me.'

'Well, let me think. School finished at three thirty yesterday afternoon, I went home and discovered my niece Ariel had bunked off school that day and –' She paused as Morwenna put a bowl of nuts on the table between them. 'Then I found a note saying she wasn't going to stay with her mother in L.A as planned –'

'L.A? How glamorous. I'd jump at the chance to leave everything behind and jet off into the sunset.' She mimed a jet taking off with her free hand and then, evidently remembering her responsibilities, took another slug of wine. 'Sorry, I interrupted, not used to adult conversation . . . I'm guessing that you weren't too thrilled?'

'You guess right. I learned from one of her friends that she'd gone off with someone called Pen. I marched straight round to Rocco's garage, practically pulled him out from under the car he was working on and demanded to know where my niece was.'

'Oh. My. God. A bad case of mistaken identity?'

'Humongous. After seeing the name Penhaligon over the garage door I thought *he* was Pen. When he came out from under the car all I could think to ask was,' she took a gulp of wine, 'how old he was.'

Morwenna snorted wine down her nose. 'Very well-preserved, though, you have to admit. Sorry, go on.'

'As you can guess, it was his son Pen that Ariel had gone off with . . .'

'Woah. Rewind. Gone off with?'

'Yes. They'd both left almost identical notes saying –'

'Let me guess. They'd had enough of studying, didn't want to go to university and –'

'– we'd find them in Scotland.'

'Scotland?'

'Apparently.' Following Morwenna's example, Harper took a large gulp of wine and stared out across the fields.

'Blimey.'

'*Blimey*'s about right. Rocco and I have formed an uneasy alliance, he wants to find Pen as much as I want to find Ariel and ...'

'Stop. Your niece is called *Ariel*?'

'Yes; her mother's an actress.'

Morwenna nodded as if that explained everything. 'Mind you – with a name like Morwenna, I shouldn't throw stones.' They clinked glasses to show no offence had been meant, or taken.

'I'm guessing your mother had a Poldark fixation from the first time round?'

'You guess right. I have a brother called Ross and, growing up, we did have a cat called *Demelza*. An evil, ginger thing it was. Go on – what happened next?'

'Rocco turned up on the motorbike and gave me five minutes to be ready.'

'Sounds like Rocco.' She laughed.

'We went to Rocco's parents' house. Thought we'd caught up with the runaways, only to find that Rocco's parents had allowed Pen to drive off in his new Jeep, in direct defiance of Rocco's wishes.'

'Man alive –'

'We spent the night there and then set out for my parents' house in Leicester. But just missed them. Since then, the trail's gone cold. We could have caught up with them, if Rocco had done what I suggested and hired a car. But he insisted on delivering the bike. Sorry –'

'Don't be. I would be worried sick if one of my girls did a bunk.

Rocco can be very single-minded. He's had no one to answer to since Pen was born. He's used to giving orders, not following them.'

'That makes two of us.' Harper reached for the bowl of nuts. 'Doesn't make for an easy relationship.'

'Rocco was due to bring the motorbike up in a few weeks, anyhow. To his way of thinking, it'd be mad to pass by within miles of Home Farm without dropping it off. Two birds with one stone, and all that. And you do need somewhere to break the journey. '

'I get it, believe me,' Harper cut in. 'However – being the male of the species, Rocco doesn't understand my concern over Ariel going off with a boy I've never met.'

'No worries on that score, Pen's an absolute sweetie.' She reached over and squeezed Harper's hand.

'Be that as it may, but how am I going to explain to my sister that her daughter, who is in my care, has gone off-piste?'

'How come you're responsible for your niece? Ok-ay . . . that was a *teacher look*. You're right; unimportant detail. You can fill me in later.'

'Sorry, old habits die hard. I'm so worried. What will happen if Ariel ends up pregnant? Rocco thinks I'm overreacting. Well, that's a bit of an understatement. He seems to think that we'll catch up with them, bring them home and . . . but they've been together for almost forty-eight hours. God knows what they've been up to.'

Harper took another swig of wine but this time it tasted oxidised, sour.

Morwenna reached over and squeezed her hand again. 'You're wrong. He understands more than you know.' Harper sensed that if she wanted to know more about Rocco Penhaligon, Morwenna was the one to ask.

'Look, I don't want you to tell tales out of school,' she pulled a face at the cliché, 'but please fill me in on Rocco's background? Just some broad brush strokes? His parents are wealthy, yet he lives above a garage in a down at heel Cornish village not chocolate-boxy enough to draw in the tourists. Where's Rocco's wife? Pen's mother? He's never mentioned her. Shouldn't he tell her what's going on?'

'Long story short?'

'Please.'

Walking back into the kitchen, Morwenna fetched the bottle of wine and topped up their glasses. 'Joe and Rocco were up at Bristol together, Joe studying Business and Management, and Rocco Philosophy Politics and Economics. They bonded over Joe's old motor car which broke down in the carpark of their Halls of Residence in the pouring rain. Rocco got it started and Joe became a lifelong friend.' Her smile wavered at the unintentional irony in that statement. Swallowing hard, she continued, 'After their end of year exams they headed to Cornwall for the surfing championships. My parents have a dairy farm near the Three Pols, I was roped in to act as a marshal at the championships, met Joe, fell in love and – sorry, this is Rocco's story.'

'Tell it your way, Morwenna.' Harper sensed that in order to understand Rocco Penhaligon, she had to know the whole story. It'd probably help Morwenna, too, make her feel that Joe was still part of her world and not an ever-fading memory.

'They wiped the board clean. The girls buzzed round them like bees round honey. I made it clear that Joe wasn't up for grabs and so they concentrated their efforts on Rocco, but he didn't seem interested. He wanted to spend the summer surfing, kicking back after a gruelling first year at university. He and Joe rented the loft above the garage at the end of the village – now Penhaligon's Garage and Engineering Works, and earned their keep sweeping floors and delivering vehicles. The owner discovered Rocco's mechanical bent and offered him a full time job in the garage. Then . . .'

'Go on,' Harper prompted.

'The raggle-taggle gypsies rolled into town.'

'The *what*?'

'New Age travellers. Posh kids pretending to be free spirits and born again hippies, living in swanky camper vans bought courtesy of the bank of Mummy and Daddy. They set up camp on the village green, just outside Rocco's garage.'

'Bet that went down like a lead balloon.' After five years living in Polzenith, Harper knew that the locals' definition of a stranger was anyone born outside the three parishes ringed by old tin mines.

'You guess right. At the end of the summer, Joe was called back to Home Farm. His father had suffered a heart attack and had no one else to turn to. His three brothers, who now help *me* run the farm, were too young to be of much use. Joe knew he would never return to finish his degree and so I moved up here to be with him.'

'I see.'

'At the end of that summer, the garage came up for sale, Rocco bought it and turned his back on university. You asked where Rocco's parents wealth came from –'

'Only to understand Rocco better, not from any ulterior motive.' Harper had savings – and while they couldn't match the Penhaligons' wealth, she didn't have to rely on any man for financial security.

'His great-great grandfather patented some kind of aileron in the pioneering days of the aeronautical industry. I'm not sure what it does *precisely*, but it ensured that aircraft held together by brown paper and string stayed up in the air. I believe a modified version is still in use. It's called,' she stifled a giggle, 'Penhaligon's Screw. Sorry, the wine's kicking in.'

'No!' Harper giggled.

'Yes! Anyhow – and please excuse the history lesson – along comes the jet engine, satellites, manned spaceflight with the Penhaligons at the forefront, inventing new stuff, patenting it, building on their predecessor's success and making a mint in the process. Living near Bristol and Filton, the home of the aerospace industry, they were in the right place at the right time. I think we have Rocco's grandfather's book: *Box Kite to Concorde* lying around somewhere. Take it with you, it'll answer all your questions.'

Harper recalled the massive, windowless building on the M5 she'd driven past every day on the way to her previous school. *Penhaligon Aerospace* it proudly announced in huge white letters on a blue background. Little did she know that she'd meet the man whose family had built it!

'So, where does the tension arise between Rocco and his parents.'

'I'm getting there. Rocco is *brilliant* at fixing stuff, as was Joe. Over the last few years they bought up vehicles held together by mud, rust and a prayer; barn finds, classic cars hidden under tarps. The motorbike was their first project, and they had plans to renovate a couple of wrecks every year, either here or at the garage in Polzenith. Our daughters were becoming more independent, Pen was all set to go off to University. For the first time in years they had time on their hands. Then –'

Morwenna gulped down another large swallow of wine.

'Joe's accident?'

'Exactly. Sorry, I'm not telling you this in logical order and it seems to have become Joe's story, not Rocco's.'

'No worries.' Now Harper understood why bringing the bike home was so important to Rocco. He'd made a promise and wanted to keep it, and not even Pen going AWOL would prevent that from happening.

'I'm guessing that Rocco dropping out of university did not go down well with his parents.'

'Yes, but delighted his grandparents who knew the Penhaligons excelled at engineering, getting their hands dirty, inventing things.'

'That doesn't quite explain the toxic atmosphere at his parents' house,' Harper opined. 'There has to be more to it than that and I'm guessing it concerns Pen. So, what went wrong?'

There was a deafening sound as, simultaneously, the girls galloped downstairs and Rocco drove up to Home Farm at the head of the Penrith Pirates. The girls came rushing out onto the decking area exclaiming *Rocco's back* and then skidded round the side of the house to catch up with him.

Morwenna shrugged and gave Harper an apologetic smile. 'Laters?'

Harper nodded. 'Laters.'

This was one story she really wanted to hear.

Chapter Eleven

Rocco saw the Pirates off, knowing they'd get a good price for the Triumph. Bone-weary, he stifled a large yawn and wheeled the precious bike into a barn and covered it with a tarpaulin. Then he injected a spring into his step. It wouldn't do to let Harper MacDonald know that he'd found the journey almost as physically and mentally exhausting as she had. Why he cared what she thought about him was more difficult to analyse. Male pride, he guessed. Further speculation was halted as Morwenna's two eldest daughters, Jane and Susan, grabbed him by the hands and dragged him over to one of the rickety camping chairs. The youngest, Mary, ran into the kitchen and returned with an ice cold beer.

'I could get used to this,' he joked. 'Being waited on hand and foot by three gorgeous girls.'

'Oi –' Morwenna interjected.

'Make that *four* gorgeous girls.' He bowed from the waist, careful not to spill any beer.

'What about Harper?' Mary asked.

'Okay – make that *five* gorgeous girls,' Rocco amended, rolling his eyes and feigning exasperation.

He sent Harper a steady look, noting how the unexpected compliment had brought a blush of colour to her cheeks. It surprised him how readily she fitted in with Morwenna and the girls, almost as if she belonged at Home Farm. He guessed that years of meeting and dealing with parents had taught her how to handle people, get them on side. Seems like he was the only person she couldn't get along with. Hiding a crooked smile he took another swig of beer. Maybe he shouldn't enjoy provoking her quite as much as he did. Without meaning to she'd got under his skin and he couldn't resist winding her up.

Morwenna, ever the romantic in spite of the hand life had dealt her, had been sending them knowing looks all afternoon as she watched their verbal sparring. Time to reel it in, he didn't want to give either of them the wrong impression. Yet, it felt good to be sitting on the unfinished decking and drinking wine with Miss Harper MacDonald even if he was under no illusion what she thought of him. Twenty-four hours ago he'd been unaware of her existence. Now, thanks to fate and two hastily written notes on purple notepaper, they were joined at the hip until their mission was over.

Shaking off his introspection, he gestured at Joe's unfinished project with his can of beer. 'I'll return with Pen and finish the decking for you, 'Wenna. It'll be a great place for you and the girls to sit on summer evenings watching the sun set over the valley.'

'Will Harper be coming back, too?' Jane inquired.

'Harper?' he prompted, lobbing the ball neatly over the net to her.

'That all depends, I've had to postpone my holiday and . . .' They turned expectant, hopeful faces towards her and she added, 'If I can, I will.'

'Thanks, Rocco, that's very generous.' Bending, Morwenna kissed the top of his head and then squeezed his shoulder. That was the cue for Mary to clamber onto his lap, put her arms around his neck and lay her head on his chest. Witnessing Morwenna and her daughters putting a brave face on things, Rocco vowed to do something, anything, to make their lives better.

More than anyone, he knew that it was impossible to turn back the clock, pointless to wish for what couldn't be. To hope that one day the door in his garage loft would open, Pen's mother would walk through and the years would roll away.

'I'm too old for this.' Pretending that the legs of the cheap camping chair were bowing under Mary's slight weight, he broke the sombre mood.

'Uncle Rocco!' they protested, 'you're not old.'

Laughing, he glanced over at Harper. 'Harper thinks I'm ancient, ask her.'

'Stop fishing for compliments, Rocco Penhaligon,' Morwenna chided. 'And, to be fair, you are over forty. We are both antiques.' It was left hanging in the air that, but for the accident, Joe would have been the same age.

'I'll be collecting my pension before I know it.' Rocco put a hand over his heart, as though his pride had been wounded. Then he collapsed on the floor and the girls piled on top of him, giggling.

'Come on, girls, give Rocco a breather,' their mother ordered.

'How old are you Harper?' Mary asked, climbing off her adopted uncle.

'That's classified information.' Rocco righted the camping chair and sat down again.

'Well, *I'm* ten, Jane is sixteen and Susan is fourteen.' They looked at Harper inquiringly and she capitulated

'Thirty-seven and a quarter,' she said, clearly understanding that such details mattered to children.

'A babe in arms,' Morwenna said, grinning at her discomfiture.

'A mere child,' Rocco agreed.

The house phone rang and the girls rushed to answer it, losing interest in the adults.

'Right,' Morwenna was suddenly business-like. 'Rocco, fetch the panniers off the bike. I'm guessing Harper's dying for a shower and to get out of those leathers. Am I right?'

'Spot on.' Harper's smile thanked Morwenna for understanding.

Morwenna rubbed her hands together and then grinned. 'Okay. Beds.'

'Beds?' Rocco asked.

'Yes. One bed – two?'

'We both need a bed,' Harper said, adding with a blush, 'a bed *each*, that is.'

'Now, you've disappointed me – I thought . . .'

'Good lord, no!' Harper said with just a little too much alacrity. Well, that was him told. 'We only met yesterday. I – we hardly know each other.'

'Morwenna's being mischievous. She loves matchmaking and has a knack for it.' Standing, Rocco slipped an arm round Morwenna's shoulders and gave her a playful nudge with his hip.

'Sorry for getting it wrong,' Morwenna said, looking not the least bit apologetic. 'I simply thought that – oh, well, never mind. Young Mary can bunk in with me and you can have her bed, Harper. Saturday's our changeover day so you won't find any girly stuff lurking at the bottom of it. Although,' she added, 'if you emerge tomorrow morning covered in glitter, I won't be held responsible. She's going through a Disney Princess phase at present.'

'That's okay, Rocco thinks I'm a bit of a princess, so the odd bit of glitter sticking to my hair won't make any difference.'

'Having heard the story, I think you're an absolute angel for getting on that bike in the first place. Let along riding pillion all the way from Polzenith. If my eldest had gone AWOL, I'd have hired a car and zoomed after her before the trail went cold.'

Harper sent Rocco a *told you so* look.

'Harper's niece is more than capable of looking after herself.,' Rocco was unrepentant.

'How *exactly* would you know that?' Harper asked.

'From what you told me in Leicester. What I've observed . . .'

'You haven't even met her. So, again, I ask you – how have you reached that conclusion? Might I remind you that your son is riding around in an expensive birthday present, in direct opposition to your wishes?'

'You don't need to remind me of anything concerning my son. He's my business.'

'He became my business when he took off with Ariel in a car without tax, MOT or insurance, too, for all I know. And, yes,' she held up her hand,' I am aware that because of the Mini's age he didn't need *all* of the above.'

God, she really was unbearable when she reverted to being Miss MacDonald who'd fought tooth and nail against the closure of her schools. But he wasn't about to let her have the last word.

'As regards vehicles, they're perfectly safe. As I just said. So, back off –'

'Back off?'

'Yes. I have a pretty good idea where we'll find them.' Damn, he'd nearly disclosed classified information to the enemy.

'Planning on sharing that information any time soon?'

'Like you shared your parents' address, you mean?'

'Children, children. Behave.' Morwenna clapped her hands to get their attention. 'Now,' she pushed Rocco towards the top step of the decking, '*you*, fetch the panniers. And *you*,' she faced Harper, hands on hips, 'come with me and I'll show you to your room. You'll feel more like yourself once you've had a shower. And, for what it's worth, both Pen and Ariel have acted reprehensibly but you two have to present a united front when you catch up with them, otherwise they'll play you off, one against the other.'

Rocco knew she was right. She and Joe had worked like a team to bring up their girls. 'Yes, Mum.' He sent her an impudent smile.

'Still here?' she asked, quirking an eyebrow.

'Going. Going. Gone.'

Clearing the steps in one bound, fatigue forgotten, he headed for the barn to collect the panniers.

Walking over to Harper, Morwenna gave her a massive hug and gurgled, delightedly. 'Oh. My. God. You two – what're you like? I love it. Are you *sure* you want separate beds?'

'Perfectly sure.' Harper squared her shoulders, suspecting that Morwenna had a way of getting what she wanted. Rocco was right, she really was a matchmaker.

'Okay. I'll say no more.' They both knew that was a lie. 'Now, upstairs before he returns with the panniers and you start fighting all over again.'

'I wasn't fighting, I was merely . . .'

'Yada-yada-yada,' Morwenna said, miming a duck's bill opening and closing as she led the way through to the hall. 'I love you giving Rocco a run for his money. I suspect that you're both wa-ay too used to getting what you want. That's why you're sparking off each other. You know what this is, don't you?'

'Er, no-oh.'

'U – S -T.' She placed a heavy stress on each letter.

That phrase was unfamiliar to Harper. 'What?'

'Unresolved- Sexual-Tension. Textbook case, Miss MacDonald.'

Harper shook her head as she followed Morwenna upstairs heading for Mary's glitter-encrusted bedroom. 'As if,' she said, mimicking Morwenna's eldest exactly.

Chapter Twelve

Dinner was a leisurely affair with Morwenna and Rocco swapping 'Joe' stories and reminiscing about the time they'd all lived together in the loft above Penhaligon's Garage. The girls cleared the table like old hands, helped by Harper who was enjoying the banter which was part and parcel of this family's life. Maybe if life at *Killiecrankie* had been relaxed and loving Shona would never have gone off the rails and *she* wouldn't feel the need to overachieve to compensate for Shona's shortcomings. Seeing Morwenna's family joshing and larking around brought home what she'd sacrificed: love, family life, children, a place to call her own.

Once Ariel returned from L.A and took up her university place, Harper's role as guardian would be over. Penhaligon had his son and Morwenna her daughters. All she had to look forward to was working until she collected her Teachers' Pension, or took early retirement from the profession. Safe. Boring. That wasn't how she'd seen her life panning out.

She wanted more.

She deserved better.

* * *

After dinner, some of the Penrith Pirates who hadn't seen Joe's renovated bike rang to announce they were on their way. Excusing himself, Rocco headed for the barn keen to show off his handiwork. His absence gave Harper time to quiz Morwenna over the comment Rocco had made at his parents' house regarding Pen –

You lost the right to have any say in his life the day you suggested I put him up for adoption.

The girls were washing up, presenting Harper and Morwenna with the perfect opportunity to slink away into the snug and curl up on opposite ends of a huge grey velvet sofa.

'So – New Age Travellers?' Harper prompted. Morwenna launched straight in, evidently keen for Harper to know all.

'The surfing championships over, Rocco and Joe were able to concentrate on the garage business.' She settled herself more comfortably, cradling a coffee mug in her hands. 'I suppose what happened next was partly our fault, Joe's and mine. We were all loved-up and Rocco must have felt like a spare part. You know what falling in love is like,' she sighed. 'All consuming. You become totally self-absorbed. A pain to be around, frankly. Yes?'

'Yes,' Harper agreed, bowing her head over her coffee mug, unwilling to admit that she'd never fallen in love. Sure, she'd had flings, relationships but nothing earth shattering like Morwenna was describing. She'd never known that glorious moment when you were no longer governed by the laws of physics, your feet sprouted wings and you floated several feet above the ground. At thirty-seven and a quarter she'd left it too late to change, to willingly surrender her whole self to a man she had yet to meet. As for children, her biological clock was not so much winding down as reaching the point when it would stop ticking completely. What a sad old maid she'd become, she laughed at herself. Not so much executive head of federation of schools, more Miss Harper MacDonald, spinster of this parish.

Better buy a cat. Buy several cats.

'One day Rocco brought this *creature* to our place above the garage,' Morwenna continued, snapping her out of her reverie.

'Creature?'

'Oh, you know the type – blonde dreadlocks, husky voice, body piercings, cropped tops and skimpy shorts. All the better to show off her legs, jacked up bosom and a huge mermaid tattoo which stretched from her left thigh to her bum cheek. She was a walking cliché, a complete fake, pretending to be a born-again hippy when she had her parents' house in Primrose Hill to fall back on when living in a camper van lost its appeal.'

'I take it you didn't like her, then?' Harper quipped.

'She was never without a spliff and Joe and I suspected her of 'powdering her nose'. Drugs were freely available so scoring them wasn't a problem.'

Harper thought of her own life that same summer. She'd been planning a gap year, longing to travel the world with her friends before settling down to the rigours of academic life. Then Shona had dropped her bombshell . . . Harper didn't think it diplomatic to point out that Rocco came from a similar background. That if the garage hadn't worked out, he could have returned home and no more would've been said about his temporary brainstorm or his crazy idea of dropping out of university.

Instead, she said: 'Rocco doesn't seem the kind to get taken in by someone like that.'

'Not now, perhaps. But back then . . . Together, they created quite a reaction in the village. Rocco tall and dark like the Penhaligons. Whereas, Lorelei –'

'Excuse me – *Lorelei*?' Harper couldn't keep the incredulity out of her voice.

'Not her given name, natch. I seem to remember she was called Camilla, Annabel, Saskia; something Sloaney like that. The other so-called travellers were a bunch of pseuds, too, adopting names such as Warlock, Caerwin, River, Autumn, Cloud. Joe and I used to joke that they'd chosen their hippy names from a Farrow and Ball paint chart. Once, Rocco would have laughed with us, but he was too besotted.'

'Go on.'

'Lorelei would disappear for days at a time and then return – make that stagger – back to the loft, totally wired; like she'd been plugged into the National Grid. Rocco was so glad to have her back he didn't ask her where she'd been, what she'd been up to.' She paused and made a face. 'To put it crudely, the loft floor was in danger of giving way beneath us, thanks to their sexual gymnastics.'

'Oh.'

'What man isn't going to fall for someone who looked like she did, who gave herself so freely? Rocco was young, inexperienced, blind to who she was, *what* she was. A user – in every sense of the word.'

Harper felt a shiver of empathy for the young Rocco, so blinkered, so smitten. This was followed by another emotion, one she didn't want to give a name to. She might not think of Rocco in – in *that way*, but she didn't relish the thought of him spending hot summer nights making love to Miss Trustafarian on the beach as the sun set over Polzenith Point.

She glanced out of the window towards the barns, willing Morwenna to finish the story before Rocco returned. 'And then –'

'And then, pouf,' Morwenna snapped her fingers. 'The first breath of autumn and they were gone, like Will O' the Wisps. We – Joe, Rocco and me, woke up one morning, looked out of the window onto the village green where they'd been camped, only to find a pile of burning rubbish and patches of yellow grass where they'd erected tepees and parked their camper vans.'

'What about *Lorelai*?' Harper tried to stop her lips from curling but failed.

'Crept out of Rocco's bed, grabbed her belongings and hightailed it back to – well, wherever she came from. I think Rocco had contemplated moving on with them, giving up the idea of the garage. Luckily – in our opinion – he wasn't invited. So it was left for Joe and me to pick up the pieces.'

'And there's been no significant other in his life since?'

'Hard to believe, isn't it? He's quite a catch.' Putting her mug on the floor Morwenna went over to the fireplace to tend the fire she'd lit earlier. She continued the story without turning round. 'To be honest, Harper, we've all been in love with Rocco at one time or another but he's a tough nut to crack. I guess that, having given his heart and it ending so badly, he'll stay single for the rest of his life. Which would be a shame. You've seen him with the girls, he's a natural and they adore him.'

'There speaks the founder of the Rocco Penhaligon Appreciation Society.'

'True.' Morwenna re-joined her on the sofa, smiled and looked out of the window towards the distant hills.

'And?' Harper prompted, but Morwenna was back in Polzenith with the man she loved and who loved her in return.

'What? Oh, then,' she shrugged, 'Joe's dad had a heart attack, followed by a stroke and Joe came back to help his mother and brothers keep Home Farm going. I came too. My family, as I mentioned before, were dairy farmers, so I could be very hands-on.'

Morwenna sighed and Harper suspected that she wouldn't get her back on track. So near to understanding Petroc Penhaligon, yet so far. Once she and Rocco set off in the car tomorrow morning and could communicate without using Bluetooth, she'd ask him outright where Pen's mother was.

Whether he chose to tell her was another matter.

* * *

Rocco had two choices if he wanted a good night's sleep. Curl up foetus-style on the sofa or let his legs dangle over the arm. He should have accepted Morwenna's offer of Susan's bed but good manners had prevented him. He preferred not to think of the alternative, that he and Harper shared a bed. Recalling the look of horror on her face at Morwenna's half-joking suggestion, he frowned, punching his pillow into a more comfortable shape and releasing some of his pent-up frustration. At the time, he'd felt like saying that he could name quite a few women who'd *jump* at the chance to spend the night with him. But that would have been crass and made him appear like a boastful eighteen-year-old, which he most certainly was not.

As she'd been quick to remind him.

Good Lord, he was only a few years older than her but she made him feel like Methuselah. Forty plus was the new twenty, wasn't it? His brows drew together as he remembered his twenties when life hadn't been easy. A single parent living above a garage in a Cornish village with a child, subject to village gossip, parental disapproval and disappointment. And now, just as Pen was ready to launch himself into the world, along comes Ariel MacDonald and screws it all up a second time.

It takes two to tango, Harper had said and she was right. He thought Pen was still a child yet overnight he'd become a man. He wasn't quite ready to acknowledge that, or prepared for Pen to fly the nest. However, the moment had arrived and he'd better accept it with good grace. He stared into the dying embers of the fire and watched the scented candles burning down their wicks. Going forward, was this how his life would look? Sitting alone by the wood burner on a beautiful summer's evening with a book for company, wondering what Pen was getting up to at Oxford; wondering why he'd stopped talking via WhatsApp?

On the plus side, he could invite his latest girlfriend to stay over, no longer having to worry about setting Pen a bad example. But where was the sense in that? Perhaps it was time he grew up, moved on, slid unprotestingly towards middle age and accepted that the glorious summer he'd spent with Pen's mother was long over. He closed his eyes, puckering his forehead as he tried to remember exactly what she'd looked like.

Instead, the only thing he could remember with startling clarity was Harper MacDonald in that damned nightdress. He suspected that the image was seared onto his brain and would need only the slightest excuse to return and taunt him. Damn. Sitting up, he leaned forward and rested his elbows on his knees and concentrated instead on how much aggregate, cement and seasoned timber he'd need to finish Joe and Morwenna's deck. That sublimated Harper's image. Then he calculated how many days it would take before he caught up with Pen and said goodbye to Harper MacDonald.

Two or three, tops.

The thought should have cheered him but, oddly, he found it disheartening. Unable to fathom the reason for that, he lay back on the sofa and stared at the ceiling until sleep found him.

Chapter Thirteen

'This had better be a joke,' Harper muttered, watching Rocco perform a perfect donut on Home Farm's gravel drive before bringing the Land Rover to a halt. The daughters of the house clapped their hands while Morwenna stood by smiling, two towels draped over her arm.

'Your carriage awaits, Miss MacDonald,' Rocco said, jumping out and holding the passenger door open.

'I thought,' Harper ground out, 'you'd organised a hire car.'

'A hire car? Don't be ridiculous. We can continue our journey in the Land Rover, it's well suited to the rough terrain where we're headed.' He made himself sound like Bear Grylls embarking on some dangerous expedition, all uneven roads, wild animals and bandits. 'It's a classic.'

'A classic piece of crap,' Harper declared.

'Miss MacDonald, really. There are children present.'

Much to Mary's delight, Rocco covered her ears with his hands and tutted like a maiden aunt. Harper glared at him, would he never allow her to forget she was a teacher? Taking a deep breath, she walked round the car and examined it. As she suspected – a rust bucket. In the past, someone had executed a very poor paint job and its coachwork was in three different shades of green. None of them, she suspected, genuine

Land Rover colours. The front grille with its two embedded headlights was flaking and rusty. The split windscreen was scratched, discoloured and only had a windscreen wiper on the driver's side. Hm, no prizes for guessing what *her* view of Bonnie Scotland would be if torrential rain set in! And to top it all, the canvas roof was ripped and the studs holding it in place were rusted or missing.

'Let me guess, a barn find?'

'Uncle Seth's barn, to be precise. He gave it to Joe and it's been in my mind to restore it. So, I was thinking –'

'Why not take it with us?'

'Exactly. That way, Pen and I can take it back to Polzenith , restore it and sell it on Morwenna and the girls' behalf.'

'Why don't we hire a car and pick it up on the way back?' she suggested, keeping her temper in check.

'We could, but I want to put it through its paces. The engine's sound and all it needs is a bit of a face lift. It's a 1951 "Series 1 80". A similar one, only a few years older, sold for just under seventy-five thousand at auction. Think what Morwenna could do with that money.'

Harper couldn't argue with that. Last night, Morwenna had let slip that Rocco had been helping out financially since Joe's death, passing the money off as payment for work he and Joe had carried out on another 'classic'. Morwenna, plainly, didn't believe a word of it. However, with her eldest applying for university she couldn't let false pride get in the way. Unlike Ariel, Morwenna's girls didn't have grandparents who'd been squirrelling money away to fund her education since the day they were born.

'Hey, keep me out of this. The main thing is to find Pen and Ariel. I can loan you a perfectly serviceable Ford Fiesta.' Momentarily, Harper's spirits were raised but Rocco quickly dashed them.

'And leave you and the girls without a car? No way.' Rocco turned to Harper. 'This old girl has done less than five hundred miles since new and has its original number plate. Okay,' he said, channelling an honest car dealer, 'granted – it does leak a little oil, but it has bench seats and a spare wheel in the back.'

'Oh well, that's made all the difference,' Harper responded, not in the least mollified. In the Land Rover's favour, however, the tyres looked almost brand new and even in her present mood she could see that it was crying out for TLC.

Exactly how she felt!

'You could, of course, stay another night with Morwenna and hire a car tomorrow. I'll go on without you. Oh, wait,' he smacked his forehead with the heel of his hand. 'I've just remembered, you have no idea where Pen's headed.'

Having done exactly the same with her parents' address, Harper was forced to suck it up. However, there was no way she was prepared to allow Rocco Penhaligon to think that he'd got the better of her. Or provide him with a cast iron excuse for dumping her at the first opportunity.

'I see what you're trying to do and it won't work. Just get in the bloody car, will you? And – yes, more foul language.'

She threw her luggage – clothes and toiletries stuffed into a rucksack borrowed from Jane, in the back of the Land Rover. Then, remembering her manners, walked over to Morwenna and her daughters and hugged each in turn. 'Thanks for everything, I hope to see you soon – runaways in tow, and spend a bit longer at Home Farm.'

It would do Ariel no harm at all to see how Morwenna's daughters conducted themselves, some of it might even rub off. Although, next to Ariel, the Copperthwaite's girls seemed practically Amish.

'Fingers crossed and,' Morwenna held her close and whispered in her ear, 'remember what I said last night . . . Rocco's *real* reason for not letting you know where you're headed is because he doesn't want to let you go. Trust me.'

'I'll remember, but you've got it all wrong. He can't wait to be shot of me.'

''Wenna, girls –' Rocco held his arms open and they walked into a group hug.

'Harper, too,' Susan declared, forcing her to join in. She tried to manoeuvre it so she was on the edge of the group hug and no part of her came into contact with Penhaligon. Immature – sure; but at that precise moment she felt like braining him, not hugging him. His knowing smile told Harper he was aware of her feelings and derived pleasure from goading her.

Morwenna had suggested U.S.T lay at the root of the tension between them. At that particular moment Harper's thoughts were veering more towards G.B.H, with a blunt instrument. Gritting her teeth and with a false smile in place, she swung herself up into the Land Rover's cab. Laughing and sending her a cheeky wink, Morwenna walked over and handed her a towel.

'What's this for?' Harper inquired, draping the towel across her knees.

'You'll find out soon enough,' was the cryptic answer.

Closing the door, Harper tried to slide the side window open but it was jammed fast thanks to moss growing on the runners. 'Permit me.' Leaning across, Rocco pushed it open. When he drew back, his elbow grazed Harper's breast and she reared back in shock.

'Sorry, does my touch contaminate?' he asked, irritated.

'Let's just get going, shall we?'

Turning towards Morwenna and the girls she hid the telling flush of heat scorching her cheeks. *Contamination* didn't quite cover it. Penhaligon read her reaction as revulsion, let him go on thinking that. Time this uneasy partnership was back on a no-nonsense footing until it was officially terminated. That included no touching, joshing, teasing. Nothing that wasn't directly linked to bringing the teenagers home.

Harper kept waving until Home Farm was out of sight and then she shrank low down in her seat and pretended to catch some shut-eye, even though it was only ten o'clock in the morning. If Penhaligon thought she was play-acting, he gave no sign of it, simply stared straight ahead and concentrated on his driving.

* * *

When they reached Carlisle the temperature dropped and wind whistled through the gaps in the ripped hood. Harper pulled the collar of her borrowed fleece higher, letting Penhaligon know she wasn't in the mood for conversation. If he started extolling the virtues of the heating system of this scrapheap, she wouldn't be held responsible. However, evidently picking up the negative vibes being directed towards him, Rocco drove northwards without another word.

Harper held her breath and crossed everything she had as the miles slipped by. The Land Rover coughed and spluttered its way north, seeming as if it would give up the ghost in the strong headwind and pouring rain. Crossing the border, two signs flashed up on their left hand side: *Failte gu Alba* – Welcome to Scotland – and a yellow weather warning forecasting more heavy rain ahead. Harper had been puzzled when Morwenna had handed them each a towel before they left, but now she understood. Rain was coming in through the ripped canvas roof and pouring down their necks.

Grimacing, she followed Rocco's lead and draped the towel over her head. She flipped down the sun visor to check if she looked as ridiculous as she felt. Of course, there was no vanity mirror; what was she thinking? Farmers had no need of one.

Then, through the late afternoon murk and rain-smeared windscreen, a sign indicating *Gretna Green Services* appeared. The engine wheezed, coughed and died. Luckily, he was able to coast into a parking space, switch off the ignition and apply the handbrake. In the ensuing silence all that could be heard was the battering of hailstones on the Land Rover's bonnet and the plop as some made it through the hole in the tattered cab and landed on the dashboard.

Reaching behind his seat Rocco found a waterproof jacket. Getting out, he stood in the icy rain shrugging on the coat and becoming drenched in the process, cursing because one of the sleeves was inside out. Then Harper's view of him was obscured as he propped opened the Land Rover's bonnet and started to fiddle with the engine.

'Welcome to Bonnie Scotland,' she muttered.

It galled her to think that the two who'd forced them to embark on this odyssey were bone dry, riding around in a top of the range jeep and almost certainly staying in bijou bed and breakfast establishments (courtesy of Ariel's generous summer allowance), while they were soaking, exhausted and anxious. She scrubbed 'anxious' off the list. She'd stopped fearing for Ariel's virtue miles back, whatever came Ariel's way would be her and Shona's responsibility. She'd had enough. For two pins she'd abandon the search and head back to Polzenith. However, that would be to admit defeat and Harper MacDonald was no quitter. Besides, if she parted company from Penhaligon now it'd make everything she'd said about worrying over Ariel's life being ruined seem nothing more than empty posturing.

Another deep sigh, one of frustration this time.

Grabbing an ancient Barbour off the bench seat in the back of the Land Rover, Harper slipped it on, climbed out of the cab and walked round to where Rocco was bent over the engine, removing plugs and fiddling with something which looked like it had tentacles. The distributor cap?

'So, what now?' she asked when he seemed disinclined to talk.

'I let it dry out and try to get it going again.'

'Why don't we call out the AA ? I left my card behind in Polzenith, but . . .'

'Not necessary.'

'You have cover? Great.' Her sigh of relief became a sharp intake of breath as a gust of wind threw a handful of icy rain in her face. 'Give me your card; I'll ring them on my mobile and . . .'

'I'm not in the AA.' His voice was muffled by the bonnet hood.

'Everyone is in the AA, or similar,' she protested.

'Well, I'm not.'

'I'm going to regret asking this, but why aren't you in the AA?'

'Two reasons.' Straightening, he used Morwenna's towel to wipe his face and then draped it round his neck like a scarf to prevent more water from running down his neck.

'Do share,' she said, tight-lipped.

'One, I'm a mechanic and can fix just about anything. Two, I don't need the same help as an old lady.'

'Implying that I'm an old lady?'

He shrugged, leaving her to draw her own conclusions. 'And, three . . .'

'Oh, I might have known there'd be a third reason. The holy trinity of how to survive on a road trip by St Petroc Penhaligon.' Ignoring her sarcasm he continued.

'. . . where would the fun be in calling out a mechanic, less skilled than I am, to fix my car?'

'You call this *fun*?' Her sweeping gesture took in the old Land Rover, the torrential rain and her soaking wet jeans.

'Isn't it?'

'I think you know the answer to that.'

He nodded in the direction of the brightly lit services. 'Why don't you go and fetch a couple of coffees and something to eat? You'll feel better after that. You might even believe in my ability to get this old girl going.'

Harper felt like kicking the 'old girl's' tyres but restrained herself. It was on the tip of her tongue to say that he didn't get to tell her what to do but he was soaked to the skin so, just this once, she complied. 'This is becoming habit-forming. Over the last couple of days our lives seem to have centred around motorway services.'

Returning to the cab she fetched her handbag.

'Yes, we have a lot to thank the kids for,' was his sarcastic response as he dried the distributor cap with an oily rag. It pleased Harper to learn that he, too, was fed up with this race to find the teenagers. But they had to see it through to the bitter end. Had they overreacted after finding those two notes? Well, it was academic now.

'Still here?' he asked without turning around.

'Just going.'

'Only . . .'

'Only, *what*?' she asked, somewhat testily.

'Don't get any ideas.'

'What kind of ideas? Hitching a lift from a passing lorry driver?

Finding some nice family who could fit me in the back of their car with the dog? Believe me, if I knew where those two were headed, I would leave you in an instant.' Turning around, he leaned back on the Land Rover and, sheltering under the open bonnet, pointed over her shoulder with the large spanner. Turning, Harper saw nothing out of the ordinary. 'So?'

'*Gretna Green.* Do I have to spell it out, Miss MacDonald?' He grinned, taking obvious delight in winding her up.

'What? You think I'd stand before the famous anvil and enter a state of holy deadlock with you? I'm not *that* desperate.' She bit her lip. Her throwaway remark implied that she *was* desperate, just not as desperate as he thought. She had to put the record straight, quickly. 'I'd as soon marry one of those Belted Galloways in the field over there.' He laughed for the first time that day and Harper realised he was teasing her. 'Do you derive some sort of perverse pleasure from goading me?'

'Now you mention it . . .' He laughed again, his eyes bright in the mid-afternoon gloom, eyelashes spiky with rain. After sending him a burning look, Harper turned on her heel and headed for the services. She shouldn't rise to the bait, she really shouldn't. Words were her forte and in some strange inexplicable way it pleased her that he could give as good as he got. Not many men of her acquaintance were as quick-witted or as articulate as Penhaligon, which made for boring company and the reason why they never featured in her life for long.

Banter, sarcasm, irony – anything was better than remembering his elbow brushing against her breast and the way she'd reacted. Pushing the door to the service station open, she went to place their order.

* * *

When she returned, Rocco was sitting inside the Land Rover with the engine running and the heating back on. She handed him coffee and a sausage roll through the window and climbed back inside.

'Okay, Mr-Smarty-Pants, how did you manage to get it going?' she asked, taking a bite out of the scorching hot sausage roll.

'If I told you that, I'd have to kill you,' he joked. 'Mr-Smarty-Pants, eh? I think I might rename my garage when I get back to Polzenith. After this, *Penhaligon's* simply won't cut it. If you must know, I brought along Joe's battery booster and it got the old girl going. Let's hope the rain lets up soon, these are far from ideal conditions for an old lady to travel in.' He slid her a look and then patted the dashboard, in case she thought he was referring to her!

Harper resisted the urge to repeat what she'd said about hiring a car. If he was Mr-Smarty-Pants she was fast becoming Mrs-I-Told-You-So. Instead, she finished her sausage roll, took a swig of scalding hot black coffee and then fished around in the paper bag to retrieve two donuts. It was reminiscent of the first leg of their journey and that gave her cause for thought. They'd only been on the road for two days but already they were creating a shared history. She couldn't decide if that was a good thing. Rocco, oblivious to the cogs whirring round in her head, carried on eating his sausage roll, no doubt congratulating himself on how quickly he'd got the Land Rover up and running.

Boys and their toys, huh?

When she absent-mindedly let him have first choice of the donuts he looked at her suspiciously. 'Not going soft on me are you, MacDonald?' he asked, choosing one filled with jam and cream.

'You wish.' Turning her head she looked out into the rain-drenched carpark through the side window and hid her smile. What was happening here? Now that she believed Ariel wasn't in imminent danger Harper was forced to admit that being in Penhaligon's company wasn't as bad as she'd previously thought.

Rocco finished his donut and then excused himself with a veiled reference to visiting the loos. He didn't switch off the engine, perhaps he didn't dare, so at least Harper was warm and snug in the cab. She watched him disappear into the main part of the service station and settled herself for the next leg of the journey. Shifting in her seat her foot came up against something hard on the floor. Bending, she picked up Rocco's mobile phone and placed it on the dashboard. As she did so, her thumb grazed across the home button and a list of recent calls flashed up on the screen.

She wouldn't have been human if she hadn't given it a quick glance, just to satisfy herself that Penhaligon was playing fair. Pen's name was at the top of the list and against it was the time he'd rung. Less than five minutes ago. While she'd been in the services, the two Penhaligons had been communicating, and Rocco hadn't thought fit to share that. Partners? She didn't think so. Feeling sick and betrayed, she returned the phone to the footwell, fighting back angry tears. Searching in her pocket she found a paper napkin and used it to blot her face, determined to act as if nothing had happened.

To keep from him how much his treachery hurt.

She'd been a fool to trust him.

She'd make certain that didn't happen again.

Chapter Fourteen

Rocco was relieved to get the Land Rover going. Harper had been annoyed when he'd rolled it out of Morwenna's garage, she'd go ballistic if it died on them for a second time. She had such a short fuse, God only knows how she dealt with people in her role as headteacher. She had a great 'game face', one which hid what she was really thinking. Bet she'd be a great poker player.

He glanced over at her. Since he'd returned from the toilets she'd been unnaturally quiet and that unnerved him. He'd never come across anyone like her. She could weigh up a situation, reach a decision over what should be done and then act on it, in ten seconds flat.

Time to break the silence. 'You okay?'

'Of course, why shouldn't I be?'

'No reason. You've gone very quiet and that makes me nervous.' He tried to lighten the atmosphere with a joke.

'You're right to be nervous. Who knows what we'll find when we catch up with the *youngsters*?' He didn't like the way she used the word to describe Ariel and Pen who were, in the eyes of the law at least, now adults. 'Don't you think that in many ways they've betrayed our trust? Played us for fools?'

'I thought we'd established that at the outset journey and got over it,' he said, peering through the windscreen at the road ahead. It was late afternoon but the lowering clouds and bad light made driving difficult. Just as they were beginning to get along and trust each other she'd reverted back to being Miss MacDonald, headteacher. What had happened to change that? His loo break had only lasted five minutes but when he'd returned she'd been sitting there boot-faced.

Women, huh?

In a show of female solidarity the Land Rover started missing, forcing Rocco to concede that Harper was right. He should let her call out the AA to take them to the nearest garage on a low-loader and have the engine properly inspected, but he held back. Call it male pride, stubbornness, what you will – but he wasn't ready to go down that road, or admit that he was wrong. Thinking about ringing the AA had him patting the side pocket in his cargo pants to locate his phone.

'Damn it,' he exclaimed.

'Something wrong?'

'I –think I may have left my mobile in the services. We'll have to turn around and –'

'Perhaps you left it in the pocket of the waterproof you were wearing earlier?' she suggested. 'Tell me your number and I'll ring you with my phone.' He complied and *Born to Be Wild*, sang out from somewhere near his feet. He did at least have the good grace to look embarrassed at her learning his ring tone. 'There,' she said in a snappy business-like manner, 'no need to turn back.' She picked up the phone, stretched across him and tossed it into the dashboard shelf in front of him. 'Disaster averted, you should be more careful. Not leave your phone lying around where it could be picked up by the wrong person.'

'Thanks, but I'm not ten years old,' he said, taking exception to the reprimand.

'That's right, you're not. But, at times, you act like it.'

'Woah, where's all *this* coming from?' He had the sinking feeling that she knew Pen had rung him. But, how could she, unless . . . *picked up by the wrong person*. Was that a clue? He didn't want to pick a fight with her because he knew the Land Rover was about to go into spasm and that would be the last straw, for both of them. She'd be back to 'what did I tell you' and insist he rented a car (if such a thing was even possible late on a Sunday afternoon, miles south of Glasgow) and he'd be forced to concede defeat. 'I'm pulling off the road, does that meet with your approval?'

'It does.'

They left the M74 at junction 19 for the improbably named Ecclefechan, Rocco genuinely worried that the Land Rover wouldn't make it much further. 'Come on, old girl,' he whispered, 'stay with me'. He sounded like a heart surgeon nursing a patient through a tricky operation.

'Look. A farm,' Harper said with false brightness. 'They'll be sure to understand all about classic Land Rovers and perhaps let us shelter in a barn, or something, until madam here gets a second – or, should that be third wind?'

'Good idea,' Rocco said, keen to keep her on side. 'Brilliant.' He cringed, he sounded like an over enthusiastic teenager, exactly like Pen.

Glancing over at Harper a suspicion began to form. He wouldn't put it past her to have found the phone while he'd been over at the toilets, realised that Pen had rung him and then put it back where she'd discovered it, simply to make a point. They were 'even' on the whole 'I'm-not-telling-you-where-we're-headed' stakes, but concealing Pen's phone call had been a bad move. He saw that now. Putting the thought aside he swung off the road and drew up in front of a farmhouse. Feeling that the onus was on him he got out of the Land Rover, walked over to the door and rang the bell.

Immediately, two border collies skidded round the corner from the back of the house, making it plain he was an unwelcome visitor. He waited patiently for someone to answer the bell and eventually the door opened a crack and an elderly man peered out.

'Can I help you?'

'I hope so. My friend and I are on our way north but our Land Rover has broken down. I wondered if I could wheel it into one of your barns, dry out the plugs and then be on our way?'

'Land Rover you say?' The door opened fractionally wider and the farmer looked over Rocco's shoulder. 'Is that a one-eighty?'

'Yes, early 50's model.'

'Och, we had one of those when I was a boy.' Now the door was pushed back on its hinges and he wheeshed the dogs with a command. 'D'ye mind?' Walking over to the vehicle, he opened the bonnet and stuck his head in, tutting at what he saw

'I've dried it out as best as I can.' Rocco felt he should apologise for the state of the engine.

'Quite collectable, isn't it?'

'Very much so. My plan is to restore it and then sell it on behalf of a friend.' The farmer nodded his approval.

'Aye, it'll fetch a pretty penny.'

'It will. I'm Rocco Penhaligon by the way.' They shook hands.

'My friend,' he nearly added, *the one sitting in the cab with a face like thunder*, is 'Harper MacDonald.'

'MacDonald, ye say? My wife was a MacDonald before I married her. Tell your young lady to go away in tae the house while we get the Land Rover into thon barn. It's empty because the beasts are in the summer pasture.'

'Thanks, I will.'

Harper was already outside of the Land Rover and waiting for him. 'I heard all that, no need to repeat it. And,' she lowered her voice, 'whenever the moment presents itself, please make clear that I am *not* your young lady.'

'With pleasure,' he said, sotte voce. Then just to annoy her he raised his voice so the farmer could hear. 'You wait in the house while we sort out the Land Rover, sweetie.'

Sweetie? Her face said it all.

He would pay for this and the deception over Pen's phone call, big time. Turning, Harper walked over to the farmer and thanked him for allowing them to park in his barn, however temporarily, very much in headteacher mode: polite, professional, charming. The dogs didn't growl when she walked over to the farmhouse, simply trotted behind her tame as you like. Was that because their master was keeping an eye on them and they knew they had to behave? Or, unlike him, knew better than to mess with her?

* * *

'Really, you've been more than kind,' Harper smiled at the farmer's wife, 'allowing us to camp overnight in your barn, drying the plugs in your Aga. And now, delicious sandwiches and a flask of tea. How can we ever repay you?'

'Och, it's nothing. If we didn't have to go to church for the Sunday evening service I'd have done more. There's a visiting preacher and the whole community will be there. I cannae miss it, but on the other hand it's not often a MacDonald rolls up on a Sunday afternoon.'

'It's sweet of you to say so, but I feel a bit of a fraud as I haven't been to Scotland since I was a child . . .'

The woman patted her on the arm. 'You dinnae need to live in Scotland to be Scottish, it's in your heart, m'dear. Once you reach the highlands, your ancestral home, you'll see what I mean.' There was an earnest light in her blue eyes which touched Harper to the core. 'Besides, does it not say in the guid book: *Do not forget to entertain strangers, for by so doing some have unwittingly entertained angels.*'

'It does, indeed.' Though, anyone less like angels than herself and her sparring partner would be hard to imagine! 'Well, thanks again.' She took the flask and sandwiches from the farmer's wife.

'And if you and your husband need anything else, we can sort it when we get home after the service.'

It was on the tip of Harper's tongue to put the record straight, but she smiled and said nothing. Outside, the farmer honked the horn of his pickup truck impatiently. The two collies jumped in the back and Rocco held the door open so his wife could climb in the cab. After waving them off, he joined Harper in the barn.

'So ...' he let out a long breath. 'Go on, say it.'

'Say what?'

'That I should have told you that Pen had been in touch.'

'Okay – *you should have told me that Pen had been in touch*,' she parroted. Placing the flask and sandwiches on a hay bale, she surveyed the barn. It was empty apart from animal fodder and the Land Rover whose vital components had been removed and put in the warming oven of the Aga to dry out. The plan was, the farmer would remove them from the oven before he and his wife retired for the night. Rocco would collect them in the morning and try to restart the Land Rover.

'If I apologise, will that do?' he asked, cocking his head on the side and sending her a look which, no doubt, had melted many a woman's heart. She remained stony-faced. He wasn't being let off that lightly.

'It will, if you tell me what Pen said. You know where they're headed, don't you?'

'I have a pretty good idea. Pen wouldn't confirm it one way or another, he simply rang because he was feeling guilty and didn't want me to worry about him.'

Pity Ariel hadn't thought to show me the same consideration, Harper huffed.

'As far as Pen's aware, I'm in Polzenith eating a late, lonely Sunday dinner waiting for Country File to come on.' He pulled a face at the picture that painted. 'I want it to stay that way. He's enjoying the freedom of making his own decisions, doing what he likes without referring to me. Thinking about it, maybe I've been a helicopter parent over the years, but he's all I've got.'

'It doesn't put my mind at rest. The thought of him and Ariel alone, getting up to what comes naturally, makes me break out in a cold sweat. As I said before, I don't want history repeating itself twice in a generation.' She poured out two cups of tea from the tartan flask, removed the Clingfilm from the sandwiches and arranged them on the bale of hay as though it was Afternoon Tea at the vicarage.

Rocco laughed. Raising her head, she shot him a look. 'Relax, I'm not laughing away your concerns, I just want you to know that you needn't worry on that score.'

'Really, how do you know?' She passed over a mug of tea and a bacon sandwich.

'Because Pen made his feelings about Ariel very clear during our brief phone call.'

'Go on –'

'She's driving him mad. She's demanding, bossy and expects him to run round after her. Nothing's right; it's too hot, it's too cold, she's hungry, she's thirsty, I could go on. Wonder where she gets that from?'

'Don't push it, Penhaligon. I still haven't forgiven you for keeping the phone call secret.'

Walking over, Rocco sat next to her on the hay bale. 'I was going to tell you, but hesitated because the Land Rover was in a worse condition than I suspected. I really thought that we'd part company at Gretna Green and I'd be left to handle your niece on my own.'

Harper laughed. 'Now that, I'd pay good money to see.' She recalled Morwenna's take on Rocco keeping their destination secret. In Morwenna's ever-romantic heart, Rocco didn't want Harper to leave him because he was smitten with her and reluctant to let her go.

Rocco's admission was nearer the truth, he needed an ally.

'Pen likes Ariel. He says she's funny, smart and good company, when it suits her. But being with her is like sitting on a powder keg which could blow at any moment.'

'I know the feeling. Poor Pen. So, Mr Penhaligon, where *are* we headed?'

'Plockton.'

Harper frowned, the name had a familiar ring to it. 'Where's that?'

'Near the Kyle of Lochalsh. I have a house there.'

'You have a house there?' Of course he did. She sent him a speculative look. The revelation that he owned a house in the highlands of Scotland made her wonder: who was the real Petroc Penhaligon?

'It belonged to my Gunn grandparents. Every summer they'd

hold open house and anyone who cared to take the overnight sleeper from Paddington to Inverness, before travelling on to Plockton, was guaranteed a good time. They're in their nineties and live in Edinburgh now, a few years back they decided the journey was too much for them and gave the house to me.'

Just like that.

'Shouldn't it have gone to your parents?'

'It should, but Father needs to be near Bristol as he still plays an active part in the business. Mother prefers big cities and shops to big open skies. Surprisingly, the cross-country line from Inverness to Kyle is still in operation, so Pen and I fly up every summer and stay for as long as I feel I can leave the garage to run itself.'

'It sounds idyllic.'

'It is. We rent garage space from an elderly villager, have done for years, and store an old jalopy in there which we use to get about. The house is kept aired and the garden in trim by a local lady, Janet Baxter. I ring her up, tell her I'm on my way and she stocks the fridge with essentials in case we arrive late and the pub's closed.'

'Forgive me for saying this, but isn't it a bit extravagant? Having a house which is empty for most of the year?'

'It is. However, Granny and Grandpa Gunn would have a fit if I sold it, or turned it into an Airbnb. Each year, fewer and fewer houses in the village remain in private hands. To be honest,' he paused, clearly wondering if sharing his innermost thoughts was a good idea, 'I'd live there permanently if I could find somewhere suitable to work on my cars. I – I don't need the money, I'm happy with very little and I've brought Pen up to be the same. However, for my mental health's sake, I need a project to work on. Does that sound cringingly new-age-y?'

New Age-y? Harper thought back to the story of Lorelei and their summer romance which Morwenna had shared with her.

'Not at all. But, leave Polzenith?' Although she was considering doing the same, the thought of Rocco Penhaligon no longer knocking wrecks into shape at the far end of the village made her feel strangely bereft. As if he was moving on and leaving her behind. How crazy was that? Until two days ago, she hadn't even been aware of his existence.

'It feels like it's time for a change. If – when – Pen goes up to Oxford, it'll be the end of an era. Foolishly,' he turned his head away, hiding his expression, 'I – I've been waiting for someone to return, who . . .' He took a long swig of the now cooling tea and chewed at his sandwich thoughtfully, choosing not to elaborate.

Harper ate her sandwich, hiding her frustration at coming so close to learning more of Rocco's story. Sensibly, she decided not to push it. They'd reached a place where they were beginning to feel comfortable in each other's company. Perhaps, with gentle probing, he'd open up to her on the road? As for her, the choice was simple – stay in Polzenith, or give a term's notice and head for a large city where there were better career prospects. Somewhere where she could achieve her full potential. And, actually, now she came to think of it, there was nothing to keep her in Polzenith.

Following Rocco's example, she drank her tea and then gasped. 'What's in this?'

'A wee dram from the Annandale distillery. The taste should be singing to you, coursing its way through your Scottish blood. Here, have a top up.' He passed the tartan flask over but she shook her head.

'My Scottish blood thinks it's had enough, thank you. I'm surprised that good Presbyterians like the farmer and his wife should be drinking the devil's brew.' She laughed to show that she was joking.

'It's not the devil's brew in their eyes, its *uisge beatha*, the water of life. Slainte.'

'Sl-slainte,' she returned the toast, clinking their mugs together, then Rocco started clearing their supper away.

'If you've finished, let's get the sleeping arrangements sorted.'

'When you say *sleeping arrangements,* what do you mean exactly?'

'Morwenna, believing that the Land Rover wouldn't get beyond the end of the drive, insisted on packing a pop-up tent, air mattress and two sleeping bags. Note the emphasis on *two*. Surely, you don't think I had plans to,' he pretended to search for the phrase, 'how did your niece so charmingly put it –'.

'*Jump my bones?*' Harper grimaced. She sounded like a dried out old stick who thought all members of the opposite sex had just one thing on their minds. Small wonder he didn't look amused at her inference.

'Exactly.' He walked over to the back of the Land Rover and started hauling stuff out. 'Morwenna has even inflated the mattress for us, thinking that by the end of the day we'd have no puff left, because we'd been arguing all the way to Scotland.'

'She was right,' Harper laughed, glad to be back on easy terms.

'However,' Rocco unfolded the sleeping bags. 'I think that zipping the bags together to make one large sleeping bag is pushing the entente cordiale a bit too far. Agreed?'

'Agreed.'

'I warned you that she was a hopeless romantic and an inveterate matchmaker. Come on, help me unzip them.' Harper complied and they soon had the tent erected, the mattress on the floor and two sleeping bags on top of it. There were no pillows so they'd have to do without.

It being high summer, it was still bright as day when Rocco rolled down the barn doors. Making the most of his attention being elsewhere, Harper stripped down to her underwear and climbed in the sleeping bag. She turned her back so that when he crawled in the tent he could do the same. She heard him moving around but didn't look over her shoulder, this was intimate enough. Her side of the mattress raised slightly when he lay down beside her and she shivered.

'Goodnight Miss MacDonald,' he said gruffly.

'Sweet dreams, Mr Penhaligon.' Harper snuggled lower in the down-filled sleeping bag, pulling it up to her chin.

Then, exhausted by the physical and emotional traumas of the last few days, the trying journey, and whisky-laced tea, they were soon both fast asleep.

Chapter Fifteen

Next morning, when Harper glanced over at his side of the mattress, Rocco was nowhere to be seen. His sleeping bag was neatly rolled up at the foot of the air bed and his clothes, which had lain in a tidy pile beside him, had gone. Flipping onto her back Harper pushed her hair out of her eyes and released a slow breath.

It'd been a strange night, full of unsettling dreams filled with nameless longings. Dreams which left her yearning for fulfilment and feeling oddly dissatisfied. She put her mood down to Annandale's finest malt and the fact that, at long last, she and Penhaligon were being honest with each other. However, that didn't quite explain the most vivid part of the dream when she'd reached out for Rocco and curled her body into his as though it was the most natural thing in the world. In the dream, he'd traced a line from her forehead to her chin ending the exploration in a drawn-out kiss. The memory of it made the blood beat thickly through her veins as she tried to remember the exact detail of the dream and how it had ended. However, the bright morning light beyond the tent flap, chased the last wisps of sleep away and, with them, the unsettling dream.

Unzipping the sleeping bag she let the cool air caress her skin, rejecting the unfamiliar sensations making her shiver. Feelings she thought had died long ago when she'd given up on finding love and experiencing the deep, deep ache poets wrote about. Releasing a pent-up breath she bet herself that no such dreams had disturbed Penhaligon's slumbers. He'd probably been up for hours working on the Land Rover, intent in travelling to Plockton, finding Pen and dissolving their partnership. PDQ.

Time to get dressed and check out when they were leaving.

She was reluctant to ask the farmer if she could use his bathroom, it felt like too great an imposition after they'd already been so kind. Last night she'd used the sink in the outside loo, usually reserved for cowhands, and brushed her teeth there. She could quickly splash her face with cold water and apply a lick of moisturiser before they left. If the Land Rover kept going, they'd be in Plockton by dusk and this would be the last time she'd have to rough it. Besides, if she insisted on taking time to wash and change she'd merely reinforce Rocco's opinion of her as a princess.

'Harper? You awake?'

Talk of the devil. 'Ye-yes, just getting dressed. Give me a minute.'

'There's a mug of tea and a slice of Dundee cake on the hay bale. Be quick as you can, I'm anxious to be on our way. The rain's stopped but that doesn't mean it won't be back.' A few minutes later, when she crawled out of the tent on all fours, he extended his hand and helped her to her feet.

'Morning. Sleep well?'

'Fine. You?'

'As well as could be expected in the circumstances.' His sideways glance before he looked away made her wonder if he, too, had experienced disturbing dreams. Probably not. Hadn't Morwenna described the love of his life as tall, blonde and with startling blue eyes? Whereas, she was on the short side, had hair that could best be described as crow's wing black and the pale complexion of her highland forebears. This morning she was glad of being unremarkable. There was no place for ambiguity in this relationship.

'Have you managed to get her going?'

'Yes. Mr Bailey, the farmer, removed the plugs and distributor cap from the Aga last night, otherwise they would've been cooked this morning. That seems to have done the trick. I started her earlier while you were asleep and she turned over first time. You didn't budge when I revved her up, and when I checked you, you were out for the count.'

Harper was perturbed that he'd been watching her as she slept. Had she snored? Was her mouth open, catching flies? Did she snort and snuffle like a farm animal? She wasn't going to ask him, natch, but the thought was there all the same. Dismissing it as vanity she concentrated instead on eating her slice of Dundee cake and drinking the tea, mercifully not laced with whisky.

'Finish your breakfast while I pack up the camping gear and we'll be on our way.' She did just that and, after bidding the farmer and his wife a fond farewell and promising to call in again on their way back to Polzenith, they left.

'Plockton, here we come,' Rocco said, driving back onto the M74 and heading north.

Clearly she had no recollection of what had happened last night, Rocco thought, bypassing Glasgow and heading north. She'd probably dismissed what'd happened between them as a waking dream in that rational way of hers. Evidently, she didn't recall stirring in the wee small hours shivering with cold, burrowing her face in his neck and breathing in his scent as though it was the most natural thing in the world. It had taken every ounce of his self-control to gather her in his arms and simply hold her there, transmitting his body heat to her. God! How he'd longed to roll her under him, cover her body with his and make love to her in the pop-up tent in a cow byre. But it would be wrong and dangerous to become involved with someone he'd only just met. Someone so completely and utterly different from him. Finally, common sense had won the day. He'd waited until she had tumbled into a deeper sleep and then kissed her once, on the mouth, before rolling her onto her side and moulding himself into her as far the bulky sleeping bags would allow. He'd stayed like that until her breathing became deep and regular and he knew her core temperature had risen. Then he untangled himself and shifted onto his back, torturing himself with the thought of how it'd feel to make love to Miss Harper MacDonald. Finally, remembering the long drive to Plockton ahead of them in the morning, he'd drifted off until the farmer entered the barn at first light and woke him.

* * *

'Highland traffic jam?' Harper inquired, as the last leg of their journey to Plockton was held up by a herd of highland cattle cropping the grass on the narrow road from Duirinish. Other motorists had stopped too, getting out of their cars to take snaps of the photogenic beasts. 'The babies are so cute,' Harper exclaimed, leaning across Rocco and clicking away on her phone. This time she didn't shy away from touching him or react as though he was a disease to be avoided.

'Cute?' he teased.

'Yes! They look exactly like large labradoodles only with strawberry blond coats.'

Rocco laughed. 'Don't let the farmer hear you talking like that. They're a prize herd of cattle and fit for only one purpose.' He didn't need to spell out what that was.

'Have you no heart?' Harper exclaimed. 'Is it okay to get out?'

'Yes, but don't get too close or the mothers will think you're threatening their offspring. Those horns aren't ornamental, you know.'

Glad to stretch her cramped limbs, Harper climbed down from the Land Rover and stood on top of an embankment to take more photos. Then the cows, clearly thinking that the photo shoot had gone on long enough, ambled off in the opposite direction with their calves close behind. Clambering back into the Land Rover, Harper flopped down on her seat and closed the door.

'I can build a whole geography lesson round these photos,' she chirruped, feeling different to the hung-over-with-sleep-and-wild dreams creature who'd clambered out of the tent at Ecclefechan.

'Are you always on task?' Rocco slipped the Land Rover into gear and moved forward.

'Sorry,' Harper shrugged, 'It's the nature of the job. I've become expert at magicking lessons out of thin air. I'm always looking for new ways of presenting familiar concepts. Anyhoo,' changing the subject, she grinned, 'are we there yet, Dad?'

'Not quite,' Rocco responded, giving her a sidelong look. 'Hmm. This is an Harper MacDonald I haven't seen before.' He followed the convoy of cars towards Plockton.

'Well, I don't suppose either of us has seen the other in the best light. We've been too worried, too concerned. Now they're almost within spitting distance I feel I can relax a bit.'

'Good. It's been a bloody awful couple of days.' At last! Buoyed up by his admission that he'd been as worried as her, Harper sent him another smile.

'Quite! And to think that it's only been a couple of days. Friday, Saturday, Sunday. It feels like a lifetime. Perhaps we're relaxing before the quest to find them is truly over.'

'I like the new you. More chilled, less frosty – or is that a contradiction in terms? But I understand why you've been beside yourself. Neither of us wants,' he took a breath, seemingly searching for the right phrase, 'history to repeat itself.' Crunching the gears, they descended into Plockton.

Harper knew what she feared most, Ariel becoming pregnant on *her* watch. But what history was Rocco referring to? How might his mistakes be repeated by his son? She tried to remember what Morwenna had revealed back at Home Farm, but it was all so sketchy. More about them living above the garage before Morwenna and Joe had headed to Penrith and Rocco had fallen hook, line and sinker for the girl with the mermaid tattoo.

Pen's mother? Morwenna hadn't exactly been clear on that point.

She tried to visualise young Rocco Penhaligon falling in love with his Trustafarian mermaid, but couldn't quite match him to the image. Not that she could imagine Rocco Penhaligon giving his heart to any woman.

They passed a large sign: BOAT TRIPS AT PLOCKTON, and

underneath – FREE IF NO SEALS. She guessed that seals were in plentiful supply, but mermaids less so. Shaking her head she dismissed the fanciful thought. Yet – there was something about being in Scotland, in this beautiful place made her feel whimsical, other worldly. Perhaps the farmer's wife, Mrs Bailey, had been right:

You dinnae need to live in Scotland to be Scottish, it's in your heart, m'dear. Once you reach the highlands, your ancestral home, you'll see what I mean.

They turned left into *Sraid a Chalaidh* – Harbour Street, and she was thrown against Rocco. This time they smiled an apology at each other and Rocco drove along the shore, eventually stopping by an imposing dwelling with a canopied porch. The porch was almost hidden under the twisted tendrils of a summer clematis but Harper was able to make out a Gaelic house name. On either side of the porch were two sash windows, while on the upper floor, three canopied windows looked out over the shore. A double set of chimneys sat on either end of a blue slate roof and Harper imagined curling up in front of a fire on a cold autumn evening with a favourite novel.

She'd guessed that Rocco had inherited a simple whitewashed two up/two down cottage from his grandparents. She should have known that the Penhaligons didn't do cheap, or simple.

'Okay?' he questioned, touching her lightly on the arm.

'Fine.' Opening the door, she jumped down and waited for him on the pavement, admiring the low whitewashed walls topped by black wrought iron railings fronting the property. Behind grew a profusion of tall perennials which Harper was surprised to find growing this far north. 'These flowers, how . . .'

'Plockton and Loch Carron are touched by the gulf stream, you'll be surprised at what we grow in our gardens across the road.'

'Across the road?' she asked, bemused.

Rocco pointed to a row of well-tended gardens on the other side of Harbour Street. The cuff of his sweatshirt grazed Harper's ear sending an electric shock zipping through her. Oblivious, Rocco continued. 'The one with the palm trees is ours. The gardens along the shore belong to other houses. See the gate at the far end of our garden? It gives access to our boathouse and the shore. When the tide's in, and the weather's set fair, we get out the skiff and go sailing up the loch. I can take you out on the loch, if time allows.'

'Looking for seals? Money back guarantee?' It was on the tip of her tongue to mention mermaids but she decided against it. 'I – I'd like that very much, once everything's settled, naturally.' She forced herself to dismiss the idyllic surroundings and focus on why they were here.

If Rocco noticed her hesitancy he didn't show it. He seemed intent on introducing Plockton to her, as though in seeing it through her eyes he was seeing it anew. 'We store a runabout in Baxter's Garage at the end of the village.'

'Let me guess, an Aston Martin DB8. One 007 left behind when he was filming Skyfall a few years back?' Good; sarcasm kept her wits sharpened and stopped her from falling in love with this beautiful place.

'It's an ancient Ford Fiesta, if you must know.' Rocco didn't rise to the bait. 'Baxter's wife and daughter keep Heron Croft in good order and their son, Iain does the gardening. A family tradition started in my grandparents' time which I see no reason to change.' Leading the way up the flight of six stone steps, each one flanked by flowerpots overflowing with summer bedding plants, Rocco paused by a glass panelled front door. The top panes were beautifully wrought stained glass: one depicting a leaping dolphin and the other a heron whose baleful yellow eye was trained on the loch, looking for prey. 'Welcome to *croit nan corra-ghritheach,* which roughly translates to *Heron Croft.*'

'The Gaelic trips easily off your tongue,' Harper was impressed.

'Well, I have been climbing these steps for almost forty years so have picked up a smattering. I am very old, as you so kindly pointed out the other day. Maybe I should have a handrail installed?' There was no rancour in his voice, simply amusement.

'Ha ha, very funny.'

'Ladies first.' Rocco pushed the door open and Harper stepped into the hall, intrigued to discover if the interior was as imposing as the exterior. She wasn't intimidated by the size of the property, or what it told the world about the Penhaligons. They had money to spare, she got it; but that didn't make them better, or worse, than anyone else.

She walked into a large modern kitchen which occupied three-quarters of the ground floor and incorporated what must have been the hall. To her left, a square sitting room complete with wood burning stove, television, squashy sofas and book-lined walls invited her to *come away in and stay a while*. To the left behind the sitting room wall, a staircase led to the next floor and Harper was curious to discover what lay up there.

'I'm sure you detect mother's hand in the house,' Rocco remarked. 'Deciding that the whole *granny's heilan hame* look was outdated, she brought a team of interior decorators up here one winter and ripped the heart out of the downstairs rooms before I realised what she had planned. That was very wrong of her but typical of her high-handedness. My grandparents – her parents – gave *Heron Croft* to me because they knew I would look after it. It's my plan to restore it to how it was, when time allows. One day it'll be –'

Harper didn't find out what his plans for *Heron Croft* were because the back door opened and three women entered the kitchen. Judging by their build and colouring they were three generations of the same family: tall, fiery red hair and dark brown eyes.

'Rocco!' they exclaimed. The youngest launched herself on him with as much enthusiasm as Morwenna's girls, but the others settled for a kiss on both cheeks and a hug.

'And who is this?' the elder of the trio asked. Rocco ushered Harper forward and did the introductions.

'Harper MacDonald, this is Janet, Margaret and Fiona Baxter.' Harper shook hands with each in turn and, after a brief conversation, the matriarch of the family, Janet, shooed the other two out of the house via the kitchen door.

'You can catch up with Rocco tomorrow. I have things to sort out with him and Miss MacDonald.' Harper's heart sank, that sounded ominous as it was bound to concern Ariel and Pen.

The younger women left promising to return and Janet closed the door after them. 'You'll be wanting a cup of tea and a wee slice of cake?' she asked, moving towards the kettle and switching it on. Then she brought a battered tin out of a cupboard, put it on the table and removed the lid to reveal a Victoria sandwich cake.

'Shop bought?' Rocco teased.

'You know better than that, Rocco Penhaligon. Will ye not sit down, Miss MacDonald?' Her voice had an attractive highland lilt to it and she pulled out a chair for Harper with the air of a grand duchess at a tea party.

'Do you mind if I stand? I've been sitting for hours in the Land Rover.'

'Nae bother.' She turned to Rocco. 'I saw the Land Rover as I walked up the street and guessed it was yours. Another wee project?'

'I'm restoring it for Morwenna and the girls.'

Janet nodded approvingly. 'Aye? Auld Baxter will doubtless be keen to have a look-see.' She placed plates and a large cake knife on the table and then, glancing towards Harper, gave a discreet cough. 'Keep your eye on the kettle, Rocco while I show Miss MacDonald to her room. And cut three slices of cake while ye'r at it.'

'Are you sure I can be trusted with such a delicate operation?'

Janet gave his cheek a playful tap. 'I'm no sure, but I'll take the risk. Cheeky boy, always the same. Miss MacDonald?'

'Of course.' Harper followed Janet up the narrow stairs wondering about a relationship which allowed Janet Baxter to address Penhaligon as *cheeky boy* and gently chastise him.

At the top, the narrow stairs doubled back on themselves to form a landing, set out as a study with desk, laptop, writing materials and an office chair. It commanded a wonderful view of the loch, just the spot for some inspiration. It was so entrancing that Harper temporarily forgot her troubles and admired the view of loch, mountains and white rolling clouds instead.

'Is it no beautiful?' Janet said, seemingly able to read her mind.

'It is. I'd love to come back once everything is . . . settled.' She didn't know how much information Janet was privy to, or the reason why she and Rocco had rocked up in Plockton at short notice. She seemed confident of her place in Rocco's life and, as a mother and grandmother, would doubtless have her own opinion about Ariel and Pen's behaviour.

'Aye, I understand that. But, let me put your mind at rest over one thing.'

'What would that be?'

'I wouldn't like you, or Rocco, to think I condoned or encouraged loose behaviour under this roof while he wisnae here. By which I mean, allowing Pen and Ariel to sleep together.' She didn't seem to think it amiss that she had the authority to prevent that happening.

Her directness caught Harper off guard. 'Why, I – th – thank you.'

Janet held up her hand. 'No need to thank me. Rocco's grandparents would have something to say if I'd done any less and word had got out. My mother kept house for them and when she passed, it became my task to look after Heron Croft and, to my mind, the Penhaligons. I wasn't too keen on them being in the house without a chaperone, Miss MacDonald, I can tell you. This is Plockton, ye ken, not Las Vegas.'

'Quite.' The unlikely juxtaposition of the two locations made Harper smile.

'But, I held my wheesht, because they're of an age to make their own decisions. Even bad ones. That's how youngsters learn. Besides, I could see that they were friends, nothing more. And, with their blonde hair and fine looks could almost pass for brother and sister.'

Never having seen a photograph of Pen, Harper had to take Janet's word for it. But she knew how quickly things could develop between young people – a few drinks too many, snuggling up on the sofa to watch a DVD, thrown together for company because there was no one else, forming a pact to run away together . . .

'Thank you for the reassurance. I've been half out of my mind with worry. Rocco, too, although he hides it well.'

Janet sent her a searching look before adding; 'Of course, it's different for the fathers of sons, isn't it?' Harper felt heartened that Janet understood her predicament. 'Well, having got that off my chest, let me show you to your room. Rocco is across the landing.' Her pause implied that, as consenting adults, the same rules didn't apply to them. 'This is you, Miss MacDonald.' She pushed open a bedroom door overlooking the back of the house.

'Harper, please. When I'm addressed as Miss MacDonald I feel like I'm on duty. I'm a teacher, you see.'

Janet sent her an understanding look. 'Ariel told me that her aunt was a headteacher, and of *three* schools, too.' Harper guessed that she'd be quizzed about that over tea. 'Now,' Janet adopted a brisk attitude, 'isn't this a grand wee room? My other daughter, Margaret, redecorated it last winter. Rocco told her what he had in mind but gave her a free hand when it came to paper, paint and so on.'

'Yes, it's lovely.' Harper studied the bedroom with its soft grey and cornflower blue colour scheme. Janet guided her over to a slim, five-drawer tallboy and invited her to admire the chalk paint finish. 'Margaret hand paints furniture and receives commissions far and wide, upcycling old furniture for Airbnb owners, and such like. The laird, Sir Michael McKinnon, has commissioned her to repaint the brown furniture in his holiday cottages on the far side of the loch. He likes to support the local economy so it's quite an honour.'

Harper walked over to the window and peered out. The land at the back of the house rose steeply and, apart from a small wrought iron table, two chairs and a polythene mini green house, there was room for little else. Doubtless the reason behind the garden across the road.

'I know you and Rocco must be anxious about Pen and Ariel,' Janet changed the subject, 'but dinnae worry. They've gone up north to photograph puffins on Handa Island, and corncrakes and bumblebees at Durness.'

At last, information, freely given and without drama. Harper allowed herself to relax properly for the first time in three days. In fact, she was so relieved that it took several seconds before the unlikely pairing of Ariel with puffins, corncrakes and bumble bees struck home. That would take some fathoming, but she'd save it for later.

She laid a hand on Janet's arm. 'Thank you for understanding,'

'Nae bother. Remember Bo Peep?' She tapped the side of her nose.

'Bo Peep?'

'See for yourself.' Pushing the door of Ariel's room open, Janet revealed a dressing table covered in makeup, bed unmade, clothes on the floor and mobile phone plugged into the mains.

Woah . . . mobile plugged into the mains?

Harper did a double take as, tutting, Janet walked over and unplugged the mobile before turning to face her. 'Your expression says it all. Ariel – without her phone? Has the world come to an end?'

'Not to mention her favourite shoes, bag, Wi-Fi headphones.'

'Aye, she takes a long while to get ready in the mornings.' Janet laughed. 'And is always taking those – what d'ye call them – selfies?'

'Yes.'

Harper regarded the room and her earlier euphoria evaporated, replaced by a slow burning rage. While *she* had been reduced to stuffing t-shirts, jeans, clean underwear, toothbrush and a pack of wet wipes in the Triumph's panniers, Miss Ariel MacDonald had found enough time to pack a full complement of luggage, makeup and buy a second mobile phone, leaving hers at home so her aunt couldn't get in touch with her.

Typical. Boy, little did her sister know what was heading her way this summer. That thought made her feel better, it was time Shona stepped up to the plate and assumed responsibility for a daughter whom she hadn't seen in over a year.

'I cannae see your niece surviving on packed lunches while sitting in a bird hide waiting for a puffin to fly past. As for the phone,' Janet explained, 'she had to leave that behind. Hugh Morrison bans them on his wildlife expeditions.'

Ah, that explains Pen's rushed phone call to his father yesterday morning before they'd set off. Plainly, Hugh Morrison was a force to be reckoned with if he could compel a couple of teenagers to abandon their phones. Harper needed to know more.

'Hugh Morrison?'

'The wildlife photographer they've gone north with. He had that program on BBC Scotland last winter – *Scottish Nature Diary*. Did ye no see it? The papers called it Scotland's Autumn Watch, although it was much better in my opinion.' Not that she was biased, of course.

'What's he like, this Hugh Morrison?'

'Popular, good looking, sure of himself. Too sure of himself, to be honest. Good at what he does. He and Rocco have known each other since childhood. In fact Auld Baxter, mah husband, had to pull them apart many a time when they were youngsters. They were always scrapping and falling out over something or other. I only hope Ariel –' Janet stopped herself, as though remembering that Harper had enough on her plate to worry about.

'So, this – this Hugh Morrison invited them along to photograph wildlife?'

It seemed unlikely.

'Ach, well, not quite. Pen's been pestering Hugh to take him on his next trip. Pen's grandparents bought him a very expensive camera last Christmas and he's been dying to try it out, or so our Fiona informs me. I think Hugh finally gave in just tae get Pen off his back.'

Photographing wildlife? It seemed unlikely. *Nightlife* was more Ariel's bag. In a flash Harper did the maths. *Pestering him for some time?* It was beginning to look as if the whole 'I'll be in Scotland' vibe was Pen's idea and he'd taken Ariel – a willing partner, for sure – along for the ride.

'I'm not sure where Ariel fits in,' Harper mused, almost to herself.

'Och, Pen's never been good at being on his own. Comes, no doubt from being abandoned by his mother when he was a bairn. You'll know all about *that*, I'm thinking. Terrible business. Poor Rocco.'

'Of course.' What else could she say? *Actually, no, I don't. Would you mind enlightening me?* Perhaps, like Morwenna, Janet Baxter could be persuaded to reveal more of Rocco's backstory once they got to know each other? Fill in a few more of the missing details.

Better still, maybe Rocco would open up to her now they were beginning to relax in each other's company. After all, he knew her family history, didn't he? It was only fair that she learned his. She sighed inwardly. Dream on, Penhaligon was the Rosetta Stone in human form – tough as granite and hard to decipher. If Pen and Ariel returned before she got to the bottom of the mystery of Pen's birth mother, she'd never find out the truth.

For the first time since leaving Polzenith, Harper found herself in no hurry to see her niece. She cast one last look round the messy bedroom before Janet closed the door.

'So, you see, Bo Peep,' Janet repeated.

'Leave them alone and they'll come home ?'

'Wagging their tails behind them.'

'I hope you're right.'

'Tea's ready,' Rocco shouted up from the kitchen. 'Would you ladies like to partake of it on the patio?'

Smiling, Janet said: 'See what I mean? Cheeky devil.' Then she leaned over the bannister. 'That won't be necessary, we're coming down. After you, Harper, and mind the turn in the stairs , we dinnae want you tripping all the way to the bottom and landing in a heap at Rocco's feet.'

'Indeed we do not,' Harper agreed, concentrating as she navigated the narrow stairs. *That* would be too embarrassing for words.

Chapter Sixteen

That evening, Rocco and Harper were in the kitchen eating supper. Janet had left a cast iron casserole on top of the Range cooker with strict instructions to Rocco not to burn it. He'd given her a mock-ticking-off for filling the fridge with groceries, making the beds and putting out towels etc. in bathroom and bedrooms. Heron Croft was his home, not a hotel and he didn't expect Janet to work herself into the ground because that's what she'd always done for the Penhaligons. However, he'd known that in ringing ahead from Ecclefechan to find out exactly what was going on at Heron Croft, that's exactly what she would do.

He was furious with Pen and Ariel for going off with Hugh Morrison without so much as a backward glance, leaving their rooms in disarray for Janet to sort out. That was two strikes, if you counted the mess they'd left behind in Leicester, they only had one more left and then the roof would come crashing down on both their heads.

He couldn't speak for Harper, but that's not how Pen had been brought up.

'What *is* this?' Harper asked, eating another delicious forkful.

'It's called *stovies*. It's really an autumn or winter dish but Janet knows how much I love it and makes it as a 'welcome home' supper, come rain or shine.'

'Is the recipe a closely guarded secret?' He watched as she poked around in the earthenware dish he'd served the stovies in, accompanied by a generous dollop of brown sauce.

'Every cook has their own recipe but basically it's tatties, onions, steak mince or left over roast beef, lard or beef dripping, water and a stock cube.'

'Low in calories, then?'

'It's a known fact that calories don't exist in Heron Croft. Slainte.' He touched the rim of her wine glass with his whisky tumbler. 'When we were weans – that's youngsters to the uninitiated – we used to wash stovies down with great glasses of full fat milk. Or, if no one was paying attention, Irn Bru.'

'Is that how you grew so tall?'

'That and good genes.'

Harper put her knife and fork together with a satisfied sigh. 'I feel as though we've *eaten* our way north. Cornish Pasties, motorway sandwiches, doughnuts, the delicious Lancashire hotpot at Morwenna's – a bit like stovies, in fact, doorstep sandwiches and whisky-laced tea in the barn.' Raising her head, she looked at him through her eyelashes, warm colour touching her cheeks.

Was she referring to last night's sleeping arrangements or remembering what'd happened while she was half-asleep? He couldn't stop thinking about how she'd spent part of the night wrapped in his arms.

With a superhuman effort he pulled his thoughts back on track. 'Scotch Pies at the last services. Carbs all the way. Thank God you're a proper trencher woman, not one of those females who nibbles round the edges of a lettuce leaf like a demented rabbit.'

'Trencher woman? Have you just invented the term?' She sent him a suspicious look and then laughed. 'Usually I barely have time to grab a cup of coffee, let alone eat. For that reason, I make the effort to cook every evening and really push the boat out at weekends. Maybe I'll cook a meal for the four of us when we return to Polzenith.' She looked away as though she'd said too much, overstepped the mark by presuming the connection between them would survive beyond the end of their road trip.

'I can never fill Pen up. At eighteen, he's almost as tall as I am and seemingly has hollow legs. I keep pizzas in the freezer for him to snack on if I'm working late on a car or an engineering project. Like you, I cook every night. We don't do badly for a couple of blokes.' She laughed at *couple of blokes* and the awkward moment passed. They were starting to relax in each other's company and while it was obvious that neither of them wanted to force the pace, he didn't want her to retreat behind a wall of politeness.

'I need to learn how to make stovies. And what was that fudge stuff Janet gave us with our second cup of coffee this afternoon?'

'Not fudge, *tablet*. And if I tell you I'd have to kill you,' he laughed. 'Making tablet is a real labour of love. Ask Janet.'

'I will.' She pushed her plate and gave a satisfied sigh. 'There, all gone. Do I get a lollipop?' He liked the way humour made her eyes sparkle and her mouth turn up at the corners.

'I'm fresh out of lollipops, settle for another glass of wine? Let's go through to the sitting room.'

'Shouldn't we wash up first?'

'I'll stack the dishwasher before we turn in for the night. You can take your turn tomorrow. Deal?' He extended his hand and she shook it. It felt natural for his fingers to curl around her wrist and to hold on to her hand a little longer than good manners dictated.

'Deal.'

Slipping her hand out of his grasp she put both hands under the table, leaving him to wonder if he'd overstepped the mark. Then she smiled, picked up her glass and headed for the sitting room. Alone in the kitchen he smacked himself on the forehead, muttering – *Penhaligon, you bloody fool. What were you thinking?*

Leaving the kitchen he found Harper hovering uncertainly on the sitting room threshold, seemingly unsure where to sit. He suggested that she took the larger of the two sofas, encouraging her to put her feet up and to cover her knees with the mohair rug draped over the arm.

Metaphorically, he kicked himself a second time. She was a sexy, desirable woman and here he was treating her like a maiden aunt. Mind you, in many ways that was safer! He couldn't explain why he felt protective towards her. They'd spent the last thirty-six hours fighting like cat and dog but now they'd reached his home it was as if a kind of magic had settled on them, causing them to be their real selves.

How had that happened?

'Television?' he asked, focusing on the dull and ordinary, the nearest thing to a cold shower. His voice was gruff and he cleared his throat, aware that those clever blue eyes never missed a trick. 'There's bound to be a late movie, although there's a shelf full of DVD's, should the mood take you. Did you know that they filmed some of the scenes from the iconic Wicker Man here and the television series Hamish Macbeth? It's a ritual of mine to watch Local Hero when I return home. I practically know it off by heart.'

He was gabbling and knew it, so presumably did Harper because she took steps to make him feel at ease. 'Let's just sit here, shall we? It's a beautiful evening and I'm happy to spend it sipping wine and looking out of the window towards the loch. It's been quite a journey.' He wasn't sure if she was referring to the miles they'd covered or everything that had happened over the last couple of days.

'Understatement of the year?'

'Possibly. I don't know about you, but I'm feeling much happier now I know we'll be seeing Pen and Ariel soon.'

'You're right. Mind you, Janet's stovies are known for their medicinal powers.' He flopped down on a sofa placed at right angles to hers, kicked off his shoes and put his feet up. Much to his embarrassment, his socks had holes in them and his big toe poked through.

Harper pointed at his feet and laughed. 'You need a good woman to take you in hand and darn your socks.' Then she raised her hand to her mouth as though wanting to recall the words. 'Not,' she breathed, looking away from him, 'that I'm applying for the job.'

'Nor is there a vacancy.' That made it sound as if there was a queue of women lining up for the chance to play wife-and-mother in his loft in Polzenith. Now it was his turn to look away, shutting out the memory of the woman he'd thought suited to both tasks but who, in the end, had wanted neither. 'I find it's easier to buy a new pair of socks than to darn old ones.'

There. That put the record straight. 'How extravagant,' she drawled.

He felt the temperature drop and he acted quickly to return to their previous conversation. 'However, should the sight offend you . . .' He pulled a tartan comforter off the arm of his sofa and covered his feet, making them both laugh.

Their laughter was followed by a more contemplative moment as they looked towards the loch where the westering sun was still high in the sky, despite it being almost quarter to eleven. Rocco loved high summer in the highlands. The long days and short nights stirred something within his soul, made him contented and restless at the same time, imbuing him with a nameless longing, sharp as a pain.

'Have you ever seen the northern lights?' Harper asked.

'Many times. Sometimes the whole tamale. Other times the aurora has taken me by surprise, appearing as ghostly sheets of light feeling their way across the sky. You're more likely to see the Perseids Meteor Shower in early August, except . . .'

'Except, I'll have returned home by then?' she finished his sentence.

'I guess so.' There being nothing more to add and feeling inexplicably desolate, he moved the conversation along. 'There's also the Plockton Regatta, round about the same time. The regatta runs for about ten days and I often crew for the laird, or race against Hugh Morrison.'

'Like a miniature Cowes? We've spent many happy summers in the Isle of Wight watching the racing, filling glass tubes in the shape of animals with sand at Alum Bay. The highlight of our trip was standing on the deck of the ferry as it sailed past Britannia anchored in the Solent and waving to the crew. It was a sad day when she was decommissioned.'

'Do you sail?'

''Fraid not. I'm too fond of terra firma. Bet you're a real Action Man, aren't you?' She raised her glass to him in ironic salute and he bowed, accepting the accolade.

'I am.'

'Tell me more about the regatta.'

'Okay – on the final day there's an afternoon of music, singing, dancing and the chance of a wee dram or two in Harbour Street. We hold open house and neighbours drop by throughout the day. Janet and her daughters make mountains of sandwiches and cake so everyone has a good time. Highland hospitality is something we take very seriously. My task is to make sure the booze doesn't run out. In the evening, there's traditional music at Plockton Inn and we all stagger down there to join in the singing.'

'You describe it all with such fondness, how can you bear to leave? I mean, I know your business is in Polzenith but, forgive me, it's not like you need the money. Why not up sticks and live here permanently?'

Put like that, it did seem perverse that he chose to live above the shop when he could live in this beautiful place. But she didn't know the memories which anchored him to Polzenith. He'd love to tell her everything that happened that summer over twenty years and the subsequent fall out, but they'd be going their separate ways soon and it didn't seem right to open up his heart to someone he didn't really know, or to burden her with the whole, sorry tale.

In one respect, however, she was right. It was time he moved on.

'Could *you* live here?' he countered.

'I could. Rediscover my Scottish roots. Tap into the Celtic consciousness which being in this amazing place has awoken in me.'

They both went silent, giving everything they'd said some thought, then Rocco moved the conversation along.

'So, how *does* a MacDonald end up in Polzenith by way of Leicester?'

'My great-grandparents moved to Leicester from Glasgow in the mid-sixties, settling in Corby. Great-grandfather worked at the Stuart-Lloyd Steel Mill and great-granny worked in a café serving Scottish soul food: mutton pies, square sausages, bridies, pan loaves, and homemade clootie dumpling to ex-pats. They retired and moved to Leicester where their children found work in the boot and shoe, hosiery and building industries. Skip forward a generation to my father, the first to go to university. Like all good immigrants, my family value education and that's where I and Shona, come in. So, you see, my Scottishness begins and ends with my surname, although –'

'Go on.'

'There is something about this place which makes me feel at home. But I guess that might be the same if my surname was Smith.'

'It is magical here,' he agreed.

'Now you. I've told you everything there is to know about me but you hold your cards close to your chest.' There, she'd said it.

'Not tonight. Maybe tomorrow?'

She pouted and he sensed that she was losing patience. 'You'd better make good on that promise, Penhaligon.'

'Trust me. I will. To return to your original question: why don't I move up here? Who knows, maybe once Pen's settled at university, I'll sell off the garage and make the move.' Shuffling up the sofa he turned round, took down a decanter of whisky from the bookcase and poured himself another drink. He offered Harper a glass but she shook her head.

'You'll hate me for saying this, but I think whisky tastes like cough medicine. I can only drink it spritzed with lemonade.'

He mimed an arrow striking him in the heart. 'I dinnae hate ye, lassie,' he said in a full-on Scottish brogue, neatly steering the conversation away from himself and Polzenith. 'But ah'd keep that information tae yerself. Ah'll no be wastin' guid uisge beatha on a Sassenach who is Scottish in name only. The only liquid we add to our dram is the peaty water off the hills and then nae mare than a drap.'

'You really are full of it, aren't you?' Then she laughed, her good humour restored. He fetched a large book down off the shelves and placed it on her lap.

'What's this?'

'Hugh Morrison's bestselling book – *Birds and Beasts of the Western Highlands*. I thought you might like to see who your niece is spending time with.'

Harper balanced the tome on her knees, flicking through pages of leaping salmon, majestic stags – some at bay, baby otters floating on their backs, sea eagles, red kites, ptarmigan in their winter colours and hares crouched low in the heather. There was a special section devoted to endangered creatures such as the wildcat, pine marten and bottlenose dolphin. Then she turned to the fly leaf where Hugh, looking suitably heroic in a Morrison tartan kilt and with a pair of binoculars strung round his neck, stood with one foot on a rock, gazing moodily towards a Scottish loch ringed by snow-capped mountains.

'Blimey.' Harper looked impressed but as she closed the book and put it onto the coffee table her brows drew together. 'He's rather . . .'

'Quite.' Rocco rolled his whisky glass round in his hand. 'They call him *Handsome Hugh*, or *Hugh More-some*.' Now it was his turn to pull a face. The man was a complete tosser and a more dangerous than a sea eagle with a baby lamb in its sights. But he wouldn't tell Harper that, he just hoped that Ariel was streetwise enough not to fall for his corny chat-up line and that Pen's presence would act as a deterrent to his amorous advances. 'He's often to be seen striding through the village in his kilt, wolfhound at his heels, checking his reflection in house windows.'

'Kilt? Wolfhound? Really.'

'Doesn't know the meaning of the word *cliché*. Or irony, either, come to that. Anyway, you'll meet him when they return. It's the pub quiz on Sunday and he usually turns out for that. It's where his fan club convenes.' Now he wished he hadn't shown her the coffee table book as she was looking more worried with every passing minute.

'Can't wait,' she yawned.

'Come on, time for bed. It's been a long couple of days. I'll show you how the shower works, the hot water supply can be a bit temperamental.'

'A hot shower would be great, although . . .'

'Yes?'

'I've just about run out of clean clothes. Maybe I could use the washing machine tomorrow?'

'Sure.' Now he felt guilty. There had been no need to restrict her to two panniers when they'd set out from Polzenith. He'd done it to make a point. He was Rocco Penhaligon and no schoolmarm was going to tell him what to do. Now that seemed pathetic and he wanted to make amends. 'Couldn't you borrow something of Ariel's?'

Tired as she was, Harper laughed. 'I'd rather walk the length of Harbour Street naked than touch madam's belongings.' Then she blushed as she realised what she'd said, appearing much younger, and dangerously more attractive.

Rocco smiled down at her. 'I'm sure it won't come to that. After you.' He indicated that she should climb the stairs before him. Partly because it was good manners but also because it gave him an unrestricted view of her pert bottom in skinny jeans. When she reached the landing and turned around he made sure he was looking elsewhere. It wouldn't do to let her know the thoughts running through his head.

Entering the bathroom he demonstrated the idiosyncrasies of the plumbing system and offered her first shower. Harper accepted and, as he closed the bathroom door behind him, Rocco reflected that if the hot water *did* run out – a cold shower was probably just what the doctor ordered.

Chapter Seventeen

Next morning, when Harper came downstairs Rocco was standing by the washing machine sorting through powder and fabric conditioner with a practised air. It was a disturbingly domestic scene and, after sharing the delicious dinner of *stovies* last night and waking to a beautiful morning, Harper felt – hoped – their relationship had turned a corner.

'Washing?' he inquired, gesturing towards the open porthole with a flourish. 'You mentioned you were running short of clothes? Janet regards looking after Heron Croft as keeping faith with my grandparents who she – and her mother before her, worked for. She'll assume the role of concierge unless I stop her. Before we know it, items of clothing will disappear and then re-appear at the foot of the bed washed and ironed, as if by magic. By laundering our own clothes we can pre-empt that and save Janet time and worry. If you don't object to your, ahem, *smalls*, jockeying for position in the machine with my unmentionables.'

'I think they'll survive the ordeal.'

'Sorry,' he grinned, 'that was a long sentence. It should have started with *Good Morning*.'

Encouraged, Harper ventured, 'Someone's in a good mood.'

'How can I fail to be? Heron Croft is my second home and beats living above the garage.' It was the first time he'd admitted that living in that draughty loft was far from ideal and Harper hoped that he'd come good on his promise to tell her everything.

'I must admit, I did wake up this morning feeling less stressed.' No need to mention that sleeping alone rather than next to him, troubled by strange dreams and unfamiliar longings, made for better sleep. She moved the conversation on to less dangerous ground. 'According to Janet, the reprobates will be home in a couple of days. Although, it's probably a good idea to keep our presence in Plockton secret. We don't want them to do another runner.'

'Correct. As I said at Gretna, Pen thinks I'm still in Polzenith. We'll steal the march on them, this time.' Rocco loaded a sturdy wooden tray with breakfast things as Harper looked on, puzzled. Weren't they going to eat breakfast at the dining table?

'*Bo Peep* sums the situation up nicely,' she said.

Rocco nodded, Janet having shared her theory with him yesterday over tea and cake. 'We'll make Operation Bo Peep the code name for this endeavour. Hugh, for all his failings, will keep an eye on them, no worries.' He didn't quite say: *or he'll have me to answer to,* but it hung in the air. He picked the tray up off the table, 'The door?' he prompted.

'What? Of course.'

Rocco carried the tray across Harbour Street while Harper followed close behind. Pushing open the gate of Heron Croft's gardens, he made for the far end where a teak table and six chairs on raised decking overlooked the stunning view. The table was covered by a plastic cloth featuring mermaids, shells and leaping dolphins and anchored in place by table weights shaped as a different sea creature: crab, seahorse, lobster and shark skeleton. The chairs were covered in thick cotton ticking, the whole effect designed to make family and guests feel immediately at home and get in the holiday mood.

The garden had a small lawn, herbaceous border, clumps of large headed agapanthus and, to Harper's amazement, several palm trees. The tide was out but small rowing boats lay on their sides on the shore and half a dozen small yachts were anchored out in the loch with their sails furled. A white picket fence separated the garden from the foreshore and, in the middle, a small gate, topped by an ornamental ship's wheel, added to the nautical vibe.

It was all so different to Polzenith with its unemployment, deprivation and families who relied on food banks to feed their children during the school holidays. Plockton looked like an idyll and pleased Harper in her present mood to take it at face value. No doubt later she would find out that half the houses on Harbour Street were Airbnb, the local school couldn't recruit staff and in the winter the road to Kyle was impassable.

'Sit, please,' Rocco gestured for Harper to choose her spot.

No hot food, obviously. Instead, Danish pastries and almond croissants wrapped in linen napkins, pats of butter, dishes of jam and a cafetiere of coffee swaddled in an insulated cover. Rocco put crockery and silverware in front of Harper, glancing up from the task and smiling. Plainly, years of taking care of Pen had made him practical and self-reliant.

Just like her, Harper thought.

'I know the view is distracting, but eat – please.'

Harper didn't need second bidding and was soon munching her way through a flaky croissant. How strange that all the travelling, arguing and rough living had led to this perfect moment: breakfast in a garden overlooking Loch Carron. The sun was on her face and the soft wind off the loch carried a unique scent towards them redolent of growing things, water creatures and a faint tang of the sea.

'I didn't expect palm trees,' she said at last, dusting crumbs off her clothes.

'Tut, tut, Miss MacDonald, these are no palm trees,' Rocco remarked in faux shocked tones. 'These are cabbage palms, Cordyline Australis. The temperature in Plockton is similar to New Zealand and that, combined with the jet stream which touches these shores, is the reason they and other tender plants, flourish here.'

'I think I would flourish here,' Harper remarked dreamily, looking beyond the garden to the small inlet which branched out into the wider stretches of Loch Carron. When she glanced up, Rocco was regarding her curiously, making her wonder if she'd revealed too much of herself and had embarrassed him.

'Aye, on a day like this, m'be, but once the autumn mists descend and the winter winds whistle along the shore you'll be begging to go home to the warm south.'

'That I won't. I'm made of sterner stuff. And, for the record, your Scottish accent is appalling.'

'I'll drop it then. It's hard work trying to sound like Auld Baxter.'

'Auld Baxter?'

'Janet's grump of a husband. He owns the garage at the far end of the village near the High School, I'll be going along to see him today. When I was a teenager I used to pester him during the summer holidays to let me help in his garage. I spent hours watching him work, restoring vehicles, being rude to his customers and charging over the odds for his services. Quite an education on how *not* to conduct a business.'

'Why has it survived, then?'

'He's the nearest garage for miles and he's good at his job.'

'Can't imagine Janet being married to someone like that.'

'He's as meek as a lamb at home, but in his garage he's a proper curmudgeon.'

'Reminds me of someone else –'

'Now you're just being 'cheeky', as Janet would say. And after I've made you breakfast, too.'

'Appalling, isn't it?' Stretching her arms above her head, Harper gave a satisfied sigh and closed her eyes. 'Was watching Auld Baxter what made you drop out of university and set up your own garage?'

There. She'd broached the forbidden topic.

'Morwenna tell you that?'

'Not in so many words.' She glanced over at him but he wasn't looking displeased, merely thoughtful. So she relaxed and decided to press on. 'Rocco,' it still felt strange to use his first name, 'you know everything there is to know about me. But I know hardly anything about you, Pen. Or,' she took a deep breath, 'his mother.'

He deflected her interest away in that clever way he had. 'I don't know everything there is to know about you.'

'For example?'

'Why you've chosen to follow the path your parents decided for you. Why you didn't rebel? No, don't argue. You've dedicated your life to your niece, your career, and living up to other people's expectations. I can't believe you haven't had offers, yet you've remained single.' He paused on the word and then smiled. 'Not saving yourself for Anthony, the ninja-next-door, are you?' His description brought back the image of Anthony in his short dressing gown wielding a cricket bat.

Harper snorted. 'No I'm not. I've had offers, as you phrase it. However,' she shrugged and turned her attention back to the loch.

'You haven't met the man for whom you'd give up everything you've worked so hard to achieve? Can't say I blame you.' He refreshed her coffee cup and she picked it up, curling her hands round it.

Sitting in this beautiful place, her eyes drawn towards the muted colours of the soft hills on the far shore, the stretch of loch reflecting back the peerless blue sky and with water birds calling to them, she should've felt pride in what she'd achieved. Instead, she was aware of what she'd let slip through her fingers – life, a family, the love of a good man. Rocco was right. She'd always been focused, driven, put everyone's wishes and needs before her own. Once, she'd seen that as a strength but today, in this beautiful place, it felt like an excuse, her way of keeping life at arm's length.

'Isn't it the same for both of us?' she said, almost to herself. 'What will you do when Pen goes off to university?'

'If he does.'

'Oh, this is just a blip, trust me. If we handle it right, we can get them both back on track.' Funny how 'I' and 'you' had morphed into 'we', making them sound like a team, united by a common goal.

'I'll bow to your superior knowledge in these matters. You've had countless pupils pass through your hands. I've only ever had Pen to get wrong.'

'Teaching children isn't the same as loving them as if they were your own. Trust me.'

'Oddly enough, I do.'

His eyes swept her face and she flushed, marvelling how the harsh planes of his face had relaxed since yesterday, making him appear younger, and more attractive. Sensing that his defences were down she pressed home her advantage.

'So, back to you. Let's start with the little things . . . like, where your earring is this morning and why you've stopped wearing your friendship bracelets. Although,' she sent him a mock-stern look, 'I did think at the time there was a Health and Safety issue around you moving under cars and using power tools while wearing them.'

'Yes, I read you loud and clear when I rolled out from under the car and found you standing there, arms folded, foot tapping. The wristlets – my preferred word, are on the dressing table upstairs, and as for the earring – I removed it before we left the dairy farm yesterday. For two reasons.'

'Go on . . .'

'One. I was beginning to look like the-dad-who-tries-too-hard to keep up with his son; to be his mate. By removing the wristlets and the earring I believe I've gained gravitas.'

'Gravitas?' Harper laughed.

'Yes. Pen is due a lecture for all the worry he's caused me, and by association, you. I've learned from Janet that he's been begging Hugh to take him on an expedition with that bloody ridiculous camera my parents bought him last Christmas. It's plain that he's had this escapade planned for months.'

'And you know that, how?'

'Hugh's Wildlife trips, along with his television series, are his main source of income. He wouldn't turn down paying customers simply to get Pen off his back. I'm also guessing he wouldn't be best pleased to have Ariel in tow.'

'I think we can safely assume that Ariel had no idea what she was getting into. She doesn't do 'mud' and she certainly doesn't do 'wet and cold'. I believe, now, that she saw this expedition as the perfect excuse to miss the plane to L.A, stay away from Shona, step-dad #3 and avoid working in the local café at the end of the summer, as I'd arranged. If she'd been honest with me from the outset, there's no way I'd've put her on that plane. Although it *is* time for Shona to shoulder her responsibilities.' She paused, adopting a rueful expression. 'Maybe I've been too hard on Ariel, not been prepared to admit that she's old enough to make her own decisions. Even if they're the wrong ones.'

'Me, too, I guess.' His mouth quirked, mirroring her rueful expression.

'And – two, the earring?' He wasn't getting off the hook that easily.

'I wasn't going to give you a second chance to call me a Wild Corsair.'

Harper laughed. 'At least you've stopped calling me Miss-Executive-Head-of-Three Schools. So we're quits.'

'Quits.' He held up his hand and high-fived her and when their palms touched, his hand was warm. Harper was overwhelmed by the need to lace their fingers together but resisted. After all, this is what she was good at. Keeping folk at arm's length, denying that she yearned for physical contact, had forgotten how it felt to make love, to spend the night with someone and to wake up the next morning, drowsy with sleep and want to do it all over again.

Too buttoned up. Too repressed. And, possibly, too late.

'You suddenly look very thoughtful, not to say glum. Come on, leave the breakfast things and let's take a walk around the village, I'll show you all the places where I used to hang out when I was a teenager.'

'The Scottish version of Swallows and Amazons?' This time, there was no scorn in her voice, just amusement.

'Just about. Then, while you do the laundry, wash up the breakfast things and prepare lunch I'll go over to see Auld Baxter.'

'I think I might have to put in for a pay rise. Tackling three household tasks before noon isn't in my job description.' Standing, she left the table and headed towards the gate which opened onto the foreshore.

'Time we renegotiated it, then.' Rocco's eyes were bright with mischief. 'You're beginning to show promise, I might consider keeping you on.' It was a flippant, off-the-cuff remark, but catching them by surprise it took on its own meaning. A meaning Rocco had probably never intended when he'd spoken the words. Harper responded with a throwaway remark of her own to demonstrate that she wasn't taking any of this seriously.

'You can't afford me, Captain Penhaligon.'

'I believe that Wild Corsairs are known for saving their doubloons for occasions such as this.'

'Wild Corsair, indeed. Whoever thought up that ridiculous name?'

By way of a reply, Rocco hurdled the gate, landed on the damp sand of the shore and grasped the ship's wheel on top of the gate. Next, he struck a heroic pose as though they were on the Spanish Main, not the foreshore of Loch Carron and invited her to comment.

'Ridiculous,' Harper repeated, laughing as she pushed against the gate, forcing him to let her pass. Once on the foreshore she concentrated on avoiding pools of water and mud left behind by the receding tide and the moment passed. However, both knew they had to take care. Not with the shifting sands but with forcing the pace of this relationship, instead of allowing it to find its own rhythm and tempo, wherever it took them.

Chapter Eighteen

Rocco left Harper in the gallery at the end of Harbour Street looking at stained glass roundels and made for George Baxter's garage. Donning sunglasses against the diamonds of light dancing on the surface of the loch, he counted the steps from gallery to garage. This ritual harked back to summers spent in Plockton with his grandparents, designed to relieve his mother of the tedium and inconvenience of having a small boy home from boarding school demanding – *craving* – love and attention. A child who got in the way of golf, bridge parties and the charitable work which had resulted in her receiving an MBE.

Rocco's lips twisted in a parody of a smile as he considered the irony of his situation. After neglecting him for years and delegating his upbringing to others, his parents seemed hell-bent on spoiling Pen, showering him with extravagant gifts Rocco neither approved of nor wanted. Was this latent guilt kicking in? A desire to compensate for their crass suggestion that Rocco put him up for adoption? Or was it a dawning realisation that their behaviour forced Rocco to live almost two hundred miles away in Polzenith when they desperately wanted Pen to be part of their lives?

Rocco returned to counting the steps . . .

Back in the day it'd taken five hundred steps to walk from the fish and chip shop to Baxter's Garage, considerably more if he started out from Heron Croft. However, as he'd grown and his stride had lengthened, the number of steps had decreased. This morning that wasn't the only thing that had changed. There was an extra spring in his step which couldn't be denied. Another wry smile, this time acknowledging that his raised pulse owed nothing to the gentle incline up to Baxter's Garage but everything to the woman browsing in the gallery three hundred steps further back.

Five days ago he'd been unaware of Harper MacDonald's existence but had now spent more time in her company than any other woman. That was disconcerting. He'd vowed, after Pen's mum, that he'd never get seriously involved with any woman. Wouldn't let one get close enough to rip open his chest, pull out his heart and stamp on the pieces.

It was simple. He couldn't get Harper MacDonald out of his head. She was the last thing he'd thought about before falling asleep and the first thing when he woke up. The image of her in *that* nightdress, forever seared into the synapses of his brain, was partly responsible for this sea change. That, and the stolen kiss in the tent which left him yearning for more, much more. Hormones, pheromones and potent chemicals were coursing through his blood, leaving him lightheaded and overwhelmed by the need to possess what was unattainable.

Harper MacDonald.

Would he tell her? Hell, no. She'd made it obvious from the moment he'd rolled out from under the car in Polzenith, clocked her slim calves and ankles and noticed how her blouse tightened across her breasts, that he wasn't her type. And, he forced himself to remember, once the teenagers returned they would go their separate ways.

He jogged the last few yards to Baxter's Garage, hoping that physical exertion would put everything into perspective.

Get Harper MacDonald out of his head.

* * *

When he reached Baxter's Garage his ears were assaulted by an impressive string of swear words directed towards the hapless apprentice who'd forgotten to shovel three spoonsful of sugar in Auld Baxter's tea.

'I take it you're not working on the Minister's car, George?' Rocco quipped from the garage threshold.

Baxter stopped his lambasting and greeted Rocco with a broad smile. 'Will ye look who's here? Young Rocco. Come away in, come away in. Janet said y'were home, and had brought a lassie with you, too. About time you were married and living a miserable life like the rest of us sinners.

'I'll be sure to tell Janet that next time I see her.,'

'Och, ye wouldnae do that, would ye?' Realising that Rocco was joking he turned his attention back to his apprentice. 'Don't stand there like a lummox! Away and make Rocco a tea.'

'There's no need.'

'There's every need.' Baxter ushered Rocco into the garage where the familiar smell of engine oil, tyre rubber, petrol and grease assailed him. He realised, with a flash of insight, that it was probably the hours he'd spent in this garage pestering Baxter to death, begging to be allowed to help which had made him want to set up Penhaligon's Garage and Engineering Works. That, family history and his natural bent for fixing things.

Shame he hadn't been so adept at fixing his own life.

'So, how's tricks, George?' Rocco asked, accepting builders' tea in a chipped mug and being invited to add his own sugar from a ripped bag plonked on the work bench.

'Ach well, to tell ye the truth, I could take on double the work but I'm getting too old for all this malarkey. I can get under the cars, nae bother, but it's a real bugger getting back onto mah feet again. Last week, Fergus had to run and fetch his dad to help me up. I was so scunnered I could hardly speak.'

Rocco didn't argue. Time was catching up with George Baxter, his skin was grey and the fire had died in his dark brown eyes. Wisps of hair sticking out from under his oily tartan *bunnet* were no longer grey, but pure white and when he sat on the edge of an oil drum he sank into his shoulders. 'I'm of a mind to jack it all in.'

Rocco, realising that he was serious, didn't speak for several seconds. 'What does Janet say?'

Auld Baxter seemed as if about to deny that he was henpecked by his formidable wife, then he let out a long breath and his whole frame appeared to shrink further. 'She said I'm a bluddy auld fool who should retire and spend his winters in the villa in Spain we bought years ago.'

'Plockton doesn't take prisoners,' Rocco agreed, thinking of the harsh winters he'd experienced when spending Christmas at Heron Croft with his grandparents.

'She says that our daughters,' he pronounced it *dochters*, 'and the grand weans can come and stay anytime they like. In fact,' he smiled for the first time, 'she says we'll soon be sick of rellies who'll treat our villa like it's a free bed and breakfast, with dinner thrown in. When I was growing up in Tranent, outside of Edinburgh, mah Mither gave away the bed settee because, during the Glasgow Fair, every bluddy cousin and second cousin would descend on us and expect to be put up for nothing. If ah do retire to Malaga I'll make it clear *that* won't be happening.'

'I can see you've thought it through.' Rocco knew that George Baxter would love having his family round him and was generous to a fault, but went along with the pretence.

'Aye, well, ah'm no the sort to go rushing into things like a headless chicken.' Rocco grinned, knowing that Janet would not allow chickens, headless or otherwise, to live under the same roof. Reaching across, George grabbed him by the arm. 'Ye'll come out and see us, won't ye, Rocco? You and your young lady? A headteacher, I'm informed.' His tone implied that Rocco had done well to catch such a prize. Rocco hid his smile, imagining sharing this conversation with Harper, later.

'She is. And I will.'

'And bring Pen?'

'You'll be so sick of us, you'll not only *give* away your bed settee, you'll take a chain saw to it.' Baxter laughed, releasing his grip on Rocco's arm.

'That'll never happen, son, and you know it.'

'You're right.' Rocco laughed and they clinked their mugs together. A companionable silence descended as they watched Fergus changing the points on a Range Rover.

'Pen called in with Hugh Morrison to see me before they headed north.'

'Did he now?' Rocco's dislike of the wild life photographer was well documented.

'Brought his young lady with the weird name wi' him, too. She was a cheeky wee besom, walked round the garage picking up things and putting them back in the wrong place. Called me *darling Baxter* and kissed me before they left. What do ye make of *that*?'

'I gather she's a handful. I just hope she doesn't prove too much for Pen.'

'But no Hugh – eh?' Their exchanged look acknowledged Hugh Morrison's high opinion of himself and reputation with the ladies. 'I think he might have his work cut out wi' that one,' George Baxter chuckled.

'How did Pen seem with her?'

'Anxious to be gone on their wildlife expedition. He spent a lot of time tutting and frowning when she set out to make mischief or said something daft, like . . .' Baxter blushed under the grizzled stubble on his sallow cheeks.

'Darling Baxter?'

'Aye. *That*. Me and Janet thought her and Pen looked like a couple of angels on a Christmas card.'

'Angels, huh?'

Rocco relived the moment when Pen's mother had climbed down from her converted military ambulance, stretched her length to give her audience a better view of her stunning breasts. Then she'd turned and flashed a very white smile at him and he'd fallen hook, line and sinker; hardly daring to believe his luck when she chose *him* to spend the summer with. And what a summer! Making love long into the night, smoking joints round the campfire, living the hippy dream.

Was there something about Ariel which reminded Pen of his mother? Is that what'd drawn them together? No, that wasn't possible; Pen had been less than three months old when he'd been brought to the garage in a Moses basket, complete with birth certificate naming Rocco as the father and with a dreamcatcher woven by his mother pinned to his shawl. His mother, it seemed, wanted to study Ashtanga Yoga in Mysore and a baby would cramp her style. The two old hippies who'd brought Pen to Polzenith assured Rocco that looking after Pen was a temporary measure and that his mother would return to fetch him before the year was out.

That had been eighteen years ago.

He'd had a tough time persuading everyone, particularly his parents, that he *was* Pen's father. With a head of thistledown-white hair and bright blue eyes Pen looked nothing like a Penhaligon, nothing like Rocco. However, DNA had put the record straight and, after some legal wrangling, Rocco had obtained full parental responsibility for Pen through the courts. No one was going to take his boy from him. Although he hadn't felt very noble or forgiving at the time, he'd left Pen's given name – *Varun Shrishti*, after the Hindu God of the sea, on the birth certificate. It would be up to Pen to change it when he was older, but he never had, insisting instead on calling himself Pen, as soon as he could talk. And it'd stuck.

Only Morwenna, Joe, Auld Baxter and Janet had stood by him during that dark period in his life.

Angels? A half-remembered illustration from his prep school history primer: St Gregory, upon seeing blond, Anglo-Saxon children for sale in the slave markets of Rome had said – Not Angles but Angels.

Twenty years ago he'd thought Pen's Mother, an earth-bound angel. Acting like a moonstruck calf, he hadn't asked any questions. Hadn't even known her real name until he'd seen it on the birth certificate: Camilla Hemsworth-Stanley. Another Notting Hillbilly pretending to be a free spirit.

'Yer tea's getting cold, Rocco, drink up.' Auld Baxter's voice came from a long way off.

'Angels? I don't think so. When I catch up with Pen, I'll hug him because he's safe and then deliver the biggest bollocking known to man for turning my – *our* – lives upside down.'

'Och now, whit did Janet tell youse?' Baxter was happy to defer to his formidable wife and clearly thought Rocco should do the same. 'Leave them alone and they'll come home . . .'

'. . . wagging their tails behind them.'

'She's a very clever woman. Dinnae tell her I said so.'

'I wouldn't dare.' Grinning, Rocco took the conversation in a different direction. 'You've heard about the Land Rover?'

'I've been waiting for you to bring it round. What's stopped you? Ah, the school teacher? Well, canna say I blame you. Janet says she's a fine looking woman. Not a girl exactly, but friendly and approachable.'

'That's her. Presents a polite face to the world even when she's raging inside and wants to throttle someone, usually me.' He reminded himself that they'd managed twenty- four hours without going for each other's jugular. Clearly, something had changed.

'Just like being married, then.' They both laughed but Rocco experienced a shiver of presentiment. Married? He had no time to ponder the word as Baxter broke into thoughts. 'Tell me more about the Land Rover.'

'It was a bit of a controversial choice bringing it up here. It leaked all the way and then broke down. But I've promised Morwenna I'll get it in good shape for her to sell. She needs the cash.'

'Bring it round to the garage and I'll have a look at it, if ye like.' Rocco adopted a grateful expression. His skills as a mechanic had outstripped George's years ago, but it pleased them to maintain the pretence that George was Obi Wan Kenobi to his Luke Skywalker.

Putting down his mug, Rocco sent George a straight look. 'You know, if you're really serious about selling the garage, I'd like first refusal.'

'What aboot your garage in Cornwall?'

'Pete, one of the older mechanics is looking for somewhere to start his own business and bring his grandchildren in at ground level. I'd sell it to him if he was interested, or rent it out until a buyer came along.'

'You'd live in Plockton, permanently?' George asked.

'Nothing to keep me in Polzenith these days.'

Fleetingly, Harper MacDonald's face flashed before him, but she'd made it quite plain that her career would take her away from Cornwall. 'Pen, as I'm sure you know, doesn't seem keen on going up to Oxford. At least, not at the moment. Also, I like to keep distance between him and my parents, stop them showering him with ridiculous gifts.'

'Aye. I've seen the Jeep.' Shaking his head, George tutted.

'If photographing wildlife's his bag, maybe Hugh can recommend some courses or places to study. Take him under his wing?' Rocco frowned, the thought of Pen hero-worshipping Hugh Morrison took some swallowing. 'If you're in agreement I'd take over your garage and make Heron Croft our permanent home. I'd like to keep you on a retainer, call upon you for help if I need an extra pair of hands.' Both knew that was unlikely, but the pretence preserved George's self-esteem. And, provided him with an excellent excuse to escape if Janet found jobs round the house for him. 'Fergus, too.'

'If you want it, it's yours. Go away, think about it and then come back the morrah and we'll talk some more, before we shake hands on it. It needs to be done, all legal like.'

'Of course. You're a canny Scot, I'd expect nothing less.'

'Aye, well – you're one, too, on your mother's side, dinnae forget *that*. Have you told Miss MacDonald of your Scottish blood?'

Rocco pulled a face. 'My mother commented upon it the night we arrived hot on Pen's trail. It didn't seem to make any difference to her low opinion of me. I don't think I'll labour the point.'

George laughed. 'Met your match?'

Rocco laughed. 'I shouldn't have asked her to ride pillion on the Triumph but she was so up herself the day we met that I thought she needed a reality check. Okay, I'll admit that was wrong.' He held up his hands. 'Bringing the kids home should've been my priority. However, travelling on the bike allowed us to cut through the holiday traffic and reach Bristol in record time.'

'Aye, Janet's told me everything.'

'I thought, if she saw how hard Morwenna worked, she might climb down off her high horse, forget she was headmistress of three schools, and . . .'

'And?'

'Stop being so bloody bossy.'

He shook his head. 'You know nothing about women, do you?'

'Apparently not. Well, she's mellowed, but I have the feeling it might be a temporary state of affairs.'

Auld Baxter laughed. 'Ah'm thinking that you're the one who's learned the lesson. No her.'

'What ever happened to male solidarity? You're supposed to be on my side, remember? Anyway, thanks for the tea. Let's keep the business about the garage between you, me and Janet until I've spoken to Pen.'

'Nae bother.'

'Catch you soon.'

With that, Rocco walked back into the sunshine, leaving George to berate the hapless Fergus for the sloppy job he'd done on an MOT.

Chapter Nineteen

Harper walked along Harbour Street taking time to admire the flotsam and jetsam arranged on some of the window sills. Rocco had explained on their walk through the village earlier that it was customary to display items washed up on the shore of Loch Carron – the weird and the wonderful. He couldn't do that at Heron Croft because the house didn't front the pavement and the windowsills were hidden behind the herbaceous border. Harper loved the quaintness of the custom which added to her sense of being in a different place, a different time.

Humming a highland air, she returned to Heron Croft, crossed the hall and entered the kitchen. The tune died in mid refrain when she caught sight of Rocco Penhaligon standing in front of an ironing board, wreathed in a cloud of steam, pressing an item of clothing under a damp tea towel. She wasn't sure what shocked her most – that he knew one end of an ironing board from another, or that he was wearing only boxer shorts and a t-shirt.

Checking round the kitchen, she saw that he'd cleared away the breakfast things, stacked the dishwasher and emptied the tumble dryer. Not only that, her clothes were neatly folded at the far end of the kitchen table, including her undies!

She coughed to announce her arrival back at Heron Croft.

Instead of reaching for the pair of jeans slung over the back of a chair Rocco carried on ironing. 'Coffee's hot,' he said, pointing at the cafetiere with the iron. 'And I left you the last slice of Janet's cake. Noble, or what?'

'Thanks.' Squeezing between the ironing board and the kitchen table, Harper accidentally brushed against his bare thigh. She took an automatic step back from him, as if scalded. Instinctively, she went to brush away the accidental contact but realised how that would look and quickly dropped her hand. 'Coffee? I'm dying for a cup.' She headed for the counter, keen to put space between herself and Penhaligon.

What was wrong with her? It wasn't the first time she'd seen a man in his underpants.

Simply the first time she'd seen *Penhaligon* in his underpants.

Out of the corner of her eye she saw him whip his jeans off the chair and put them on. Was he sparing her blushes or his own? No way of knowing. She heard the rasp of the zip as he did up the fly and she shivered again, this time picturing a more intimate scenario. One where he was getting dressed after making love to – well, *her*.

Holy Moses. Where had that thought come from?

Unthinkingly, she took a gulp of hot, black coffee, scalding her tongue and palate.

'M-milk,' she gasped. Going over to the fridge she drank some straight from the carton. The very thing she spent half her life reprimanding Ariel for. She held the milk in her mouth without swallowing until the burning abated somewhat. When she turned round Rocco was leaning back against the counter top regarding her curiously.

'You okay? You seem a little agitated.'

'Sorry. Hot coffee. Burnt mouth. Nothing more.'

'There's a tube of Bonjela in the first aid box. Want me to fetch it?'

'No. I'm fine. See?' After sticking out her tongue she took another swig of milk.

Rocco looked unconvinced. 'I didn't think you'd be back so soon, hence –' He indicated his long legs with a sweeping gesture. 'Too hot to be ironing in jeans.'

'Too hot to be ironing, full stop.'

'Hope I didn't shock you . . .'

'I *was* shocked at the sight of you ironing.'

'I know how to use an iron. Don't you?'

'Well, of course, but you're . . .'

'You weren't about to say – *but you're a man,* were you, Miss MacDonald? Now *I'm* shocked.' The teasing light in his eyes gave the lie to the statement.

'Of course not. It was simply, unexpectedly,' she sought for the right word, 'domesticated.'

Nothing to do with you being in your underpants. Nothing at all.

'I'll have you know I am fully housetrained. I know the correct way to pour milk from a bottle but sometimes I prefer to drink it like this.' Picking up the carton of milk he took a long swig, his mouth covering the spot where hers had been only minutes before.

'I've just drunk from that carton!' she protested.

'I take it that you don't have a communicable disease. Ebola? Beriberi?'

'Of course not.'

'Well then.' After several thirsty gulps he replaced the milk in the fridge. 'Remember, usually it's just Pen and me. Two guys living above a garage with no woman around to make sure we observe all the niceties. FYI, we ran out of doylies three years ago.'

'Such hardship,' she quipped.

'As for doing my own ironing, it does have certain advantages.'

'Such as?'

'Keeping the ladies at bay.'

'I don't understand. Explain.'

'When I'm in a new relationship, nine times out of ten my girlfriend–' he paused, sending her a challenging look. 'I can say *girlfriend*, can't I? Or am I too old for that term? Woman-friend sounds wrong and *lady* doesn't quite cut it.'

'Let's settle for girlfriend.'

'Imagine the scene. New *girlfriend* visits, takes one look at how Pen and I live and is overcome by a burning desire to sort us out, mother us even – which is pretty weird, I think you'll agree. I refuse, politely of course. Stop her from washing so much as a mug in case it creates a precedence, takes our relationship to a place I'd rather it didn't go. Then when things don't work out and we go our separate ways it makes breaking up easier.'

'Do you always break up with your lady friends?' She couldn't resist sending him a sharp look.

'Nine times out of ten. Don't give me that look, Miss MacDonald, simply being honest. Take ironing, for example. There have been some unseemly tugs-of-war around the laundry basket when my latest squeeze tries to collect our dirty washing, launder it and bring it back ironed and smelling of fabric conditioner.'

'You must date some pretty weird, not to mention desperate, women.' Harper knew he was teasing and suspected that none of it, apart from his unwillingness to show commitment, was true.

'Desperate in general? Or desperate to date me.'

'Both.' Laughing, Rocco moved round to her side of the table and perched on the edge, their knees almost touching.

'So, is the same true for you?'

'What? Do men try and steal my laundry? No. That would be seriously weird. Although,' she sent him an unconsciously coquettish look through her eyelashes, 'they often tried to put up shelves or hang pictures for me. To prove their manliness I suppose.'

'Little do they know that uber-capable Miss MacDonald can hang her own pictures and they can go –'

'– hang.' She laughed at the pun. 'To be honest, Jim the premises officer is on hand to do stuff like that for me. As for ironing –'

'I'm all ears.'

'I farm mine out to *Iron Maidens*. They pick up our laundry and return it within a couple of days. Haven't you seen their vans whizzing round the lanes? You should give them a try?'

'What, and lose my get-out-of-jail card?'

'Do you need one?'

'It's probably hard for you to believe this, but some women actually find me attractive. But they aren't as high-minded as you.' He edged closer, their knees touched and his aftershave wafted towards her.

'High-minded, is that what I am?' She pretended to give the idea some thought, hiding how affected she was by their closeness. 'Maybe I'm just –'

'Picky?'

'Selective.'

'Know how to hurt a guy's feelings, don't you?' Feigning dejection he sighed. 'I've accepted that I can't measure up to Anthony, the ninja-next-door. But, a boy can dream, can't he?'

'Now who's being sarcastic? Poor Anthony.'

Rocco laughed. 'Okay, let's steer the conversation away from our love lives.'

Or, in her case – lack of.

Harper squashed the depressing thought that she'd left it too late to meet Mr Right and would have to settle for Mr-Right-Enough. When she glanced up, Rocco was regarding her curiously, as if wondering what was going through her mind. She needed to keep things light, frivolous. Time enough for thinking about the future when she left Plockton.

'Before we finish discussing the rights and wrongs of ironing I'll let you into a little secret.' Leaning closer, she glanced behind her checking they were in no danger of being overheard. 'Sometimes,' Rocco moved closer, their noses almost touching, 'sometimes, I pick Ariel's discarded clothes off her bedroom floor, spray them with Febreze, fold them flat and put them back in her wardrobe.'

'Seriously?'

'Seriously.'

Their exchanged look made it plain that neither was talking about what was really on their mind.

'Right. Back to the ironing – unless, you . . .' His questioning look invited her to take over.

'Dream on,' was Harper's response. 'Besides, you wouldn't want me getting ideas, would you?'

'Damn. Hoist by my own petard. Although you don't seem like the type to get ideas. Didn't you tell me back in Leicester that you want to leave Polzenith and take a sabbatical, before training as a Schools Inspector? Doesn't leave you much time for popping round to our loft to undertake a little light dusting.' Laughing at the image, he pushed himself off the table and walked back to the ironing board.

Harper laughed too, but his readiness to believe that there was nothing more to her than a desire to further her career, stung. Wasn't that just like her parents expectations of her? However, she played along, keeping up the pretence that those were her goals. No need to say that taking her foot off the gas these last couple of days and being free of responsibility (now she knew Ariel was safe), reminded her that there was a world out there, just waiting to be explored.

'Okay. Leave the ironing board out, will you? I might as well iron the clothes you washed this morning.'

'Sure you wouldn't like me to iron them for you.'

'No. For all the reasons you mentioned earlier.' Too personal, too familiar. He nodded, his expression acknowledging that she was serious. Harper, keen to return to their earlier flirty repartee walked over to the ironing board and raised a corner of the damp towel. 'I'm intrigued. What's under there.'

'I'm pressing my kilt.'

'As you do –'

'As you do,' he agreed. Whipping back the tea towel he removed the kilt from the ironing board, shook it and then brushed the pleats with a suede-backed brush. Next, he hung the kilt on a special hanger via four metal clips which attached to the waist.

'Is that the Gunn tartan?' Harper asked, remembering what his mother had said about their highland connection a few nights ago.

'Excuse me,' he said, squeezing between her and the table. 'It's the ancient or 'weathered' version of the tartan to be precise. Muted colours: grey, black, sludgy green with a red stripe making a wide checker board pattern.' He held it in front of him and struck a mock-heroic pose, not unlike the one Hugh Morrison affected on the fly leaf of his wildlife book.

'I like it, it looks very modern.' She followed Rocco out of the back door and on to the patio where he suspended the kilt from the washing line by its hanger. He then put a clothes peg over the hanger's neck to stop it slipping off the line. 'Is the kilt still damp?'

'Only slightly, I'm hanging it out here because there's a faint whiff of mothballs following it, and by association, me, everywhere I go,' he laughed.

'Tell me about the Gunns.' Harper sat down on one of the wrought iron chairs and Rocco perched on a low wall.

'Well, we're noted for our ferocious fighting spirit.' He adopted a strong-man pose, hands made into fists and arms raised.

'Natch.'

'Gunns are known for their long-standing feud with clan Keith which only ended in nineteen-seventy-eight, after five hundred years fighting over land and political position.'

'Best not to rush these things,' she said poker faced, making him laugh.

'Our clan motto is: *Aut pax aut bellum* – either peace or war. Our clan badge,' he rooted in the pocket of his jeans, 'is a hand holding a sword.' He passed over a heavy silver brooch to her. She weighed it in her hand and then handed it back. 'What about the MacDonalds?'

'I've never researched my Scottish roots, never had time. I know the MacDonalds were once Lords of the Isles and owned vast tracts of land along the west coast of Scotland. Then the king – one of the Jameses, not sure which one, took away their titles and territories fearing that they would overpower the Stuarts and assert their independence.'

'A trait they exhibit to this very day,' he joked.

'I'm sure the MacDonalds got on famously with clan Gunn.'

'Famously,' he repeated, unconvinced.

'What about the Penhaligons? Where do they come in?'

'Mother started researching the family name, lost interest, and handed over to a genealogist who traced the family back as far as the Tudors. Then they were known by another name: Penhallows. She had his findings printed, bound in leather by a small press and gave us all a copy a few Christmases back.' He shrugged, as though it was of no interest to him.

'Morwenna mentioned that your grandfather wrote *Box Kite to Concorde*, about your family's involvement in the aeronautics industry?'

'Now *that* is a book worth reading. I think there's a copy kicking round Heron Croft somewhere, if you'd like to read it.' Rocco looked more enthusiastic about that.

'Anyway, back to the Gunns. Do you usually wear a kilt when you're in Plockton?'

'Not every day, but I do like to give it an airing. It feels right, somehow, like I'm honouring my ancestors. Also, I like to give Morrison a run for his money.'

'Without the wolfhound, though.'

'Exactly. Though I suppose I could borrow Janet's Highland Terrier if I felt it would add something to the overall effect.'

'Hate to say this, but I think the wolfhound might have more impact.'

Rocco stood up. 'I'll be wearing my kilt at the pub quiz at the Plockton Arms on Sunday night. I thought we could make up a team – you, me, Pen, Ariel, the laird and possibly Janet. It'd be a good way to draw your time in Plockton to a close, before you and Ariel head home.'

'Oh,' Harper was beset by confusion. 'Ariel and me? I don't understand, aren't you and Pen travelling back to Polzenith with us?'

'I have some loose ends to tie up which might take some time and require me to be in Plockton. On top of which, I need a heart-to-heart with Pen, free from distractions.'

'Distractions?' she questioned, suspecting that she and Ariel came under that heading.

'Yes. The bright lights of the Three Pols,' he joked, pulling a wry face.

'Of course.' Harper sensed there was more to this than he was prepared to share. Earlier, she'd felt they were getting to know each other but now she felt snubbed, excluded. She'd assumed that they'd travel back to Polzenith in Pen's Jeep with her and Penhaligon sharing the driving. Call in at Mr and Mrs Bailey's Farm at Ecclefechan and stop overnight at Morwenna's to break the journey before heading to Bristol via Leicester.

Their original journey in reverse.

Now it looked as if they were singing from two versions of the same hymn sheet. Annoyed that it mattered, she shrugged away the hurt. What were they to each other, after all? Reluctant allies, brought together by events, not choice. Adopting a false, bright smile she followed Rocco back into the kitchen.

'A pub quiz sounds an ideal way to spend our last evening in Plockton. Once Ariel returns, she'll have had enough of highland life and will be champing at the bit to head south. That's fine by me.' There, that put the record straight. 'I'm hoping that, if I can persuade Ariel to get on a plane to LAX, I'll find a last minute cancellation for the tour of Nepal I was originally booked on and finally enjoy my summer.'

'Wouldn't have thought that'd be a problem,' Rocco joked, implying that her choice of holiday wouldn't appeal to many people but was perfectly designed for spinsterish headmistresses, geography teachers and trekking enthusiasts.

'Quite.'

'That won't be for a few days. I thought, tomorrow.' He smiled at her, having missed how she'd practically spat out, *quite.* 'We could go over to Skye and –'

She cut across him. 'Sorry, I'm taking the train to Inverness tomorrow. The owner of the studio told me that the line follows the shores of Loch Carron and it's a stunning journey. I can't see that appealing to Ariel so I'll set out bright and early and make a day of it. I gather the station is a request stop and I can buy a ticket on the train.'

'Yes – yes, you can. But you can buy one online and check the train times there, too.' Now it was his turn to look confused. 'I'll drive you to the station, if you like. It's a bit of a hike –'

'If you think the Land Rover's up to it.'

'Now you've really wounded me.' Harper sent him an unsympathetic look, she knew the feeling.

'You're a big boy, you'll get over it.'

With that she swept out of the kitchen, leaving Penhaligon openly wondering what had just happened and why their brief rapprochement had, seemingly, come to an abrupt end.

Chapter Twenty

Next morning, it took Harper twenty minutes to walk from Heron Croft to Plockton Station. Her resolution to take a step back from Rocco Penhaligon was evident in the set of her shoulders and determined stride. Time to make clear that she wanted *nothing* from him, including a lift to the station. His throwaway remark about her leaving Plockton after the pub quiz had touched a raw nerve. Who was he to tell her what to do? Didn't it occur to him to have found out what her plans were before dropping that little gem into the conversation?

I thought we could make up a team – you, me, Pen, Ariel . . . It might be a nice way to draw your time in Plockton to a close, before you . . . head south.

Penhaligon was a wild card, but his casual dismissal smarted. What's more, she wasn't used to be treated so cavalierly. Of course, she'd put on an act, smiling and making easy conversation for the rest of the evening as if nothing had changed. She was good at that. If he'd noticed that her smile didn't quite reach her eyes, he hadn't commented. He was a man after all, and didn't it take a man twenty minutes to register a change in a woman's expression?

Twenty minutes. The exact time it had taken her to walk to the station. He'd had all night to realise that she was seriously pissed off, but had missed the opportunity and with it the chance to put things right.

She'd thought to stay on in Plockton for a few days after Ariel's return, have a breather before making the long journey home. However, it was clear Penhaligon wanted time alone with Pen and staying on at Heron Croft was no longer an option. She got that. It was the casual way he'd delivered the message which had brought her blood to simmering point. Prolonging her time in the village, albeit staying at the Plockton Hotel, would send out the wrong message. Make her appear as one with the women who wanted to tidy Penhaligon's loft, do his laundry, wheedle themselves into his life.

Glancing at her watch she made her way on to the platform to wait for the six-twenty-seven from Kyle of Lochalsh which would get into *Inbhirness* for ten to nine. It was hard to believe that it would take two hours and twenty-four minutes to travel the fifty-five miles to Inverness, but that's what the timetable said. The train had over a dozen small stations to pass through and had to slow down at each one, prepared to stop if requested.

Waiting on the platform she experienced an uncharacteristic flutter of anxiety. What if the train driver didn't see her raised hand and steamed right past, forcing her to walk back to Heron Croft and wait for the next train? Rocco Penhaligon would doubtless be awake by then and would make good on his offer of giving her a lift to the station.

But that wasn't what she wanted, wasn't what she wanted at all.

Get a grip MacDonald, of course the driver'll see you. This is a tried and tested method, like hailing a taxi in London.

Staring down the track towards Kyle she bit her lip in consternation. She wasn't usually nervous when encountering new experiences. Quite the reverse. Evidently, spending time with Penhaligon, being forced to consult him, take his opinion into account and to act as a team had had an impact. She wasn't used to spending large swathes of her time with anyone other than Ariel, and she spent most of the evening in her room on her MacBook. Apart from Jim the premises officer, her staff were exclusively female and they worked together in a peculiarly feminine way.

Penhaligon, was mercurial, secretive. She really didn't know much about him, his background or where she stood with him. Her attention focused on a large sign in front of her showing two arrows pointing in opposite directions: Inverness to the left, Kyle to the right. This morning it seemed like a metaphor for her life. She wanted to stay but felt compelled to bring this brief chapter in her life to an end.

Seems that Rocco felt the same.

Bright lights coming along the track heralded the arrival of the train. Enough thinking for one day. Taking a deep breath she held out her hand and the train slowed to a stop. Relieved, she climbed on board, found her reserved seat on the left hand side of the carriage and settled down, banishing Penhaligon from her mind as the train pulled out of Plockton and the refreshment trolley made its way towards her. Her lips curved in a Mona Lisa smile as she pictured Rocco finding the note propped up against the cafetiere informing him that she'd already left for the station and wouldn't need a lift – thank you, very much.

Let him make of it what he would

* * *

Even at this early hour the train was busy with tourists snapping the beautiful scenery as the train swept through glens, mountains, lochs and tiny stations. The names rolled by: Stromeferry, Strathcarron, Attadale and its gardens, Achnasheen. Names to conjure with. A sense of peace settled on Harper as she gazed in wonder at the Torridon Peaks at Achnashellach Forest, the deer on the downhill route from Lochluichart and, just after Dingwall, the isolated peak of Ben Wyviss. Although she'd decided to leave Plockton she felt her Scottish roots keenly that morning. Here was where her heart belonged, close to the mountain fastnesses of Glencoe where her MacDonald ancestors had lived until the Campbells, breaking every tenet of highland hospitality, had turned on them and massacred them in the snow.

Recently her mother, in her role as consultant forensic geneticist, had been called in to date artefacts excavated in Glencoe. Now Harper wished she'd paid more attention to the paper her mother had written, attended the lecture she'd given at Leicester University. However, getting her schools out of special measures had taken up all her time. Travelling through these hills, lochs and mountains brought home a sense of who she was, where she'd come from, in a way that reading about her ancestors never could.

One day, she'd return and trace her roots, she owed her forefathers that much.

* * *

She was on her second cup of not-terribly-good coffee when her phone rang.

Reaching out, she picked it up off the table and then hesitated. What if it was Rocco, ringing to ask her why she hadn't waited for him. Then she shrugged – so what? She was past caring what he thought. The Caller Id flashed up as Unknown, but she answered the call. because she had a pretty good idea who it was.

'Auntie Harper, thank God, I've got through to you.'

'You certainly have,' she kept her voice upbeat. 'Are you enjoying your holiday with Pen, Ariel?'

A groan. 'Auntie, you have no idea. It's like *hell,* honestly. We're staying in a small hotel near Loch Eribol – or, Loch 'Orrible as I've nicknamed it. Just when I think we've run out of mountains there's another one waiting round the corner. I'm verging on clinically depressed, honestly.'

'Sounds wonderful,' Harper said, earning a snort of derision.

'Are you nuts? It's vile. The only bits I've enjoyed are the pie shop at Inverbervie and Cocoa Mountain in Balnalkeil where I overdosed on chocolate to keep my spirits up and threw up in Pen's jeep. He was so not amused. I've got break-out spots on my chin, nose and forehead and haven't taken a selfie in *days.* And even if I did take a decent photograph I wouldn't be able to upload it on to Instagram because I can't get a 4G signal. My five thousand followers will think I'm dead. I'm *this* close to being classed as a nano influencer, and being able to make money from vlogging.'

Harper didn't have any idea what Ariel was talking about – nano influencer? Vlogging? But she knew enough to understand that she should make appropriate noises. 'Oh dear, sorry to hear that. But I'm sure you're having a lovely time with Pen –'

'Pen? He's a total *dork*. All he does is sit in the hide or lays low in the bracken waiting for some animal to swing by. Then he photographs it and almost has an orgasm if the shot turns out.'

Harper did her best not to laugh. 'I thought –'

Ariel cut across her. 'Every time I utter so much as a word I'm shushed. By both of them. So what if some random animal gets spooked, there's plenty more where they came from, for feck's sake.'

Now was not the time to pick Ariel up on her language, so Harper pressed her for more details. 'You're with Hugh Morrison, aren't you? What's he like?'

'A total knob-head. Thinks he's God's gift to women and he's *old*. Older than you and Pen's dad. Imagine that.'

'I'm trying . . . I saw a photograph of him on the cover of one of his books. I thought he looked rather dishy.'

'Dishy? Are you for real? No one's said *dishy* in like, forever. I totally get that you haven't got time for men, and aren't interested in sex,' *Thanks, Ariel,* 'but Hugh Morrison has a personality disorder. If he's not being admired and adored 24/7 he sulks like a baby. He wears a kilt almost like it's a badge of honour and keeps banging on about the Highland Clearances – whatever they were. He has horrible hairy legs and his knees are scaly and chapped and in need of a good moisturiser. Or WD40.'

'WD40?'

'Yes. You should hear his joints creak when he stands up after sitting on his wee fold-up camp stool in the hide, camera poised for action. I try not to look in his direction too often as I have a feeling he goes commando.'

Harper gulped. 'What does Pen think?'

'He think the sun shines out of his ar . . . bottom. He *adores* him. It's sick making.'

Harper was careful not to overplay her hand. 'I bet your wildlife safari has brought home the contrast between Sutherland and L.A.'

'At least in L.A there's constant sun, no midges and you can get a burger when you want one. The hotel where we're staying is in time warp – tartan *everything*, swirly patterned carpets, dead things mounted on the wall and, get this, huge fish in glass cases. What's that all about? I asked for a burger for dinner and they made one from venison. Venison! How gross is that? Like eating Bambi, or something.'

'You must have enjoyed some aspect of your holiday –'

'This isn't a holiday,' she exploded. 'Pen totally sold me a pup. *Let's go to Scotland*, he said. *It'll be fun*, he said. All he wanted was someone to tag along in case he got bored; someone to deflect the heat away from him when you oldies found our letters. Not to mention sharing the punishment which we know is waiting for us when we return.'

'I'm not sure that's –'

Ariel, however, hadn't finished her rant. 'Being in L.A and forcing myself to be polite to douchebag #3 is beginning to look a walk in the park compared to spending more time with these two.'

Well, that was something, at least. 'So what did you enjoy?'

'Let me think. Oh yes, when Hugh Morrison's foot sank in a bog and came out minus his boot. That was pretty awesome. Oh, and riding around in Pen's jeep is super cool, if I ignore the slight whiff of vomit. If only I had rich grandparents who loved me enough to buy me a jeep. He's *so* lucky.' Not quite how Rocco saw it. Harper was about to say that Ariel's grandparents wouldn't dream of buying her a jeep, and that any money they'd put away was earmarked for her education. But she wasn't given the chance.

'And another thing –'

'Go on.'

The PA system kicked into life announcing that the train was pulling into Dingwall and Ariel stalled. 'What's that? Where are you?'

'I'm on the train to Inverness.'

'Inverness! Pen said you were with his dad in Plockton. Please don't leave without me, Auntie Harper. I wanna go home.' There was a catch in her voice, reminding Harper of the sweet child who'd come to live with her years earlier.

'I won't. You're sure you want to come home to Polzenith?'

'By 'home', I meant fly over to L.A to see mum and wait for my A level results there.'

'Of course,' Harper kept her voice level, her tone light. In other words, do exactly what'd been planned for her before she'd taken off with Pen Penhaligon.

'My grades are bound to be *pants*, and I don't want to open my envelope alongside that cow Tamsyn Trethowan who'll crow over me because she's going to university and I'm not.'

Having taught them both, Harper knew which one was more likely to go to university, but kept her counsel. 'Look, you're coming back to Plockton soon and –'

'No. That's the thing. Hugh-Bloody-Morrison wants to extend the trip because a great yellow bumblebee has been sighted on the machair near Durness. Apparently, if he captures it on film he can earn megabucks flogging the photo to wildlife magazines.'

Harper was surprised that Ariel not only knew what machair was but had pronounced it, correctly, "*mak'r*", that she didn't at first register that she wouldn't be seeing her niece for a few more days.

'Anyhoo, gotta go, I'm calling you from a bar in Scourie.'

'Scourie?'

Ariel rushed on, ignoring the question. 'Hugh-Up-Himself-Morrison banned us from bringing our mobiles and Pen – the wimp – meekly did as he was told. I bought a spare burner in Inverbervie when Morrison was looking the other way. I have to use public telephones to contact the outside world when he's got his beady eye on me. Which is 24/7, by the way. When he isn't on guard and I can get a signal I ring my besties and try to tap into my social media profile.'

'Oh dear.' First world problems, Ariel, Harper felt like saying, but *held her wheesht*.

'I'm pretty sure that denying me access to the internet and a mobile phone contravenes my human rights.'

'Not sure that would stand up in a court of law,' Harper ventured.

'Y'know, I actually think I hate Hugh more than I do Pen right now. Hugh sighs all the time, looks at me as though he hates me, moans that the light's fading and they haven't got the best 'shot'. Like that's my fault. We're not allowed back to the hotel until he's good and ready and,' she paused for dramatic effect, 'he won't allow Pen or me to order anything stronger than a coke from the bar. I've begged him to leave me behind each day, or kill me. But, he says he's in loco parentis and has to keep an eye on me. He's worse than you.'

Too wrapped up in herself, Ariel failed to register her aunt's huff of annoyance and ended the call. Harper was left looking at a blank screen. 'Yep, selfish people are the worst,' she said, even although Ariel couldn't hear.

Putting the phone in her bag, she wondered if Hugh Morrison had contacted Rocco to let him know of his change of plans. Well, nothing she could do about it except accept things as they were, enjoy an extra few days in Plockton, even though her relationship with Rocco Penhaligon had taken a turn for the worse.

Chapter Twenty-One

Rocco sat in the Land Rover outside Plockton station attempting The Times cryptic crossword. It was almost a quarter past eight and the last train from Inverness was due in at eighteen minutes past. He hoped Harper was on it. After spending the last few days joined at the hip it'd felt strange having Heron Croft to himself. Sure, he'd been busy enough, spending most of the day with Auld Baxter and Janet discussing his proposed purchase of the garage and time had slipped by.

However, after he'd returned to Heron Croft, made lunch and eaten it in the garden, time had slowed down. Hoping Harper might've caught the early train he'd driven to the station at four o'clock to meet her, but she was a no-show. Returning to the garden he'd read the paper and then spoken to his senior mechanic Pete about selling the garage in Polzenith and ascertained that he was interested in buying it.

Now, waiting for the twenty-eighteen to pull into the station Rocco went over yesterday's events trying to pinpoint the exact moment when the frost had set in. They'd got on really well in the morning, laughing and joking over breakfast before parting company. So far, so good. When she'd returned to Heron Croft he was pressing his kilt under a tea towel. Also fine. They'd laughed over his too-keen girlfriends and he'd teased her about Anthony the-ninja-next-door.

In fact, at one point their heads had been so close together that it'd taken all his willpower not to lean forward and kiss her. Then he'd jokingly offered to iron her clothes and she'd rejected it in the same vein. He tapped his teeth with a biro, remembering. The temperature had dropped after he'd mentioned the pub quiz and that she and Ariel would be travelling south while he and Pen stayed on in Plockton.

Was that it? Was she aggrieved that they'd have to undertake the seven-hundred mile journey by plane and train, rather than share the driving with him? But then, she'd gone on to say: *A pub quiz sounds a great way to spend our last evening in Plockton*, mentioned her postponed holiday in Nepal and getting Ariel to L.A. So it couldn't have been that.

He'd planned to take her over to Skye via the bridge and show her the Fairy Pools. But she'd cut him off mid-sentence and rejected his offer of a lift to the station.

She was good at hiding her feelings so he'd never know what he'd done wrong unless she chose to enlighten him. All he knew for certain was that he'd missed her today. Had felt hollow, incomplete and none of the usual distractions: reading, walking on the hills or tinkering with cars in George's garage had made it more bearable.

Puzzled, he folded up his newspaper, pushed the biro behind his ear and headed for the platform to meet the train.

* * *

Harper gathered her bags together, tucking the large green Loch Ness Monster she'd bought in Inverness under her arm. 'Nessie' would be a brilliant teaching aid, help her to discuss myths and legends with the older children while entertaining the younger ones with stories about Nessie and her watery lair.

The train came to a halt and she stepped down onto the platform and stood there for several minutes watching the train pull out of the station and disappear round the bend. The next time she saw the Kyle train she'd be on it heading south with Ariel. Hitching Nessie more securely under her arm she headed for the exit and the walk back to Heron Croft.

'Need any help, lady?' Rocco Penhaligon stepped out from under the verandah of the former station house, now an Airbnb. Harper's chest tightened and her breath caught in her throat at the unexpectedness of finding him waiting for her.

'I – I can manage, thanks.' Although she was still madder than hell with him, some part of her was glad to see him. Work that one out!

'Bit old to be playing with toys, aren't you?' He pointed at Nessie with his rolled up newspaper.

'Never too old to play with toys,' she retorted. 'Why are you here, Penhaligon?'

'To meet you off the train.' She walked past him, making it clear that she didn't expect – or want – such consideration. But her traitorous heart gave a glad leap when he followed close on her heels.

Without turning, she stopped in her tracks and asked: 'Why?'

'I thought, after exploring Inverness, you might welcome a lift home.'

Harper tightened her grip on the carrier bags. 'Well, I don't.'

'Nessie looks exhausted,' he said, closing the gap between them. 'Och, the puir wee monster.'

'Plesiosaur, *if* you don't mind.' She feigned annoyance at his lack of knowledge of prehistoric creatures.

'Puir wee plesiosaur, then.' Reaching round, he took the toy from her. 'You'd like a ride home, wouldn't you Nessie? Swimming around for thousands of years in Loch Ness and a long train journey from Inverness to Plockton – you must be worn out. How could you be so unfeeling, Miss MacDonald?'

She turned to snatch the toy back and to give him one of her dampening stares. However, he looked so ridiculous clutching the large green monster to his chest that she bowed her head to hide her smile. Then she hardened her heart. He needn't think he could ooze charm after serving notice on her stay at Heron Croft.

'Knock it off, Penhaligon. You aren't in the least bit amusing and if anyone's too old to play with toys, it's you.'

'Well, I think Nessie likes me, even if you don't.' Gathering the toy to his chest he stroked its felt scales and ruffled the fur between its ears, sending her a *go-on-deny-it* look.

So, he knew she was displeased with him. Good. Even if he probably had no idea why. Let him stew! Harper snatched Nessie out of his arms and handed him her bags instead. 'You can take my bags home, if you like. As for Nessie and me, we'll be walking. I've been on the train for over two hours and I feel as if my legs have seized up.'

'I'll go home and put the kettle on then, shall I?' He acted as though Nessie was an unplanned for but welcome visitor. 'How does our guest take her tea.'

Our guest? His use of the pronoun reminded Harper that they were no longer a team united by a common goal. The teenagers would be home soon, their partnership dissolved, she would head south and that would be that.

End of.

'Black and with no sugar. She's sweet enough, just like me.' Flashing him a saccharine smile, she tossed her head and started off down the hill with Nessie under her arm, not caring how she looked. Left with no other choice Rocco climbed up into the Land Rover and headed home without her.

* * *

Rocco was in the kitchen when Harper and Nessie arrived back at Heron Croft. Flicking the switch on the kettle he gestured towards the tea tray set out on the table. 'Tea, coffee, cake?' he asked, pulling out two chairs. Taking Nessie from her, he sat the wee plesiosaur in a chair at the end of the table like an honoured guest.

'Actually,' Harper began, 'I think I'd rather have a drink of water, I'm feeling a little overheated.' Slipping off her light jacket, she picked up a flyer off the table and fanned herself with it.

Rocco looked at her concernedly. 'You seem rather flushed. Look – I'm sure you go yomping over the moors after a long day at the chalk face, just for the hell of it. However, maybe a sightseeing trip to Inverness sandwiched between two long, slow train journeys – not to mention a twenty-minute walk at either end – has proved too much. '

He paused, obviously expecting her to snap his head off. When that didn't happen, he took her by the hand and moving her closer to the kitchen window, laid his palm against her forehead. His hand was so deliciously cool against her hot skin that Harper closed her eyes, leaned back against the sink and took in a deep breath. She released it, and when she opened her eyes he was regarding her concernedly. He stretched out his arm, reached behind her and she flinched.

'Calm down, I have no ulterior motive other than helping you.' He held a small mirror in front of her so she could see her reflection.

'Oh. My. God.' Sounding exactly like Ariel, she snatched the mirror from him and examined her face more closely. Her lips were swollen and bright red hives dotted her skin like large weals. 'What is it? What's happening?'

'Are the blobs itchy and are your lips tingling?'

'Uh-huh,' she cast a helpless look in his direction.

'Did you have lunch in Inverness?'

'Sushi.' She placed the mirror on the draining board and then clutched her stomach with both hands. 'I think I'd better . . .' She dashed to the back of the kitchen where there was a small cloakroom with toilet and sink. She'd barely sat on the toilet before the sushi headed south. Then, simultaneously the contents of her stomach decided to head north. 'Oh, God,' she groaned.

She searched around frantically, wondering how she could remain seated on the toilet while managing to be sick over the sink. The bathroom door opened a fraction. 'Rocco, for the love of God, don't come in –'

'I wasn't going to. Here.' He placed a Victorian chamber pot on the floor within reach and then, turning sideways, pushed it towards her with his foot, without glancing in her direction. Harper scooped up the chamber pot just in time to be violently sick into it. Her bowels, not to be outdone decided to join in the action. This went on for about five minutes and all the while she was acutely aware that Rocco was on the other side of the door, listening, trying to be of help but knowing she wanted to be left alone in her misery.

To die from shame and embarrassment if the food poisoning didn't finish her off.

Roughly half an hour later, when she'd stopped vomiting, Harper reached behind her and flushed the toilet once more. It sounded gross, but the skoosh of water round her nether regions was strangely refreshing. She groaned, how could she face Penhaligon after this?

When there was a hiatus she got shakily to her feet, emptied the chamber pot down the toilet, swished it out with fresh water, squirted some toilet cleaner into both, then left it on the floor until she felt able to deal with it. Straightening, she walked over to the sink and grasping hold of the edge glanced at her reflection in the mirror. What a sight – the hectic blobs had disappeared, leaving her grey and drawn, hair hanging in greasy tendrils round her face. She did her best to wash her hands, rinse her mouth out with the bottle of anti-plaque liquid on the shelf and then raked her fingers through her hair.

Feeling marginally more presentable she inched open the bathroom door and peered round. Rocco Penhaligon was sitting by the kitchen table working on his crossword. He was at her side in seconds.

'Sluices open both ends?' he inquired, in a feeble attempt at humour.

'Apparently.'

'Come and sit down . . .'

'No thanks, I want to have a shower, brush my teeth. That is, if my innards will permit. Once, my school was beset by the norovirus and we had to cancel the Christmas Concert, but *this* is worse, much worse.'

Rocco glanced at his watch. 'That sounds particularly horrible, children throwing up everywhere . . . sorry, shouldn't have mentioned the war. Here, gruesome as it sounds, I think you should sit on this chair near the toilet door, just in case. I can fetch your face flannel, toothpaste and toothbrush, if you like?'

'Please.'

He did just that, arriving back in record time and handed her a scrunchy. 'Tie your hair up and allow me.' Walking over to the sink he filled a bowl with lukewarm water and rinsed out the facecloth. 'I'm sure I should be putting a few drops of essential oil in the water. But I haven't got any, even if I knew what it looked like.' Once her hair was clear of her face and neck he gently wiped her skin all over with the facecloth. Then he passed her a stick of chewing gum. 'Easier than brushing your teeth and just as effective.'

Harper chewed the gum and her mouth felt a little fresher. She nodded towards the cloakroom. 'I've cleaned up as best I could, but it's pretty grim in there. Sorry.'

'Don't be. I've cleaned up after Pen often enough. And at least I haven't had to strip you and put you in the shower along with your clothes.'

Harper winced at the thought of standing naked in the shower being sluiced down by Rocco Penhaligon. 'Really?' she managed at last when the image left her.

'Really. It's a rite of passage for an eighteen-year-old –'

'But possibly not for an almost thirty-eight-year-old?'

'Possibly not. We'll put yours down to the sushi and not sixteen-point-six ABV St Petroc's Hard Cider on offer at The Tipsy Fisherman. Once he'd stopped being sick, Pen remained cross eyed and bilious for days afterwards. Rather poetic that the cider was named after his father, don't you think?' Harper groaned, sympathising with Pen. 'It taught him a lesson though, more effectively than anything I could say.'

'Kids, huh?'

'Exactly.'

'Ariel has seen her mother and her louche friends drunk too many times to find the prospect enticing. I –' Pushing Rocco out of the way she headed back to the cloakroom to repeat the humiliating experience, emerging later when things had settled down.

Rocco placed a glass of water and a packet of salt crackers on the kitchen table.

'I d-don't think I can,' Harper protested, her shoulders sagging.

'Try a few sips of water at least and see if you can keep it down.' He pulled a chair out for her and guided her over. Placing his arm around her shoulders, he handed her the glass of water. By now, Harper was used to the peaty brown water off the hills, but it didn't make her feel any better about drinking it, especially in her present condition. 'Go on, a few sips. Just rinse your mouth out if nothing else and spit it down the sink.'

'That's my street cred gone,' she said, pulling a face.

'I won't tell anyone if you don't,' he said, helping her over to the sink and turning on the tap. Much against her will, Harper swilled out her mouth and spat in the sink. Rocco led her back to the table where she flopped down and laid her head on her arms.

'Urgh, send for the vet,' she managed a weak joke, then shuddered. Her earlier fever replaced by a cold sweat that trickled like ice water down the length of her body.

'Cold?' Rocco went over to the coats hanging near the utility room, fetched a fleece and wrapped it round her shoulders, raising the collar and pulling it up to her ears. Harper was immediately assailed by Rocco's distinctive aftershave and she gave a shudder of a reaction which had nothing to do with feeling cold. 'Sit there quietly and – if you don't dash to the loo in the next ten minutes, we might think of letting you go upstairs to your bedroom. Okay?'

'Okay.' She managed a weak smile thinking, he would have made a great doctor, full of practical advice, calm and unflappable. 'How come you're so –'

'Unfazed? Being a single parent helps, if I don't deal with such emergencies, no one else will. God,' he pushed his thick hair off his forehead, grey-green eyes bright as he remembered. 'Pen's first nappies were disgusting. The first time I changed him I was so unused to a baby's sewage system that I threw open the window and was sick over the dustbins. Considering a baby eats hardly anything I couldn't imagine where all the poo was coming from. If you get my drift.'

'I get it. But, can we please change the subject?'

'Of course. You sit there sipping your water and I'll plough my way through this nightmarish crossword. When you feel ready, you can head upstairs, I'll walk behind you, just in case. . .'

'Thanks, Rocco,' Harper managed, looking up at him through her eyelashes. Tentatively, she stretched out her hand and was about to touch his, her way of showing how grateful she was. Then, remembering that she'd started the day annoyed with him, she changed her mind and curled her fingers into her palm.

If Rocco saw the moment of hesitation followed by a subtle withdrawal he gave no sign.

'No worries.' Picking up his pen he returned to the crossword while, on the other side of the table Nessie sent them a baleful look, demanding that she be returned to the primordial depths of Loch Ness where life was much, much simpler.

* * *

Half an hour later Harper emerged from the shower, wrapped in a large bath sheet towelling her hair dry with a separate towel. Standing still for a few moments she listened to her body, waiting for another spasm of pain to send her scurrying back to the loo. Nothing. Phew. So far, so good. She hadn't been sick or . . . worse for about half an hour. Pray God that her torture was at an end.

'Everything okay in there?' Rocco knocked at the door and waited for her response.

'Yes – yes. Fine. Give me a minute and I'll join you . . . '

'Don't even think about getting dressed. It's late, get ready for bed and we'll see how you are in fifteen minutes.'

It was on the tip of Harper's tongue to say *Yus Sur* and salute. But that would be churlish after he'd been so kind. Sighing, she carefully stepped over the edge of the bath, planted bare feet on the tiled floor and then perched on the side of the tub, tying the towel more securely round her.

It felt odd to have someone looking after her. Usually, she was the one who handled emergencies and disasters, sorted everything out. She stared unseeingly at the weighing scales over by the door and frowned. She'd be lying if she denied that some part of her enjoyed 'letting go', allowing Rocco Penhaligon to take control. Just this once, mind. She'd make that plain when she got her sea legs back and then it'd be business as usual.

Talking of which . . .

Walking over to the bathroom door she opened it a fraction and peered round. The door to Rocco's bedroom was wide open and he was sitting on an armchair in the dormer window reading his kindle. Although she tiptoed out of the bathroom he obviously heard her because he put the kindle on the floor and rose to greet her.

'Come in, Harper.' Pushing the bedroom door open wider he beckoned her forward. Being the master bedroom it commanded a view of the loch and the mountains beyond. The soft wind blowing off the loch brought with it the scent of the pine woods and the last of the gorse flowers. 'I – I took the liberty of stripping and remaking my bed while you were in the shower. I want you to sleep here tonight, it's closer to the bathroom and . . .'

He didn't have to say anything more. Harper's stomach gave another lurch at the thought of being sick again. She didn't argue as she might have once done. It made perfect sense to be closer to the facilities, nor did she think, to use Ariel's inimical phrase, that *he'd jump her bones* in her present condition.

'Thanks, where will you sleep?'

'In your room.' He looked surprised that she meekly agreed to his suggestion and ploughed on, seemingly keen to press home the advantage. 'I glanced in earlier and fetched your pyjamas, I hope you don't mind. I also found a dressing gown in the wardrobe and since you're feeling the cold I've brought that, too. It might smell a bit fusty, but otherwise it's clean.'

'Thanks.' She was so wiped out that she couldn't think of anything else to say.

'And, you've got a visitor.' Reaching behind the arm chair he retrieved Nessie.

'I'm allowed visitors?' Harper gave a weak smile.

'Ordinarily, no. However, Nessie has promised she'll put the light out in half an hour. Isn't that right, Nessie?' No reply. 'Also, wait . . .' He went onto the landing and returned with a bucket holding several inches of disinfectant-laced water. 'Just in case.' Simultaneously, they pulled a face at the thought. 'Hopefully, you won't need it.'

'Thanks.' Draping the wet hair towel over the foot of the massive brass bed Harper drew her fingers through her tangled curls. Rocco brought a hairdryer out of an old-fashioned armoire in the corner and laid it on the bed. 'Thanks.' Harper bit her lip, couldn't she think of something more original? Sound more grateful? She switched on the hairdryer rendering further conversation impossible.

Picking up the kindle, Rocco shouted something which sounded like *you know where I am if you need me* over the din and then left the room.

Feeling weak and shaky but slightly more human Harper dried her hair, got into bed, snuggled beneath the covers and hoped she wouldn't need to use the bucket in the middle of the night.

* * *

Rocco was woken just before dawn by a heavy thud. Remembering why he was in Harper's bed he threw on a t-shirt and dashed for his bedroom where he found Harper lying in a crumpled heap by the window. Without asking or waiting for permission he scooped her up and returned her to bed.

'My head,' she whimpered. Worried, Rocco placed the back of his hand against her forehead and felt heat emanating from her. Deciding she could come to no further harm he dashed to the bathroom and returned with a dampened guest hand towel, folded over to act as a cold compress.

'What were you trying to do?'

'Open the window. I was sick again and needed fresh air.' She turned her head sideways, saw the offending bucket and went a whiter shade of pale. 'Oh . . .' Straightaway, Rocco emptied the bucket and brought it back filled with fresh disinfectant and water. Placing it by the side of the bed he wiped Harper's face, neck and décolletage with the guest towel.

'Water?'

'A little.'

Helping her to sit up he allowed her to have a few sips and then took the glass from her.

'Stay there –'

'I ain't going nowhere,' Harper managed with a weak smile.

'Good.' Walking over to the sash window he lowered the top half and let fresh air waft in to the bedroom. It was a beautiful summer's night and, at two o'clock, the darkest point before dawn in half an hour. 'Do you want to sit up or lie down?'

'Lie down, but with a few more pillows?'

'Your wish is my command.' He left, returning with two large pillows which he used to prop her up. 'Better?'

'Better. I'll be fine now, you can go.' She waved a limp hand in the direction of the door. 'You've gone above and beyond the call of duty.'

'I'll stay here until I'm sure you're okay.'

'Fine.' Seemingly lacking the will to argue she flopped back on the pillows and positioned the compress over her forehead and eyes. Before long her breathing was rhythmic, steady and Rocco stood at the foot of the bed wondering if he should stay or go. Wondering, too, where this overwhelming feeling of wanting to make her better, to take care of her stemmed from.

He let out a slow breath as the night air stirred the curtains and the purple half-light beyond the window called to him. He recalled other summer nights when, unable to sleep, he'd stood by this window thinking his life was over. Then it'd been just him, Pen and the memory of the summer when Pen had been conceived. But now he was older and had life experience, he knew that memory could be selective, remembering only the good times and forgetting the gut-wrenching moment when he realised that the love of his life had dumped him without a word, or a backward glance.

What a fool he'd been, mourning a love that hadn't been real, yearning for something which could never have worked out. Laying his forearm on the meeting rails of the sash window he rested his temple against the cool glass and tried to analyse his emotions.

It was less than a week since Harper MacDonald had stormed into his life. She'd turned everything upside down. Made him examine everything he'd thought sorted, decided: Pen's place at Oxford, the freedom Pen's moving out would give him. The chance to do what he wanted with his life for the first time in years.

Suddenly, that freedom didn't seem so enticing if it meant Harper MacDonald wasn't part of it.

Tiptoeing over to the bed he looked down on her lying there, dark hair spread over the pillows, so pale and wan. With the fight gone out of her she looked younger, less confident and assured. Reaching over, he removed the compress from her slack fingers and his heart contracted with a range of emotions he couldn't classify: compassion, concern – and, something deeper, something he wasn't ready to let in or give a name to. Not yet.

For now, it was enough to acknowledge that he wanted to put right whatever it was he'd got wrong the day before. He didn't want them to part as enemies; didn't want them to part, if he was being totally honest. However, there was much to resolve in his and Pen's lives. As for Harper, she had her own dreams and aspirations and, if today was anything to judge by, they didn't include him.

He sat down on the opposite side of the bed, put his elbows on his knees and held his head in his hands, bone-weary. Surely, he thought, turning sideways and flopping back on the pillow, it wouldn't hurt to lay down beside Harper for a few moments. Just long enough to make sure she was settled for the night. Just long enough to . . .

His eyelids drooped, his breathing settled into a rhythmic pattern and he felt content. He was in the place he loved most in the world and was with a woman who tested him, made him question where his life was going but who also made him feel more alive than he had in years.

Chapter Twenty-Two

'Harper, wake up.' Janet's voice broke into Harper's dreams. Opening her eyes and blinking in the early morning light, Harper pushed her hair off her face. 'Are ye no well?' Bustling round the bed Janet discovered the bucket and its contents, the still-damp compress on the dressing table, the hairdryer on the carpet.

'Sushi. Inverness.' Harper groaned, covering her face with her hands and reliving every ghastly minute. 'Food poisoning.'

'And, whit's this?' Janet pointed at Nessie lying at the foot of the bed.

'A teaching aid for next term,' Harper supplied, reaching for the glass of water on the cabinet to her left.

'And *this?*' Janet stood at the door waiting for an answer. Harper followed her gaze and nearly died of shock when she found Rocco Penhaligon lying beside her, face buried in the pillows, one arm dangling off the bed, fingers almost touching the floor. Looking as if he'd been there all night.

'I – don't know. I thought he'd gone back to his own room after he helped me back into bed and . . .'

'Och, wheesh.' Janet waved away her protests, laughing. 'Ah'm only kidding, whit you get up to is none of my business. Good morning Rocco,' she greeted as he stirred and then flipped over on his back.

'Morning, Janet. What time is it? I must have fallen asleep.' He didn't look in the least concerned at being found in the same bed as Harper. 'More to the point, how's the patient?' Rolling over onto his left-hand side he propped his head on his hand and sent Harper a concerned look.

'Grim,' the reply came back, 'but better than last night. Thank you for looking after me. You went above and beyond the call of duty.' There, that should let Janet know that nothing untoward had gone on during the wee small hours of the night. Not, as she'd just said, it was any of her business.

Still . . .

'I would say it was a pleasure but we know that isn't true.' He leapt off the bed, apparently refreshed by a good night's sleep. 'I'm heading for the bathroom and a shower. Do you want to use it first?' He paused, meaningfully. Harper listened to her body but the gurglings and groanings had stopped.

'I think I'll just lie still.'

'Breakfast?' Janet asked.

'I might never eat again,' Harper said.

'Och, you'll soon get over it. I never touch fish unless I've cooked it myself. And certainly none of that fancy-schmancy sushi-stuff.' Giving a shudder Janet left the room. 'See you downstairs, Rocco. I'm guessing you want breakfast?'

'Yes, I'm starving, but in deference to Harper's delicate state I'll forgo the Full Scottish and settle for toast and coffee.'

'Thanks.' The thought of the smell of fried food wafting up the stairs was more than Harper could stomach.

Walking round, Rocco picked up Nessie and sent Harper a long look. 'At least you look less like twins this morning. You've got more colour in your cheeks. When you feel up to it, come downstairs and sit on the decking at the back of the house. No need to get dressed, you might want to go back to bed before the morning's over. The decking gets the sun this time of day and,' he made a feeble joke, 'it has the added advantage of being close to the downstairs loo.'

'Don't.' Harper covered her face with her hands. 'I've never been so ill, or so embarrassed in all my life.'

Sitting down on her side of the bed Rocco removed her hands from her face and held them. 'Look on the positive side –'

'There's a positive side?' Harper pulled a comical face, unconvinced.

'Yes, I didn't have to hose you down in the shower, like Pen.'

'Thank the lord for small mercies.' Rocco continued holding her hands and seemed in no hurry to release them. Raising his head, their eyes met and something passed between them, an acknowledgement that some things had resolved themselves. For a few seconds neither spoke. Then he released her hands and headed for the bedroom door.

'Wait until I've showered and we'll go downstairs together, in case your legs buckle under you.'

'Okay.' Harper replied, vowing that the last thing she would sanction was being helped downstairs by Rocco Penhaligon as if she was his granny. She'd see how she felt after sitting on the patio in the sunshine. She had to be fighting fit for Ariel's return.

Having food poisoning hadn't changed a thing.

* * *

The following evening Harper felt confident enough to venture across the road and into the garden overlooking the loch. Her stomach had stopped doing an impression of Krakatoa before it erupted and she hadn't vomited for twenty-four hours. So far, so good. She took her iPhone out of her pocket, fitted her ear pods and chose a track on Spotify. She'd persuaded Rocco to leave her on her own as she suspected he had business of his own to attend to. Business which didn't include her. Well, whatever it was, it hadn't necessitated him driving there in the Land Rover so she assumed he'd stayed in Plockton visiting old friends and acquaintances.

He'd mentioned something about visiting the laird, but beyond that – nothing.

As she'd reminded herself a couple of days ago, Rocco Penhaligon was an enigma wrapped in a conundrum. He might have looked after her with kindness and consideration while she'd been ill but nothing had really changed. Sighing, she adjusted the volume on her phone and let the temperate air wrap itself around her, breathing in the scent of roses and honeysuckle in the herbaceous border.

Counting on her fingers, she tried to work out how long it had been since she left Polzenith. Tried to make sense of the whirlwind which had been the last few days.

Friday – end of term and the mad race to Bristol only to find the birds had flown. *Saturday* – Leicester and then Penrith where she'd met Morwenna and her daughters. *Sunday* – travelling along the M6 and M74 with a towel draped over her head, spending the night in a cow byre. *Monday* – Plockton and a respite after all the travelling, discovering that the youngsters were okay. *Tuesday* – breakfast in this lovely garden and the feeling that she and Rocco could, at the very least, remain friends when all this was over. Then he'd dropped, oh so casually, into the conversation that he'd prefer her to leave after the pub quiz. *Wednesday* – Inverness and food poisoning. Yesterday *Thursday*, being looked after and treated as if she was somehow precious to him.

Today, *Friday*, left to her own devices but with strict instructions to ring him on his mobile if she felt unwell.

Suck it up, Harper, she advised herself. This is how it's going to be from now until you leave. She huffed, annoyed at herself for missing Rocco's company and the attention he'd shown her whilst she was ill. Pathetic. She stared cross Loch Carron chewing her bottom lip.

Earlier, Hugh Morrison had rung saying he planned on being home for the pub quiz the day after tomorrow, bringing the teenagers with him.

Rocco had played the conversation over speaker phone so Harper could listen. Morrison's tetchy tone had been unmistakable and Harper had mirrored Rocco's amused grin. Morrison had spent five days in Ariel's company and it was clear he couldn't wait to hand her over to her aunt for safekeeping – or for throwing down a well.

Whichever suited her best.

'Bo Peep,' Rocco had said at the end of the phone call. 'Janet was right.'

Harper had joined in with his laughter while keeping from him that having Ariel staying at Heron Croft, even for a couple of days, would require her to up her game.

Heaving a sigh, she shuffled her song list and one of her favourite tracks played. The best thing about listening to music through headphones was that no one knew what you were listening to and couldn't judge you. She closed her eyes letting her mind concentrate on the music, enjoying the peace and tranquillity.

When she was tapped lightly on the shoulder she sat upright and removed her ear pods. Turning, she found Rocco behind her, rug draped over his shoulder and carrying two glasses and a bottle of wine. 'Warm enough?' he inquired.

'Perfect, thanks.'

Putting the bottle and glasses on the garden table he joined her on the bench and draped the rug over her knees.

'Really, there's no need. I'm much, much better.'

'You're breaking the basic rules of the doctor/patient code, I'm the one who decides if you're well enough, or not.'

'Really?' The old fire was back in her eyes.

'Please, indulge me. I'm enjoying the moment.'

'What moment?'

'You. With your defences down. Spending time with an Harper MacDonald who is a million miles away from the starchy creature who came into my garage breathing fire a week ago.'

Ha. So! He'd been counting the days, too.

'I was stressed over Ariel, no change there. However, looking back I can see that I was out of order and shouldn't have shouted at you in front of your men.'

'No, you shouldn't,' he agreed. 'Neither should I have made you ride pillion all the way to Penrith.'

'Agreed. So, we're quits?' She presented her knuckles to him for a 'fist bump'. Rocco reached for her hand, turned it over and uncurled her fingers. Startled, Harper shied away but Rocco caught her hand, twining his fingers through hers.

'Harper –'

'Rocco, I –'

'No, listen. It's taken a bout of food poisoning to let the real you shine through. And, guess what? I much prefer *Harper MacDonald 2.0.* The other day, I did or said something which seriously pissed you off. I don't want to go back to how we were: arguing, being awkward just to prove a point. We have so little time before the kids return and we have to act like responsible adults.' He looked at her with a steady gaze. 'Except, I don't feel like acting as an adult, responsible or otherwise.'

Harper let his words sink in. 'I'm not quite sure what you're proposing.'

'Neither am I,' he laughed. 'As a starter, let's have a couple of glasses of wine and watch the sun disappear behind the hills. It'll start to get cold soon and we should go indoors.'

'O-h-kay,' Harper drew out the syllables.

Rocco poured out the wine and touched her glass with his own. 'Slainte.'

'Slainte Mhath.'

'Spoken like a native.' They drank their wine in silence and then Harper, deciding it was her turn to move things along, topped them up. 'A cheeky little wine, wouldn't you say, Miss MacDonald?'

'To the point of impertinence, Mr Penhaligon.' Their glasses chinked and the wine started its slow progress through Harper's bloodstream, making her relax and forget all about the day after tomorrow. She gave a contented sigh. When they'd finished their wine Rocco took Harper's glass and put it on the table.

'Is it me, or has it suddenly become much colder?'

'The temperature has dropped,' Harper agreed, although it would have been more accurate to say it had risen by several degrees.

'In which case, shall we –'

Standing, he draped the rug over his shoulder as a highlander would his plaid and extended his hand. Harper was no teenager. In taking his hand she knew exactly what she was agreeing to. Momentarily she faltered, and then looked into his face for reassurance. His countenance was open and his eyes, bright in the fading twilight, made it clear that the final decision was hers. No pressure. Harper took a deep breath and then released it. Dammit; it was time she took a risk. The risk being that at the end of her stay she would find it hard to walk away from Rocco Penhaligon, Plockton and the promise of a different life.

A life that possibly wasn't on offer but the thought of which beguiled her nonetheless.

In that instant she decided whatever happened, she wouldn't return to the same old/same old in Polzenith. She'd give a term's notice, hand in the keys of her rented house and, on the last day of term, leave Polzenith. Go somewhere hot, kick back and decide what she *really* wanted from life.

A great weight lifted off her shoulders and she smiled at Rocco.

'Let's go indoors,' she said, taking his hand.

'Sure?'

'Never surer.' That might have been stretching the truth but she didn't want to appear like some buttoned-up spinster who hadn't had sex in a l-o-o-n-g time. Rocco's lopsided smile told Harper that he didn't know where tonight would lead, either, but was willing to take a chance.

'You know,' he said slowly, 'everyone assumes we're sleeping together. It seems a shame to disappoint them.' Harper nodded and then frowned. She'd spent most of her adult life worrying about what people thought of her. Tonight would be different.

Holding hands they crossed Harbour Street to Heron Croft and entered the house. Rocco closed the front door and led her into the kitchen, still warm from the summer heat, the air redolent of Janet's cock-a-leekie soup. After draping the rug over the back of a chair he turned, picked her up and sat her on the edge of the kitchen table. Prising her knees gently apart he stepped between her thighs, pressing himself close. There was no mistaking his arousal as he removed the scrunchy and pins from her hair, allowing the dark tangle of curls to settle around her shoulders.

'There, that's better,' he said, teasing out tendrils to frame her face.

His touch was gentle, non-threatening. Harper closed her eyes and drew in a shaky breath, all this was new, uncertain. She tried to remember the last man who'd touched her like this but no man had ever been allowed to get this close. In her mind's eye she saw a procession of 'men in suits', county advisers, education officials and other headteachers – men she'd dated because there was no opportunity to date outside her circle. However, because of the incestuous, gossip-ridden nature of the profession she had never allowed matters to progress beyond a good night kiss. Like Caesar's wife she had to be above suspicion; she couldn't allow her professional reputation to be tarnished by dating married men or those with a dubious track record.

'Harper, open your eyes, sweetheart.,' Rocco tilted her chin. 'When I kiss you I want you to know it's me, not Anthony, the ninja-next-door.' Opening her eyes, she laughed and slapped his hand away, disguising that his use of *sweetheart* had made her last defences crumble.

'Not funny, Penhaligon.'

'That's better, relax. More like the old you, but not too much.' Moving his head closer he pressed his lips against her, the lightest of kisses. Then he pulled back, 'Strawberries –'

'What?'

'Strawberries. Bad, very bad.'

'Because ?'

'Because it means you've eaten the last strawberry yoghurt. The one I hid at the back of the fridge. Such underhand tactics might be the norm for Pen, but quite frankly I expected better of you. I'm shocked, I tell you Miss MacDonald. Shocked.' Shaking his head, he turned away.

Harper laughed and, emboldened, turned his face back towards her. 'It was a macro-biotic yoghourt and I thought, given my delicate condition over the last couple of days, you wouldn't object. Let me make it up to you.'

'Not sure that's possible. But, if you insist . . . what do you propose?'

'I thought, perhaps, a kiss?'

He appeared unconvinced. 'I should warn you, in these matters the first kiss is generally considered a deal breaker.'

'That so?'

'According to every authority on the subject,' Rocco feigned surprise at her ignorance.

Grabbing the collar of his polo shirt she pulled him closer and kissed him for all she was worth. When they drew apart their faces were flushed and their breaths came in shallow gasps as though they'd run a marathon.

'Wh-where did you learn to kiss like that?' Rocco asked, stunned

'Well, not at Sunday School, that's for certain,' Harper quipped.

'Behind the bike sheds?'

'I couldn't possibly comment.' She adopted a lofty expression, hiding her pleasure at their teasing war of words. Delight fizzed through her like a firework, leaving a trail of joy in its wake, making her feel alive and as far removed from her usual circumspect self as was possible to imagine. Taking the light-hearted flirting a step further she regarded him seriously. 'More evidence is needed before I can reach a proper conclusion.'

'Of?'

'You as a great kisser.'

'Indeed?' Rocco's raised eyebrow suggested he couldn't believe further proof was necessary.

'Absolutely. There is a precedence, I believe.'

'Based on what, exactly?'

'The accepted rule that scientific fact should always be subjected to further experimentation, to eliminate the chance of a fluke occurrence.'

'You think that kiss was a fluke?'

'I'm simply saying it could be. Best of three?'

'Very well,' he sighed, as though kissing her was too taxing for words. 'If we must.' They exchanged another passionate kiss and this time Rocco's fingers teased the shirt out of the waistband of her shorts. Then he drew back. 'How did I do?'

She pulled a face and wiggled her hand from side to side, implying that the kiss had been so-so. 'Good, but slightly ruined, if I'm being honest, by your churlish attitude regarding the yoghourt.'

'Sorry about that. Do you think more proof is needed?'

'I do.'

He bent his head towards her for another kiss but she forestalled him, laying her hands on his chest and keeping him at arm's length.

'Normally, raised blood pressure and heart rate are more accurate indicators. However, we lack the proper equipment for measuring physical changes. We might have to abandon this experiment and return to it another time.'

Rocco struggled to keep a straight face.

'I do have a smartwatch. We could, in theory, continue this quasi-scientific experiment right here, right now.' Rocco curled an arm round her waist and held his wrist at an angle so they could both see the watch. 'Ready?'

'I think so.' Harper wriggled her bottom trying to find a more comfortable position on the table. She sent him a severe look. 'Just remember, this is for the advancement of science and no other reason.'

'The Penhaligons have long been engaged in the advancement of science, albeit in a different field.' When their lips touched, Harper felt the curve of his smile against her mouth. Taking in a deep, shuddering breath which made his ribcage rise and fall, Rocco kissed her as though their lives depended on it. When they pulled apart, Harper took hold of Rocco's wrist and pretended to read the stats on his watch. This was all for show because she wasn't wearing her reading glasses and could only focus on his face

'Hm, aerobic activity un-n-naturally high,' she stammered.

'Unsurprising.'

'Should we be making notes?'

'There's pen and paper on the bookcase in the sitting room. We should do this properly. Then, if either of us is dissatisfied with the result, we'll bring the experiment to a halt and settle instead for buying more yoghourts from the village store when it opens in the morning. Agreed.'

'Agreed.' They shook on it.

'Shall we?'

'Why not?'

Rocco scooped her up into his arms and carried her across the sitting room threshold, like a bride on her wedding day. After laying her on the squashy sofa he walked over to the bookcase and began searching for writing materials.

'Pen, paper,' he said, laying them on the coffee table. Then he knelt on the floor by her side. 'Let's move on to stage two, shall we?'

'How many stages are there?' There was a slight tremor in her voice, a mixture of nerves and anticipation.

'As many as you like, it's your call. We can stop or –'

'I don't want to stop,' Harper was full of conviction. 'Do you?'

'What do you think?' Remaining on his knees he shuffled closer to the sofa and was suddenly serious. 'Can I lay down beside you?' Harper nodded. 'Hooch up, then.'

Harper wriggled further back so that he could lie alongside her. He turned towards her until they were practically nose to nose, which made Harper's eyes cross. She giggled. Inching closer, Rocco began unfastening the buttons on her shirt. Each unbuttoning followed by a brief, teasing kiss.

'Wait.' He removed his watch and dropped it on to the floor. 'It might spontaneously combust. Here,' he laid her hand over his breast bone. 'That's down to you, Miss MacDonald.' His heart beat out, strong and true under Harper's palm and hers matched his, beat for beat.

'Oh,' she said as he parted her shirt and unfastened the clasp of her front-fastening bra with deft fingers. 'Wh – where did you learn to do that?' Harper didn't really want to know the answer.

'I'm a paid-up member of the Magic Circle,' he joked. 'That move can be found on page one of Magic for Beginners.' Propping himself up on one elbow, he traced a line from her throat, past the hollow between her breasts and all the way down to her waist before peeling back the lacy cups of her bra. Then he fell silent as her breasts were revealed, nipples rosy and erect. 'Also, one doesn't spend all day wielding ratchet spanners without developing *leger de main.*'

'*Leger de main* – oh, sleight of hand. Why – you – ' Feigning disapproval, Harper made as if to slap him but he caught her hands and trapped them beneath her.

'Resistance is futile, you know that, don't you?' Lowering his head he released her imprisoned hands and then, with her off guard, took her nipple in his mouth and circled it with his tongue before sucking on it.

'F-futile' she stammered, scarcely able to breathe.

Knowing she couldn't endure the exquisite teasing a moment longer and retain the power of speech Harper raised his head so that she could kiss him on the lips. So much easier to cope with. Next, she unfastened the belt of his shorts, dragging it free of the loops before dropping in onto the floor. Surprised at her audaciousness, she undid the top button of his shorts and slid her hands downwards until she encountered the curve of his buttocks.

'Wait.' Rocco pulled his t-shirt over his head and removed her bra, burying his face in her breasts again. Harper revelled in his weight pressing her into the sofa, the rough touch of chest hairs against her hyper-sensitive breasts, his warm breath stirring her hair.

A voice Harper barely recognised as hers, let out a low moan and said: 'Oh, my good God – Rocco,' as he traced a line from the hollow of her shoulder to her ear and back to her breasts. Then he drew back, leaving her cast adrift on a sea of sensation. 'Please, don't stop.'

'I may have to. There's a small problem,' he whispered in her ear, 'I don't have any condoms. I don't usually need them when I'm in Plockton.' *Unlike when he was in Polzenith,* Harper read the sub-text but shut her mind to its implications. 'So, unless,' he raised himself up on his elbow again and looked down on her, face flushed, his expression wry and apologetic.

'Go on.'

'Unless you have a better plan, we'll have to wait until the chemist opens tomorrow –'

'– by which time, we might have,' she gulped, 'gone off the boil.'

'Unlikely, however –'

She cut across him. 'It's okay. To proceed, I mean.' That sounded as if she was directing traffic! 'I'm on the pill,' she added, which sounded *much* worse. 'You see, I – oh, never mind.' Get a grip, Harper, he doesn't need to know about your irregular, painful periods. All he – they – needed to know was that it was safe for them to make love without worrying about consequences.

He nodded and then held up a finger. 'One more thing.'

'Go on . . .' *But make it quick, or I'll think of a hundred reasons why us becoming lovers is sooooo not-a-good-idea.*

'I don't want the first time we make love to be on this sofa. We're hardly teenagers, as you so rightly pointed out in my garage.' Harper nodded and then shivered. First night nerves, closely followed by second-thoughts were starting to crowd in. Rocco seemed to understand. 'Here,' he dragged the tartan comforter off the back of the sofa and handed it to her so she could cover herself. Getting to his feet he fastened his shorts and then held out his hand. Harper took it, trustingly, and he led them back into the hall and then up the stairs. Pausing on the landing, he grinned: 'Your place or mine?'

'Yours,' Harper said without a moment's hesitation. 'Bigger bed.'

'Good choice.'

Rocco led them into his bedroom and headed, not for the bed, but for the armchair by the window. He pulled Harper on to his knee and gathered the comforter round her, holding either end and drawing her closer until she was cocooned in his arms. Then he kissed her – face, lips, throat, until she threw off the comforter and the last of her inhibitions. Nerves vanishing, she found the courage to straddle his legs. That was all the signal Rocco needed. Picking her up, he carried her over to the bed, then returned to the window and made as if to draw the curtains.

Harper held out her hand, forestalling him.

'No. Don't.'

She wanted to remember this moment, making love in the purple, golden and red of a highland summer sunset, as though they were free of responsibilities, free to choose the life they wanted. Pen and Ariel would return soon and the happy bubble of desire and contentment they were living in, would burst.

Instead of drawing the curtains Rocco walked over to the large brass bed and peeled back a corner of the duvet. Harper wriggled under it, skin goose-pimpled from a mixture of longing and trepidation. Rocco walked to the foot of the bed where Nessie was regarding them with fine Presbyterian disapproval. Picking up the toy he gave it a severe look before putting her out on landing and closing the door.

'Three-in-a-bed was never my thing,' he laughed. 'And that includes plesiosaurs.'

Laughing, Harper raised a corner of the duvet. Rocco, only too happy to comply, slipped off his shorts and climbed in beside her. And, before she knew it, the heart-hammering, mind-blowing kisses started all over again, taking them beyond the point when nothing short of a nuclear explosion could have stopped them.

Chapter Twenty-Three

Later, in the middle of the not-quite-dark Highland night, Rocco played with Harper's hair and nuzzled her neck. Their breathing was measured and regular, each heartfelt sigh echoed.

'I never knew that –' Harper struggled to find the words.

'– it could be like that?'

'Yes.' Lifting his arm she curled it round her.

'Believe me, it isn't. Not ordinarily. At least, not for me. These things take time. But since we met, our lives have been on fast forward, rushing towards this moment.' Rocco's leg stretched across her, pressing her into the mattress. 'If I'm being honest, you bewitched me from the outset, drove me crazy and made me angrier than anyone had in years.'

'I did?'

'You know you did. At the time I put the angst down to concern over Pen and my reaction to your bossiness.'

'Thanks –'

'I didn't realise at the time it was –'

'What?'

'Foreplay.'

'Really?' His breath was warm on Harper's neck and she felt a rumble of laughter deep within him.

'Of course! Think about it. I've spent more time with you over the last week than I have with any woman in the last twenty years. Except,' he paused, 'Pen's Mother. But that seems unreal, like it happened to a different me. Does that make sense?'

'Yes, I understand.' Then she laughed and snuggled closer.

'What?'

'Morwenna claimed that the tension between us stemmed from U.S.T.'

'Sounds like a particular nasty urinary tract infection.' Harper dug him in the ribs, feigning disapproval at his unromantic response.

'For your information, Penhaligon, it stands for Unresolved Sexual Tension. Ask Morwenna next time you see her.'

'I stand corrected, Miss MacDonald. I would say that's been well and truly resolved, wouldn't you?'

'Several times.' Harper marvelled that she felt relaxed enough to joke about their love-making.

Rocco came back with, 'And better each time. However, the night is young – half past three, to be precise, and I don't feel like sleeping. Do you?'

'I can't get used to these long summer nights,' Harper fudged her reply. Being intimate with Rocco was new, exciting and she alternated between boldness (more of the same, please) and shyness (I can't believe this is happening).'The way the sun barely disappears below the horizon before it rises again.'

'The downside – because, naturally there has to be one, is that winter days are long, dark and dreary unless there's a frost to paint the sky blue.' Harper smiled, from his poetic turn of phrase, it was clear that Rocco loved Scotland. 'It's trade-off, everything in life is.'

Harper moved the conversation along. 'Can I ask two questions?'

'Go ahead.' Rocco flipped over on to his back and put his hands behind his head.

'The first one's easy. That night in the tent, did you kiss me, or did I dream it?'

'You snuggled up to me for warmth, nuzzled into me as a matter of fact. What's a man to do?'

'I knew it felt too real to be a dream! However, you stopped at a kiss. Very commendable.'

'It took more willpower than I knew I possessed, however –'

'Go on –'

'At that point I believed you hated me and you can be one scary lady. I thought that, if I took matters any further without you being fully aware, you would have probably punched me on the nose. Also, that isn't how I operate.' Rocco turned sideways and kissed Harper so thoroughly that a fresh wave of desire washed over her.

'Okay, I get it.' Rocco Penhaligon didn't force himself on women because he didn't need to.

'Next question –'

'More personal. Sorry. When we were at my parents' house, I told you everything about myself. Sang like a canary. Not quite sure how that happened.' She laughed and turned on her side.

'I can be pretty persuasive when I put my mind to it.'

'I'm usually more circumspect,' she went on. 'However, on that occasion I was overwhelmed with the desire to brain you with one of my mother's awards. Telling you my backstory seemed safer.'

'Narrow escape, then?' He laughed, walking his fingers from her navel to the shadowy space between her breasts, cupping her left breast with a warm hand. Harper smacked his hand away, she wasn't going to be side-tracked. This chance might never present itself again.

'Indulge me.'

'Anything.'

'I understand, from Morwenna, that Pen's mother moved in and then –'

'In the words of the song: like the autumn leaves she drifted away. Actually, drifted is the wrong adjective, I woke up one morning to discover that Lorelei –' Harper felt rather than saw Rocco wince at the pretentious name. Then he'd been naïve and infatuated; but time and distance put a different spin on their relationship.

'Go on,' she encouraged.

'– had done a bunk along with the others, leaving me, Polzenith and a pile of debts behind. Debts, I later discovered she could easily have paid. But that was all part of the game, pretending she was a free spirit, untrammelled by material possessions. Nothing could have been further from the truth. I paid what she and the other *free spirits* owed the village store, cleared their slate at the Fisherman's Arms. After all, I planned on making my life in the village and didn't want people blaming me for their behaviour. Polzenith isn't like St Ives and other Cornish holiday towns – it's less tourist-y, people are poor and every penny counts.'

'And then?'

'Not so much as a postcard. I knew they were planning to spend the winter in Goa and naïvely assumed that I'd be travelling with them. Plainly, they had other ideas. The morning I discovered they'd left, I stood at the window overlooking the churned up village green believing that, if I stared long and hard enough, I could conjure them up. Bring them back. Time and subsequent events put paid to that romantic idea.'

'Oh, Rocco.' Harper manoeuvred herself so that she was lying close to him. 'You must have felt awful.' Taking his face in her hands she attempted to kiss away the pain, hurt and bad memories. Rocco gently put her aside and carried on with his story, as though sharing it helped to expiate his demons.

'Then reality kicked in. She didn't want me, she just wanted a respite from living in a converted ambulance and sharing rudimentary sanitary arrangements with half a dozen other hippies. Sharing each other's beds, too, for all I knew. I felt a bloody fool for falling for her lies and with hindsight, realised that all I represented was a shower and a shag.' Harper winced at his bitter tone. 'Did I mention how miserable I was?' Rocco joked, lightening up.

'Once or twice.'

He pulled Harper back on top of him as though the physical contact helped him to retell the story. Having started unburdening himself he seemed unable to stop. 'All I could hope for was that they'd return in the spring and we'd pick up where we'd left off. One of the reasons I bought the garage was so I'd be there when she returned. I then discovered how much I enjoyed mending things, tinkering with cars, fixing broken agricultural implements, nursing old tractors back to health – just about anything. It's in my blood. Hardly along the same lines as Penhaligon's Aeronautics, but good enough. Anyway, in August of the following year, just as I'd given up hope of ever hearing from her, two old hippies rocked up at the garage with Pen – three months old, in a Moses basket.'

That much she knew from Morwenna and Ariel.

'That must have been quite a shock.'

'You could say that. Seemingly, his mother had flown back to the UK from India while it was still safe to travel and given birth to our son in the Lindo Wing of St Mary's Hospital.'

'Where the royals have their babies?'

'The same. However, she wanted to return to the commune in Mysore to study Ashtanga yoga which, seemingly, was more important than bringing up our son. The hippies' parting shot as they left Pen in the Moses basket at my feet was: *she'll be in touch.*' Something in the pit of Harper's stomach contracted at *'our* son', however she was given little time to examine her feelings because Rocco ploughed on with his story. 'After that, and over the intervening years, nothing. Zilch. I've made it clear to Pen that when – *if* – he wants to take the *Who Do You Think You Are?* path and seek her out, I'll support him every step of the way.'

'But how?'

'Her name's on the birth certificate. Tracing her wouldn't be too hard, not these days when we're all stamped, catalogued and indexed.'

'Oh, Rocco.' Reaching out, Harper found his hand and linked fingers. 'But what if she *did* return?'

He shrugged. 'Unlikely after all this time. I imagine that she tired of the hippy dream, married some wanker-banker and is living in the Home Counties, pretending she doesn't have a son. Didn't spend a summer living above a garage in a Cornish ex-mining village with a university dropout.' Raising her hand to his lips, he kissed each finger in turn.

'It's almost five am and soon it will be morning. Time's running out. Morrison will bring Pen and Ariel home the day after tomorrow and *this* – our needs and desires will take second place to sorting them out. Let's make the most of the time we have left.'

He traced a line downwards, his questing fingers seeking out the sweet spot which brought Harper fulfilment. Arching her back, she gave herself up to the physical release her body craved – and backstories, vanishing mothers, runaway teenagers and worries about the future were temporarily forgotten.

* * *

At first, Rocco thought the commotion outside Heron Croft was the bin men. Then he remembered it was Saturday and even the most conscientious refuse collector didn't work at the weekend. Getting out of bed he took a long drink from the glass of water on the bedside table and ambled over to the window to see what was causing the ruckus.

'Fuck-a-duck,' he exclaimed.

On the pavement below was Pen and a leggy creature with a thick golden plait hanging down her back. They were arguing furiously and Pen's usually untroubled countenance was dark as thunder. Thinking on his feet, Rocco collected Harper's clothes, raced across the landing to her room and threw them on the bed. Then he dragged the dressing gown off its peg behind the door and dashed back to his bedroom with it.

'Harper, Harper, wake up.'

'Mm? What is it?'

'The kids. They're a day early. Come on. They can't find us like this.'

'Oh, my good God.' Rocco draped the dressing gown round her shoulders, bundled her onto the landing and propelled her towards her bedroom with a cheeky pat on her bottom. Glancing over her shoulder she nodded to indicate his nakedness, made a face and then closed the door behind her.

Rocco pulled on pyjama bottoms and a t-shirt just as the front door opened and Pen called up the stairs.

'Dad it's me. Pen.'

'*And* Ariel,' a voice asserted.

'And Ariel,' Pen confirmed, wearily.

Rocco checked the time, almost twelve o'clock. Being in pyjamas was going to take some explaining, and as for Harper . . . Sensibly, she appeared back on the landing and, after some furious miming, headed for the bathroom. Once the shower was running, Rocco leaned over the bannister and shouted down to his son.

'Be with you directly. You and I need to talk.' There, that'd put him off guard, distract him.

'Yes Dad,' was Pen's resigned reply.

'We are *so* dead,' Ariel hissed at Pen before stomping further into the kitchen and opening the fridge so forcibly that bottles in the door rattled. Rocco hoped that he and Harper could keep the teenagers on the back foot and prevent them from picking up on what was going on between them.

The front door opened and Hugh Morrison entered dragging a couple of rucksacks behind him. 'I'll leave your bags there, shall I? No, really, it's no problem. No need to thank me.' His sarcasm soared right over the teenagers' heads and he received a '*Cool*,' from Pen, and a casual '*Whatev's*' from Ariel.

Dumping the rucksacks, Morrison glared at his erstwhile protégés. Hiding a smile, Rocco stopped himself saying: *Welcome to my world* as he walked downstairs. Greeting Morrison with a curt nod he received a snarled 'Penhaligon,' in return. If Hugh was surprised to find him in his pyjamas he gave no indication. He looked more concerned with returning the teenagers and high-tailing it for his cottage where he would doubtless down a dram or two of Laphroiag.

So far, so good.

Rocco walked over to Pen and Ariel who were shoulder barging each other out of the way and raiding the fridge. Asserting his authority Rocco stopped them with: 'You two. Come away from the fridge and sit down at the table.' Apparently deciding that getting him onside was a good idea they did as instructed.

Rocco looked at his son and then raised an enquiring eyebrow.

'Sorry, sorry. Dad, Ariel. Ariel, Dad.' Then he slumped down in his chair and looked out of the window, evidently anticipating the dressing down heading his way before the day was out.

'Hello Mr Penhaligon,' Ariel greeted, seemingly unfazed by the situation. 'Or can I call you Rocco?' Pulling her plait over one shoulder she played with the end of it, teasingly, and sent him a coquettish look.

'I think, given the circumstances it should be Mr Penhaligon.'

Ariel, openly displeased at having her friendly overture rejected, countered with: 'Why are you wearing pyjamas at this time in the morning? And where's my aunt?'

Resisting the urge to reply: *we'll be the ones asking the questions,* like a badly drawn character in a war film, Rocco ignored her. 'Sit down Morrison, I was just about to make brunch. You're welcome to stay, unless you have other plans?'

'Thanks, I'll take you up on it. I'm not sure if my housekeeper received my text about us returning a day early and stocking the fridge. Also, I would like to meet Ariel's aunt.' He and Ariel exchanged a significant look then she tossed her plait over her shoulder, followed by another *whatever* shrug.

'To be honest, we weren't expecting you until tomorrow.'

'Things didn't work out quite as planned,' Hugh explained. 'The weather forecast predicted a front moving in from the north so I thought it sensible to head home.' Sensing tension between him and Ariel, Rocco willed Harper to join them. Dealing with Pen was one thing, but he felt woefully underequipped when it came to handling her niece. Judging from his glowering expression Hugh Morrison felt exactly the same.

Walking over to the pantry he returned with a skillet, fresh eggs, bread and butter. He slapped them on the counter top and then headed to the fridge for bacon, tomatoes and mushrooms. Standing in front of the fridge brought back last night, the strawberry yoghurt and what had happened afterwards. What he wouldn't give to send them all packing, return to his warm bed with Harper and spend all day making love?

He sighed; that wasn't possible.

'Any chance of eggy bread, Dad?' Pen asked in a blatant attempt to remind Rocco of brunches shared in their garage eyrie.

'Not today.' Turning, Rocco leaned against the sink and sent his son a severe look. He needn't think everything was forgiven and forgotten because they'd decided to return to Plockton of their own accord. He and Ariel had caused a major upheaval in his and Harper's lives, they needed to learn that actions carried consequences and that the day of reckoning was at hand.

'Okay. Cool.' However, his glum expression didn't quite match his nonchalant response.

Ariel walked over to the counter top, took one look at the food and pouted. 'I don't eat bacon or eggs, I'm vegan.' It was plain from Pen's expression that her conversion to veganism was a new development. 'Is there anything else to eat?'

'Not unless you fetch it from the village shop and cook it yourself. Leave what you can't eat.' How did Harper cope with her twenty-four-seven? The word *Minx* sprang to mind, old-fashioned but appropriate. Pen, despite his grandparents' best efforts to spoil him, was far easier to handle. Rocco gave silent thanks for that and instructed Pen to lay the table. He didn't ask Ariel to help, for the moment she was a guest in the house and other than tidying up her bedroom and packing for the journey south, nothing more was required of her. Also, he had a sneaking suspicion that she'd refuse to do anything he asked, which would lead to more confrontation and make things worse.

Suppressing his annoyance he made his way over to the coffee pot. It was then that he noticed a large purple and green bruise on Morrison's forehead.

'Wildlife fight back, Morrison?'

Acting as if he'd forgotten the bruise, Morrison raised his hand to it and winced. 'Oh, that. Banged my forehead on the low ceiling in the hide where we were trying to photograph corncrakes on their nest.'

'Who knew that photographing wildlife could be so dangerous? Must have hurt,' Rocco said, his expression dead pan.

'Oh, it did,' Ariel confirmed, gleefully. 'Saw stars, didn't you,

Hughie?' A look passed between them, alluding to something other than her temerity at addressing the BAFTA winning wildlife documentary maker, *Hughie*.

'At least I got my photograph,' he said, changing the subject.

'Result, then.' Rocco turned his attention to cooking the bacon, mushrooms, and tomatoes in the skillet and whisking eggs to scramble in the microwave.

'Of a kind. The bumblebee eluded me, I'm afraid.'

'Bumblebee?' Rocco asked.

'*Bombus distinguendus*, to be precise. Did I say that right, Hughie?' Rocco could almost hear Morrison grinding his teeth as he kept his temper in check.

'Yes. Or, in layman's terms,' he glanced at Rocco, making plain that he fell into that category, 'the great yellow bumblebee.'

'Don't you just hate it when that happens?' Rocco couldn't resist adding.

Ariel snorted while Pen looked displeased at his father not showing his hero due deference.

Fortunately, Harper, freshly scrubbed and with damp hair hanging round her shoulders, descended the stairs. She paused on the bottom tread and surveyed the scene with one hand on the newel post. Although he remembered every second of last night's lovemaking, Rocco guarded his expression to hide the exact nature of their relationship from Ariel and Pen.

And, although he was relieved to have his son back safe and sound, part of him felt cheated by the cuckoos' early return to the nest, ruining his and Harper's last day together.

There were things he wanted, *needed* to say to Harper which would now be left unsaid unless the right opportunity presented itself . . . buying the garage, relocating to Plockton, his plans for the future, a future he hoped would include Harper. Maybe they could snatch a few moments alone later this evening?

Another quiet groan, this time of despair. Turning his back, he got on with making brunch.

Chapter Twenty-Four

Ariel ran over to her aunt. 'Auntie Harper, I've missed you. So much.' 'Really? Could have fooled me.' Harper's response was cool, suspicious. If Ariel thought for one minute that she could charm her way out of this she was mistaken. However, Harper was relieved to find the runaway safe and sound, so she hugged her and pushed the too-long fringe out of her eyes. Ariel was the closest she'd get to having a daughter and, in spite of everything, Harper loved her. Although at that precise moment she was less concerned with welcoming her home and more with letting her know how far she'd overstepped the mark.

She guessed that Rocco felt the same about Pen. However, when she glanced over at him the thought went out of her head as she remembered... how his eyes had lit up the first time he'd seen her naked, the way his mouth had quirked when he'd said: *God, you are beautiful*, using humour as a foil against their runaway emotions.

Now he was studiously ignoring her and she totally got that. Right now, she and Rocco occupied the moral high ground. However, if Pen and Ariel found out that they were lovers, everything would be flipped on its head. Coughing to draw attention to himself, Hugh got to his feet, moved Ariel none too gently out of the way and extended his hand to Harper.

'Hugh Morrison,' he announced somewhat unnecessarily. 'Enchante dear lady, enchante.' Then he raised her hand to his lips and kissed the air above it with old-world courtesy. There was something about Morrison that struck Harper as phoney. From 'dirty blond' hair swept back off his forehead like a lion's mane, golden highlights artfully woven through it to appear as though burnished by the sun and not his hairdresser in Inverness. His eyebrows were a tad too well-shaped, teeth too perfect and his skin showed no signs of the weathering one might expect from a man who spent hours in the driving rain waiting for the money shot.

It all jarred with Harper and plainly Ariel thought the same.

Taking a backward step, she made the twitter 'hashtag' symbol behind his back with crossed fingers and mouthed: *knob head*. Plainly, standards had slipped during the time she'd spent in his company. It would be the devil's own job to rein her in.

'Harper, would you and Ariel mind laying the table? I asked Pen but he's got better things to do, evidently.' Pen was perched on the end of the kitchen table looking through the viewfinder of his expensive camera at the shots he'd taken on his wildlife safari. Removing her hand from Morrison's grasp, Harper sent Rocco a silent thanks.

'Sure.' She smiled, but her expression advised Ariel to do as Rocco asked.

'By the way, Morrison, do let us know if you're out of pocket as a result of taking Pen and Ariel north with you.'

Hugh turned towards Rocco and waved away his concern. 'Not at all, old man. My pleasure to show them the beauty of Durness. Pen's beginning to show real promise as a wildlife photographer.' He didn't mention what talents Ariel had demonstrated on their trip. 'It was a surprise, although a delightful one,' he assured Harper with an insincere smile, 'to discover Pen had brought a friend along with him.'

'I can imagine,' Harper commented.

Now she began to wonder if Pen actually *had* dragged Ariel all the way to Durness to stop him from being lonely and to deflect the flak which would descend on him once he and his father were reunited.

With his white blond hair, blue eyes and winning smile it was clear he'd learned to charm the birds out of the trees as soon as he could walk. However, judging from Rocco's expression, he'd have his work cut out to win his father round.

'It was really, cool, Dad.' Putting down his camera, Pen turned towards Rocco with shining eyes. 'I've got some amazing shots, thanks to Hugh. He's a great teacher.' Morrison dismissed Pen's fulsome praise with a gracious wave of his hand.

'Come off it, Penhaligon.' Ariel walked over to the table, picked up Pen's expensive camera and flicked through a few frames. 'Tell the truth and shame the devil, isn't that what you always say, Auntie Harper? Okay, looks like it's up to me to tell it like it really was. The hide where we spent most of our time smelled of pee. Seriously.' Ariel shuddered. 'It's alright for men, God's given them the right equipment for peeing in the heather. When I wanted to *go*, Pen had to keep lookout in case a walker went past. Humiliat-o! Then both gave me an earful because one day I got bored, went off on my own and disturbed those cornflakes –'

' – *crakes!*' Pen and Morrison chorused, tutting. Ariel's innocent look made it plain that she was deliberately antagonising them.

'You two made it perfectly clear from the get-go that I was unwanted, just so much excess baggage. To think that I turned down a trip to L.A to spend days in the heather with only the midges and glassy eyed sheep for distraction.'

'Oh, be fair Ariel,' Pen began.

'I am being totally fair. I've been put off Scotland for life.'

'Brunch,' Rocco announced, and then paused midway between the cooker and the table. 'Plates? Cups, saucers, cutlery? Anyone?'

'Of course.' Unconsciously taking on the role of chatelaine, Harper moved Pen's precious camera out of the way and organised him and Ariel to lay the table, the light in her eyes brooking no refusal. They were in trouble and they'd better remember it. Then she got the coffee machine up and running and after a few minutes, they all sat down to brunch.

* * *

Later, when Hugh Morrison had taken his leave and Pen was stacking the dishwasher, Harper and Ariel climbed the stairs to the latter's bedroom and closed the door. Soon after that, Rocco and Pen left Heron Croft and made their way across Harbour Street to the garden overlooking the loch.

Show time.

Harper sat on the edge of Ariel's bed as she rooted through the clutter on her dressing table and picked dirty laundry up off the floor. It was so out of character for Ariel to tidy up that Harper suspected – no, *knew*- she was using it as a distraction technique.

'So?' was Harper's opener.

Ariel joined her on the bed. 'I screwed up. I shouldn't have taken off with Pen. My bad.'

'Indeed. You should have talked to me about not wanting to stay with Shona. We could have sorted something out. Instead –'

'Instead I went off in search of adventure and ended up eaten alive by midges, getting mud on my best jeans and spending time in the company of two of the most boring men on the planet, obsessed with photographing a freakin' bumble bee.'

'Not to mention forcing me to cancel our travel arrangements and come in search of you.'

'To be fair,' Ariel ventured, pushing her luck, 'you didn't *have* to come in search of me.'

'To be fair,' Harper snapped back, 'I did. This may come as a surprise, Ariel, but until you are with your mother, I stand in *loco parentis*, and am responsible for you.'

'Not really. I'm eighteen – legally and mentally capable of looking after myself.'

'You have a strange way of showing it. Taking off with a boy I'd never heard of. As far as I, or his father knew, you were going to rock up at Gretna Green, get married and ruin both your futures.'

Ariel burst out laughing.

'You've read too many romances, Auntie Harper. Rock up at Gretna

Green? If you want to shack up with a boy, you just do. You don't have to be married these days to have sex.'

'You know all about that, I suppose?' She willed Ariel to contradict her.

'FYI – Pen and I haven't slept together. We don't see each other in *that way*. In fact it would almost be incest –'

'Incest?'

'Relax. I simply mean that everyone says we could pass for brother and sister. Just because we are both drop-dead gorgeous, have blond hair and blue eyes. ' No one could ever accuse Ariel of false modesty. 'Credit me with some intelligence. He's just a mate, right? Unlike in your day, back in the dark ages, girls and boys can simply be friends.'

Harper ignored the *dark ages* comment. 'If you say so.'

'I do say so.' Cue exaggerated eye-rolling.

'That doesn't let you off the hook for leaving your grandparents' house looking like a tip, waking half the neighbourhood, upsetting the neighbours . . .'

'Neighbours? You mean Anthony? Oh, he's such an old woman and he hates me. Kept saying that he could expect no better from me, given how my mother has behaved.'

Harper frowned, it was not his place to chastise her niece or run down her family, but she wasn't going to be side-tracked. Ariel was good at that. 'Okay, let's forget about him. Before we leave Plockton you will ring your grandmother's cleaner, ask her to put everything straight so that when they return from holiday everything will be hunky-dory. I believe your mother's paid your summer allowance? You can pay her out of that. I'd take you back there myself and stand over you until it was done but I don't see why you should clean the house while the Penhaligon boy gets off Scott free.'

'*Scott free?* Nice one, given where we are,' Ariel chuckled. 'Of course, I'll make everything good. I would have done so at the time but Pen was so anxious to keep his date with Hugh Morrison that he practically dragged me out of the door.'

'Okay.'

'Honestly, talk about kiss his ass. No need to give me 'the look', Auntie. It's been Hugh-this, Hugh-that, Hugh-three-bags-bloody-full for the last week. Nauseating. I can't believe that I thought he was a cool dude.'

'Morrison?'

'God, no. Pen. All the girls in the sixth form loved him. Felt sorry for him because he was dumped on his father's doorstep by some saggy-titted hippies, in a Tesco's carrier bag.'

'Moses basket,' Harper corrected.

' -and was forced to live above the garage with his scary dad.'

'Scary?' She didn't see Rocco in that light.

'Yes, scary. To be honest, Auntie Harper, Mr Penhaligon makes you seem laid back.'

'Thanks.'

'I will admit, though, he is kinda hot, for an old guy I mean. It's a bit weird though, you have to admit.'

'What is?' Harper stopped herself leaping to Rocco's defence

'Well, over brunch, Hughie,' another snort of derision, 'kept flirting with you, passing you the salt, freshening your coffee. That sort of thing. He calls it good manners, old world charm, I call it being seriously creepy. He can't see a woman under eighty without hitting on her, it's almost pathological. Mr Penhaligon, on the other hand – I'm to call him that until further notice, *apparently*,' a toss of the head, 'barely looks at you. It's as if –'

'Go on.'

'– he doesn't even like you.'

'That's to be expected. In his eyes, my niece encouraged his son to turn his back on a promising academic career.'

'Is that what he thinks? He needs a reality check. To be honest, Pen's no brain box. He only got his place at Oxford because his great-grandparents endowed the college with a bursary to ensure state school pupils stand a chance at getting a place there. Apparently, the Penhaligons always study there. Except for his dad who dropped out of Bristol Uni, got some grungy hippy chick pregnant and brought Pen up single-handed. He's in no position to lecture his son, is he?

'You seem to know a lot about it,' Harper commented, thinking that if she wanted to know about the Penhaligons all she had to do was ask Ariel.

'Apart from which, Pen had this trip planned months ago but was too chicken to tell his dad. Apparently, Daddy and Hughie don't get on. Never have. So, you see, this was all Pen's idea, nothing to do with me. I won't be taking the rap.' She folded her arms across her breasts with a huff of indignation.

So there!

'I'd never heard you mention Pen before. That really got me worried,' Harper confessed. 'After I got to know Rocco and learned a little of his family background I did wonder if you and Pen had struck up a friendship because of the parallels in your lives.'

'Parallels?'

'Having mothers who –' *How can I put this delicately,* Harper wondered, 'have put their interests before those of their children.'

'No that had no bearing. Although there is another parallel.'

'There is?'

'Both mothers landed us with daft names.' Ariel grinned, seemingly happy that Harper was accepting her version of events.

'Pen isn't such a daft name, as you put it. Although I have wondered why he's called Pen Penhaligon.' And, no doubt Rocco would have explained that, too, if they hadn't come home a day early!

'His mother named him after a Hindu god, something like Shr-shriti but he chose to call himself Pen. So, there you have it – feckless mothers who named us after a Hindu deity and a character from Shakespeare. You couldn't make it up. Besides, you've been more of a mother to me than Shona will ever be. Never doubt that I love you.' Leaning across the bed, Ariel took Harper's hands and squeezed them. Harper blinked away the tears and swallowed hard.

'I love you, too,' she said in a husky voice. However, her straight look let Ariel know that she wasn't out of the woods.

'I have no illusions about my mother. She is what she is. Maybe part of me wanted to make her sit up and take notice, put me first for a change. Perhaps that's why I went off with Pen? Guess she wasn't too put out that I didn't want to stay with her as planned, huh?'

'She doesn't know what's been going on. I thought I'd be able to sort things out, smooth the way. Keep everyone happy.'

'As you've always done.'

'As I've always done. I simply said your visit was postponed until later in the summer, a last minute change of plan. And, as it's turned out . . .'

'You were right. I didn't want to play piggy-in-the-middle with her and douchebag #3, all I wanted was some fun. Instead I ended up with Pen, king of the dorks. That brought a shedload of trouble down on my head and introduced me to Hugh Morrison.' She pulled a face and her expression clouded. Harper's stomach gave an anxious lurch.

'Meaning?'

'Okay, I'm going to share something, but don't freak out. And, above all, don't do anything to embarrass me.'

Oh God. 'Go on.'

'Promise?'

'Promise.'

'He didn't get that bang on the head in the hide. One night, he came to my hotel room, all friendly-like, said he wanted to show me some photos he'd taken that day. Wanted to get my opinion as a lay person. Pen, he said, was too invested in the project and wouldn't tell him if a shot was rubbish or not. The last bit at least was true, Pen is a major suck up.'

'W-what did you do?' Harper's chest tightened and she rubbed away the pain travelling the length of her breastbone with her knuckle.

'Slammed the door in his face, nearly knocked him out. Dirty old goat. Now he's terrified in case I take it further. Imagine the headlines:

Housewives' Favourite tries to grope teenager in hotel bedroom. Don't look so shocked, Auntie, I'm used to men finding me attractive. I know how to handle it. I've had plenty of practice with mother's live-ins, not to mention three 'dads'.'

She stated it all so matter-of-factly. Harper was shocked, feeling she'd let her down.

'Oh, Ariel, you should have told me. I would have –'

'Done what? Overreacted? Rang Mum and had a slanging match over the phone?'

'Both.'

'Don't worry, living with you – and that self-defence course you sent me on last winter, has taught me to look after myself. If a door in the face hadn't put Hughie-boy off, I was ready to stick two fingers in his eye or knee him in the nuts.'

'Oh, Ariel.' In spite of everything, Harper laughed.

'You've shown me how important it is to have a career, to depend on no man for money or security. I don't want to end up like Shona, relying on alimony and palimony to keep the wolf from the door. Don't worry about me, three years at university, more if I decide to study for a PhD. will keep me away from L.A and mother's questionable husbands.'

'University?' Harper's heart gave a glad leap. 'I thought your letter, said –'

'If you read it again you'll see that I only wanted time out, to have fun. Not that the last week could be described as fun.'

'I overreacted. Guilty as charged.' Adopting a rueful expression, Harper squeezed Ariel's hand.

'It's what you do. It's why I love you.' She shuffled closer on the bed and hugged Harper. 'I know I've been difficult to live with these last few years, a right cow, in fact.' *Understatement.* 'I'm a teenager, it comes with the territory. But I'm more than capable of looking after myself, you've taught me well. It's time for you to stand down, get on with your own life.'

'Ariel. I –'

'No, listen. You're still relatively young. Quite good looking. Who knows you might find a man who's your equal, who can measure up to your exacting standards.' She grinned. 'Stop trying to please everyone – and that includes the grandparents. You can't keep compensating for my mother letting them down. Follow *your* dreams for a change.'

Harper held her niece at arm's length and regarded her in wonder. They'd been apart for just over a week but in that time Ariel had grown up. Or maybe it was that she'd been so preoccupied with getting the three schools out of special measures that she hadn't noticed Ariel's transformation from girl to woman.

Woman! Now she wanted to march over to Morrison's house and give him a piece of her mind. Ariel apparently had anticipated that, too. She tapped the side of her nose with a long finger. 'As for Morrison, don't worry about him. I have a little surprise up my sleeve for Hughie-boy.'

'You aren't going to tell me what it is, are you?'

'Nope. I'm saving it for tomorrow night at the Pub Quiz. Should be fun. Now, am I forgiven?'

'Of course.'

Without Ariel she would never have met Rocco Penhaligon, embarked on this crazy road trip, taken stock and realised that life was passing her by. Would not, she swallowed hard, have spent the last few days falling in love with a man she probably wouldn't see after she left Polzenith. Still, she reflected, biting her lower lip, better to have spent a long summer night making love to Rocco Penhaligon than any other man.

Leaving Plockton and Rocco Penhaligon was going to be a wrench.

'You've gone very quiet. You, okay?'

'I am now you're home safe and sound. Come on, leave the tidying up, I want to show you round Plockton. Tell you about the summer time we were up here on holiday and Shona inveigled her way into a crowd scene they were filming for an episode of Hamish Macbeth and was bitten by the acting bug.'

'Sounds like Mom, alright.'

Harper zoned out, wondering if Rocco had been staying with his grandparents that summer and, like her, had watched the filming from the sidelines. What if they'd met that day, what if . . . Shaking herself free from her introspection she concentrated on Ariel instead.

'When we return, I'll get on the internet and organise tickets for our journey home. Tonight, if Rocco's in the mood, we'll have a bar-b-q in the garden overlooking the loch.'

'Cool.' Plainly, Ariel had had enough of Scotland, Pen and Hugh Morrison and everything connected with them and, uncharacteristically, it didn't occur to her to ask why they were travelling south without the Penhaligons.

Grabbing their handbags, they headed downstairs and out into Harbour Street. Harper glanced over at Heron Croft's garden where Rocco and Pen were having a heart-to-heart. Judging by Pen's woeful expression his father wasn't cutting him any slack and for that Harper was grateful. Not everything that had happened was Ariel's fault and she hoped that when they next spoke Rocco acknowledged that.

Chapter Twenty-Five

Next morning, Harper, Rocco and the teenagers sat down to breakfast. The previous evening Ariel had expressed an interest in visiting the Fairy Pools on Skye and demanded that Pen took her there. Alternatively, Pen could hand over the keys to the Jeep and she would drive herself. Pen had looked horrified, sighed and then pointed out that it being the height of the tourist season, they'd need to be on the road to Glen Brittle at crack of dawn.

'Are you prepared,' he asked for a second time, as Rocco packed sandwiches and Harper filled a flask with hot chocolate, 'to walk twenty minutes over uneven ground to reach the pools?'

'Duh. It'll be a stroll in the park after what I've had to put up with Horrible Hugh this past week.' Again, Pen looked displeased at his hero being referred to in such disparaging terms. 'Besides, I want to get my money's worth out of those walking boots he insisted I buy in Thurso. I don't suppose after today I'll be yomping across moor and heather for quite some time.'

Pen muttered something which sounded suspiciously like: 'Please God.'

'I heard that, Penhaligon.' Reaching across, Ariel twisted his thumb back in sisterly fashion.

'That's enough, Ariel.' Harper wondered how she'd ever imagined that Ariel was showing signs of maturity.

'Given my name, and in recognition of the fact that I was conceived during a run of The Tempest, it is only right that I should pay my respects to the wee folk.' She struck a pose over by the sink, laying the back of her hand against her brow in dramatic fashion.

Pen gave a resigned shrug while Rocco, amused at the interaction between the teenagers, grinned at Harper over his son's head. Briefly, happiness wrapped itself around her like a cashmere pashmina as she imagined herself in the centre of a loving, squabbling family, secure in the love of a good man with whom she shared children and a happy home.

It struck her that, in choosing career over family, she'd passed up on the chance of that ever happening. She dismissed the feeling of regret. Surely a night of mind-blowing sex wasn't enough to make her question her life choices? To dismiss everything she'd worked so hard to achieve? Her life had changed the moment she'd clambered on Rocco Penhaligon's motorbike – fact – but there was no point of yearning for what could not be. This brief interlude would come to an end tomorrow when she and Ariel caught the 6.27 to Inverness.

Unexpected, tears stung her eyes and she dashed them away with the cuff of her borrowed dressing gown before anyone saw them.

'Five thirty. Time you were off. We've made sandwiches, packed you a flask of hot chocolate and some of Janet's cake. Everything else you can buy on the other side of the Skye Bridge at the Co-op in Broadford, including petrol.' Walking over to the worktop Rocco handed two twenty pound notes and an ancient rucksack to Pen. Then he marched the teenagers to the front door giving them no opportunity to change their minds.

'Take lots of photos of the Fairy Pools.' Harper joined them by Pen's Jeep once she'd regained her composure.

'Why don't you come with us, Auntie Harper?'

'No can do, Ariel. I have to organise our return home to Polzenith.' She had no intention of squandering her last day with Rocco trudging over to the Fairy Pools, no matter how stunning the waterfalls were.

'Okay,' Ariel gave her a hug and then looked at Rocco, evidently wondering if she should kiss him on the cheek. Deciding against it, she turned to Pen. 'How about letting me drive some of the way, Penno?'

'Dream on, MacDonald.'

'Don't be so mean. Unlike you, I passed my test first time, so don't lord it over me. Give me the keys. Oh look,' she pointed over his shoulder to the hills on the far side of the loch, 'a greater crested bustard.'

'A greater crested *what*? Where?'

'Nowhere,' she laughed, snatching the keys out of Pen's slack fingers. 'I made it up. Got you going though, didn't I?' She dangled the keys above her head just out of his reach.

'Ariel, give Pen his keys. I don't want you two squabbling all the way to the Fairy Pools and ending up in a ditch.'

'See, Rocco, that's Auntie Harper for you: Queen of the Worst-Case Scenario.' Laughing, she tossed the keys in the air, Pen caught them and she climbed into the Jeep and fastened her seatbelt. Rocco sent Harper a *how do you put up with her?* half-amused, half-appalled look.

She pulled a face, her expression telling him that he didn't know the half of it.

'Have fun,' she said as Pen turned over the engine.

'Unlikely,' was his gloomy response.

'Don't be late back. It's the Pub Quiz and we're on Hugh's team,' his father added.

That cheered Pen up. 'I won't.'

'Play nicely children,' Ariel called out as Pen crunched the gears, drove to the end of Harbour Street and executed a U-turn. As he drove past he gave three staccato blasts on the horn breaking the Sunday morning silence.

'Kids, huh?' Rocco said. Waiting until the Jeep was out of sight he caught Harper's hand, swung her into his arms and kissed her. 'Been wanting to do that all morning.' Then he led her up the six steps to the front door. 'Better get you inside. It's hardly fitting for the Executive Head of Three Schools to be seen on Harbour Street on the Sabbath kissing a man wearing nothing but a dressing gown.'

That made her laugh. 'Now I'm confused; who's wearing the dressing gown, you or me?'

'For the sake of clarity, you.'

'And how do you know that's all I'm wearing?'

'I did your laundry the other day, remember?'

'Only too well.'

'By my reckoning, you're about to run out of clothes. If you weren't leaving tomorrow, I'd have to put on another load.' He tutted like an old washer woman, folded his arms and looked down on her from the top step. Banishing the thought that this was her last day in Plockton, Harper focused instead on the unforgettable image of her undies doing five rounds with Rocco's boxer shorts in the washing machine.

Intimate, but not as intimate as what followed.

'You have such a hard life,' she quipped, entering Heron Croft and closing the door behind them. 'Cooking, shopping, picking folk up from the station . . . '

'. . . making love.'

She stopped, overwhelmed by the need to be in his bed, his arms. To forget time was running out and concentrate instead on what was important: *the moment*. Should she initiate their love-making or would that make her seem desperate? Truth be told, she was feeling pretty desperate. If they didn't make love soon she'd spontaneously combust. Time to return to the flirty banter, the trade mark of their relationship, and banish dark thoughts and misgivings.

'What's made Miss MacDonald smile?'

'The idea that it's okay for a Wild Corsair to be seen in his pyjamas by Presbyterian ladies on their way to church with bibles under their arms. Whereas, a respectable headteacher in a borrowed dressing gown several sizes too big, comes in for censure?'

'That's because you're a woman and I'm a man. That's how it works in the highlands.'

'Ah, so you noticed that I'm a woman, then?'

'Several times the other night and twice yesterday morning.' Rocco's veiled reference made Harper's stomach flip over.

'You kept score?'

'I only mention it in case you want to repeat the experience.'

'The laundry, or – ?'

'Happy to oblige with either, ma'am.' Leaning against the door he burst out laughing, humour lighting his eyes.

'What?' she demanded.

'Curious how we've spent the past week trying to catch up with our children, but now –'

'– can't get rid of them fast enough?'

'Exactly. Shouldn't it be the teenagers chasing the adults out of the house so *they* can indulge in hanky-panky?'

'Hanky-panky?'

'I've thought of nothing else since I got out of bed this morning. How about you, Schoolmarm?' The last word was said with an exaggerated Western drawl, then he reached out and pulled her close. 'However, I feel I should explain, to one who has led such a sheltered life, what hanky-panky actually involves.'

'Please do.' Harper kept her face straight.

'There's this –'

Sitting down on the stairs he pulled her onto his knee and started untying the dressing gown belt. 'That's quite a knot. Were you in the Scouts?'

'Guides, actually.'

'Guides – of course. What was the old adage? A boy scouts and a girl guides.'

'Blatant sexism, Mr Penhaligon.'

'Prepared to be shocked further, Miss MacDonald. Ah, there, done. Or should that be – undone?' Unknotting the cord he parted the dressing gown, revealing her nakedness. 'Just as I remembered.' He dipped his head and kissed her shoulder.

'*Just* as you remembered?'

'*Better* than I remembered.' Tipping her back, he planted light kisses all over face, neck, ears, everywhere apart from her mouth. Unable to bear the teasing any longer, Harper pulled him close and kissed him. The silk dressing gown slithered off her warm body, pooling across the bottom step and hall floor like liquid gold. Rocco slid his hand along the inside of her thigh and deepened the kiss. Shamelessly, Harper guided his hand higher as her body remembered those magical hours spent in his bed and craved more.

'God – you are perfect, Harper. Perfect.' His skin was flushed beneath a day's growth of beard, his eyes wide and his pupils dilated – all the better to see her with.

'You have me at a disadvantage,' Harper murmured.

'I do?'

Getting to her feet Harper picked up the dressing gown and slipped it on. The look of disappointment on Rocco's face made a bubble of laughter rise in her throat. 'You're very overdressed.'

Happy to please, Rocco pulled his pyjamas top over his head. For several pleasurable moments Harper marvelled how his muscles, used to lifting heavy weights and hoisting engines on chains, contracted and expanded. Reaching out, she traced the line from his shoulder to his wrist, turned his hand over and drew a line across his palm with her nail.

Rocco shuddered. Pleased at his reaction, Harper looked at him through tangled, just-got-out-of-bed hair and then laughed.

'What?'

'Ariel said you were kinda hot for an old guy.'

'And?'

'Those were my exact thoughts when you slid out from under the car the day we met.'

'And . . .' His winding up gesture suggested more was expected.

'You do very well for your age.'

'Not only ageist but impertinent.'

She grinned. 'You weren't exactly complimentary the day we met. Your exact words, stop me if I'm wrong, were – *you don't call the shots round here, Miss Executive-Head-of-Three-Schools.*'

'I don't think those were my *exact* words.'

'I'm paraphrasing,' she said, squeezing past him on the narrow stairs. Rocco chased up the stairs after her, making her trip over the dressing gown hem and land face down on the landing. Standing over her he rubbed his hands together in the manner of a Music Hall villain and twirled an imaginary moustache.

'I was heading for the bedroom, but if you prefer the landing, my proud beauty, I'm more than willing. '

'I choose the bedroom. By my reckoning, the kids won't be home before mid-afternoon, giving us plenty of time.' Reaching for his hand she led the way towards his bedroom at the front of the house.

'For?'

'Everything our hearts desire.'

'That could be rather a lot.'

'In that case, we'd better get to it before Pen's Jeep draws up under the window and curtails our enjoyment for a second time.'

* * *

Later, Harper lay in Rocco's arm tracing the eagle tattoo on his shoulder. Rocco drew in a long breath, revelling how his body responded to her touch even after making love several times. God, he couldn't get enough of this woman, she was an addiction but he was happy to declare himself an addict. Closing his eyes, he put his hands behind his head and let her trail her fingers along skin super-sensitised by lovemaking.

'Do you think that the kids have any inkling of our relationship?' Harper asked. He didn't feel like answering, he wanted the world beyond the four walls to remain outside the bubble they'd created for themselves. However, Harper, being Harper, needed T's crossed and I's dotted. He opened one eye, caught a glimpse of her breasts and lost the thread of what he was about to say.

'Luckily, at this age they are more interested in themselves,' he managed, after a few seconds.

'We'll have to be careful, though. Pen might have his head buried in a bird book but Ariel is sharp as a tack. The quiz will keep her occupied tonight and by this time tomorrow we'll be flying out of Inverness on our way to Gatwick.' Her expression became serious and the corners of her mouth drooped. He understood perfectly. These last few days had been idyllic, hinting at how things could be if all obstacles were removed.

'I understand the need to be cautious, ' he said huskily.

'It's not just the kids, Rocco.' Harper raised herself on one elbow to look down on him. 'I've always been careful to keep my personal and professional life separate. I can't allow gossip to circulate round the Three Pols. It would make my position untenable.'

He pulled the duvet up to his chin, like a maiden aunt surprised in bed by the window cleaner. 'I have my position as proprietor of the local garage to consider, too.'

'Not funny,' she pinched his ear between her thumb and forefinger, 'be serious.'

Rocco lowered the duvet, took her by the shoulders and gave her a gentle shake. 'I'm being serious. I make it a point of honour that my dates never appear at breakfast the following morning wearing one of my shirts. I don't want Pen to grow up in that environment. Lying here with you,' he kissed her gently, 'talking, making love, laughing, has been the best thing to happen to me since – well, let's just say, a long time.'

'Snap. I couldn't bring 'men',' she pulled a face, 'back to our house. Could you imagine Ariel's reaction? In her eyes I'd be no better than her mother. This,' she took in the room with a sweeping gesture, 'has been . . . unexpected.'

'Nice unexpected or bad unexpected?' he teased.

'Let me think – hey,' Harper protested as he started tickling her. 'Nice unexpected,' she gasped out.

'That's okay, then.' Straddling her, he pushed her hair out of her eyes. 'Although . . .'

'I know, we need to talk. We said that we'd get the kids settled before we started thinking about ourselves, the future. That still holds true, doesn't it?'

Rocco nodded. 'It does. You also said, that morning in the garden, that you thought you could flourish here. Does *that* still hold true?'

'Ye – es.'

'You sound unsure.'

'I've never been more certain of anything in my life. Only yesterday, Ariel told me it was time I started putting myself first.'

'She's right. Maybe it's time you allowed her to make her own decisions. A summer spent with her mother could be just the thing to send her winging back to Polzenith, collect her results and head for Uni.'

'You could be right.'

'During our head-to-head in the garden yesterday Pen told me he wants to pursue his love of wildlife photography, make it his profession. I'm keen for him to do something – anything with his life that makes him happy, even if that involves sitting cross legged at Morrison's feet gazing up at him, like he's some kind of guru and not a total . . .'

'Knob head?' Harper laughed. 'Ariel's description.'

'An astute assessment I'd say.'

'How come you don't like him?'

'Oh, ancient history. We've been giving each other black eyes and bloody noses ever since we were old enough to put up our dukes. His family lived on Harbour Street and he was always around when I stayed with my grandparents in the summer. They saw something in him, encouraged him to go to university to study Natural History, helped him out financially.'

'Sounds commendable.'

'They thought we'd become friends, learn from each other. Didn't work out that way. Chalk and cheese. Then, when Pen was less than a year old, I brought him up to Plockton to meet his great-grandparents. During that visit, my parents flew up to join us for a family conference. Over dinner, Morrison made a disparaging remark about Pen's mother and sided with my parents who were keen for me to give Pen up and return to university. Naturally, I've never shared that information with Pen, which makes it all the more galling that he should consider Morrison the dog's bollocks. Sorry!' He flipped himself onto his back and stared up at the ceiling.

'Forgiven.' Reaching out Harper squeezed his hand.

'Bloody Morrison has agreed to help him realise his dream of becoming a wildlife photographer, which is amazingly generous of him. But I can't help thinking that he's doing it to get one over on me. Does that sound cynical?'

'Having met him, I'd say no.' Pushing herself higher up in the bed Harper hugged one of the large feather pillows. 'I probably shouldn't mention this but, Ariel told me that Morrison tried it on when they were staying in the highlands. That bruise on his forehead has nothing to do with the low ceiling of a hide and everything to do with Ariel's bedroom door being slammed in his face.'

'The bastard, I'll –' It surprised him how protective he felt towards Harper and her niece.

'You'll do nothing. Ariel made me promise not to mention it to anyone. If she finds out, she'll – well, I'm not sure what she'll do. Kill me probably. Like you, my instinct was to march round his house and punch him in the face. Of course, I didn't. Ariel is pretty good at handling herself and assures me that she has a little surprise up her sleeve for Morrison.' Rocco didn't say another word. She'd trusted him with a secret, one he couldn't act on without betraying her confidence. 'I won't interfere. Much as I'd like to.'

'Good. Now, back to discussing the kids. Won't you miss Pen if he's up here in Scotland and you're in Polzenith?'

Rocco took a deep breath and, much as he wanted to, held back from telling her about his prospective purchase of Baxter's Garage. By the time she got back from Nepal it'd all be settled and he could share the news without jinxing it. Would the fact that he was leaving Polzenith have any influence on her future plans? She had a range of options to choose from and he didn't want to pressurise her, one way or another. Frowning, he stared past her to the landing where the length of the shadows on the wall told him that time was moving on; running out.

'Rocco?'

'Sorry, miles away. Yes, I'll miss Pen, we'll have to see how *everything* pans out.' He emphasised the word, hinting that he had things on his mind, too. 'Now,' changing the subject he threw off the summer weight duvet and sat on the edge of the bed. 'I think we should consider getting changed, tidy up the kitchen, otherwise it might seem that we've done nothing but make love since cock crow.'

Harper raised an eyebrow at the unintentional double entendre and they both laughed. Drawing him back on to the bed she cradled his head in her lap and dropped a kiss on his brow. 'Once more for luck?'

Rocco marvelled at how far she'd come since the first time they'd made love, learning to throw off her inhibitions and allow her instincts free rein. He loved her for it. Feigning resignation he caught her hands and kissed her face, upside down.

'If we must.'

'We must.'

'Okay. But with the proviso that we share a bath afterwards. It's our duty to save the planet's resources for future generations and conserving water is a good place to start.'

Laughing, Harper lowered her head towards him. 'I heartily concur.'

Twenty-Six

Harper made herself as presentable as possible, given the few outfits at her disposal. She wanted to look her best so that when she got on the train for Inverness tomorrow she'd leave Rocco with a memory that would stay with him forever.

However long forever turned out to be.

Putting the thought aside she fetched wine from the pantry, placed bowls of nuts and crisps on the table for anyone dropping by to pre-load before heading for the Plockton Arms.

'Not sure why Pen's getting away with doing nothing,' Ariel grumbled, spilling crisps and cashew nuts on the counter top in response to her aunt's request that she helped. 'Typical. Useless. Bloody. Male.' Harper allowed herself a wry smile, how had she ever imagined Pen and Ariel madly in love and heading for Gretna Green? Perhaps, as Ariel said, she read too many romances.

'Rocco wanted a quick word with him and asked if we could get the drinks ready.' Her reply was calm and measured, her usual response to Ariel's strops.

'Couldn't that Janet-person be called in to do this?'

'No, she couldn't. She's regarded as a family friend even if she does cook and clean for them. She's not a member of staff, not in the way your mother has staff in L.A. So mind how you behave.'

'Of course, I'm not a child.'

'Course not.' Harper sent her an ironic look.

Tossing her head, Ariel went into the sitting room where she draped her legs over the sofa arm, got out her phone and immersed herself in social media. Having been deprived of the internet for almost a week she had to ensure her legion of Instagram followers knew she was back online. Time spent in the land of her ancestors hadn't put her in touch with her inner Celt, she hated Scotland and couldn't wait to escape. Whereas, Harper's heart was breaking at the thought of leaving Rocco and this beautiful place behind.

'Changed your mind about helping,' Harper asked, snapping out of her reverie when footsteps echoed in the hall.

'Looks like everything's been taken care of, no help required,' Rocco replied.

Heart leaping, Harper turned to find him and Pen on the threshold of the kitchen wearing kilts, walking boots and thick socks. Pen wore a navy blue Scotland rugger shirt over his kilt while Rocco favoured a tight fitting black microfleece, giving the traditional outfit a contemporary edge.

'You both look amazing,' Harper managed once she was capable of speech. 'There's something heroic about a kilt.' Sexy, too, but she didn't say that. Recalling the morning when Rocco had hung the kilt on the washing line she marvelled at how swiftly their relationship had progressed.

Smiling, Rocco opened a bottle of Sancerre while he explained. 'Most of the residents wear kilts to the Pub Quiz. It pays to get them out of mothballs in readiness for the regatta in two weeks' time.'

'Last year we almost won the laser class, but Hugh pipped us to the post,' Pen said, helping himself to some crisps.

'We want to win this year. Right, Pen?'

'Totally.' Father and son high-fived each other.

'What a pity I didn't think to pack my full highland regalia,' Ariel said snarkily, sauntering in from the sitting room. 'Given that I'm probably a descendant of Flora MacDonald who smuggled Bonnie Prince Charlie over the sea to Skye.'

'I thought you hated everything about Scotland,' Pen reminded her.

'Oh, I quite like the romantic bits. The rain and midges, not so much. I'd be a brilliant Flora if ever they make a movie of her life . . . I can see me now, standing on the shore wrapped in a shawl, watching Bonnie Prince Charlie disappearing into the mist –'

'– being sent to The Tower of London for treason,' Pen added, darkly.

'That, too,' she replied, popping an olive into her mouth.

'You can't pick and choose the bits of Scottish heritage and history you like and discard the rest.' Clearly Pen found her facetious remarks annoying, which was rather the point.

'Is that so, Pen-*elope*.' Spinning on her heel, she took a couple of photos of him in his kilt. 'Up-kilting. Woo hoo.'

'If that ends up on Instagram, I'll kill you.' They started chasing each other round the kitchen until Rocco intervened, standing between them and holding out his hand for the phone. To Harper's astonishment, Ariel handed it over. After deleting the photos Rocco returned it to her.

At that point, the back door opened and Hugh Morrison entered along with Janet and a distinguished looking gent in his early seventies. Both men wore kilts, V-neck cashmere sweaters and casual shirts while Janet sported a pleated tartan skirt and Pringle jumper. Harper steeled herself for another snippy remark from Ariel but she levered herself onto the worktop and sat, cross legged, scrolling through her phone.

Rocco made the introductions.

'Harper, this is Sir Michael McKinnon, the laird. His family and the Gunn branch of the Penhaligons who settled in Plockton have been friends for more years than anyone can remember. Hugh and Janet you already know. Michael, this is Harper's niece Ariel. We four usually make up a team at the quiz but you ladies will provide an added dimension tonight. Hell, we might even win.' The laird stepped forward and shook Harper's hand.

'I've been looking forward to meeting you, my dear. Rocco was singing your praises the other day when he dropped by for a wee dram.'

'Was he, now?'

Rocco's *what can I say?* shrug was followed by an enigmatic smile which recalled how they'd spent most of that day. Harper swung her attention back to the laird who was still holding her hand.

'Are you well, my dear? Your hand is burning.'

'Yes. I'm afraid I'll never make a pastry chef,' she quipped, withdrawing her hand. Looking between Harper and Rocco, Janet crossed the kitchen and opened the back door.

'It's awful close,' was her dry comment.

'Our houses are built for keeping the heat in, not staying cool,' the laird joked. 'We've had a week of sun but we'll pay for it in a couple of days. I only hope it stays fine until after the regatta. Will you be staying on for the racing, my dear?'

'Sadly, Ariel and I must leave tomorrow morning. But, maybe another year?' She glanced at Rocco and then lowered her head, hiding her expression. Would there be 'another year' as far as they were concerned?

'I don't know if Rocco has mentioned it to you,' the laird glanced between them, 'there will be a vacancy for a headteacher at the primary school – *Bun-sgoil a' Phluic,* when Mrs Munro retires at Easter. You wouldn't be interested, I suppose, Harper? We could do with a teacher of your calibre, but other than beautiful scenery, we have little to offer. Rocco says you're destined for great things – Ofsted, Her Majesty's School Inspectorate?'

'Thinking about it.'

Her heart plummeted to her boots and she wondered why Rocco hadn't mentioned the vacancy. Clearly, he had his reasons even if he hadn't shared them with her. She pulled herself together, she wasn't going to ruin her last night in Plockton by overthinking the situation. He probably hadn't mentioned it because he knew she had a lot of soul searching to do over her future plans.

Yes, that'd be it.

'Pen, pass round the nibbles.' Reaching for the wine, Rocco sent Harper an anxious look, evidently guessing what she was thinking.

'Come on, Penhaligon. Forget the wine, get out that bottle of

Macallan I know you keep in reserve. We must give the ladies a proper send off.'

Morrison bowed in Harper's direction, his lion's mane flopping forward. Pushing it back with a practised sweep of his hand he glanced over at Ariel perched on the worktop and fleetingly his self-possession wavered. It was evident that far from *giving the ladies a proper send off*, he wished Ariel to Hell, or at least on the train to Inverness with her aunt.

Rocco returned from the sitting room with the Macallan and five whisky tumblers. 'Pen, fetch some cans of mixers and bottles of Highland Spring from the fridge while I pour the uisge beatha.'

'Sure thing, Dad.'

'I should warn you, Michael,' Rocco attempted a feeble joke, 'Harper thinks whisky tastes like cough medicine and dilutes it with lemonade. Isn't that right, Harper?'

Harper replied in similar vein. 'You beast, Rocco, that was supposed to be our secret.' Colour stung her cheeks at the exact nature of the secrets they shared, but she kept her composure. 'I'll stick to wine, if that's okay.'

'I'll take the – what did you call it –'Ariel declared, putting her phone down.

'Uisge beatha.' Rocco looked at Harper for permission. Knowing Ariel wouldn't rest until she'd tried the Macallan, she nodded. 'Sip it,' he added. However, Ariel knocked it back in one like a gold prospector in a saloon bar. Unsurprisingly, she coughed and spluttered as her throat burned.

'Girls, huh?' was Pen's lofty observation as he sipped his whisky with a practised air.

'Indeed.' Morrison clinked glasses with the men while Ariel sent him a hard look.

A definite atmosphere was building, like on a hot summer's day when the air thickens before a thunderstorm. Morrison: openly wondering if Ariel had said anything about his ill-advised midnight visit and how he'd come by the bruise on his forehead. Ariel: sitting so meekly on the worktop that Harper suspected she was up to something. Pen: handing round cans of mixers and small bottles of water in an attempt to curry favour with his dad. Michael and Janet: openly observing the dynamic between the players' interaction and wondering what it was they were missing.

And Rocco: willing Harper to understand why he hadn't mentioned the vacancy.

'Is your husband, George, taking part in the quiz?' Harper asked Janet in an attempt to lighten the atmosphere.

'Och, no. He'll hide away in a corner of the Plockton Arms with his cronies and ignore us until the quiz's over. Which suits me just fine.' She raised her glass, implying that a night off from family responsibilities was a rare thing.

'So, Hugh,' the laird turned to Morrison. 'How was your trip?'

'Perfect in all respects, except one.' Morrison rolled his tumbler between his hands. 'I was monitoring the crofters in Sutherland managing their grassland and wondering if their methods could be improved upon.'

'Is that important?'

'It is, if we're to increase the habitat of breeding corncrakes, great yellow bumblebees and over-wintering passerine populations.'

'All very admirable. So which aspect of the trip was less than satisfactory?'

'Hugh was desperate to photograph bumblebees on the flower-rich machair, where traditional crofting is still carried out,' Pen put in, eyes shining. 'There's a chance of funding for the farmers and crofters via the Scottish Rural Development Program, if Hugh can make a good enough case to the conservation authorities and powers that be. Once, the bees were common all over the UK but now they're restricted to north-west Scotland. I'd've loved to have seen one; maybe on our next trip?' He looked at Hugh for confirmation.

Ariel, bored, picked up her phone and started scrolling through her photos. 'Ariel,' Harper hissed, appalled at her display of ill-manners. She was about to apologise to Morrison, then remembered how he came by the bruise on his forehead. He deserved everything Ariel sent his way.

'The queens use old mouse nests, rabbit burrows and other holes under grass tussocks as nest sites. I thought,' Pen looked across at Ariel, 'that queen bees and their habitats would be of great interest to you. Seeing how you're a bit of a qu –'

'Okay, Pen. We geddit. No need to labour the point.' She glared at him and then gave Hugh a saccharine sweet smile. 'Shame it didn't work out for you, eh, Hughie? I'm guessing that a photograph of a queen emerging from a mouse nest would command a high price, especially if syndicated? The very thing dab for your new book.'

'It would,' Hugh ground out.

Pen, evidently believing that his hero was being denied the honour due to him, turned on Ariel. 'Hugh will get that photo, no mistake. He always gets what he wants.'

'Not always,' Ariel drawled, sending a dark look in Hugh's direction.

'For example,' Pen continued, 'Hugh has given his name to a species of six-eyed sand spider he discovered in Africa. Haven't you, Hugh?'

Morrison waved away his praise as though it was of no matter.

'What, there's a spider called *Hughie* out there?' Ariel asked, pretending astonishment. Michael, Harper and Rocco spluttered in their drinks but Pen was unamused.

'I meant its scientific name . . . *Loxosceles haddadi* Morrisonii.'

'Gesundheit,' Ariel said.

'Oh, grow up,' Pen snapped.

'That's okay, Pen,' Hugh laid a restraining hand on his arm. 'Ariel's just having a little joke at my expense.' Ariel returned to scrolling through her phone and an uncomfortable silence descended once more.

'We probably should get going,' Rocco said, glancing at his watch.

'Good idea,' Harper agreed, thinking a change of scene wouldn't hurt. They drained their glasses and headed for the back door. Ariel leapt off the worktop and held out her phone so Hugh and Pen could see the screen.

'I don't suppose *this* is one of tham thar great yellow bumblebees, is it?'

'Let me see.' Morrison snatched the phone out of her hand. 'When did you take this?'

'When you told me to stop talking, moving and, if possible, breathing because I was spooking the wildlife. I went off to lie down in the machair and catch a few rays. I was so still and quiet, you would have been seriously impressed. Soon, the bees starting landing on the wild flowers and grasses drinking nectar or whatever bees do. Then one, bigger than all the rest, emerged from a nest of twigs, grass and moss. It looked so cute, I snapped it.'

'*Cute?*' Morrison appeared to find breathing difficult.

'Yes. So swee-eet. Whatd'ya think Harper, Rocco?' She handed the phone to her aunt and Rocco looked at it over her shoulder.

'Impressive. That is one big mother of a bumble bee, Hugh. How much would a photo like this be worth? Would it, for example, go towards paying Ariel's university fees for a year?'

Morrison gave the question serious thought. 'It depends on a number of factors. Rarity, quality of the jpeg, and so on. Luckily, I have the contacts who would be able to help.'

'That would be very kind,' Harper began.

Cutting across her, Morrison pulled out his own phone. 'If Ariel wouldn't mind airdropping me a copy –'

'Airdropping you a copy? You're kidding, right?' She laughed in Morrison's face. 'I'm not quite as naive as you imagine. When I'm in L.A, I'll have time to consider what to do with the photograph. For the first time in her life my mother and her contacts can actually prove useful.' She put her phone away in her bag. 'This is *so* cool, Hugh, you have your spider and I have my bee. Happy days.' Aware that only he and Harper could see her face, she mouthed *knob-head* at Morrison. Then she took Michael's arm. 'Quiz time, your lairdship?'

'I believe it is.' Michael led Ariel out of the back door, down the side of Heron Croft and in the direction of the Plockton Arms. Hugh, Pen and Janet followed while Rocco, under the pretext of locking up, hung back.

Sitting on the edge of the table he pulled Harper towards him and held her close, mutely acknowledging that things were changing between them. Harper sighed, the sex between them had been good, that was undeniable. Better still, they'd started to relax in each other's company, to understand what the other wanted almost before they knew it themselves. Inevitably, Pen and Ariel's arrival had altered that dynamic. Harper feared that once the train pulled out of Plockton, their relationship would unravel further due to time, distance and what was left unsaid.

Until there was nothing more left to connect them.

With that thought in mind she moved out of his arms.

'We should go –'

'You're right, of course.' Rocco pushed himself off the table. 'Tonight'll be sheer torture; being with you but not being with you. I'm not sure how much longer I can keep up the pretence.'

Harper sent him a bright smile. 'Luckily, that won't be a problem after tomorrow, will it? As for tonight, everyone's so wrapped up in their own affairs they won't give us a second thought: bumble bees, spiders called *Hugh*, finding a new head for the primary school.' She paused long enough to give him a chance to follow up with: *I was going to mention the vacancy, but –*

However, the words remained unspoken. Stung, she moved away from him and picked up her bag from the kitchen chair.

Rocco's helpless look showed his awareness that Harper'd taken a step back from him. There being nothing more to say, he gestured for her to leave the house, locked the door and then followed her up the path to Harbour Street.

Chapter Twenty-Seven

Entering the Plockton Arms they found the others seated at a large table overlooking the loch. Locals dropped by to greet the laird, slap Morrison on the back and renew their acquaintance with Pen. After some time, tourists emboldened by the relaxed atmosphere asked Hugh for his autograph or had selfies taken with him. When Rocco and Harper appeared, Hugh made room for Harper to sit next to him and indicated that the laird should make room for Rocco. Pen and Ariel, seemingly having patched up their differences, were laughing over something that had happened during the last week of term. After ensuring that Harper was okay sitting next to Morrison, Rocco walked up to the bar where Auld Baxter and Janet were standing.

'Rocco, hope ye dinnae mind, I'm going to sit with my family this evening. You have Ariel, Pen and Harper on your team while my family is short of players.' Janet nodded in their direction.

'Fine by me,' Rocco replied, ordering drinks.

'Are Ariel and Harper away the morrah?' Baxter inquired.

'Yes. They're catching the six twenty-seven to Inverness, a plane to Gatwick, another to Newquay and then hiring a car to drive the last leg to Polzenith .'

'That's quite a journey.'

'The original plan was for us to travel back to Cornwall in Pen's Jeep, Harper and me sharing the driving. Now, with Pen wanting to stay on in Plockton and having to sort out the purchase of your garage, that isn't going to happen.'

'Why doesn't Harper hire a car and drive home, maybe staying off at a bed and breakfast on the way?' Janet asked.

'We did the maths. It's roughly seven hundred and thirteen miles door to door. Plus, Harper knew that if she hired a car Ariel would want to drive some of the way. She's only just passed her test and Harper doesn't think her skills are up to it. It's a tough call because Pen drove all the way from Bristol and, by all accounts, Ariel is a better driver.'

'I for one wouldnae want to argue with Ariel all the way from Plockton to Cornwall,' Janet said, sending a sympathetic look in Harper's direction.

'She's a bonnie lassie,' Baxter agreed, 'but a right wee besom.'

Rocco nodded. 'Exactly. Harper wants to get her over to L.A before she changes her mind – again. On top of which, Harper's keen to see if there's a place available for her on the second tour to Nepal, having missed the first one. God knows she deserves it after everything that happened.'

Zoning out, thinking about things he and Harper had shared over the last week, he stared ahead unseeingly.

Janet sent him a straight look. 'You'll miss them when they've gone, especially Harper.' She'd been better than a mother to him over the years and, apart from Morwenna, no one understood him better.

'That goes without saying.' Turning, he focused his attention on the barman.

'You've told her that, then?'

'What?'

Janet tutted in exasperation. 'That you'll miss her.'

'Not in so many words.'

'Och, Rocco – how many words dis it take?'

'Not many, but more than one might imagine.' He glanced over to the laird's table where Morrison's head was close to Harper's and she was looking cross and uncomfortable.

'I gathered from what was said in the kitchen that you hadn't mentioned the vacancy at the primary school, either?'

'I didn't Janet, but with good reason.'

'Go on.'

'Harper's a high-flyer and, no disrespect to our local primary, destined for greater things. Also, everything is in a state of flux: buying your garage, selling my garage and moving from Polzenith , settling in Plockton for the foreseeable future.'

Baxter sent him a sceptical look. 'Och, Rocco, come on, son, you'll have to do better than that. It's no like you need to sell the garage in Polzenith tae buy oors. Is it? The way I see it, it's simply a case of you and Pen packing your stuff into a van, moving to Heron Croft, and letting estate agents and solicitors do the rest.'

'Put like that it all sounds very simple.'

'It is that simple.' Baxter sipped his whisky.

'There's Pen to consider.'

'If he's serious about making a career photographing wildlife then there's no better place than Plockton and the Western Isles. Not tae mention learning first hand from Hugh.' They glanced over to the laird's table where Hugh was knocking back whisky like it was mother's milk, a few more drams and he'd be in his cups.

'Pillock,' Rocco muttered.

'Tell me you aren't still hoping that Pen's mother will return?'

Rocco laughed. 'Good God, Janet, no.'

'I hope ye dinnae mind me asking?'

''Course not. Who else cares enough to ask?' He put his arm around Janet's shoulder and gave her an affectionate squeeze. 'However, you're right, it's time to move on. This wild goose chase to catch up with Pen and Ariel has been a game changer. To be honest, this last week has been the best week of my life, no contest.'

'At the risk of repeating myself – have you told Harper that?'

Rocco grinned and repeated his earlier answer: 'Not in so many words.'

Janet tutted, but then laughed. 'Well, you're too big to listen to anything me and George Baxter have to say.'

Baxter picked his glass up off the bar. 'I'm away over tae play dominoes with the lads. Catch youse all later.'

'Aye, later,' Janet said. Rocco made as if to leave but Janet laid a hand on his arm. 'Just one mair thing, Rocco. Dinnae let Harper slip through your fingers because you feel the time isn't right. Waiting for the time to be right can lead to regrets which stay with you for the rest of your life.' Fleetingly, she glanced over at Auld Baxter but didn't elaborate.

'I won't.' Rocco kissed her cheek just as the laird, Ariel and Pen joined them at the bar.

'Rocco. I've just discovered, via Harper that I was in the village the day they filmed the episode of Hamish Macbeth when Ariel's mother was in a crowd scene, along with other village children,' said the laird. 'It was a grand day. Afterwards, the crew came up to our house and filmed location shots of the loch from the sunken garden.'

'How about that?' Ariel seemed genuinely delighted. 'Mum will be thrilled when I tell her. Come on, Michael, let's go outside before the quiz starts. I want a photo of you and me with Plockton as a backdrop.' Ariel held out her hand and the laird took it, pleased to be the focus of a lovely young woman's attention.

'I'll take the photo if you like,' Pen offered, his friendship with Ariel restored to default setting.

'Cool,' Ariel said and they left the pub and headed for the loch.

Somewhat unsteadily, Morrison walked over to the bar and ordered himself another whisky. It was on the tip of Rocco's tongue to tell him to lay off but it was clear from the set of his shoulders and the ruddy colour spreading along his cheeks that he was in no mood to take advice from anyone.

Least of all, Rocco Penhaligon.

Getting to her feet Harper moved away from the table, miming that she was heading for the Ladies as she sashayed past Rocco and Morrison. Rocco raised his hand in acknowledgment, noticing how the other men watched her make her way through the crowded bar. But only he knew how it felt to make love to her and the very thought made his blood sing. A tsunami of hormones and memories swamped him; he sucked in his breath, holding on to it until Harper disappeared headed into the Ladies and the pleasurable wave of sensations ebbed away.

Janet was right he was a bloody fool. He should declare his hand tonight, tell Harper how he felt. Make a point of asking her to return to Plockton once everything was settled in Polzenith: her job, the garage, Ariel's future. Tell her about Baxter's garage, his plan to settle in Plockton and see what her reaction was and take it from there. If she felt he was assuming a relationship that didn't exist she'd be sure to tell him.

These last few days, he mused, had been a crash course in falling in love. Now it was time to consolidate, to ensure that those feelings were real.

'There she goes,' Morrison joined Rocco at the bar, lurching against him. Rocco steadied him and then made as if to walk away but Morrison grabbed him by the arm. 'So prim, so proper. Butter wouldn't melt. It's obvious that while *I* was babysitting your ch -children, paying for their accommodation and food, the pair of you were at it like knives. Don't bother to deny it.'

'I did offer to pay you, if you remember. Still more than happy to do so.' Opening the flap of his leather sporran, Rocco pulled out a wad of money and started peeling off tenners. 'So how much do I owe you?' Morrison knocked his hand and the money fluttered onto the floor. Bending, Rocco picked up the notes before anyone was aware of what was going on. Plainly, Morrison was spoiling for a fight and Rocco didn't want to say or do anything which would make the situation worse.

'At the very least, Ariel could have airdropped the photo of the bumblebee to me,' Morrison whined. Rocco was tempted to say: *maybe of you hadn't paid her a midnight visit she might have viewed your request more sympathetically.* But he'd given Harper his word and could say nothing.

'A bottle of house white, Bob,' he ordered, hoping that concentrating on the ordinary would get Morrison off his back. Morrison, however, was on a roll and obviously feeling sorry for himself. His words were slurred and his native highlander brogue threatened to override the upper-class English accent he'd spent years acquiring.

'It's nauseating; the covert glances, the way she looks at you, your self-satisfied smiles. Whereas *I* have the temerity to sit just a fraction too close to her ladyship, accidently graze her thigh with my hand, and she brings her heel down on my fuckin' foot. Almost broke my toe. I've had it up to here with her *and* her bloody niece. You're welcome to them, pal. They're nothing but a pair of cock teasers.' He poked Rocco on the chest as he pronounced the last two words, then knocked back his whisky with a deft flick of the wrist. 'Must sh-ay, though, I didnae have you down as a three-in-a-bed man, Penhaligon. Which do you have first? I'd take the aunt, I bet she knows all the tricks of the trade. Then move on to the niece, if you've got the energy.'

Desperate not to react to Morrison's provocation Rocco took a deep breath. He felt like knocking Morrison's block off but reminded himself that they weren't kids any more. Aware that people were beginning to glance in their direction he took Hugh by the elbow and starting walking him towards the pub entrance.

'Go home, Hugh. Sleep off the whisky and your bad mood. I'll give your apologies to the others.'

'Get your fuckin' hands off me.' He pushed Rocco away.

Rocco held up his hands to show that he was happy to comply. However, Morrison's blood was up and Harper and Ariel's perceived show of disrespect had cut him to the quick.

'Come on, Hugh, let some of the lads see you home.' Rocco beckoned over the farmers and fisherman they'd grown up with and who were in the pub. 'You don't want photos of you tired and emotional to appear on social media tomorrow.'

'I said, get your fuckin' hands off me.' Repeating his earlier command, only much louder, Morrison took two steps forward and pushed Rocco hard up against the bar. The roll top edge of the mahogany counter crushed into his vertebrae and he grimaced in pain.

In that instant, it was as if all the scraps they'd had throughout childhood and adolescence, pushing and shoving each other on to the mud on the loch shore, giving each other bloody noses, vying for Rocco's grandparents' attention, confirmed to Morrison that, no matter how famous he became or what he achieved, he would never be Rocco Penhaligon.

'Here she comes,' he said loudly, pointing to Harper as she made her way through the crowded bar. 'Pure as the driven snow.' He snorted in derision before adding, 'Slut.'

'Okay, that's enough.' Rocco signalled for his friends to encircle Morrison, aware that if he touched him, Morrison would explode.

'C'mon, Hugh.' The laird's gamekeeper stepped forward. 'Show the lady some respect.'

'Shee'sh no lady,' Morrison slurred, 'shee'sh a cock teaser.'

Closing the gap between them, Rocco enlisted the other men's help and guided Hugh towards the door. There they collided with the laird, Pen and Ariel, the very sight of whom incensed Morrison further.

'And *she*,' he pointed his finger in her face, 'is another one.'

'Another one, what?' Ariel demanded, squaring up to him.

'Never mind.' Forgetting his earlier resolution Rocco propelled Morrison out of the Plockton Arms. Morrison drew back his arm and elbowed Rocco on the side of the head. A firework display of stars and lights danced before his eyes and a hollow, rushing sound filled his ears. He took two faltering steps backwards and was caught by Janet's son who helped him outside to sit on a bench and get fresh air.

Regardless of his protests, the men frogmarched Morrison towards his house at the opposite end of Harbour Street to Heron Croft.

'Oh My God, Rocco.' Harper was at his side, pushing his hair off his face, touching his rapidly swelling eye with gentle fingers, their differences forgotten. 'What was that all about? Are you hurt, can you stand? Come on, we're going home.'

Even in his dazed state, Rocco liked the way she said *home,* meaning his house. He would willingly have crawled on his hands and knees to Heron Croft if it meant the two of them could have five minutes alone. Time to sort everything that was going wrong, time to repair the damage caused, not by him saying too much, but because he hadn't said enough.

'I'm okay, don't worry.'

'We're coming too,' Ariel pronounced, directing Pen to help Rocco to his feet. 'Here, Michael, you take Rocco's other arm, I'll go back into the pub to collect our things and meet you back at Heron Croft.' In spite of a thumping headache, Rocco smiled. It was plain that Ariel was more like her aunt than any of them realised.

Reluctant to relinquish Harper's touch on the side of his face he nevertheless allowed Pen and Michael to take him home.

* * *

Within ten minutes, the kitchen at Heron Croft had turned into a three ring circus. Janet, George, the men who'd taken Morrison home, the laird, Pen and Ariel had assembled there and were drinking Rocco's best Macallan. Harper bathed Rocco's wound and gave him a pack of frozen peas wrapped in a tea towel to hold against his temple to reduce the swelling.

'It's a pity it wisnae the other way round, Rocco, you thumping Hugh,' one of the fisherman said.

'Aye, he's due a black eye,' another agreed. This was followed by lots of nodding, clinking of glasses and cries of *slainte.*

'Ever since the BBC commissioned his wildlife series he's been a bugger to live with,' the laird's gamekeeper said. 'Sucks me dry for information – what birds have been seen, where they're nesting and then I don't get as much as an acknowledgment.'

'Sadly, only too typical of Hugh,' the laird agreed. 'Although, I'm sure he'll regret his behaviour in the morning. Luckily, I don't think any of the tourists were aware of what was going on.' The others nodded.

They might think that Hugh was an idiot but he was their idiot and, in Plockton, that counted for something.

'He isnae all bad,' one fisherman opined. 'His celebrity status and him living in Plockton attracts the tourists and the talks he gives in the village hall during the winter months, raises money for local charities.'

'Rocco seems to bring out the worst in him, nothing has changed since they were weans,' Janet added.

'That doesn't give him the right to get drunk and throw his weight around,' Harper said in her best headmistress voice. That solicited more 'ayes' and head nodding. Then she stood in the middle of the kitchen and, with a look, made plain that the sideshow was over. Janet made the men drink up and then escorted everyone out of Heron Croft, closing the door behind her with a sympathetic wink in Rocco's direction.

'Thanks, Harper,' Rocco said, putting his hand over hers as she readjusted the compress. In typical teenage fashion, Pen and Ariel had failed to notice the tender exchange but made themselves useful by collecting the glasses and putting them in the dishwasher. Harper tutted, knowing she'd have to take the cut glass tumblers out of the dishwasher when they weren't looking otherwise the lead crystal would turn cloudy. Then Pen turned and addressed his father. 'Dad – I hope this doesn't affect Hugh's offer to help with my wildlife photography.'

Ariel rounded on him.

'You selfish pig, Pen. You don't know Hugh Morrison half as well as you think you do. And if you did, you'd learn that your idol has feet of clay.' That reference seemingly puzzled him. She looked as if it would give her the greatest pleasure to tell Pen exactly how Morrison had come by the bruise on his forehead. However, catching Harper's eye she settled for her favourite expression: 'He's a total knob head.'

'That's fine, Ariel.' Rocco turned his head so he could see her with his good eye. 'I'm sorry this happened on your last evening in Plockton.' He winced as his eye hurt. 'This could have been our chance to beat the doctors team from the surrounding villages. Don't worry, Pen, I'll square it all with Morrison tomorrow . . . after he's slept off his bad mood.'

Harper's heart contracted with love because she knew that no matter what Rocco thought of Morrison, he wouldn't let it stand in the way of Pen's dream. Letting out a long breath she turned to Ariel. 'Let's leave the boys to it. We have to finish packing and have a long day ahead of us t-tomorrow.'

She couldn't bring herself to say *when we leave Plockton*. Ariel nodded, as if she understood more than Harper realised. Only Harper saw the dejected slump of Rocco's shoulders and the look of utter dejection in his uninjured eye as he followed their exit from the kitchen.

* * *

The ScotRail to Inverness rounded the bend into Plockton on time. Harper was happy to allow tourists and hikers to board the train ahead of her because it gave her precious extra minutes with Rocco.

'You really do look like a Wild Corsair,' she said, touching his bruised eye with tender fingers. Swallowing back a sob, she held out her hand and attempted to communicate what she felt, wordlessly. 'Thanks for everything.'

'Everything.' Echoing her words, Rocco pulled her into his arms not caring who saw. 'I'll be in touch,' he whispered, kissing her on both cheeks and, once, on the mouth.

'Only if you want to.' Harper tried to affect diffidence but failed.

'Why wouldn't I?' Rocco looked puzzled.

'Oh, you know, I'll be busy, you'll be busy.' She didn't add: *absence doesn't always make the heart grow fonder*. 'Ignore me. I'm all at sea, not thinking straight. I still feel out of sorts and haven't recovered properly from the food poisoning.'

Rocco took hold of her hands and pulled her close. 'Well I am thinking straight, so – know this, Harper MacDonald, I will be in touch. Having found you, I won't let you walk out of my life.'

Harper blinked back the tears and was about to respond when Ariel called from the door of the carriage. 'Come on, Auntie. You're holding up the train.' Sure enough, the guard blew the whistle.

'Kids, huh?' Rocco joked and released her. 'Who'd have 'em?'

'Not me, that's for sure.' Harper managed a weak smile.

'Laters,' he said, channelling the teenagers in a heavy-handed attempt to make the parting less painful.

'Yes. Laters.' Climbing into the carriage she added: 'Soon?' She sounded needy, so unlike herself.

'Soon,' he confirmed, closing the carriage door behind her.

She smiled down at him, outwardly calm but with her stomach churning away like a cement mixer full of bricks. Tearing herself away from the door she made her way along the short carriage and sat down opposite Ariel. She'd booked a window seat on the left hand side so that Rocco would stay in view as long as possible. Ariel stuck her tongue out at Pen who responded with a royal wave and an extravagant bow which set her giggling. Rocco, standing stock still on the edge of the platform mouthed something Harper didn't catch.

Having nothing to lose, Harper responded with – *I love you.*

Words she'd wanted to say but had lacked the courage until now.

'Goodbye Plockton, hello L.A.' Ariel dusted off her hands as the train pulled out of the station and Pen and Rocco vanished from sight. Retrieving her headphones and iPhone from her tote bag she gave Harper a steady look. 'You know, auntie, if I didn't know better, I'd say –'

'Yes?'

'Stop me if I'm wrong here, but I thought that maybe Rocco had a bit of a thing for you.'

'Bit of a thing?'

'Crazy, right?' She laughed and then adopted the demeanour of a relationships councillor. 'Though, to be honest, I think you've missed an opportunity there. You're in last chance saloon and the fat lady is about to sing the final aria. That's all I'm saying.' Putting the headphones over her ears she brought the conversation to a close.

'Too many mixed metaphors, Ariel, but thanks for the advice.'

However, Ariel'd already lost interest and was scrolling through her phone for Spotify tracks while beautiful highland scenery sped past, unseen. Sighing, Harper opened the new Val McDermid she bought in Inverness and attempted to read it.

Inverness!

Oh no, Nessie! She'd left her in Rocco's bedroom. What if Pen saw it, put two and two together and . . . she stopped herself. Pen thought about nothing except his wildlife photographs. If Ariel hadn't picked up the vibe, he certainly wouldn't.

Releasing a pent-up breath she tried to focus on the long journey ahead and what would happen if they missed any of their connections. However, all she could see was Rocco standing on the platform looking as wretched as she felt, knowing that their highland fling had come to an end.

Chapter Twenty-Eight

Familiar scents greeted Harper when she entered Polzenith Primary School five days before the start of the autumn term: varnish, fresh paint and the lingering smell of school dinners. Same old. Same old. Smiling wryly, she walked across the newly polished hall keeping to the edges so as not to undo Jim's hard work. Pushing open the door of her tiny office she stood on the threshold and reflected on everything that had happened since the last day of the summer term.

Rocco Penhaligon.

The mad dash to Plockton.

Falling in love.

For the first time she didn't experience the buzz which usually accompanied the start of a new term. Or the missionary zeal she'd felt five years ago when taking up her post as head of the three schools. She'd accomplished everything she'd set out to do: bringing the schools out of special measures, recruiting enthusiastic teachers, gaining Outstanding status and raising standards. Should she decide to bow out at the end of term she would be leaving everything in good order.

So – why didn't she feel more upbeat?

Fancifully, she recalled Alexander the Great who, upon seeing the breadth of his domain, stood and wept because there were no more worlds to conquer. Was that it? Had she reached the end of her five-year plan and had nothing to look forward to?

Get over yourself, MacDonald, move onwards and upwards to greater things, as you'd planned, before –

Before meeting Rocco Penhaligon.

She missed him so much that it was almost a physical pain, a 'Rocco-sized' hole in her heart which nothing could heal. The only thing keeping her going was the thought of walking to Penhaligon's garage later today, climbing the rickety stairs to Rocco's loft and surprising him. She shivered, feeling nervous and excited at the same time, as skittish as a teenager on a first date.

Harper MacDonald having a bout of whimsy? No way.

Sitting at her desk she reached for the in-tray and started sorting through the mail. She didn't hear Jim crossing the hall until he tapped on her office door.

'Jim!' she greeted.

'Welcome home. Good holiday? How was Nepal?'

'Bit of a disaster. We all went down with a tummy bug during the first week. It was ghastly, my second bout of food poisoning this summer. I'm still not over it.' In fact, the lingering smell of school dinners was almost enough to set her off again.

'That doesn't happen in Newquay. Not much, anyway,' he laughed.

'How's Ariel?' Jim had a soft spot for her and she knew exactly how to twist him round her little finger.

'Good, thanks. She achieved really good A level results and her place at Imperial College London to study Geology has been confirmed. Lured there, not so much by the course and the promise of a year's study abroad, as the bright lights of the city. Apparently, she's had enough of Polzenith and Pl –' She stopped herself saying *Plockton*. 'She'll be returning soon and I'll take her shopping to Truro for bed linen, duvet, pillows and – special request – a coffee machine, prior to Fresher's Week. It's all so organised these days, unlike when I went to uni and we sort've muddled through.'

'You'll miss her.'

'Yes – and no.' They both laughed, knowing exactly what she meant. 'So, what's been happening in the Three Pols in my absence?'

'Of course, you won't have heard, seeing as you only got back from Nepal last night.'

'Heard what?'

'About the Penhaligons.' At the mention of their name Harper relived the *ice bucket challenge* she'd taken part in several years ago, a douche of cold water dropping on her head and travelling all the way down her spine.

'What about them?'

'They've sold up, lock, stock and barrel, left the village and moved to Scotland.' His enquiring look prompted her to fill in the gaps. As predicted, news of her storming into the garage on the last day of term, accusing Rocco of cradle-snatching her niece, forming an uneasy alliance and heading after the runaways on the back of his motorbike had spread round the village like wildfire.

So unlike Miss MacDonald. Usually so professional, so circumspect.

Although, no more than expected from Rocco Penhaligon, judging by Jim's expression. 'No one saw it coming. Rocco's left a trail of broken hearts and some very disappointed ladies behind, I can tell you *that*.'

'Really?' She kept her features neutral. She liked Jim, but at the end of the day the sooner people forgot about her Highland Fling the better.

'By the way, before Rocco left the village he dropped a package off at our house.' Another enquiring look as he handed over a large carrier bag. 'You okay? You've gone very pale.'

'Ye- yes.' She forced a smile. 'The tummy bug has left me tired and washed out.'

'You should see a doctor. You never know what you've picked up abroad. I know someone who picked up an intestinal river fluke and –'

'Thanks, Jim, I will.' Taking the hint, Jim left the office and headed for his inner sanctum where, among mop buckets, cleaning materials and bin bags he listened to the Test Match on an ancient transistor radio.

Harper opened the carrier bag and her breath snagged as Nessie's green ears and felt spine poked out. Removing the wee monster from the bag she noticed that a luggage label was attached to its chest, like Paddington Bear.

It read: *Please look after this plesiosaur, thank you. Rocco.*

'Oh, Rocco,' she breathed shakily, giving Nessie a hug before putting her on the desk.

When they'd parted at the station Rocco'd said: *Having found you, I won't allow you to walk out of my life.* However, he hadn't mentioned moving out of Polzenith . She wouldn't jump to conclusions, she'd stay calm, give him a chance to explain. Looking at her in-tray and then back to Nessie, she reached a decision.

She'd go home, phone him and listen to what he had to say.

* * *

Later, settled in an armchair with a hot drink, Harper dialled Rocco's landline. There was lot of crackling as Polzenith and Plockton connected.

'Hello.'

'Hello. Is that Pen?'

'Yes.'

'Is your dad around?'

'Dunno.'

'Would you mind checking? Tell him it's Harper and –'

Pen put the phone down before she'd finished. Her hand had been shaking as she'd dialled Heron Croft's number but now she felt like exploding, annoyed by Pen's off-hand manner. Then she reminded herself that Ariel would've acted similarly and Pen had probably forgotten who she was.

'Penhaligon.'

'Hello, Penhaligon,' Harper replied, her voice husky. For a few moments the line went dead, then it crackled back into life.

'Harper? *Harper!* Pen didn't say who was on the phone.'

'That's because he didn't wait to find out.' Remembering their conversation at Plockton station she laughed. 'Kids, huh? Who'd have 'em?'

'Not me.' Harper wondered if, like her, he'd gone over those last precious moments so often that the memory was blurred round the edges. There was no time for further reflection as Rocco continued. 'He's being a nightmare at the moment. All he can think about is going away with Hugh Morrison. I could cheerfully strangle him.'

'Hugh or Pen?'

'Both.'

'Please don't. I have no desire to visit you in the Scottish equivalent of Wormwood Scrubs.'

'That'd be Barlinnie,' he supplied, then a brief silence. 'Why are we talking about Her Majesty's Prison Service when . . . hang on a minute.' Seven hundred miles away Rocco got up and closed the sitting room door before crashing back on to the sofa. 'Not that Pen has the slightest interest in what his dad says to his friend's auntie. However, in case I say something which might scar him for life, I'll keep our conversation private.'

'Is that likely? Traumatising Pen, I mean.' They'd slipped back into their easy way of talking, as though they'd never been apart. Her anxiety disappeared and she settled more comfortably in the arm chair, putting tired legs and unusually swollen ankles up on a foot stool.

'Very likely. First up, however, let me start by saying that watching you get on the Inverness train was the hardest thing I've ever done. Things were left unsaid because I thought we'd have more time, but with the kids arriving early and the business with Morrison at the Plockton Arms, everything went pear-shaped. Things were left unsaid. Important things – sorry, repeating myself.'

He sounded keen to put the record straight. Steeling herself for the worst, Harper urged him on.

'I'm listening.'

'I need – *want* – to explain. About my selling up, re-locating to Plockton and buying Auld Baxter's garage.' Auld Baxter's garage? Ah, now it was starting to make sense.

'You don't have to, I understand.' She didn't, not really. However, she didn't want to come across needy and desperate. If he was about to deliver the *it's not you, it's me* speech, she wanted to hang up with her dignity and self-respect intact.

'No you don't understand.' He was quite firm. 'I didn't mention buying the garage for the same reason I didn't mention the vacancy at the primary school. I didn't want to get in the way of your plans for the future or pressurise you into making a decision you might later regret.'

Time to lay *her* cards on the table.

'My decision has been made. I'm leaving at the end of term. Head teachers have to give a term's notice and I want the school to be in a good place when the new head takes over. My legacy, if you like.'

'When will you leave?'

'Right after the Carol Service, slipping away as quietly as possible. I'm seeing the chair of governors tomorrow to hand him my letter of resignation.'

'Just like that?'

'Just like that.'

Now she knew how he felt, everything had become secondary to her desire to be with him. 'I'll inform the staff during the INSET days planned for next week, swearing them to secrecy. I don't want Chinese whispers flying round the village at the start of a gruelling sixteen-week term.'

'Sixteen weeks? I don't know if I can wait that long until I see you.' His disappointment was tangible. 'When can you come up to Plockton?'

'Not before half term. School starts back next week and I have Ariel to get settled at university.'

'I thought you were stepping back and letting her mother do more?'

'I was. But it's hardly practical for Shona to fly over from L.A.'

Rocco gave a non-committal huff. 'To repeat the question, when *might* we expect to see you in Plockton?'

'The last week in October.' Silence.

'That's a long way off.'

'It'll give us a breathing space.'

'I don't need a breathing space. I need you in Plockton – where you belong. To paraphrase the song – my bed really is too big without you.'

'God, Rocco,' she whispered, overcome by his passionate declaration.

'Isn't that what you want, too?'

'It is. But –'

'Go on. I know you, there's always a caveat; dot the i's, cross the t's.'

'Exactly. You have responsibilities, too, what about Pen?'

'He's about to travel to Africa and India with Hugh, making a documentary commissioned by the BBC. I'll talk to him before he goes; explain how things are.'

'I hope he won't be too upset by the . . . change in circumstances.'

'He's a big boy, as he keeps telling me. He'll get used to it.'

'Africa? India? Wow, that'll be quite some trip. I hope they find time check on *Loxosceles haddadi* Morrisonii' she joked. 'Hugh's spider.'

'I'm sure they will.' He laughed. 'I take it that Ariel's holding on to her photograph of the bee?'

'Yes, she's hoping to make a little money from licensing it but keeping the copyright. Her mother's advising her.' Harper rolled her eyes even though Rocco couldn't see her. 'I think that was the incident that tipped Morrison over the edge on the night of the pub quiz. That, and seeing me with you.'

There was a knock on the door and Pen entered the room.

'Dad. Your mobile's ringing.'

'Damn. Okay, thanks, Pen. Now, listen up MacDonald, I'll ring you later; tonight and every night to make sure you don't *slip through my fingers.*'

'Shakespeare?' she queried.

'Janet. That night in the pub when we were talking at the bar she said: *Dinnae let Harper slip through your fingers because you feel the time isn't right. Waiting for the time to be right can lead to regrets which stay with you for the rest of your life.*'

'Oh.' Her voice caught in her throat.

'Look, gotta go, ring you later.'

'Later.'

Harper cradled the phone long after their connection had been severed. A sigh escaped, quickly followed by another wave of nausea. Reaching for the packet of ginger biscuits which were never far from her side she wondered when the after effects of the Nepalese tummy bug would leave her.

Jim was right. Next week, if she wasn't any better she'd go and see the doctor.

Chapter Twenty-Nine

The first day of the autumn term Harper was at her desk ticking items off her to-do list.

Talk with chair of governors/hand over letter of resignation – done

Inform staff of intention to leave at end of term – done

Book taxi to pick Ariel up from Heathrow – done

Find free weekend to buy everything Ariel needs for university – done

Confirm date when taking Ariel to university – done

Make appointment with GP in Truro – pending

Ring Rocco this evening – top priority; code red

Naturally, the chair of governors had been disappointed but not surprised to learn of her intention to leave Polzenith. To sweeten the pill Harper had suggested that assistant head, Sue Trevithick, be appointed Acting Head for the Spring Term. The chair's parting shot had been: 'Sue's a most able teacher but she isn't you, Harper.' That was undeniably true but she was leaving Polzenith after the Carol Concert and *that* was non-negotiable.

As expected, the staff had been shocked at learning her news. Their stunned expressions suggested that they hadn't seen it coming, which made her feel guilty and a little sad. But the thought of living seven hundred and thirteen miles from the man she loved hardened her heart and she knew from experience that no one was irreplaceable.

Luckily, no one linked her decision to leave the school with the Penhaligons' departure from the village, which suited her fine. She didn't want her private life to be the talk of the Three Pols.

She'd spoken to Ariel on the phone and she'd seemed genuinely excited about going to Imperial. Typically, she'd emailed a long list of 'essentials' they would need to purchase before she headed to London. Harper had sent it back with most items ticked, some crossed out and a couple left open to negotiation. Once Ariel returned to Polzenith Harper would share her plans with her. Hopefully, the excitement of Freshers' Week would take Ariel's mind off the fact that those plans included Rocco Penhaligon. What was it she'd said on the train to Inverness? *Maybe Rocco had a bit of a thing for you.*

Little did she know!

Moments later, Sue Trevithick entered the office. 'The troops are waiting, Boss. Have you chosen the hymn for this morning's assembly?'

'I'm going to tell them about the legend of the Loch Ness Monster and show them Nessie. Perhaps, *When a Knight Won His Spurs?* I know they love it.'

'Me, too. I'll go and flex my fingers.' Sue was the only member of the staff capable of bashing out a tune on a piano. One of Harper's first moves on being appointed, had been to recruit a retired music teacher on an ad hoc basis to provide recorder and violin lessons. She also helped out by accompanying the singing at end of term concerts.

End of term . . .

Harper followed Sue into the hall and, as her foot touched the newly polished floor, it dawned on her that she was taking the first step towards a new life.

A life with Rocco Penhaligon.

* * *

'You sound tired,' Rocco commented a week later. 'Not overdoing it, are we?' Harper laughed, he sounded like some crusty old village doctor pre-NHS who accepted poached game, rough cider and home grown vegetables in lieu of payment from his poorest patients.

'Hard not to if I'm to get the academic year up and running in the three schools.'

'Well, you can be thankful for one thing,' Rocco said.

'What's that?'

'You haven't got Auld Baxter under your feet.'

'Oh, dear.'

'Exactly. By the end of the month the purchase of his garage will be finalised, the money in his bank account and then he and Janet will head off into the sunset. Well, their villa in Spain to be precise. Until then, I'm obliged to accept his help because I don't want to hurt his feelings. He has promised to help me set up the engineering side of the business when they return from Spain in the spring, so I haven't seen the last of him.'

'It will be quite a wrench for him,' Harper mused and then giggled. 'No pun intended.'

'Naturally, I'll keep his name over the garage door until he leaves and then change to *Penhaligon – automotive engineer.*'

'Just like Polzenith.' Harper remembered that hot afternoon when she'd stormed into the garage and torn a strip off him in front of his workforce. 'I can't wait to see it.'

'And me?'

'And you.'

'At the risk of repeating myself, you sound tired. Something bothering you?' Harper loved that he could detect the slightest change in her mood, even over the phone.

Her shoulders slumped and she groaned. 'That's because my parents have just rung, trying to be helpful.'

'Great. They're academics, aren't they? I'm guessing that they've offered to replace you as head of the three schools, releasing you from your obligations and allowing you to fly up to Inverness on the next available flight. You said 'yes', I take it?'

'If only,' Harper sighed. 'No, it was about Ariel. I know, I know,' she heard Rocco's huff of annoyance. 'But it's not what you think.'

'Surprise me.'

'They want to take Ariel up to university in my place.'

'Sounds like a plan.'

'It is, but a crazy one.' Harper settled herself more comfortably on the settee, took a sip of coffee and explained. 'They plan to drive down to Cornwall, load Ariel and her belongings into the back of the Range Rover, drive up to London and settle her in. During Freshers' Week, they'll stay over and take in a show or two, be around for a few days in case she needs anything, then they'll drive back to Leicester.'

'I don't get it. Why is that a problem?'

'It isn't, except I've always thought I'd be the one to take Ariel to university, see her settled. Discharge my commission, if you like. I know it's absurd, but this is probably the last thing I'll ever do for her, it'd provide closure for me – and her.' She teared up at the thought of waving goodbye to her naughty, difficult niece.

Rocco laughed. 'Seriously? Somehow I think you'll be sorting Ariel out for years to come. You should take your parents up on their offer, unless . . .'

'Unless?'

'Anthony, the ninja-next-door's travelling down with them. Trying his luck with you, one last time?'

'Stop it, you are too bad.' Harper laughed and then relaxed. 'So, you think it's a good idea?'

'I think it's a great idea. I'm guessing that Freshers' Week is the first week in October? It'd be insane for you make the return trip over a weekend with everything else you have to do and then travel up to Plockton a couple of weeks later. If you don't come up at half term, I don't know what I'll do.'

'Oh, Rocco.' Harper loved him making his feelings clear and showing how much he felt for her, how much he hated them being apart. They'd never actually said the 'LOVE' word during any of their phone conversations and Harper knew that was because, when they said it for the first time, they wanted to be together.

'Do this one thing for me, Harper. Please?' Put like that, how could she refuse? She frowned, knowing she should let go, let her parents take the strain, but it was hard to change the habits of a lifetime.

'I will.'

'Promise?'

'Promise.' A sigh, followed by another yawn. 'I've been looking forward to talking to you all day, but dealing with my parents has exhausted me – no change there – I can hardly keep my eyes open.'

'You had the doctor check you over when you came back from Nepal, right? Your resistance was low after the food poisoning bout you had in Plockton. God only knows what you picked up in those teahouses.'

'I've been in touch with a couple of others who were on the trip and it turns out that they've been similarly affected.'

'By 'they' you'd better mean retired Geography teachers called Rodney or Gerald, who wear baggy shorts, favour a socks and sandals combo, and have more hair sprouting out of their ears and nose than stuffing from a busted mattress.'

'That is an uncanny description.' She laughed, cradling the mobile to her ear, heart swelling at the thought of him being distrustful of other men and their intentions. 'Not jealous, are you?'

'Of course, I am, I know what a catch you are. Yet here I am, hundreds of miles away, unable to keep other guys at bay and damning them all to hell. My eyes are greener than Nessie's.'

'Stop it,' she gurgled, tiredness forgotten.

'No, really. Once you're in Plockton I'm never letting you go.' He repeated his earlier promise.

'Well, you'll have to, for now, I'm contracted right up to December the twentieth, don't forget.'

'As if I could. But, I see what you're doing, you're distracting me and not answering my question. Back to the doctor. Have you had bloods taken, or been checked for parasites, viruses, et cetera?'

'Relax. I'm bunking off school tomorrow for the last hour and heading into Truro.'

'Truro?'

'I'm registered with a private GP there. When I was first appointed, I didn't relish the village knowing every time I went in to the local surgery to see a doctor.'

'I get it. Now, can I give you some advice?'

'You can try,' she said with some of her former spirit.

'Have an early night. I don't want you arriving in Plockton worn out and unable to enjoy –' he paused.

'Walking and such like activities?'

'Among other things,' he laughed. 'Hang up, we'll talk twice as long tomorrow. Deal?'

'Deal.'

Reluctantly, Harper ended the call, made herself more comfortable on the sofa and closed her eyes, remembering his face, the light in his eyes, the way his lips quirked when he was teasing her and . . .

Within seconds she was fast asleep.

Chapter Thirty

In the end, Harper was more than happy to accept her parents' offer. Ariel had been a complete nightmare since returning from L.A, having been spoiled and indulged by her mother. She, along with other former sixth formers waiting to go up to university, had decided to spend the last days of summer, riding round the Three Pols shouting and making a thorough nuisance of themselves. She had hoped that Ariel would volunteer to help in school, under supervision, naturally, maybe even get a liking for teaching. However, Ariel flatly refused to work with the rug rats, as she called them, informing Harper that this was her last hurrah and she planned on making it memorable.

There was little Harper could do, except fume in silence and cross off the days until Ariel went up to Imperial. In fact, she was so annoyed with Ariel's attitude that she postponed the planned heart-to-heart to explain her and Rocco's relationship. More annoyingly, having Ariel home meant she was forced to ring Rocco from her bedroom every night if she wanted privacy.

At times, she wondered who exactly was the teenager!

As far as she was concerned the day Ariel left for university couldn't arrive quickly enough. But arrive it did, and although she experienced a pang when her parents' Range Rover rounded the bend and out of the village, it was quickly replaced by a massive sense of relief. She loved her parents but they had proved a headache of a different kind, demanding to know what she planned to do after the end of term.

In their eyes the only sabbatical one could justify was the one which occurred at the end of a long, successful teaching/academic career. So it was with a light heart that she went back into her cottage, picked her phone up off the hall table and rang Rocco.

'The family has left the building,' she said when they were connected.

'What was that sound in the background? Like a wave crashing on the beach. A deep sigh of relief?'

'You said it.' Laughing, she kicked off her shoes and pulled the comforter off the arm of the sofa and over her bare feet. 'What are the chances of us suffering empty nest syndrome now the kids have gone?'

'Remote. The house is quiet and I do miss Pen but he recently started prefacing every sentence with "Hugh says," or "Hugh thinks."'

'Galling.'

'Very. He doesn't yet realise that his idol has feet of clay, as Ariel pointed out back in the summer.'

'He will. Trust me.'

'So, my lovely,' he said in a faux Cornish accent, 'what have you got planned for tonight?'

'A quick tidy up and a long, relaxing bath.' Silence on the other end of the phone. 'You still there?'

'Yes, just thinking of that bath we shared – any chance of repeating the experience in, say, a month's time?' Now it was Harper's turn to be silent as she remembered the tender way he'd soaped her body, lingering over her erogenous zones as he'd rinsed off the lather before wrapping her in a huge bath towel, not caring that water pooled at their feet on the bathroom floor. Sometimes, the days they'd spent together seemed like a dream and she prayed that when he met her off the train they wouldn't feel awkward in each other's company, only managing to relax when it was time to return home.

'We might fit it into the itinerary I've drawn up.'

'Itinerary? You're kidding.'

'I thought we could go walking over the hills, maybe visit the Fairy Pools, pay Sir Michael a visit, that sort of thing.' She kept her voice light, glad he couldn't see her struggle to prevent herself from laughing. 'I'll pack my walking boots and we can take a flask and sandwiches and go yomping over the hills. Hours of endless pleasure.'

'My itinerary is somewhat different. Although it, also, involves hours of endless pleasure.'

'Surprise me.'

'Well, apart from the aforementioned baths, I envisage long, lazy mornings spent in bed, making up for lost time. Hell, some days we might never get out of bed. Then, in the evenings, it'll be dinner in the sitting room in front of the fire, planning our future. How's that for starters?'

Harper couldn't keep up the pretence any longer. 'Beats my itinerary, hands down.'

'Glad to hear it. Roughly five weeks from today I'll be meeting you at the station. Are you sure you don't want me to pick you up from the airport?'

'Just be there when the train pulls in.'

'How will I recognise you?'

'I'll have a wee green monster tucked under my arm and . . .'

'Thanks, I think I can fill in the gaps –'

'And join the dots?'

'Without a safety net.'

'Good night, Rocco.'

'Good night, Miss MacDonald.'

Chapter Thirty-One

Five weeks later, the Inverness to Kyle of Lochalsh train pulled into Plockton Station. Harper's hands were shaking and her legs hardly seemed able to support her weight as she collected her luggage. She let the other passengers off the train and then, taking a deep breath, stepped down onto the platform.

'I'm here, Harper.' A longed for voice, sounding vivid and real after weeks of phone conversations made her spin round. At first, she hardly dared look at Rocco in case he'd altered in some subtle way. He must have guessed how she was feeling because he gathered her to him in an embrace designed to reassure that nothing had changed.

Harper held on to him wishing the moment could last forever.

At last, Rocco put her from him and tucked a long strand of hair behind her ear. 'Is it you? Is it really you?' he asked.

'It is,' Harper said, finding the courage to look into his face. If he'd changed, if it seemed as if he didn't want her there, she'd know immediately. However, there was a light in his eyes, a look which told her she was everything he'd been looking for his entire life. And, she knew in that instant that everything was going to be alright.

'Better kiss me before you disappear in a puff of smoke.' Rocco laughed, seemingly not caring that the tourists who'd rented the former station house *Off the Rails* for the holidays were watching them with interest over afternoon tea. Happy to comply, Harper dropped her bags at her feet and did just that. When she pulled back, Rocco looked down at their feet and frowned.

'Disappointing.'

'What is?'

'The fact that the paving stones haven't melted beneath our feet. Clearly we're out of practice, let's go home and work on our technique. Ah, I see you've brought an old friend with you.' Bending, he picked up the carrier bag holding Nessie.

'A much-travelled plesiosaur pining for the highlands, just like me. Take us home, Rocco.' Harper slipped her tote bag over her shoulder, put her arm round his waist and leaned into him. 'This is where I long to be.'

'Thank God for that.' Rocco wiped imaginary sweat off his brow and, taking her hand, led her out of the station. Harper looked for the Land Rover with the ripped roof but could only see a Volvo 4x4 with a personalised number – R100 PEN.

'Nice motor, John,' she commented in a mockney accent as Rocco opened the passenger door.

'I didn't think you'd relish getting in the one I'm renovating for Morwenna. Although, I do have a certain romantic attachment to it.' Putting Nessie in the back with her luggage, Rocco fastened Harper's seat belt taking care not to touch her, although plainly it was on his mind; on both their minds. Getting into the driver's seat, he turned over the ignition and headed downhill into the village. Neither of them spoke during the short drive to Heron Croft, there was too much riding on this long weekend and they knew it.

Harper calmed her nerves by observing the changes brought about as summer slipped into autumn: mist over the loch, the colour of the vegetation on the far hills, the flowers in the gardens touched by the first frost. Even the clematis round the door of Heron Croft had lost it leaves, its skeletal fingers twisting arthritically round the wooden porch waiting for spring.

Rocco had warned her that winters here could be punishing and she didn't doubt it. She smiled inwardly, envisaging evenings by the fire, long mornings in bed and walks over the hills. That beat playground duty, INSET days, planning meetings at County Hall and evenings dealing with admin at the dining room table.

Climbing down from the Volvo, Harper looked across Harbour Street towards Heron Croft's garden remembering the breakfast she and Rocco had shared there, the turning point in their relationship. It seemed so long ago now, and so much had changed that she worried if they could make this long distance romance work.

Glancing at her over his shoulder Rocco led the way, pushing open the front door and depositing her things in the hall. Harper followed, removing her coat and scarf while he attended to the wood burner in the sitting room. The house smelled of apple logs and peat turves and she took in a deep breath, savouring Heron Croft's signature scent. It felt as if the house was wrapping its arms around her. She was startled out of her reverie when Rocco returned from the sitting room.

'Welcome home, Harper.' His light kiss was designed to reassure her that he understood the need to take things slowly; give them time to ease themselves back into the physical relationship they'd enjoyed back in the summer. Harper was glad for his sensitivity.

'I'm glad to be here,' she replied, 'at last.'

'You must be tired. Go through and sit by the fire while I make us both a drink. What'll it be – wine, whisky, tea, coffee?'

'Tea would really hit the spot.' Walking into the sitting room she soon relaxed, mesmerised by the flames dancing behind the glass door of the wood burner. Glancing across to the other sofa she remembered when Rocco had imprisoned her there, saying: *Resistance is futile.*

How right he'd been.

* * *

Fingers clumsy with nerves, Rocco poured tea into mugs aware that he couldn't afford to screw up, to do anything which would send Harper high-tailing it back to Polzenith. They were beyond pleased to see each other, but there was a tension between them which was hard to pinpoint. It had been so much easier talking on the phone. They'd fallen in love during those nightly phone conversations but now things felt awkward, forced. He wanted her so much, longed to take her upstairs to his bed and make love until evening settled around them. However, he knew it was up to Harper to decide how quickly things moved forward. Taking a deep breath, he carried the mugs through to the sitting room where he found Harper staring into the fire, deep in thought.

Anxiety made his mouth dry. 'Tea, m'lady?' Uncurling her legs, Harper smiled and reached out for the mug. She cradled it in her hands, as if deriving comfort from its warmth. 'Cake?'

'You've been baking? I'm impressed.' Good, some of her old spirit and their easy way of talking was returning.

'Sorry to disillusion you but it's shortbread from *Plockton Shores,* I know my limitations.'

'I don't recall too many limitations,' she said, straight-faced, though her eyes danced. His body reacted to her smile, reminding him that he might be taking things slowly but the hormones beating through his blood had other ideas. Picking up his mug he sat down on the other sofa, his eyes drawn to the goodie bag on the table which suggested Harper had caught the train to Inverness.

'The Caledonian Sleeper? I thought you were flying up?'

'Circumstances changed.'

Harper pushed the bag towards him, indicating that he should open it. Intrigued, he removed a cellophane-wrapped Cornish pasty, two scones, a small pot of clotted cream and cake from Polzenith village bakery. 'Saffron cake, how did you know I was suffering withdrawal symptoms?' He arranged everything she'd brought on the coffee table.

'There's more.'

Dipping back into the bag he pulled out an envelope and frowned.

Opening it, he pulled out several grainy black and white polaroid photos. He knew straight away what they were. His bowels clenched and he felt sick. How *could* Pen have been so stupid? So irresponsible? Getting Ariel MacDonald pregnant and then swanning off to Africa with Morrison as though nothing had happened? How could he and Harper have misread their relationship, dismissing it as almost fraternal?

So much for the heart-to-heart they'd had before Pen left for Africa when he'd poured out his soul and revealed his feelings for Harper. Why hadn't Pen mentioned Ariel's pregnancy then? This explained the slight distance between him and Harper, no wonder she was acting strangely towards him.

God, what a mess.

Letting out a long breath he cut his son some slack. Perhaps Pen didn't know about the pregnancy? Maybe it wasn't his? For a moment relief washed over him before reality kicked in, accompanied by a sickening feeling of dread and déjà vu. Of course it was Pen's. History had a way of repeating itself, didn't it? Both of them fathers before their twenty-first birthday?

Christ. What a legacy.

'You okay, Rocco? You look as though you've seen a ghost.' Harper came over and sat next to him.

'I h-have. The ghost of pregnancies past.' The scan had unmanned him, made his hands shake and his knees tremble. He coughed to clear his throat and tried to speak. 'I can't take it in. Stupid. Stupid. Stupid.'

Harper looked equally troubled, understandably weighed down by the thought of Ariel and Pen becoming parents. Now he understood; she'd travelled all the way to Plockton to tell him something she couldn't share on the phone and for no other reason. Nothing to do with wanting to see him, to be with him. He'd misread her from the moment she'd stepped off the train.

Plainly this bombshell was responsible for the sense of detachment between them. God, what a car crash. If he was angry she must be apoplectic but, as ever, was good at hiding her feelings. What was it she'd said back in Polzenith months ago: *don't you know that it's different for girls?*

'What an idiot!' He smacked his forehead with the heel of his hand. Stony-faced, Harper took the scan from him and returned it to its envelope with a finality that was disquieting. It didn't take a genius to figure out that once she'd said her piece she'd most likely move into the Plockton Hotel and head home on the first train tomorrow.

'Stupid? We're both to blame, aren't we?' When she glanced up her eyelashes were spiky with tears.

'What did you expect?' Disappointment at his son's irresponsible behaviour made him speak more harshly than intended.

'Something a little more considered. A little more supportive.'

Barely registering what she'd said, Rocco ploughed on, struggling to contain his anger and disappointment. The day was ruined, their longed-for reunion a disaster. 'I can't believe that Pen could act so reprehensively. His prospects, his life, ruined. Same goes for Ariel,' he added, somewhat as an afterthought.

'Pen? Ariel?'

Rocco ploughed on. 'That's it. I'm bringing him home. Now is not the time for him to be off enjoying himself when he has responsibilities to face up to. I'm sorry, Harper this must be a shock for you, too. But I'm guessing that you've had a week or two to get used to the idea. *What*? Why are you looking at me like that? God, is there more?'

What more could there be?

Harper drew her sleeve across her eyes, blew her nose using the paper napkin next to her piece of shortbread and took in a shaky breath.

'It's not Pen's baby.'

'Not – then, whose?'

'Whose do you think?' Raising her head, she looked him straight in the eye.

'I – I'm not . . . Y- you don't m-mean –'

'The baby is ours. Yours and mine.' Her cheeks burned as she gave him time to absorb the news.

'But, how –'

Visibly upset, she nevertheless managed a weak smile. 'Bit old for a biology lesson, aren't you?' she asked, with a touch of her old asperity.

'Well, obviously I know *how*, but when?'

'The first time we made love after I'd had food poisoning. Clearly, the birth pill was flushed out of my system along with the sushi. It's not unheard of.'

Reaching over, he removed the envelope from Harper's fingers and re-examined the scan, this time in wonderment. 'Yours and mine,' he repeated.

'Apparently.'

'God –'

'My feelings exactly.'

Realising that his reaction to the baby scan wasn't the one Harper had been expecting or deserved, he quickly made amends. He placed the scan on the table, carefully, reverentially and turned to her.

'Harper. I am such an idiot; can you forgive me for spoiling a precious moment?'

'I should have foreseen that you'd reach a false conclusion.'

'I am so sorry. Please –' He opened his arms and was relieved when Harper melted into them, put her head on his shoulder and curled an arm round his waist. A baby. Their baby. He was overwhelmed by a new gamut of emotions: a need to protect Harper and their unborn child, pride and satisfaction that they'd created this new life and, inappropriately, the desire to make love to her.

'Right, madam,' he said shakily, kissing the top of Harper's head and putting her from him.

Walking over to the other sofa he arranged the cushions so that Harper could recline there. Taking her hand he guided her over, made her put her feet up and then drew the cashmere comforter over her knees. Harper watched in obvious amusement as he pushed the coffee table out of the way and sat at her feet with his back against the sofa.

'I won't break, you know,' she laughed, reaching out and running her fingers through his hair. He reached over his shoulder for her hand and kissed it.

'Sorry I acted like a complete jerk, you caught me off guard. I know first-hand how hard it is to bring up a baby on your own and wouldn't wish that on any teenager, let alone Pen, or Ariel.' Turning round, he knelt up and cupped her face in his hand.

'No, I'm sorry. I've had a few weeks to get used to the idea, I should have anticipated that you'd be shocked and –'

'– delighted.' Poking fun at himself, he raked his fingers through his hair and presented his best profile. 'You don't think this Wild Corsair is too old to become a second-time dad? I seem to remember you had reservations about my age, first time we met.'

'For Ariel, not for me. Since then you've kinda grown on me. And you have to admit, 'second time dad' sounds better than 'elderly primagravida', which is how I am referred to in gynaecological terms.'

'Okay, I'm going to ask you a series of stupid questions about pregnancy, please bear with me.'

'But you've been through all this before, with Pen.'

'No I haven't. His mother left the village without my knowing she was pregnant. I only learned of his existence when he was delivered to my door in a Moses basket.'

'Okay. But first, come and lie next to me on the sofa.'

'Done.'

He lay beside her, turning onto his left-hand side so they could lie nose to nose. Her soft curves pressed tantalisingly against his body, her perfume overwhelmed him, improper thoughts overruled practical considerations and his earlier resolution to take things slowly. Would it be safe to make love without harming the baby, he wondered? Time for all that later. For now, he had to reassure her that he welcomed the news and would be at her side, every step of the way.

Rocco pulled the comforter over them and they snuggled up together as the soft highland dusk settled round Plockton. Rain pattered on the window and the turves of peat hissed and flamed in the wood burning stove. Their breathing settled into a regular pattern, each sigh met with a corresponding breath as they dreamed of the future. Rocco closed his eyes, knowing there was no place he'd rather be, no one he'd rather be with.

Time to make that clear to Harper.

'I'm guessing your being unwell after Nepal was the baby making its presence felt and nothing to do with Nepalese cuisine?'

'You guess correctly. It wasn't until I went to see the doctor and they got bloods back from the lab that I found out the reason behind the nausea. I –' she blushed. 'I've always had irregular periods and put the changes down to an early menopause. Sorry, TMI?'

'Don't apologise, I'm just sorry you had to face that alone. If you'd called me I would have been down there, PDQ.'

'I know that. But that would have made sorting out my eventual exit from the Three Pols harder to arrange. ' He stroked her cheek, marvelling at her calm demeanour.

'How are things now?'

'Sickness gone, well just about, in exchange for a new set of symptoms. When I return to Polzenith I'll be fifteen weeks pregnant, a few weeks after that I'll have another scan when the doctor will be able to determine the baby's sex. Should we want to know. Do we?'

'Not sure, something else to discuss this week. One of the many things – the others being: where the baby will be born, when we tell our families and how soon you can leave the Pols.' He kissed the top of her head and then laughed. 'My parents will die of shock. To paraphrase Oscar Wilde: *'to father one child out of wedlock may be regarded as a misfortune; to repeat the mistake looks like carelessness.'* He pulled a face, suddenly very serious. 'They'd better behave themselves this time round or they'll have no part in our child's life. On that point there's no room for negotiation.'

She nodded. 'I'm hoping I can keep the pregnancy secret until the end of term, but I doubt I'll manage it. I'll be twenty-one weeks pregnant and with a significant bump. I usually wear business suits for work –'

'Yes. I remember that tight skirt and jacket combo you were wearing when you walked – make that *stormed,* into my garage back in July.'

'Rocco, focus.' Pointing two fingers at his eyes and then back to hers, Harper laughed. 'I'm thinking much looser clothes will be the order of the day. As for your parents, what about mine? They'd set their hearts on my becoming an H.M.I.'

'They'll get over it,' he dismissed her concerns in an instant. 'All that matters is that you know I love and want to protect you both.' Pushing the comforter further down their bodies he laid a gentle hand over her almost undiscernible bump. Then he laughed.

'What?'

'I had it all planned: champagne, steak and all the trimmings, one of Janet's amazing puddings out of the freezer, cheese, scented candles and glittery stuff scattered aesthetically around the dining table – the works. Instead I blurt out *I love you*, like a jackass.' Harper laughed, laying her hand over his on her baby bump.

'It's perfect, don't worry. And, for the record,' she laughed again, 'I've wanted to say I love you for so long I'm surprised it wasn't the first thing I said when I got off the train. I thought the moment might lose its impact if I'd said it down the phone.'

'Same here.' Propping himself up on his elbow he smiled down at her. He'd forgotten how blue her eyes were, the glossy sheen of her dark hair, the pale complexion so typical of her highland DNA. 'My delivery might not win an Oscar but never doubt that I love you, Miss MacDonald.'

'I love you too, Wild Corsair.' Then they went quiet, until Harper giggled, breaking the mood. 'Know what I want more than anything else right now?'

'The same thing I do?'

'Well, unless that's a bath I couldn't say.'

'A bath?'

'Like the one we shared this summer, lots of bubbles, fluffy towels, you washing my hair. Remember? I've been dreaming about it all the way from Cornwall.'

'You should have been dreaming about *me* all the way from Polzenith.'

'I was, naturally. Only, the bath, more so.' She sent him a sassy look and kissed him.

'Good. No man likes to take second place to plumbing in the affections of the woman he loves.'

'Loves? I'll never tire of hearing you say that.'

'Happy to oblige.'

'The bath in our rented property is pathetic whereas you have a humongous roll top bath.' She returned to the original subject.

Rocco laughed. 'You're serious, aren't you?' She nodded and they fell silent, as the vision of them making love in the bath presented an alluring and distracting image. Rocco shook himself and then explained. 'Granny was a great one for long baths. The shower over the bath is a recent innovation. Anyway, we have other things to discuss, first. Your travel arrangements for one; why didn't you fly up to Inverness?'

'I didn't want to risk flying, although everything I've read suggests that after twelve weeks I wouldn't be putting the baby at risk. I booked a rather luxurious superior double on the Caledonian Sleeper because it came with an ensuite shower room. The nausea has almost disappeared, but I don't like to stray too far from a loo. I won't go into more detail because it's a bit of a passion killer.' She pulled a face.

'Nothing you say could ever stop me wanting you.'

'I'll remind you of that in two months' time when you come down to bring me home.' She took his hand, turned it over and held it palm upwards. 'Right now, our baby is the size of a pear, but come the end of this term it'll be more like a pumpkin.'

'No chance of you leaving before then?'

'Naturally, I'd like to. But, unless advised otherwise by the obstetrician, I'll see the job through to the end. It'll be my last act as a headteacher and I want to go out on a high.'

'You won't regret leaving the profession, will you?'

'Are you kidding?'

'I suppose you could always apply for the headship of the village school after Easter. Keep your hand in?' He smiled to show that he was aware how not mentioning the vacancy back in the summer had temporarily put a wedge between them.

'No way.' Harper punched him playfully on the shoulder and then became serious. 'I never considered motherhood, didn't think it was for me, especially seeing how it messed up Shona's life. Bringing up Ariel over the last few years was almost like having a child of my own to love, nurture and,' she grinned, 'argue with. However, falling in love with you, becoming pregnant has changed everything. This feels so right. Look, I've been giving it some thought. Why don't you come down to Polzenith and stay with me for the last few weeks of term? If the garage can spare you?'

'Fergus can manage' he said quickly.

'By then, my reputation as a scarlet woman and a disgrace to the teaching profession will be established. I'll be the talk of the Three Pols.'

He felt fiercely protective of her. 'The first person to say anything untoward in my hearing will be putting themselves at serious risk.'

'Not that I condone violence, naturally. But I like your style.'

'Are you hungry?' Then he grinned. 'You don't have weird cravings do you? Like eating coal or kippers covered in salad cream?'

'Only for the bath,' she laughed.

'You're like a woman possessed. Okay, your wish is my command. You stay there while I take your things upstairs and run the bath.' Pushing himself off the sofa he headed for the hall and then paused, half-turning towards her. 'I take it that you want your things put in my bedroom?'

'Nessie would settle for nothing less.' Stretching out, she picked the scan off the table and lovingly regarded their child. Rocco stood in the doorway, transfixed by the scene, his heart so full of love that he thought it might burst. 'Still here?' she asked.

'Sorry, ma'am, one bath coming up.'

'Don't forget the scented candles . . .'

'I won't. I'd forgotten how bossy you can be, but I can learn to live with it. What I can't do, is learn to live without you.' His voice thickened and his eyes were bright as he turned and headed upstairs.

Left alone, Harper kissed the twelve-week scan and spoke softly to their unborn child. 'It's all going to be alright, little one. You see, I've chosen the best man in the world to be your father.'

Chapter Thirty-Two

In the end, leaving Polzenith had been as easy as One. Two. Three.

One: shake hands with vicar and chair of governors after Carol Service, hug staff and friends, walk down path from church; join Rocco in waiting car.

Two: Stay overnight in posh hotel/spa north of Bristol; by-pass both sets of parents and inevitable recriminations. Break journey at Morwenna's then head for Plockton.

Three: Arrive at Heron Croft; twist engagement ring round finger . . . and breathe.

Harper had imagined that Heron Croft would be cold and unwelcoming when they arrived. However, in a cinematic moment, snowflakes fluttered down out of steel-grey sky shot through with crimson and landed on their hair and faces. Bright pin lights, twined through the wrought iron railings at the front of the house and the iron fretwork of the door canopy, welcomed them home. And, in the place of the usual winter hanging baskets, an arrangement of tiny lights on copper wires fashioned into mistletoe branches twinkled in the dusk.

Two prelit wicker roe deer stood sentinel on either side of the path, looking so realistic that Harper suspected she wouldn't be able to walk past them without stroking their twiggy heads.

'Who? How?' she asked, blinking in amazement and climbing out of the Volvo V60.

'Janet's home for Christmas and she and the girls were desperate to decorate the house, inside and out, as a wee surprise for you.' Rocco joined her on the pavement. 'Although, be warned, Miss MacDonald, this is a one-off. Next year it'll all be down to you.'

'As a primary school teacher of twenty-odd years' experience, I think I'll cope.'

'Big words, Miss MacDonald. I'll remind you of them.' Rocco came round to her side of the car. 'Oh, and no paper chains, can't stand 'em.'

'Duly noted.' She pretended to make a note on her phone but took photos of the front garden and Rocco instead. 'Smile.'

Rocco, happy to oblige, struck a suitably heroic pose, opened the wrought iron gate and walked up the path ahead of her. Pausing beneath one of the mistletoe-shaped decorations he turned, sent her a warm look. 'Welcome home, my darling.'

Then they kissed, their breaths coalescing in the frosty air. Rocco's lips were warm and tasted of the coffee they'd bought at the last services. The kiss triggered familiar longings and they held each other in a seemingly never-ending embrace.

Rocco was the first to draw back.

'Shall we?' Resting his hand lightly on her back to ensure that she didn't slip, he guided her up steps rimed with a tell-tale icy fern pattern. When they entered Heron Croft, the warmth melted the snowflakes on Rocco's dark hair and eyelashes. The house smelled of Christmas: gingerbread, cinnamon and the clootie dumpling Rocco was keen for Harper to try. This was all thanks to Janet who was as keen as Rocco to ensure everything was perfect for Harper's arrival.

'Richard Curtis eat your heart out,' Harper shouted, laughing and throwing her arms wide to encompass everything,

'Four Weddings and a Funeral?' Rocco suggested.

'One Man, a Kilt and a Baby,' Harper supplied, unable to contain her excitement at finally being in Plockton with the man she loved. A new life lay ahead of her; of them. A delicious shiver of prescience traversed her as she thought ahead to next year when their child would be seated in a high chair at the far end of the table, celebrating their first Christmas together as a family.

Mistaking Harper's shiver for her feeling cold, Rocco rubbed her hands to warm them. 'You okay?'

'Never better.' Standing on her tiptoes she kissed him, her heart so full of love that she could hardly speak. Their baby, not wishing to be left out, kicked against Rocco's stomach.

'We hear ya,' he laughed. 'Getting overexcited because it's Christmas Eve the day after tomorrow, are we?'

'Better get used to it. I have a feeling this one's going to be trouble.' Harper laughed, unwinding her scarf and dropping it next to her beret and gloves on the table.

'Don't get too excited,' Rocco warned Harper. 'Christmas is a sedate affair in Plockton, the real celebrations begin on Hogmanay when Sir Michael opens MacKinnon House to friends and family.'

Detecting a sad note in his voice, Harper reached out and squeezed his hand. 'Will you miss Pen not being here?'

'Yes and no.' She sent him a puzzled look and Rocco explained. 'He's having a great time with Morrison out in the Far East. I'll be lucky to receive a phone call on Christmas Day. From here on in, it'll be just you, me and . . .' he looked down at Harper's five-month bump.

'The wee one,' she said, sounding exactly like Janet.

'Exactly. Let's relish the moment of peace and quiet, next year it'll all be different.' He picked up the mail thoughtfully stacked on the table for him and had a quick flick through before turning back to Harper. 'Tomorrow we'll drive over to Skye and drop our M10 form off at the registrar's office in Kyle before it shuts for the holiday.'

'M10. Such a romantic name for our Marriage Notice.' Harper rolled her eyes. 'Not.'

Rocco was suddenly serious. 'Are you sure you won't find the journey too tiring? Only one of the intended party needs to drop off the forms in person, as long as the other party has filled them in correctly and attached their birth certificate.'

'That's one trip I won't be missing out on,' she said in a firm voice.

'And, are you positive that you're happy to settle for a civil ceremony, with Janet and Michael as witnesses, instead of a full blown white wedding? I don't want you to feel you're missing out because I want us to be married before the baby arrives.'

Harper sensed that he was remembering Pen being dumped unceremoniously on his doorstep and the lengths he went to ensure that no one could take Pen away from him.

'Quite sure. We'll be too busy getting ready for the baby's arrival in April – decorating the nursery, shopping trips to Inverness for new clothes for me, not to mention prams and other baby paraphernalia. Before we know it, I'll be *huge,* refuse to go anywhere and spend all my time reading or watching box sets while you cater to my every whim.'

'Not much change there then.'

'Cheeky.' She feigned annoyance. 'Besides, trying to get everyone up here in the depths of winter for a wedding could prove tricky. Pen's unsure how long he's going to be away with Hugh, Ariel will be back at university, Shona's in the middle of filming and my mother's about to embark on a lecture tour from which she can't be released. Besides –'

'Yes?'

'I'll be more romantic renewing our wedding vows on July 31st, the anniversary of the day when we met. I'll have lost my baby weight and look gorgeous for our wedding photos, and . . .'

'You'll always look gorgeous to me . . .'

'I know, but us elderly primagravidae have our standards.'

Rocco laughed. 'If you're happy, then I'm happy. Let's talk more about this when we're less tired. Michael said he had a little surprise up his sleeve which he'll reveal when we all meet up at Janet's on Christmas Eve. But for now –'

Harper nodded. 'I don't know about you but I'm pretty knackered.'

Rocco pulled a face which would have done a dowager duchess

proud. 'Not quite the words one expects to hear from the executive head of three schools, Miss MacDonald.'

'*Former* executive head, if you don't mind. Get used to it, husband-to-be, those days are over. Now, fetch our things from the car, let's head upstairs, and . . .'

'Not the *bath thing*, again? You're like a woman possessed.'

'Not tonight. But I'm not ruling it out for tomorrow.'

Grinning, Rocco left the kitchen and headed back outside. Alone, Harper stood in the middle of the room admiring the greenery and lights Janet and her daughters had used to decorate the kitchen, including twining holly branches, heavy with berries, through the banister and handrail. Rocco was right, she had a lot to live up to next year. Walking through to the sitting room she paused to admire the Christmas tree decked out with heirloom crystal and glass ornaments the Penhaligons had used to celebrate Christmas in Heron Croft longer than anyone could remember.

Next year, there would be huge vases of flowers, presents round the tree, carols playing on the sound system and the three of them would be preparing to welcome their friends and family to their home on Christmas Eve.

Before she knew it, Rocco was back in the kitchen carrying two holdalls and looking dog-tired, although he struggled to conceal it.

'And so to bed?' she questioned.

'My thoughts exactly, Miss MacDonald.'

Sending him an inviting look over her shoulder, Harper climbed the wooden hill to Bedfordshire, giving out a little squeal as Rocco pinched her bottom and chased her into their bedroom.

Chapter Thirty-Three

Seven months later, Rocco and Harper stood on the battlements of Michael McKinnon's ancient pele tower, having sneaked away from the party celebrating the renewal of their wedding vows.

'So, Mrs Penhaligon, how does it feel to have made an honest man of me, twice over?' Rocco asked, straightening the fur capelet over the shoulders of Harper's ivory silk dress.

'Good, although . . . '

'Go on.'

'I'm rather worried in case the Wild Corsair has disappeared for good.'

'He's simply having a well-earned rest.' Laughing, Rocco popped open the bottle of Pol Roger he'd smuggled out of the hall and sent the cork soaring through the air.

Taking the proffered champagne flute, Harper let out a contented sigh.

'Mind you, I don't mind him going into semi-retirement if it means you wearing full highland regalia. I've never seen so many kilts in one place. It's quite overwhelming to be honest.' Pretending to fan herself she gave her husband an appreciative once-over.

'And, have *I* told you how my heart almost stopped when you came down the main staircase, walked through the hall and joined me to renew our vows before our family and friends? That moment will stay with me, forever.' He raised her hand to his lips, the light in his grey-green eyes telling her never to doubt his love.

'Oh, Rocco . . .'

'It's up there with the moment I first held Flora in my arms and welcomed her into the world. You'd done all the hard work while all I'd done was cheer on from the side-lines.' His voice thickened as he remembered the moment when he'd looked into Flora's blue eyes and vowed to protect her from the dangers of the world. 'It didn't seem a fair trade then and it still doesn't.'

They clinked glasses together, mindful of Michael's best crystal and looked over the parapet to the gardens below where guests were spilling onto the terrace to sit under large umbrellas and canvas sails while the hall was made ready for the dancing. 'Talking of Miss Flora Penhaligon, where is she?'

'She was last seen being pushed round the gardens in an ancient Silver Cross pram Ariel discovered in Michael's attic. She and Morwenna's daughters have spent the last couple of days scrubbing it to within an inch of its life and decorating it with ribbons, flowers and baby mobiles. Even Pen has helped.'

'Talking of whom, have you witnessed him and Ariel arguing over who has precedence when it comes to holding Flora and helping out at bath time. Pen thinks that being Flora's half-brother trumps Ariel who – in his words – is merely her cousin.'

'He hasn't quite braved a nappy change,' Rocco laughed. 'That's what separates the men from the boys.' Leaning over a granite crenulation he surveyed Michael's famous tropical gardens which rivalled those at Inverewe and Attadale. 'I was a bit worried about the weather, but . . .'

'Michael's events manager assured me everything would go off without a hitch and that she had a back-up plan if the weather turned. She understands Plockton's climate better than most, having organised weddings, christenings and family parties at McKinnon House since it was licensed five years ago.'

Rocco raised his glass to their friend and benefactor, Michael, who'd gifted the whole package: family dinner last night, vow renewal ceremony, buffet lunch, evening party and ceilidh as a belated wedding present. He'd also offered to host Flora's christening in the church on his estate when the time was right.

'It was kind of him to accommodate our family and friends in the Big House and guest cottages around the estate. I don't think I could have stood another minute of my mother and father's pointed looks, designed to remind me what I've 'thrown away'. Their words, not mine.' She released a huff of annoyance. Rocco turned away from the view and rubbed her back soothingly.

'Hey, why should you get off lightly? I'm in trouble for fathering a child – as my mother so delicately put it, *at my age.*'

'Shockingly ageist,' Harper gurgled, despite knowing that it was a year to the day since Rocco rolled out from underneath the car he was working on, and she'd demanded: *My God, how old are you?*' Both sets of parents, she'd noticed, had struck up an unlikely friendship, seemingly united in disappointment. The only wobble being when Harper's father dropped, oh so casually, into the conversation that he'd been awarded the Order of the British Empire for services to education, while Heather Penhaligon had been awarded the less prestigious Member of the British Empire medal for her charitable work.

'Sneaking away to get married in a civil ceremony with only two witnesses when we could have been married in the Order's chapel in St Paul's Cathedral dealt them another blow,' Rocco commented, not in the least repentant.

'Better not tell them that Flora will be christened in Michael's church later this year. They've already been badgering me to have her christened in the chapel.'

'As if we'd schlep all the way down to London for a fifteen-minute ceremony. Plockton is our home, it's Flora's home and that's where she'll be christened. It's not open to negotiation.'

'Let's forget all about them.' Harper slipped her arm through Rocco's.

'I have been disappointed in one respect,' Rocco said, 'I had hoped your ninja-next-door would have made the trip up to Argyll in one last attempt to spirit you away, like a middle-aged Young Lochinvar. We could have fought it out up here.' He mimed a sword fight to the death or, at least, until Anthony cried: *I yield.*

'Stop it.' Harper poked him playfully in the ribs. 'You've met my sister, let that be enough.'

'Ah, yes, Shona.' Rocco had made it plain from the moment they'd shaken hands and exchanged an air kiss that a little of Shona MacDonald went a *very* long way.

'Did you notice her eyeing up the antiques and family silver over dinner last night? She even turned over her plate to see if it was back-stamped *Crown Derby*, or whatever. After dinner, she pinned me in a corner and demanded the lowdown on Michael's widower status and whether or not there were children waiting in the wings to inherit 'this pile', as she put it. She fancied herself as Lady Shona until I pointed out that, should Michael choose to remarry, his wife would be known as Lady McKinnon. That seemed to put her off.'

'I don't imagine she takes kindly to second billing?'

'Exactly.'

'Seeing her in action has made me realise what a great job you've done bringing up Ariel, of keeping her on the straight and narrow. I hope Shona will acknowledge her debt to you.'

'Unlikely.' Harper leaned back on the crenulation and grinned. 'But no worries. Exercising my right as a bride, I drew up the seating plan and ensured that Shona was on the same table as Hugh Morrison. She might be family but there's no way she was sitting on the top table getting drunk, causing mischief and recounting how this was all *so different* to her three weddings. If she tells me once more how lucky I've been to – what was her word, *snare* you, I won't be held responsible for my actions.'

'She does have a point, though,' Rocco said, neatly sidestepping before Harper could exact vengeance. 'I'm the lucky one, let no one dispute that.' Taking Harper's glass and placing it next to his, he drew her into a kiss. 'You're like chalk and cheese, thank God. Did you see Ariel sending her daggers because she's been knocking back the booze and flirting with Hugh, and any other eligible man, throughout the meal?'

'To give Mother her due, she has had words with Shona threatening dire consequences if she ruins the day, Luckily, when we left the hall she seemed to have settled for regaling anyone within earshot about her bit part in Hamish Macbeth all those years ago.'

Rocco, having heard the story several times, groaned and put a hand over his eyes.

'I've just had a brilliant idea,' Harper said. 'Why doesn't Shona earmark Hugh for husband #4? They could get married in the fancy-schmancy chapel at St Paul's and everyone would be happy.'

'Plan,' Rocco said, high-fiving her.

At that moment, the wooden trap door leading up from the floor below opened and Pen stuck his head through.

'Dad, the event's organiser wants to know if you and Harper are ready to be piped into the hall for the ceilidh.'

'Thanks son, we'll be down in a minute.'

Pen retreated and Harper and Rocco drank the last of their champagne.

'Shall we?' he asked, extending his arm. Laughing, Harper hitched up her skirts so she could negotiate the spiral stairs. Rocco, catching a glimpse of her Gunn tartan garter, grinned and waggled his eyebrows up and down in a suggestive fashion. Harper, anticipating him sliding it down her leg later when they were alone, blushed. Going ahead to prevent Harper from losing her footing on stone steps worn down by the passage of many feet over time, Rocco led them back to down to the lawns and gardens below.

* * *

Miss Flora Na Guinnich Penhaligon was cooing contentedly in the McKinnon heirloom pram playing with the mobile of miniature Nessies dangling in front of her. Unable to resist, Rocco scooped her up and buried his face in her neck, breathing in her unique baby scent. Kissing her, he moved her into the crook of his left arm and took her mother's hand.

'Ready Mrs Penhaligon?'

'Never more so.'

Taking that as his cue, the piper by the iron-studded door of McKinnon House blew air into his bags and played *Gunn's Salute* as family, friends and well-wishers lined up behind Rocco, Harper and Flora to process into the hall.

Then, a sound much louder than the bagpipes filled the air and a cloud of dust travelled up the drive from Loch Carron. It was some time before Rocco realised that the dust and commotion was created by the Penrith Pirates.

'What the – ?' Sending Rocco a knowing smile, Harper took Flora from him and put her back in the pram. 'Did you know about this?' Rocco asked.

'Might've done,' she replied.

'Rocco. Dude.' Dismounting, the leader of the convoy came over and gave Rocco a man hug. Then, delicate as you like, he kissed Harper on both cheeks. 'Thanks for the invitation, Harper. Did we get the timing right?'

'Bang on,' she confirmed, smiling as the other bikers dismounted and joined them.

Rocco still looked puzzled. 'I don't get it. Why have you brought the Bonneville all the way up here? I thought Morwenna had sold it. Has the buyer backed out?'

'No,' Morwenna replied, joining them and receiving a kiss from the biker. 'The new owner paid up just after Christmas, cash on the nail. However, we received instructions not to deliver the bike until today. Right, Harper?'

'Harper?' Rocco spun round on his heel and looked at his wife and then back at the bikers. 'Sorry. Being dim here. What would Harper know about it?'

Reverting to full-on schoolmarm mode Harper tutted and Morwenna came round and linked arms with her. 'Men, huh?'

'Exactly. *I've* bought the bike, Rocco. How could I let it pass into someone else's hands knowing how much it meant to you, to Morwenna and,' she gave a resigned shrug, 'me. It's what brought us together . . .'

'. . . and nearly drove us apart,' Rocco added, his expression lightening as the penny dropped.

'Although, I'm not entirely certain that a family man with responsibilities should be riding along the highways and byways of Wester Ross on a classic motorbike.' Harper frowned, pretending that she was beginning to regret her romantic gesture, then gasped in surprise as Rocco picked her up and spun her round several times.

'God, I love you,' he declared.

'Just promise me that you'll be careful.'

'I promise.'

Ariel sauntered over and joined them. 'You can display it in pride of place in your new garage, Rocco. It'll bring in the punters and be a permanent reminder of how much you and Harper owe Pen and me. Without us . . .'

'The jury's still out on that one,' Rocco reminded her, but winked to show that he was joking.

At that point, the events manager approached the bikers. 'This way gentlemen, I've arranged for you to get changed in the library.'

'Changed?' Rocco queried.

'You don't think they're going to pass up on the chance to wear a kilt and wow the ladies this evening, do you?' Morwenna asked. 'It's all been taken care of – by me and the girls, and paid for by Harper. Laters, lads, eh?'

The bikers gave her the thumbs' up and followed the events manager into the house via a side door. Rocco, rendered speechless by the turn of events, unconsciously took a step towards the precious Bonneville, evidently intent on checking it over.

'Don't even think of it,' Harper warned sotto voce, 'or I'll be adding a rider to those vows we exchanged earlier.'

'To include first degree murder?'

'Got it in one.'

Laughing, Rocco stepped back and put his arm around her shoulders. 'But I haven't got you anything –'

Harper placed her finger on Rocco's mouth to shush him. 'You bought me these antique Scottish freshwater pearls to wear at the civil ceremony in January, the Volvo to drive Miss Flora around Plockton in. What else is on offer?'

Rocco leaned in and whispered something. His breath fanned the curls which had escaped her up-do and the tiny hairs on the back of her neck stood to attention.

Harper giggled. 'Really?'

'Really.'

'In that case – Piper, *Gunn's Salute,* if you please.'

Resignedly the piper struck up the tune again and Miss Flora Na Guinnich Penhaligon was wheeled into McKinnon House by Ariel and Pen. Rocco held his hand out and Harper placed hers over his with a gracious nod. And so it was that Penhaligon, his Highland Bride – and baby – took a step forward towards a long and happy life together.

THE END

Acknowledgments

In order to produce a typo-free manuscript, I had help from eagle-eyed Nina Kenchington. My novel, both paperback and kindle has been formatted by Sarah Houldcroft of www.goldcrestbooks.com. Thanks, also, to Gail Bradley at www.gailbradleydesign.co.uk for producing such a fabulous cover for *Harper's Highland Fling*. I adore it, and hope to work with Gail to update my other five covers over time. Special mention is also due to sounding boards/beta readers and all round wonderful 'critical' friends: Isabella Tartaruga (aka the Diva from Dumbarton), Jan Brigden, Miss Wrafter, Jane Little, and Miss Davies of Edge Grange who've been with me and supported me every step of the way.

Thank you, ladies, you rock!

Whilst searching Google et al for images to illustrate the cover of my novel I was fortunate to find amazing wedding photographer Stuart McIntyre of www.boundbylight.co.uk. Stuart's portfolio of wedding photos is amazing and I've spent many happy hours browsing through them, gaining inspiration for subsequent novels set in the highlands of Scotland.

Thank you, also, to Samantha and James, the bride and groom featured on the cover of *Harper's Highland Fling* for granting permission to use the photograph of their special day to illustrate my novel. I hope they and Stuart enjoy reading the signed copy of *Harper's Highland Fling* I've sent them and will relive happy memories of their wedding day as they thumb through its pages.

A Personal Note from Lizzie

Dear friends and readers,

Thank you so much for buying *Harper's Highland Fling* I do hope you enjoyed it.

When I published *Tall, Dark and Kilted* in 2012 I thought that'd be my first, and last, attempt to write a novel. However, I found myself bitten by the writing bug. *Harper's Highland Fling* is my sixth novel but it certainly won't be my last. I've drafted the outline for number seven and hope to get started on that once *Harper's Highland Fling* is out of the trap.

As some of you may know, I was the deputy head of a large primary school for the last sixteen years of my thirty-four year teaching career. When I took early retirement to concentrate on my writing everyone assumed that I'd write children's books, or at least a series set in a school. This is the first time I've drawn upon my former career for inspiration. Harper MacDonald is exactly the kind of teacher I aspired to be and I hope you like her as much as I do. As for Ariel . . . there's quite a lot of me in her, too. But, don't tell anyone that.

No writer can write convincingly about the journey her heroine takes until she has fallen in love with her fictional hero. For me, this happened the moment Rocco Penhaligon slid out from underneath the car he was working on and landed, fully formed onto the page. If that sounds fanciful, trust me, that 'wow' moment is what makes authors of romance keep writing. And, in my book, there's nothing wrong with that!

I am aware that 2020 has been a very difficult year for us all. Leicester has been in lockdown from early June, so being able to escape to the Scottish Highlands through the pages of my novel (even if we did have to cancel our research trip) has kept me sane. As has the unstinting support of my husband Dave who takes my obsession with magicking characters out of the air and living in another world as a given.

Stay well, stay safe and, above all, keep reading and reviewing all the gorgeous romances out there.

Let's hope that 2021 is a better year for us all.

Much love and best wishes,

Lizzie

November 2020

Contact Lizzie

I'd love to hear from you so do get in touch:

Find Lizzie on Amazon	viewAuthor.at/LizzieLamb
Email Lizzie	lizzielambwriter@gmail.com
Facebook	www.facebook.com/LizzieLamb
Twitter	www.twitter.com/lizzie_lamb
Website	www.lizzielamb.co.uk
Pinterest	https://uk.pinterest.com/lizzielamb/
Instagram	www.instagram.com/lizzielambwriter

"When I'm not writing – I'm dreaming"

More books from Lizzie

Take Me, I'm Yours

A Wisconsin love story: an uplifting small town romance

India Buchanan plans to set up an English-Style bed and breakfast establishment in her great-aunt's home, MacFarlane's Landing, Wisconsin. But she's reckoned without opposition from Logan MacFarlane whose family once owned her aunt's house and now want it back. MacFarlane is in no mood to be denied. His grandfather's living on borrowed time and Logan has vowed to ensure the old man sees out his days in their former home. India's great-aunt has other ideas and has threatened to burn the house to the ground before she lets a MacFarlane set foot in it. There's a story here. One the family elders aren't prepared to share. When India finds herself in Logan's debt, her feelings towards him change. However, the past casts a long shadow and events conspire to deny them the love and happiness they both deserve. Can India and Logan's love overcome all odds? Or is history about to repeat itself?

Some reviews for Take Me, I'm Yours

'Yet again Lizzie Lamb has written a thoroughly enjoyable book, crackling with sparks and humour as well as painting a wonderful image of rural Wisconsin.'

'Ladies take note – Logan MacFarlane is yet another incredibly hot hero. India Buchanan is just the sort of woman needed to challenge him and from their first meeting the chemistry is buzzing.'

'The dialogue is witty, warm and deft and the cocktail of love, dating and passion is deliciously handled. That the reader is kept on tenterhooks to the end is the mark of a captivating writer who weaves unexpected patterns.'

Girl in the Castle
A heart-warming romance set in the Highlands of Scotland

Her academic career in tatters, Dr Henriette Bruar needs somewhere to lay low, plan her comeback and restore her tarnished reputation. Fate takes her to a remote Scottish castle to auction the contents of an ancient library to pay the laird's mounting debts. The family are in deep mourning over a tragedy which happened years before, resulting in a toxic relationship between the laird and his son, Keir MacKenzie. Cue a phantom piper, a lost Jacobite treasure, and a cast of characters who – with Henri's help, encourage the MacKenzies to confront the past and move on. However – will the Girl in the Castle be able to return to university once her task is completed, and leave gorgeous, sexy Keir MacKenzie behind?

Some reviews for Girl in the Castle

'It was the first paragraph that did it. A ghostly lament, images of an ancient Scottish castle above a loch, swirling mists and – yes – the word Sassenachs. Hey, I'm a huge fan of Outlander. How could I resist?'

'Lizzie must have done hours of research to get the facts right and they fit into the book beautifully. There's also a bit of paranormal activity too, buried treasure and of course, lots of her trademark humour.'

'One of Lizzie Lamb's big strengths is her descriptive settings; the history and Gaelic references she includes add such sparkle and authenticity to the story.'

'I was totally hooked from the moment the heroine, Henriette, stepped off the train & walked into the swirling mists & the great adventure awaiting her.'

'I wonder how many people are inspired to visit Scotland after reading one of Lizzie Lamb's books? I bet quite a few ...'

'Girl in the Castle is a lovely, escapist romantic read which is expertly executed by this talented writer.'

Scotch on the Rocks

Family secrets, love and romance in the Highlands of Scotland

Ishabel Stuart is at the crossroads of her life. Her wealthy industrialist father has died unexpectedly, leaving her a half-share in a ruined whisky distillery and the task of scattering his ashes on a Munro. After discovering her fiancé playing away from home, she cancels their lavish Christmas wedding at St Giles Cathedral, Edinburgh and heads for the only place she feels safe – Eilean na Sgairbh, a windswept island on Scotland's west coast – where the cormorants outnumber the inhabitants, ten to one.

When she arrives at her family home – now a bed and breakfast managed by her left-wing, firebrand Aunt Esme, she finds a guest in situ – Brodie. Issy longs for peace and the chance to lick her wounds, but gorgeous, sexy American, Brodie, turns her world upside down.

In spite of her vow to steer clear of men, she grows to rely on Brodie. However, she suspects him of having an ulterior motive for staying at her aunt's B&B on remote Cormorant Island. Having been let down twice by the men in her life, will it be third time lucky for Issy? Is it wise to trust a man she knows nothing about – a man who presents her with more questions than answers? As for Aunt Esme, she has secrets of her own.

Some reviews for Scotch on the Rocks

'A cracking book that stays with you long after you have finished.'

'I like the way she weaves 'older characters' into the story; how love isn't just for the young.'

'Lots of romance, humour, quirky secondary characters and a mad parrot. I was kept engaged, right up to the last page.'

'A five star romance from a five star romantic novelist.'

'A delight to read. Loved the Scottish'ism and the bits of history and the evocative imagery of a highland castle. Oh and the hero completely rocked.'

Boot Camp Bride

Romance and Intrigue on the Norfolk marshes

Take an up-for-anything rookie reporter. Add a world-weary photo-journalist. Put them together . . . light the blue touch paper and stand well back! Posing as a bride-to-be, Charlee Montague goes undercover at a boot camp for brides in Norfolk to photograph supermodel Anastasia Markova looking less than perfect. At Charlee's side and posing as her fiancé, is Rafael Ffinch award winning photographer and survivor of a kidnap attempt in Colombia. He's in no mood to cut inexperienced Charlee any slack and has made it plain that once the investigation is over, their partnership – and fake engagement – will be terminated, too. Soon Charlee has more questions than answers. What's the real reason behind Ffinch's interest in the boot camp? How is it connected to his kidnap in Colombia? In setting out to uncover the truth, Charlee puts herself in danger ... As the investigation draws to a close, she wonders if she'll be able to hand back the engagement ring and walk away from Rafa without a backward glance.

Some reviews for Boot Camp Bride

'Loved it.'

'Another sparkling read, full of passion and laughter, but with a sinister undertone that keeps you turning the pages.'

'A definitely great read, as was Lizzie's Debut book, Tall Dark & Kilted... roll on book 3!'

'That good I read it twice!'

'The dialogue between the two main characters, rookie journalist Charlee Montague, and world-weary photographer, Rafael Ffinch is brilliant and full of repartee.'

Tall Dark and Kilted

A contemporary romance set in the highlands of Scotland

Fliss Bagshawe longs for a passport out of Pimlico where she works as a holistic therapist. After attending a party in Notting Hill she loses her job and with it the dream of being her own boss. She's offered the chance to take over a failing therapy centre, but there's a catch. The centre lies five hundred miles north in Wester Ross, Scotland. Fliss's romantic view of the highlands populated by Men in Kilts is shattered when she has an upclose and personal encounter with the Laird of Kinloch Mara, Ruairi Urquhart. He's determined to pull the plug on the business, bring his eccentric family to heel and eject undesirables from his estate – starting with Fliss. Facing the dole queue once more Fliss resolves to make sexy, infuriating Ruairi revise his unflattering opinion of her, turn the therapy centre around and sort out his dysfunctional family. Can Fliss tame the Monarch of the Glen and find the happiness she deserves?

Some reviews for Tall, Dark and Kilted

'This story is full of romantic Scottish themes; Kilts, bagpipes, scenery, Gaelic whisperings, Clan Urquhart tartans and Strathspey reels. Definitely an enjoyable read.'

'I really couldn't put it down. Makes me want to buy my hubby a kilt.'

'No complications just a relaxing story that drags you in to the end. Quite sad to finish it.'

'You won't be disappointed ladies and men, you could learn a thing or two.'

'I truly enjoyed this book. I stumbled across it on Twitter. I was looking for a light read. However, I had trouble putting this one down.'

Made in United States
North Haven, CT
30 April 2022

18737865R00190